MAIDSERVANT THE GOD

MAIDSERVANT THE GOD

B C HOWELL

"I will always be least in any room with other people in it."

...Maidservant

***

PROLOGUE – DR PAUL BENJAMIN

THE MAN DROVE HIS DILAPIDATED PICKUP from the security gate up through steep forest watching the house rise castle-like over the crest of the hill ahead. Reaching the top, an automatic gate blocked the direct way, forcing visitors to take a meandering route through acres of self-indulgent gardens. He sped through the narrow lanes mocking the overabundance of artsy-fartsy European statues so out of place in the American Northwest until reaching the semicircle driveway to the house and sliding sideways into it with squealing tires.

A frantic security man ran out waving him away and pointing to a visitors' lot in the distance, which was next to the gate where he had detoured, so he jammed the brakes in front of the main entrance, revved the engine and switched it off, prompting loud backfires out the tailpipe. He knocked the bent door open with an elbow, got out and pounded it closed with the side of his big fist.

More resembling an itinerant day-worker than Professor of Classical Languages and Civilizations wearing a rumpled flannel shirt, rough work boots and permanent scowl, Dr Paul Benjamin pulled the bill of his '62 Seattle World's Fair cap lower over his eyes. Then he sauntered to the back of the truck, ignoring the furious man waiting for him to state his business as if the gate guard had not called ahead.

Taking his sweet time, he worked free two rusty screwdrivers holding closed the bashed-in tailgate, stepped back and let it crash to the pavement. Then he stood on it, removed wheel blocks securing a battered Radio Flyer Red Wagon piled high with cargo hidden by black plastic leaf bags tied in place with dirty clothesline. The man was about to explode with threats and demands, so he preempted with a curt wave of the hand. "Hey, Bub, use the hands God gave you to help, why don't you?"

He facetiously refused to leave the wagon outside because someone might steal it then followed behind the man, enjoying red anger splotches spreading and darkening on his neck with every creak, wobble and bump the wagon made. Passing through room after room chock full of rare, hand-loomed rugs and ooh-and-ah artwork worth fortunes, Dr Benjamin reckoned selling all of it would feed an impoverished nation for a year.

They entered a humid gymnasium-sized room with a two story waterfall cascading from a wall into a pool on one side and a glass enclosed tropical nursery on the other. Just past the pool, his guide motioned him down a hallway with an arched ceiling and heavy medieval oaken door at the end.

Behind an enormous wooden desk sat the famous man, more boyish than his pictures. He did not bother getting up and was surly. "I made it clear to my team those tapes were confidential and not to be shared under any circumstances. I demand you tell me who gave them to you."

Dr Benjamin shrugged. "You should be thankful one of them was intelligent enough to consult an expert."

"They were experts! And they concluded there was nothing on them but noise and gibberish, so how am I to believe someone five years later claiming to have gleaned hundreds of pages of information, especially when his background is dusty old languages known only to a handful of academics? I know you spent a year in an Israeli prison for dealing fake antiquities, too, so don't think you won't suffer consequences demanding money for nothing."

An overstuffed chair in front of a big fireplace across the room looked comfortable so he went and sat down, giving the man no choice but to move from behind his oversized symbol of authority and take the smaller chair across from him. As his host sat, he began explaining. "The so-called gibberish is a mix of obscure classical dialects, including some that are unknown. Every few sentences, the speaker changes languages, making it impossible to piece together anything intelligible. Mind you, that conclusion was reached with the assistance of the five top classical experts in the world."

The man sputtered. "How many people have you involved? And if it's impossible to make sense of it, where did you get information?"

"First things first. Since all the tapes seemed to be the same voice, I was in a bit of a conundrum because it's not possible for any one person to know so many dialects. Long story short, I took the tapes to a sound guy I know in Berlin to be analyzed before wasting more time."

He half rose from the chair. "You took them out of the country! Why didn't you just put them on the internet, for god's sake? How do you know this man can be trusted? Who is he?"

Dr Benjamin gave him a cold stare. "With your connections, you must know the work I used to do for the government, so stop playing games. He is a wizard with recorded sound. He didn't understand a thing he heard and only cared about the money I paid. However, my academic colleagues helped more as personal favors than for money, which was not nearly enough. I included a folder in the wagon with additional amounts you should give them. I expect to be reimbursed for all my expenses above and beyond the bonus you offered the other group, too."

"Awfully cocksure of yourself, aren't you?"

"You be the judge. It is one voice, a young female by all indications, but the breakthrough came when my man examined the areas where she makes those strange, high-pitched sounds that your people wrote off as nonsensical noises. By slowing the tapes in incremental steps, he discovered that it is extremely fast speech. For want of a better comparison, think of something akin to electronic data streaming."

"That's absurd. No one can speak that fast."

Dr Benjamin shrugged. "Yet, that's what it is. Some of my people thought you created the voice artificially for high speed communications or encryption programs and offered all that money to see if anyone could crack them."

"What do you think?"

"That doesn't explain the impossibility of anyone knowing so many dialects. Regardless, in those areas, she uses only one language for each chapter. Most of what we translated was early Egyptian, Greek or their precessors, which are dialects that evolved into the mainstream languages."

The man stared intently. "Chapters? About what?"

"They are a series of stories repeated over and over, always in the same order. They begin with a book name and chapter title. Most are about a young girl from ancient Egypt. The rest are people who figured prominently in her life."

"Can you be more specific?"

Dr Benjamin laughed nervously. "They are fantastic stories about gods, demons and immortality, not to mention the destruction of an island some people claim was Plato's Atlantis." Seeing the man's surprised look, he quickly added, "I still expect you to pay, however."

The man leaned closer. "Immortality?"

"Yeah, and more, including explanations how a person can speak so fast, if you care to wade through all the nonsense that comes…!"

The man jumped up, grabbed the wagon handle and ran with it through a hidden bookcase door that slammed closed behind him. Astonished, Dr Benjamin stared after him before going to push and pull on it, but to no avail.

The security man came in from the hallway with two large companions. "He asks for your patience while he studies the materials you brought. You will remain here as his guest until he is ready to meet again. Please give me your cellphone."

PART ONE

OF

DR PAUL BENJAMIN'S

TRANSLATIONS

ONE

THE BOOK OF MAIDSERVANT: THE MOUSE

T HE YOUNG GIRL SCURRIED SHADOW TO SHADOW along a dimly lit
stone block corridor, paused to wipe sweat from her eyes then darted
into a narrow, seldom used way that led to the crypts where ancient
texts were stored. Vaguely, she wondered how she knew all this having never
been here before then tried desperately to clear her mind of thoughts about
her other life, but it was too late.

Pain erupted in her head, driving her to knees inside a dim but dangerous
glow-circle cast by an oil lamp on the wall. Shaking violently, she fought
against the part of her that would not accept that the other life was only a
symptom of her madness, finally resorting to punishing herself in the face
with fists until the forbidden thoughts returned to the dark places inside her.
She got up, wiped her bloody nose and hurried on, admonishing to keep her
mind on the job. If discovered in this part of Pharaoh's Library, they would
execute her even if she looked younger than her twelve years and they thought
her to be no more than an ignorant household slave.

She arrived at an intersection as approaching voices echoed from the right
turning. Backtracking, bare feet making the tiniest noises, she dived into a
dark alcove holding a statue of Isis and squeezed into a slight cavity in the
wall behind, not allowing herself to wonder how she knew it was there. Heart
pounding, she fished out the pill that would make her invisible from a patch
pocket on the front of her coarse dress and cupped it close to the mouth, ready
to swallow. But she must not panic and take it too soon. Her master had
warned the magic would work for three minutes only, barely enough time to
return to the public areas.

The voices and echoing footfalls went silent suddenly. She waited, but
there was nothing else. Mouthing a prayer to the statue, she darted a quick
peek then went motionless in the shadows, holding her breath because they
were directly in front of her.

One was the ruthless Captain of the Guard, a hero renowned for a glorious victory that turned the tide of Pharaoh's last war. He would kill her without afterthought, yet she smirked because her mistress hung on his arm with her body pressed tight against his as she pulled his head down for a long kiss.

Breathtakingly beautiful with her face fashionably painted and made up, she wore a perfect black wig adorned with a fortune in jewels that cushioned her head against his chest as she purred words remindful of a pampered temple kitten stroked by hot hands. "But Ahkmen, they won't notice if you're gone a few hours. Everyone is in the basements moving documents up from the flood waters."

He was adamant. "I told you, I'm the only interior guard watching the sacred storerooms today. If I'm missed, I'll be disgraced, or worse."

She pushed him away roughly and fixed devastating brown eyes highlighted with vibrant green outlined in black upon him. "Then I'll have to find someone else to while away a long hot afternoon. Pepi is on the other shift, isn't he?"

He grabbed her hard. "I'm crazy for you, but duty takes precedent over everything else."

She kissed him again, arching her back and pushing into him, then she shoved away. "I'll be off then, shall I? Say hello to your wife for me."

He was desperate. "We can go to a storeroom."

Instantly, the temple kitten became a vicious alley cat. "So, you think me no better than a common street girl to play, pay and go away. Why am I wasting my time with you? Goodbye!"

He grabbed her arm. "You're driving me mad! Very well, we'll go to my private apartment in town if you'll hurry for once. Where's that maid of yours gone? I must account for her before we go."

She stared straight into the dark next to the statue then took his hand and pulled him down the hall. "Sent the useless creature home because Father had an errand, but let's talk about all the fun things we're going to do instead of that useless worm. This will be a day you'll remember, I promise."

The girl carefully returned the pill to the pocket then jumped up and ran fast as her legs could carry her. It would be easy now that she knew no one was on guard.

***

CURVED PALMS AND EXOTIC PLANTS shaded the villa's back garden from a summer sun blazing in uninterrupted blue sky. Exquisite painted statues were placed tastefully along walks while boats and barges passing languidly on an eternal river, lifeblood of a timeless land, created the ideal backdrop for a scene of perfect harmony and tranquility. Yet, an exceptionally tall man, the wealthiest of merchants judging by clothes and adornments, dominated the surroundings as he fed documents piled next to him into a hungry fire. His eyes went to the only ugliness in sight, a slave waiting with eyes cast down and hands clasped behind her back. Although he resented having to converse with someone so common, he felt compelled to give her just due. "I never dreamed you'd do so well, girl. You're certain you found everything?"

Her voice trembled. "Great Thoth's seals were on the storage jars just as you said they would be, Master. Kalli's name was on some of them, too. I was careful to check them all. Sorry if none of it is of use to you."

The last sheaves disintegrated in his hands as he put them into the flames. "That things so old even exist is remarkable. That time ruined them disappointing, but not surprising. And to think, I've spent more than two hundred years trying to discover whether the One Master discovered any of the ancient words of power and hid them in Pharaoh's Library, and you answered the question in a single afternoon. You've earned my appreciation, so I'll forgive the loss of the magic pill and forego the punishment that would normally follow such a careless mistake."

She looked up in surprise, eager to express gratefulness. "Oh, thank you, Master. It was a very tiny hole in my pocket, but I should've checked better."

"You've already told me all that! Keep your eyes down in my presence as instructed by your mistress."

She expected discipline for messing up again, but just then a man dressed as a tradesman but with the barrel chest, scars and bearing of a soldier came fast down the long walk from the main house. He stopped and saluted, right arm across the chest, then waited for permission to speak.

"Why did you come here, General Antwah? If my snoopy daughter finds out, I'll have your head."

"She's on the river with that foppish captain again, Lord. Perhaps you could send this slave away. I have important news."

"I asked why you're here, not for advice how to manage servants."

The general stiffened, fighting to hide his fear. "Lord! A few months ago, stories came to my attention that an island had miraculously appeared near a busy sea-lane. It fit the description of Kalli's last stronghold with an enormous volcano, fabulous cities and harbors. I decided…"

The man cut him off. "Those wild tales have been told by sailors to impress brothel girls for hundreds of years. Surely you didn't come all this way to repeat such tripe to your master."

Carelessly, the general let show how pleased he was for a chance to prove him wrong. "Two of my most credible agents visited there, Lord. It is named Kalliste after Kalli and temple priests teach her ways to students from many lands. It is under the protection of King Ermiticus of the Keftiu Empire, but he has stationed none of his navy there. Without defenses, or so much as a militia, I can take it in a day if you will give permission."

The man was careful not to show excitement. "If your information is correct, they surely wield great magic and don't need to rely on the King. That is the only reasonable explanation for the lack of soldiers and navy."

The general bridled. "Although visitors are restricted from leaving the harbor areas, my agents sensed no old magic anywhere on the island. I recommend we attack at once. Think of the glory."

The tall man could only tolerate so much stupidity. "You think people descended directly from the most powerful followers of Kalli live on an island bursting with wealth, have no means to defend themselves and can magically hide it from sight, yet decided to come out into the open. Don't you think it might be wise to investigate before charging in blindly?"

Antwah reddened. "Yes, I see your point, Lord."

"What do the islanders say about it appearing so suddenly? Or did your people not think to ask them?"

"They claim it has always been there and don't understand the fuss. Ridiculous, of course, as it's all everyone in the region is talking about."

"Doesn't the Keftiu Empire worship cows or some such nonsense?"

"Bulls, my Lord. Kalliste has symbols of them everywhere, too. Those people are just bunch of superstitious ignoramuses."

The man wanted to incinerate the fool before another breath escaped his lips, but it was not a convenient time. Instead, he sniffed loudly and smiled, a dangerous sign to those who knew him well. "Kalli's followers can't possibly believe in bulls, General, or any other religion. It goes against all her teachings. I want you to report to Shelitine and ask what she'll charge to remake all the warriors in my oldest battalions. I don't need to warn you to be careful around her, do I?"

At the very mention of Shelitine, the general blanched. "No, Lord."

"I'll discuss this matter with the Master and concoct a way for Egypt to establish a presence on the island that will not cause concern then go assess the situation personally. It will take at least two years to get everything in place so have the soldiers ready by then. If you have no questions, dismissed."

Antwah saluted, glad to hurry away.

The girl had not moved the whole time. The man noted her grimy neck and frayed barrette holding tangled brown hair back on one side. Typically, she had forgotten or lost the second one. Weakest of his thousands of servants, he tolerated her because she possessed a single, unique ability that he needed. He whispered, "Have you made any headway with the scraps of text I gave you to study?"

Caught by surprise, she looked up and answered too loudly. "I'm sorry, but no, Master. If some of Pharaoh's Library documents had been legible, it might have been enough for me to decipher. Then you could rule the world the way you want."

Quickly, he sent awareness around the garden making certain no one spied on them. "Don't say things like that outside, you idiot!"

Terrified, she blurted something else stupid. "I still don't understand how merely saying words makes someone powerful."

"You don't need to know. Do you never listen?"

"Yes, Master. I mean, no, Master. I mean..." Stinging sensations peppered her arms and legs, causing her to jerk and dance. "I'll do better, Master!"

He stopped the punishment and moved close over her. "You must try harder to be a good girl, not sometimes, but all the time."

She could not stop shaking. "Yes, Master."

"You've earned more than I've given. Perhaps I'll let you accompany your mistress when we leave here if you learn to control your fits better. She told me that they have been getting worse and...ugh!" He clapped a hand over his nose and backed away. "Do you never bathe? Return to work!"

She bowed and ran up the walk, doing her best not to smile because the onion water she used to rinse her hair had kept him from getting close enough to look into her mind and discover she had found a bundle of the old documents in good condition and kept them.

***

EVERY NIGHT FOR A MONTH, SHE STUDIED under a small table shoved into a corner of the big kitchen cupboard where she lived. A moth-eaten red blanket draped over the open sides sheltered the tiniest flame she could manage from a cracked oil lamp salvaged from garbage. Servants venturing into the kitchen hurried away after seeing the eerie red glow, certain the new kitchen maid's madness created an evil aura that would infect them if they stayed too long.

Never before had she come across a language she could not decipher. Yet, even though a brilliant scholar-scribe left a lifetime's notes about his attempts to understand the fifty pages of ancient text and four pages of painted objects with inscribed names, she kept having the same problems he experienced eight hundred years ago. The characters simply did not fit together in consistent ways to form words. She set aside the page she had worked on for days and looked at his notes, in spite of knowing them almost word for word.

He said a waxy substance had preserved the pages though she found no evidence of it now, probably accounting for everything having faded almost beyond recognition. The strange composition of the pages did not help, either, as it was thinner and flimsier than skins or papyrus, nor did the tiny groups of characters written so precise and uniform that it was impossible any hand other than a god's could have made them. In addition, the scribe's frequent ramblings about religion broke her concentration when she skipped ahead. She reread his final comments, presumably just before his death.

Descended from the eternal Shining Ones, the First Gods lived more than nine thousand years before the beginning of our modern times. There was Siris, who made Kalli, who made Thoth. Kalli betrayed the other gods after learning to use the awesome power left behind in the secret writings of the Shining Ones, yet Thoth defeated her and ruled over a glorious age. Surely Great Amon-Ra, divinely fused, intervened on his behalf and...

Pharaoh believed if he could wield the magic of the Shining Ones same as Kalli, he would be immortal upon earth as well as in the heavens. In my youth, I believed it, too, but now we've grown old, he is dying and cynical, and I am wiser. Yesterday, he ordered me to destroy these documents then prepare to join him ascending into the afterlife, an honor I do not deserve.

Because, Mentho, ever-obedient Chief Scribe, must disobey my master this one time. Destroying the words of the eternal Shining Ones will unleash retribution upon us in the afterlife so I am sealing them away with Thoth's secret histories where they will remain guarded until time diminishes both their relevance and existence.

But now, O, Reader, you have found them. I curse you! Snakes and scorpions will bite and sting you to death. The Four Crocodiles of the West will rip your body asunder. The Devourer of the Dead will chew your bones eternally. Your spouse will erupt in flames and burn alive for one hundred years. The seeds of your sons will rot and the wombs of your daughters shrivel. Your family name will cease to exist. Heed Mentho. Return these holy documents to their resting place and run away fast as you can to avoid my curse. Never forget---Mentho's vigilance and vengeance is eternal.

She could not imagine how being cursed would make her life any worse, especially since she could not figure out the text and become an all-powerful god. She gave her arm a twisting pinch for failing, causing another black and blue mark among the many. But, at least, she had gotten something for all the trouble.

She reached into her pocket, pulled out a dirty rag and unfolded the pill. Tomorrow she would go to the market, become invisible and steal a pretty brush and comb for her hair. Humming tunelessly, she spread the rag on the floor and placed beside the pill a piece of flatbread she had brought to share with the mouse that lived in the grain bin. Bone-tired, she yawned and closed her eyes to rest for a few seconds, but fell into a deep sleep and dreamed.

A full moon illuminated tranquil desert. Cold sand made her feet ache. Spindly black creatures in all sorts of strange shapes danced around her, casting frenetic moon shadows with stick arms waving her to join in. She declined, but returned their smiles and waved back.

One skipped up, chirped in her face and twirled back into the circle. Others did the same, each making a different sound. Laughing at their antics, she repeated them. But when nine remained, seven walked away and stood solemnly outside the circle. The other two jumped up and down excitedly. Then their shapes changed and they were perfectly still.

This was not the first time she dreamed solutions to translating languages, so it did not surprise her they were the documents' symbols. The seven outsiders had to be superfluous characters, in spite of their use spelling names on the four pages of labeled objects. She admired how simple and clever a trick that was. Already, she had surmised the eighth and ninth characters might be markers to separate words and end sentences. Now, that she could see individual words, she would figure it out. She relaxed for the first time in weeks, dreams drifting back to childhood when she and her sister competed against each other to learn lessons fastest.

Suddenly, her mistress' face---washed and scrubbed free of paint and makeup as only her personal maid had privilege to see it---came out of the darkness at her shrieking and threatening to smother her life spirit. She screamed it to leave her alone and woke up hitting her head and fists against the stone wall.

She stretched, rubbed her eyes then saw the mouse spinning and doing crazy flips around the lamp. She thought it was funny until he ran into a table leg and rolled onto his back, kicking cute pink feet in the air before he went still.

She poked him with a finger then slapped the hand over her mouth. He had made a mess eating the bread, and the pill was gone, of course. Through fingers, she whispered, "An invisible pill. I am such an idiot sometimes. Sorry I caused you to die, Mousey."

Her screaming had wakened the other servants along the two halls adjoining the kitchen, but it was so common an occurrence that no one bothered checking anymore. Cook-Servant, the stranger they insisted was her mother, would beat her if she did not have the kitchen prepared on time. She had to rush to her mistress' rooms to help her bathe and dress, too. It would be even worse if she was late for that.

She wiped blood from her knuckles with the blanket, rolled the documents in it and threw them under the table. No one bothered her stuff, which was the only benefit of being mad. She took the mouse by the tail, ran into the kitchen and tossed him into the smoldering fire. Then she added wood and stoked it.

She did not feel anything in particular about him dying or her master's unconcern about killing her. Just like the mouse, she was small and weak, and that was what happened to defenseless creatures like them. She smiled. But not for much longer, because soon she would be a god then make him and her hateful mistress squirm and bow down to her. She could hardly wait.

It seemed forever, but she figured out the text and a night arrived with everyone out of the house. Hardly able to contain her excitement, she sequestered in the cupboard under the table with the documents propped on her knees to read aloud finally. She translated the first line and waited, but nothing happened. Throwing caution to the wind, she skimmed down the page sorting words then read the entire first paragraph in a rush. Seconds ticked by. She kicked her feet. "This isn't going to make a god of anyone. It's no different than the hundreds of others I've done."

Aggravated, yet not surprised to be disappointed yet again, she decided to read it anyway. She picked up a piece of partially eaten fruit and took a big bite. Then she began again. "The Book of the God Thoth: Kalli and the Mud Men. The day dawned steamy…"

TWO

THE BOOK OF THE GOD THOTH: KALLI AND THE MUD MEN

THE DAY DAWNED STEAMY and saturated with earthy odors after a series of brief showers. Hiding in thick foliage atop a high hill on a steep slope to a plateau high above, twenty warriors watched a female stranger slowly making way up a winding trail toward them. Dumfounded by her creamy skin and long silver hair, they had never seen anyone except ebony or brown people with dark hair before now. Known as the Mud Men because they plastered themselves with sticky clay and crushed dried plants to protect from sun and insects, their enemies also called them Orange Ghosts for their ability to attack seemingly from nowhere.

One warrior, who considered himself more articulate than the others and talked too much, whispered, "She sparkles more than the wet leaves." Then he compared her to his youngest mate, needlessly reminding that her hair was a dull reddish-brown and unusual, too. He prattled on about how the Life-Giver, the great god-river, stretched out on the wide plain below them, sometimes honored aged ones by changing their hair to white and mentioned their former leader's amazing forty-two season-cycles. "I can remember when his hair was black as night."

Siris, the present leader, hissed for silence. He was deeply concerned because he saw two images of the female at the same time. First, a tiny figure more than three-quarters mile distant, and a second that seemed no more than a few feet away. And, although the sun glared off the Life-Giver, he could make out every minute detail of the land around her in both instances. Never had his weak eyes worked so well. He could tell his men experienced the same things, yet not one questioned it. A couple even smiled back at him, pleased by his attention.

By the way she moved, Siris knew she had traveled many days, too. Not even a skilled warrior from another tribe dared walk this side of the river alone, and no man was stupid enough to allow his females outside the village unguarded, yet this one acted nonchalant---whether from arrogance or ignorance, he could not tell. Then she stopped beneath a towering palm, slung a heavy bag off her shoulder and stretched.

Forgetting the need for silence, several men gasped when she whipped off a cloak of skins, revealing spectacular white skin offset by a flimsy dress blue as the sky. Samus, son of Thoth, a mere boy and youngest in the party, exclaimed loudest of all. "She's a god!"

Siris backhanded him across the mouth to the ground and straddled him. "After I feed your so-called god's entrails to the lions tonight, you will stand before the village and sing a song of love to her head mounted on my spear." He glared at the men until they choked off snickering.

Samus dared not move or utter a sound, recalling his best friend who stepped on a thorn and scared away a herd of antelope they had tracked most of a day. Siris had forced him to hold his tongue out and pierced it with three thorns as a lesson. Because the boy suffered the punishment silently, Siris declared he would be a good warrior someday. Unfortunately, he died a few nights later when red demons swelled his tongue up so big he suffocated. Samus shuddered. Sometimes, there was no accounting for the harsh will of the Life-Giver.

Siris kicked the boy in the ribs, took his hand and jerked him up roughly. "Time to set up the ambush. Talik will come in a few minutes with more instructions. Make sure this piece of dung, Samus, doesn't foul things up."

The men melted into the thick vegetation without disturbing the loud morning birdsong. Siris grunted satisfaction to his brother and second-in-charge, Talik the Strong. Then, resolute as a boulder, he scanned every foot of the land stretched out below them, returning finally to the female, drinking too much water from a skin. His heavy brow furrowed. "What manner of bow is that? It is too long to be any good in the heavy brush. And what's that white pole she had tied across her back? It is too thick for a spear. Hmm, a battle staff, maybe. Strange, isn't it, a female armed same as a warrior?"

Talik snorted derisively as she stooped to smell white flowers next to the trail. "Whoever heard of a female warrior, Siris? She simply bears weapons for her man, that's all."

Siris voiced another worry. "The wind's getting stronger, coming down off the plateau. I hope she doesn't detect our scent. She looks fast and I don't want to waste time chasing her in case a war party is nearby."

The most skillful hunter in the tribe, Talik sniffed the air. "A bad storm is coming, but we'll capture her before it arrives, no problem."

Siris shook his head. "Best to kill her quickly then backtrack to find her companions."

Talik grinned, showing missing and broken teeth. "Ah, let's enjoy her first, brother. Let's make little Samus' god cry for the mercy of the Life-Giver many times. Maybe even give the boy his first taste." He jabbed Siris in the ribs good-naturedly. "What do you say, brother? Many times, eh?"

Indeed, Siris experienced unusually strong desire for the woman, surprising since he seldom felt such urges since passing thirty season-cycles. He imagined how hot her white skin would feel in his hands. "Very well, but I'll keep watch from here for companions until you have her in case she was sent to bait a trap."

"We can see to the river and along the shore for miles. She is alone."

Siris responded in the same patient, strained voice he explained things to his many children. "Think, Talik. She crossed the Life-Giver alone, which means she traveled through the lands of the Crocodile People, where even we dare not go without a large force. More importantly, how is it we can see her so well from so far away? Consider the sun is in your eyes and that you haven't questioned a single thing about it. Does that not suggest something?"

Talik closed his eyes tight then looked again as she resumed moving up the path. "Yes, it must be witchery. Our father chose well when he named you leader over me."

Surprised by the admission, Siris grabbed Talik's forearm and they exchanged fierce stares until Siris smiled sheepishly and looked away. "Witch or no, I desire this strange female as much as my first wife. Do you remember?"

Talik laughed. "You were so miserable until Father bought her for you. You know what they say---fires burn hottest for the first one, but to have that experience again is surely a gift from the gods. We'll hold her for you to go first."

Embarrassed, Siris stepped back. "Just be sure to keep close watch on that useless son of Thoth. I don't want him getting himself killed like his stupid father did."

Battle cries sent clouds of protesting birds into the sky. Siris broke cover and raced down through waist high grass, exhilarated by the excitement of the hunt, but then heard shouts of alarm. He veered down the steepest, most dangerous part of the hill, tripped and crashed through thick brush onto the trail where his men caught him. A warrior was dead on the ground with an arrow through the left eye. He had been in charge of the group cutting off the trail behind the woman.

Siris led pursuit down the trail and found the brother of his youngest wife with his head twisted nearly off a broken neck. Siris knew no one with strength to do that other than Talik, who the men said had left with Samus before the ambush and not been seen since. Mystified, Siris had no time to worry about that now.

At the base of the hill, the last member of the small party, their best spear maker, was dead from a blow across the left temple. Siris could not believe a female could use a staff with so much force but had no other explanation. Furious, he shouted the dazed warriors into designated places as they charged down the path toward the river, two scouts ahead reading tracks, two bowmen guarding the flank and everyone in between watching for ambushes and signs the scouts missed. Siris set a fast pace, yet they ran all the way to the broad mud flats along the Life-Giver without so much as a glimpse of her.

Moving along the bank, their best tracker, uncharacteristically nervous, pointed to the ground. The tracks simply stopped in the center of a wide area of mud. Some of the men gazed up into the sky as if expecting to see her flying away while others mumbled about witches and gods. Silencing with a withering glare, Siris ordered them into a rest and ready formation---sitting in a circle facing out, weapons on the ground by their sides.

The only answer that made sense to Siris was the female made the tracks before going up the trail, though he had difficulty believing a female could plan something so clever. And where were Talik and Samus? Furious, he shouted the men back up the trail, searching into every tree and brush fifty paces either side, but they found nothing. Finally, they reached the bodies of their fallen comrades, which were putrid and swarming with ants and flies. It was a full hour past midday. Siris ordered a rest break.

Thunder grew ominously louder from the plateau above, but they were not prepared for the ferocity of the storm that roared down at them thrashing treetops, shredding foliage and ripping off boughs. Then, as Siris turned to order the men to cover, an arrow whisked by his left ear, striking a man in the shoulder. Instantly, everyone had weapons ready, scanning every direction for the enemy. Then someone shouted and pointed.

On top of the hill, at the precise spot where they had watched, stood the woman in the blue dress, platinum hair spreading and reflecting lightning as the storm bore down behind her. So fast her arm was a blur, she fired two arrows that whizzed either side of Siris' head before he could even think to dodge, striking down two more warriors. He was astonished.

The storm engulfed the hill, whipping her hair and dress violently. She put the bow down between her knees, unfastened a wide belt holding a long black knife and arrow bag and hitched the dress up. Then she refastened the belt, bent forward and stretched her arms straight out over her head. The wind whipped the dress off. A tumbling blue shape-shifter, it flew straight at Siris, who tried to swat it away with his spear, but it came up the shaft over his arm into his face. It had the smell of her and he was slow removing it.

Strange light flared around the woman, glistening wet and naked except for a short underskirt and the belt. A warrior cried out, "Life-Giver, protect us from this evil creature!"

Siris yelled to attack, sure she could not use a bow with so much wind, but then she fired an arrow that struck the ground precisely between his feet. His anger exploded. Ducking and dodging, he led a charge up the hill, men fanning out to attack on a wide front, a common strategy against bow and spear attacks.

To Siris' left, lions attacked his men out of high grass. To the right, Talik came out of nowhere swinging a small tree trunk, driving the men back. Dismayed, Siris stopped. How could he defeat a witch so strong she turned wild beasts and his own brother against them? Then he spotted the tribe's fastest runners closing on her blind side. They hurled spears, certain to strike at that range, but at the last second Samus jumped up from brush in front of her and knocked one away. The other one struck him in the gut.

The woman stared down at the fallen boy then took the end of the white staff in both hands and pointed it at Siris. "Stop this foolishness before all of you die for no reason."

He was staggered. The words had been inside his head, and in the language of the Mud Men, not the pidgin language tribes used to communicate with each other. Then her face was close to his, concerned, earnest and appealing while crystalline green eyes overpowered his resistance. He whistled the fighting stopped.

More witchery occurred. The lions withdrew and sat in the grass, no longer concerned about the men. Talik tended the men he had just been fighting, and it was as if everyone had forgotten his role in the battle. A buzzing noise sounded around Siris, and he, only vaguely aware, climbed the rain swept hill with the spear bearing the dress held straight out before him.

The woman took the point of the spear and pressed it against a glowing symbol of crossed double-axes above her left breast. The warriors expected Siris to kill her, but he waited docilely until blood trickled down her abdomen then handed her a water skin that she used to catch it. Handing it back, she stepped away from the spear, pulled the dress on and announced, "I will tend to the seriously wounded."

She healed everyone by putting hands on them and saying magical words except Samus, who, the warriors agreed, would soon die. But she pulled out the spear, hitched up the dress and removed the underskirt, unmindful of their gasping and gaping. She made bandages and forced Samus to drink all the blood-water from the skin, which should have killed him with that type of wound, the warriors reckoned, yet the bleeding stopped and he fell into deep sleep. She turned to Talik. "Are other children in the family of Thoth?"

Observing custom, Talik deferred to Siris for an answer. Surprised, his brother hesitated to gather his wits before responding. "He had two older sisters, but we wed them to the Life-giver to stop a drought."

She gave him a very sour look. "You mean you sacrificed them?"

"Yes," he answered proudly. "Then the rains resumed and not a single warrior went hungry next season-cycle."

She seemed about to say something else then threw her head back, waved the staff in the air and shouted the Mud Men's hunting cry. "Eee-yahhhh-heeeee! What say you, Talik, are you hungry?"

"I could eat two hyenas raw!" he yelled, mimicking the animal's yelping and striking the ground with the club. Then everyone danced and imitated animals, causing the lions to snarl and roar and agitated birds to fly into the sky.

By the time the last of the storm clouds disappeared in the east far beyond the Life-Giver, it seemed natural the woman knew all their names. As the air became thick and still again, it seemed natural that she spoke their language and knew all their customs. As the sun boiled steam out of the trail to the plateau, it seemed natural that she was a great god that the Mud Men must heed and honor.

***

"I AM KALLI," SHE ANNOUNCED, "come to make you prosperous and powerful beyond your wildest dreams. All you have to do in return is share your good fortune with other tribes, tolerate no more killing and at the end of each season-cycle celebrate a Feast Day renewing your vows to me. Do this for three hundred season-cycles and I will make your descendants as near to gods as men can be, each living longer than the time I ask you to commit."

An elder stepped forward. "It is not possible for mortals to live so long."

She pointed to Samus, propped up on a litter at the side of the crowd. "I will make it so this boy does not age as proof of my claim. Furthermore, Siris will live much longer than anyone you've ever known."

When the incredulous murmuring died down, a different elder carped, "Our descendants will reap the benefits of our sacrifices. What do we get?"

Her anger frightened them. "You live in squalor. You kill each other without second thoughts. You explain anything you do not understand with superstition. You starve much of the time. And you greet promises that you will live better than kings do with stupid, selfish questions. Ask another, and I'll leave you to scratch in the dirt for bugs to eat."

They shrank back, afraid to say anything else, except for Siris. "What's the catch?"

To everyone's relief, she seemed to think it was a good question. "After you become rich and powerful, a powerful enemy like none you have experienced will come to make you serve them. I will show you how to defeat them."

Siris did not hesitate to show anger. "We need no help fighting enemies!"

"While they have vast armies, they prefer to infiltrate and conquer by turning segments of a society to their evil ways then use them against you. You will not understand you are under attack until it is too late."

"No man alive can fool the Mud Men so easily."

"They are hideous monsters created in darkness that you will see as people until becoming one of them. They are known as the Corruption."

Only Siris understood. "You mean the bogeymen the shaman rails about after chewing the roots of insight, don't you? Oh my, I'm all a-tremble."

Kalli cut off the laughter. "If you are not ready, you will serve them. I propose to stay with you for thirty season-cycles to help you prepare then return on the Feast Days to assess your progress and give advice. If you remain faithful for three hundred season-cycles, you will be the most amazing people who ever walked any land. If you fail to keep our pact, I'll return you to the life you now have."

After only a short amount of discussion, they agreed with little concern for consequences because three-hundred season-cycles were a ridiculously long time and returning to this fine life was not punishment. The woman might be a god, one observed, but she was also irrational like all females. In high spirits, they knelt before her and sealed the agreement.

Kalli tirelessly taught the Mud Men how to recognize the temptations of Corruption while showing them ways to improve every aspect of their lives. Very quickly, where had been camps and villages sprang up towns and cities. They began calling themselves the Obsi, meaning the Chosen, and they were mighty. When Kalli departed after thirty season-cycles, the entire nation lamented.

It seemed almost no time before she was back to celebrate the fifty-fifth Feast Day, a somber time, for Great Siris' recent death still weighed heavily. A grandson, a long time elder, received Kalli's blessing as new leader. From that point, the Obsi turned evermore to matters of business. Prosperity fueled growth and growth fueled prosperity. A golden age ensued, marked by fabulous construction more suited to modern needs. They tore down older buildings, including many of the small austere temples of Kalli, to make way for fabulous recreational and business complexes. Good-natured competition amongst the larger cities to erect the most fabulous statuary and temple complexes began.

**

KALLI INSISTED SAMUS LIVE WITH HER. Initially, he felt honored, but she treated him as a servant and said he should be grateful, not complaining constantly about petty matters. There was something else, too, but he was still too ignorant and ashamed to understand it. He desired Kalli, maybe even loved her, and experienced growing frustration that she did not consider him an equal. She was completely unobtainable.

People made pointed comments about his age because as season-cycles passed, he grew older. Late one night, having just moved into Kalli's smallest temple in the new capital and filled with beer courage, Samus nagged her. "You lied about my not aging, huh?"

She sat next to the altar, restringing her bow by light from a white globe she created overhead. "Your breath stinks."

"Least you can do is look up when you speak to me."

She did not, of course. "It hasn't been convenient for me to do without you."

He staggered sideways. "Liar, liar, liar---that's what you are."

She sighed. "Go to the garden and dig a hole next to that pile of leftover stone blocks. Make the depth and length the same as your height."

He thought it was make-work, something she often required when he bothered her. "It's past time for bed already."

"You'll have it done before I come out if you know what's good for you."

It took a long time to finish, but even so, she kept him waiting. Fuming, he sat on the ground guzzling the last of the beer when, from behind, she pushed him into the hole. Too drunk to climb out, he cursed her. She handed him a cup of rank liquid and told him it would make him feel better, but after drinking, he fell to the ground unable to move.

Terrified that she meant to kill him, he watched her push two huge stone blocks over the opening. Then, moments later, it seemed, he was on his back next to the hole staring into blinding sunlight with her forcing a different bitter liquid down his throat, after which she left him to crawl into the house on his own. A full day passed before he recovered enough to confront her, again at the altar, where she meticulously made marks on dried animal skins, a senseless activity far as he could tell. "What did you do to me the other night?"

"You were asleep five season-cycles," she answered as if discussing nothing important. "Now, for a time, you'll age so slowly it will seem to people you stay the same."

"Pull the other one, why don't you?"

"Go look outside."

He rushed back. "How is it possible?"

"Learn to read and write then I'll show you where to find answers."

"What's read and write?"

She held up a skin and explained. "Do you understand?"

For the first time ever, he earned a smile of approval from her. "It'll revolutionize everything."

"Long sleep improves inherent abilities, but studying is required to hone them. Sit down, and I'll give your first lesson."

Eagerly, he complied. "Did you pick me because you thought I had potential for this kind of thing?"

"Yes, but I didn't realize how big a pain in the ass you are or I would have taken Talik."

At first, Samus was happy with the changes because his physical prowess developed fast as mental skills. He became popular as he developed into a wrestler and runner without peer, but inevitably, not growing older and the fact no one could win against him caused envy and resentment. Of course, no one said anything when Kalli was nearby, but the insults and threats became so bad when alone that he stopped going out except when she made him. Their relationship soured quickly after that.

Twenty-seven season-cycles after entering into the pact with the Mud Men, Kalli told Samus he had to sleep again. He assumed it would be another five season-cycles and that she would be gone when he awoke. He had already resolved to run away when she left and considered the sleep a chance to get away from her sooner.

Late one night, twenty-one season-cycles later, Samus crawled in from the garden naked and muddy. An old woman, squatting in the main room eating, got up without a word, went to the kitchen and came back with a jug of bitter liquid for him to drink. He paid little attention to her as she departed, not realizing it was Kalli, cloaking her identity.

The next evening, Samus packed provisions and left town, but after a few hours, escalating panic attacks sent him scurrying back. He tried numerous more times to leave with the same result, which caused him to despise Kalli so much it made him physically sick, but, at least, she had done something to protect him. Inside the temple, the hundreds of people who used the altar room each day did not recognize him, nor would they go into other rooms or the walled garden, even if he invited. Moreover, he found a fortune in gold and jewelry under the floor of Kalli's closet, so poorly concealed he concluded she meant him to have it, but rather than being grateful, he was angry she had not simply told him.

He settled into a lonely routine, buying everything he needed through an agent and only going out late at night, biding time until no one remained who recognized him. Fascinated by science, he studied everything he could get his hands on and became adept at conducting experiments. He developed a unique talent for mathematics and designing monuments and buildings, a growing passion of his people, whose cities had become marvels. He formed a partnership with a man who did not ask too many questions and sold plans for elaborate houses and gardens that became the talk of the capital. His business evolved into designing and constructing whole communities and large complex structures. When his partner died, no one knew Samus any longer, and he operated their many businesses with assumed names and numerous partners, even discreetly visiting worksites when necessary. In all that time, Kalli did not bother to come see him, and he was glad. In fact, he seldom thought of her anymore.

Then, on a rainy, chilly day, Samus came in and found Kalli wringing water out of her hair next to a roaring fire. She looked up at him with critical eyes. "You've certainly let the place run down. The new fireplace is nice, though."

He was annoyed. "It has been there for thirty season-cycles. I'd tear the whole place down and leave if you'd let me. The neighborhood has gone to seed."

"Yeah, I noticed the Mud Men have become obsessed with money and material goods while the poor starve. Not surprising."

He struck his chest with a fist. "We are Obsi!"

She gave him an appraising look. "The Council Elders said I was sick in the head when I told them I was Kalli. When I asked why they're not observing Feast Days any longer, they threw me out. They even warned me to stop dressing like a god or they'd have me whipped and sentenced to construction labor in prison."

"What did you expect? It has been forever since you visited them."

She took a deep breath. "I wasn't wanted. Regardless, the Corruption is here."

He was sarcastic. "Of course they are. Whatever will we do, Great Kalli?"

"It is a serious matter. You must try to make your people understand what is happening before it is too late."

He kicked the dining table, converted from the old altar. "We can take care of ourselves! Go away and leave us alone!"

Without a word or look back, she walked out into the cold rain.

***

THE PROPHET APPEARED IN THE BIGGEST CITY OF THE SOUTH preaching a religion of nationalism, wealth and power. He claimed immortality and the ability to bestow it. People were used to far-fetched pronouncements because new religions making wild promises came and went constantly. Yet, almost overnight, his became the primary faith in the south with magnificent new temples in every town.

The richest man in the south subscribed to the new religion from the outset and had much to do with the Prophet's success. He had three sons. The third was foul, cruel and sadistic, but the man paid little attention to his family and ignored complaints about the boy. Late one night, the oldest brother found the youngest in the female servants' quarters drawing pictures of demonic creatures on walls and floors with the blood of three maids horribly mutilated. To protect the family name, the father concocted a tale of thieves breaking in then kept the countryside in turmoil as the older sons searched towns and villages for the culprits, eventually accusing and executing a group of recent immigrants, closing the matter.

The man planned to send the third son to a faraway country, but a delegation representing the Prophet intervened with a message saying he had chosen the boy for acolyte training at his Temple of Divine Contemplation. The man turned them away with profuse thanks, contributions and excuses, prompting the Prophet to come see him personally. The man broke down and confessed what had happened. To his surprise and immense relief, the Prophet forgave the boy, guaranteed he could rehabilitate him and assured no one else need ever know. The man cried from relief and joy when the Prophet took his son away.

The third son grew into manhood without equal. Inexplicably strong, towering and possessed with unparalleled warrior skills, he was also brilliant, seductively handsome and beguiling. Rumors of ill temper and sadistic acts popped up from time to time, but as he was the Prophet's right hand, no one believed them. Not that it really mattered, everyone said, because as third son he could not rise higher, for his father was healthy and the law of the land was wealth and position went only to the eldest son.

The father invited the leading people of the south to the eldest son's wedding at his country estate. A fire in one of the Prophet's largest temples delayed his arrival, his good fortune because on the eve of the wedding, a savage band of rogues broke into the house and murdered everyone except the third son, who escaped out a window then crashed back in to avenge the family by killing all twenty of the assailants single-handedly. It was a fantastic story not widely believed at first, but after countless retellings in the Prophet's temples, the people heralded the third son as one of the Obsi's greatest heroes.

Meanwhile, people realized the Prophet truly did not age, causing rampant speculation that he could grant immortality, too. Thousands across the country flocked to his religion.

The Prophet and King Ramond, who ruled the country with a Council of Elders from the capital in the north, had strained relations. The Prophet politely declined every invitation to visit the north and present himself to the King because the government did everything it could to stem his growing power.

Then the Prophet denounced two kingdoms to the far south for plotting to invade and sent a deputation with an appeal to King Ramond to create a real army to protect them. Ramond threw the delegation out because the kingdoms were peaceful allies. In response, the Prophet proposed a southern militia be created with the third son as general to protect them. He offered high wages and, in the unlikely event of battle, generous division of spoils. Recruits poured in from all the Obsi lands. The government could only watch nervously, fearing what would happen if they told the south to desist.

The militia attacked the two kingdoms, killing and enslaving thousands. With exciting stories of glorious battles and brave deeds preceding them, the army marched home to wild celebrations, culminated by the Prophet proclaiming the third son the personification of the religion's prophesized god, Seth, who was to rise up and lead his people to conquer the world. Then the Prophet gave him immortality.

The new god, Great Seth, proposed King Ramond and the Council cede rule to him in return for naming them Regents of all the northern districts, which were ceremonial titles with no authority but allowed them to keep their riches. Relieved, they agreed at once. Then he outlawed the worship of other gods and renamed the Obsi the Horutep, meaning Wisest Ones, because he said they alone were responsible for their rise to greatness. Then, finally, he announced a visit to the capital. The people rejoiced.

***

SAMUS, AN EARLY CONVERT TO THE PROPHET'S RELIGION, used his immense wealth to undermine King Ramond and his council of weaklings. As Seth's power grew, he came more into the open, failing to realize his activities were under scrutiny by Ramond's network of spies. He expected Seth to depose Ramond, not leave him and his cronies in positions of influence in the capital.

In keeping with the religion's family values, Samus had taken two wives and expanded the small ramshackle building into a fine big house, very conspicuous in the slums. He did not realize the first wife schemed from the beginning to steal his wealth and suspected he practiced black arts that hid his aging. Her brother, who Samus considered his closest friend, conspired with her, passing weekly reports to the local magistrate, a cousin of a Council Elder. The second wife and her children, marginalized and mistreated by the first, doted on him.

Kalli's two hundredth Feast Day loomed near, but Samus gave it no more thought than anyone else did. Then, during a typical rowdy family supper late one evening, the first wife spat out a mouth of food and jumped up. "Who are you? Get out of my house!"

Stepping out of shadows from the new foyer, Kalli looked exactly as depicted in the faded paintings on older buildings that showed her with a white gown and staff. "All these snotty young'uns yours, Samus? My, my." Answered by nothing but incredulous stares, she shrugged. "The Corruption is taking over. I've returned to keep my promise to the Mud Men and be done with it."

Samus found his voice. "Are you completely mad? Get out of here!"

Just then, a loud commotion came from outside. Soldiers burst in behind Kalli and a melee ensued. More soldiers stormed in the back way, easy since the remodeling removed the courtyard walls. They overwhelmed and imprisoned the house's inhabitants.

An enormous dust cloud shadowed the land and a thousand drums beat a slow, ponderous cadence, marking the army's progress up the slope from the Life-Giver toward the sprawling capital on the high plateau. It demonstrated the power of Great Seth.

Arms outstretched and tied to the white staff across her shoulders, the one Ramond dubbed the Kalli-Pretender stood resolute in spite of a shattered right leg and having been beaten near to death. Noting the irony, she watched the army's approach from the same grassy hill she first encountered the Mud Men. Nearby, tethered by the necks to long poles driven into the ground, two vicious criminals and several hapless politicians awaited death, also. Bound and saturated with lamp oil, five hundred other prisoners, including Samus and family, were to be tinder for the sacrificial fires.

Arrayed close to the prisoners in best positions to see the approach of Great Seth as well as the sacrifices, King Ramond, the Council and royal court celebrated. Ramond's entire royal guard, decked out in splendid black and red uniforms, the colors of Great Seth's battle standards displayed on a thousand golden flagpoles, crowded the lower part of the hill. Ramond glanced up a flagpole and wished for wind so the standards did not hang so limply.

Excitement was at fever pitch when the army halted a short distance from the hill. Seth had granted Ramond the ability to make everyone hear and see him close-up, amusing the southern soldiers to no end as this kind of power was new and frightening to the northerners. To begin the ceremony, Ramond went to the staked prisoners and directed the simultaneous slashing of wrists. Then he declared the last one standing would receive a proper burial rather than a beheading and left for wild animals, which the Prophet taught would keep them from entering the afterlife. The army catcalled and wagered who would last longest while Ramond marched with four guards to the Kalli-Pretender.

The King mixed bawdy jokes into an account of how the Kalli-Pretender had shown up claiming to be the old god and making demands of him. All the while, he struck and challenged her to defend herself. Then he lifted her gown and pointed at her nakedness. "If you ask me, she's nothing special."

The warriors hooted, whistled and yelled obscenities. Ramond drew his sword and struck her in the face with the hilt. "Will anyone volunteer to die in her place? If so, I will spare her life."

The soldiers quietened almost immediately. Angry murmurs rippled through the ranks. He would allow her to live? What would Great Seth say?

Samus' second wife stood up. Ramond ran and beheaded her, the sword's arc slinging blood on a group of elegant ladies of the court, which made the soldiers roar with laughter. Then Ramond made it even better. "This one doesn't count because she's already dead! Now, does anyone alive want to volunteer?"

The soldiers jeered, cheered, clamored and yelled. Nearly out of time, Ramond had his men grab the ends of the staff and jerk the Pretender back upright. He sliced her right wrist half through and blood spouted. He waved the sword over his head. "Damn the old gods! Hail, Great Seth!"

Drums struck a fast syncopated rhythm and the army ran in place screaming a song extolling the wonders of Seth. Ramond ran back to his court and joined in. Meanwhile, as tethered men fell one by one, they had their heads lopped off, the last suffering the same fate as the others. Hardly anyone noticed the reneged promise because Ramond had wine and beer passed through the ranks. The celebration had started in earnest.

Great Seth, astride a black stallion remade by the Prophet into something huge, monstrous and seen by even the uninitiated, made a dramatic appearance from behind a curtain of banners. His red armor and plumed helm shined from inner light. His shadow was twice that of other men, a god if ever a god there be. Ramond, waving one of the standards, ran down the hill and threw himself on the ground before the god, who drew his famous black-bladed sword and held it over the King's neck. "By granting Ramond life, I accept him into my service. Soon, my people, the rest of the world will bow down before our might and pay dearly to join us. This, I pledge to you!"

Meanwhile, courtiers taunted and threw rocks at the Kalli-Pretender, standing stoical with eyes closed, but the guards were concerned because already she had lost enough blood to empty ten people. Taking matters into his own hands, a lieutenant rushed over intending to behead, but the ropes binding her to the staff began writhing and twisting untied. Then they fell to the ground and became huge hissing hooded vipers. The guards stumbled backwards from them into the ranks of courtiers, creating a loud commotion. No one noticed the snakes vanish, the Pretender push the staff overhead and begin fast-speaking incantations.

All Ramond's people on the hill moved in unison like jerky marionettes. They turned in her direction, drew bladed weapons and hacked each other. No one tried to escape, resisted or cried out. At the same time, Seth's warriors went berserk, yelling and flailing weapons at unseen enemies. Seth grabbed one and asked what he saw, but the soldier attacked him. After he killed the man, Seth said words to remove the protections shielding himself from mind tricks and witnessed giant snakes coming out of the ground, but before he could act, the images transformed into a vision of the Kalli-Pretender holding the staff overhead. Torrents of blood gushed from both her wrists, feeding a network of glowing, pulsing blood vessels covering the entire hill. Then the wounds closed, the network of veins vanished and she lowered the staff.

Seth knew he faced the real Kalli. Trying to decide whether to fight or withdraw to consult the Prophet, he used his power to gauge her strength and determined how weak the torture had left her. He suppressed her vision and replaced it with one of himself, which rallied the stunned troops. He glanced down at Ramond, on the ground with arms over his head babbling. "But I killed her. I did. Everyone saw me. I killed her."

Seth kicked him. "The Prophet showed me drawings of illusions Kalli employs. The blood and network of veins she calls Heart of the Land. You brought the real Kalli here, fool."

Ramond looked up. "But Kalli is just a myth, isn't she?"

Seth jerked him off the ground by the arm and swung him into a tree trunk so hard his body flew to pieces. Beating shields with weapons, the troops roared approval. Seth spoke a spell infusing them with even more bloodlust, drew his sword and pointed to the hill. "Kill everyone!"

Ramond's people were dead or dying, and the prisoners could do nothing to escape the crazed hordes swarming toward the hill. Some screamed to Kalli for help, but she stood with eyes closed and lost in trance. It seemed hopeless.

Suddenly, the charging soldiers staggered, overwhelmed by visions of the mutilated bodies of Ramond's people, putrid odors from their deaths and certain knowledge the same fate awaited them on the hill. Seth could not break the spell but could tell it required all Kalli's remaining strength.

She was easy prey. His glory would have no bounds if he killed her personally. He pushed through the men onto the hill, ignoring the spell assailing his senses. He closed the distance to her quickly and noted Kalli's closed eyes and that her only weapon, the staff, hung loosely in the left hand. Insuring he reached her on the correct foot, he summoned all his corrupted power and strength. Black-tinged flames blazed from him to the sword as he swung a wide arc to cut her in half with a single stroke, but the weapon met no resistance whatever, carrying him forward off balance. She was an illusion.

Kalli rose up from the prisoners and struck him across the face with the staff, sending the god-giant crashing to the ground on his belly. The blow would have killed anyone else but only stunned Seth. She bent down, gingerly took the sword from his hand and straddled his body. But, as he raised his head, he sensed the danger and twisted violently as the blade struck his neck, wresting it from her, but it was too late. Head half-severed from the body, Seth slumped to the ground, dead.

The warriors who attacked the hill were human and fled, but the demons and soon-to-be-demon converts had waited. Moreover, they could sense that she had all but depleted her energy. Kalli, sitting on Seth's body, watched them coming, knowing she would not win this battle. But then Samus was there, keeping them at bay with the threat of her staff until the frustrated demon leaders huddled to quarrel whether there was really anything to fear from it in his hands.

Kalli reached up to Samus with a hand dripping Seth's blood. "You must taste this. Do it!"

He did as told. Terror and disbelief seized him as for the first time he saw their true demon forms. He cursed her. "What have you done to me?"

She reached up again, taking his hands and guiding them to lift her up. "Now that you have an evil master's blood in you, you can see the Corrupted."

"Why didn't you show us this before?"

"Because, except for people with exceptional abilities, ingesting their blood without initiation kills them."

He actually laughed. "So, am I going to die?"

"Possibly. How do you feel?

"Nothing's changed. Mostly, I hate you."

"That's good. Give me the staff." With his help, she pointed it at the demon leaders. "You have two days to get out of these lands or I will burn your life-spirits for all eternity."

Her voice had boomed inside their minds, and when they looked up, they saw the sky turning to fire. Then flames erupted on the ground between them and the woman. Terrified, they ran.

***

KALLI, LEG WRAPPED AND PROPPED ON A STOOL, watched the smug way the new Council of Elders considered the furnishings of Samus' family room and did not ask them to sit. Shuffling uncomfortably, they began explaining the Prophet and his clerics had disappeared without a trace. She cut them off. "Samus, son of Thoth, convinced me to give you a chance to redeem yourselves by constructing a new city he designed. It is a ridiculously ambitious project and I don't think you can do it, but I'll leave it for you to decide."

They looked at each other with surprise. They had expected her to demand sacrifice of a large portion of the population or forfeiture of much of the country's wealth. Eckarius, First Elder, whispered under his breath to the others. "This god is not only lame, she's weak."

Kalli motioned Samus to pull back curtains covering three walls. The Second Elder blurted, "No one can build all that!"

She shrugged. "So I take it you want a different punishment?"

Eckarius answered before anyone else could. "Indulge us a moment, Great Kalli, while we confer." They gathered in a tight knot filled with whispers then, with a smug smile, Eckarius said, "We'll do it, but it'll take at least seventy-five cycles."

She looked bored. "You may have a hundred. After all, I always keep my word."

They shared puzzled looks, none of them remembering the details of the bargain struck with the Mud Men two hundred cycles ago. Eckarius bowed to her. "We accept and give thanks to Great Kalli."

She smiled, and they thought she was pleased, but then she said, "Just so you do not think I am weak as well as lame, I will add a second, more difficult requirement. When you're finished, none of the monuments in the new city may be dedicated to me or any other god, nor will they bear inscriptions of any kind."

The Council clustered around the Second Elder, all but pushing Eckarius away from the group as more whispered discussions ensued. Finally, the Second Elder addressed her. "Uh, we don't understand why you think that is more difficult than building it."

She surprised them by laughing, deeply and robustly, until they joined in. Later, they agreed the god had a strange sense of humor.

Several weeks later, Kalli sat at the Thoth family's dining table, watching Samus pace. "One day you'll understand, but the damage to my leg is too severe to heal properly, but that's not the main reason I want you to go with me. You possess amazing abilities that require guidance and long sleep to develop properly."

He was angry. "We can't leave. The projects have just begun. You want us to fail, don't you? You've always wanted us to fail. A real god takes care of people! A real god fights for them! A real god protects them!"

"With all the studying you do, you should realize by now that there are no gods, Samus."

He waved his arms wildly. "Gods created the world! They watch over us! At least, the good ones do!"

"Okay, okay, believe what you will, but I'm certainly not a god. Letting your people think I was seemed the best way to get them to change at the time, but I understand now that pretending to be a god is a flawed strategy."

He yelled in her face. "Strategy? Is that what you gods do for kicks, play with people's lives then cast them off when you tire of them?"

She pushed him away. "There are better prospects than the Mud Men elsewhere."

He grabbed her shoulders and shook her. "We are Horutep! You promised three hundred season-cycles! If I was a god, I would never forsake my people, you lame witch!"

In spite of excruciating pain, she stood, twisted him onto the dining table and pulled up on top of him. Pinning his arms, she whispered something that rendered him helpless. She cut open her palm, forced a large amount of blood down his throat and made him drink a large jug of water. She squeezed his right wrist, yelled an incantation and struck his upper left chest so violently with her fist that it rendered him unconscious.

Fighting back tears, she climbed off the table and stared down at him. "We could have been together for a very long time, but now, I just hope that Nun records you succeeded where I failed. Good luck to you, Samus."

Sunlight streamed through the high eastern windows of an enormous room of lavish furnishings. Sprawled across a long ornate banquet table, Pharaoh jerked awake with a throbbing hangover and raised a hand to his forehead. A glowing symbol of three golden pyramids on his inside wrist caused him to avert his eyes down to his chest where another symbol of crossed double-headed axes glowed and offended his eyes even more. With a loud curse, he rolled off the table into a big golden chair, where he sat rubbing his temples, wishing he could stop the nightmares about her.

A heavy door at the rear creaked open. Two priests in long robes waited until he looked their way then followed a luxurious crimson carpet across the room, stopping to bow every nine steps. They placed brimming trays of food and drink before him. Chief Priest Eckarius spoke. "Great God Thoth will find the fruit especially sweet this morning."

He swept the trays from the table with a mighty arm and screamed up at the ceiling. "Kalli, damn you, why did you do this to me?" Frightened for their lives, the priests cleaned up the mess, brought more wine and scurried away.

For fifty-five season-cycles, he had driven the Horutep to finish the project, yet they were hopelessly behind schedule. Good wages and incentives failed to get results. Harsh disciple brought no remedy. There were numerous strikes and outright rebellion. Executions of demons he spotted only created discord and disloyalty as no one else could see them and believed his accusations were madness. Legions of spies could not root out traitors and troublemakers. Queens, wives and consorts could not endure more than a few season-cycles living with him. He had lost track of all his children and relatives plotting to take the throne. He drank incessantly, suffered fits of depression and committed horrendous acts of violence against anyone who stood in the way.

One evening, drunk, despairing and cursing Kalli for his miserable life and his people's failures, Great Thoth stumbled from the palace during a heavy rainstorm and was last seen walking next to the flooding Life-Giver. No one ever found his body and he passed into history and legend.

***

MIRACLE! THE NEW PHARAOH BRINGS BACK THE GREAT PROPHET with a new religion more suited to the times. Together, they issue a decree to complete the new city of temples and monuments on schedule as a demonstration of the power of the Horutep to a world that has begun to doubt them.

REJOICE! They complete the task and gather to celebrate and count off days until the wondrous morning when priests climb onto the back of the mighty new lion-god that watches over the most fabulous temple complex in the world. They will call him into service by shouting his secret name to the people three times.

PRAISE! The day arrives, and with it, another miracle. An unknown god flies down from the heavens with Head Priestess Raiku of Khemenu City to witness the Ten Priests of Exaltation sacrificing ten virgins on the back of the lion-god. Plunging ceremonial daggers into the virgins' chests, they bring forth hearts steaming in the coolness of the wonderful new day and perform a holy chant. "In the name of the Great Prophet and the mighty Horutep, the time has come for the world to bow down to our new god, Great…Great…!"

DISASTER. They cannot remember the name. They mill in confusion until a sacrificed virgin stands, removes the ceremonial wig and shakes out long, white-blond hair. Suddenly, everyone in the land remembers the oath to Kalli and the significance of this, the three hundredth Feast Day. After begging her for another chance and seeing the reply in her emerald eyes, the Priests leap from the great cat to their deaths.

RETRIBUTION. Kalli turns slowly and speaks without malice or emotion, yet everyone feels them in her words. "You will destroy all evidence that your enemies, the Horutep and the Obsi, dared walk in your lands. When you finish, you will not remember they existed. Now, take back what is rightfully yours and restore your former glory, proud Mud Men!"

***

SAVAGE TRIBES CRISSCROSS LANDS FILLED WITH RUINS of an ancient people long forgotten. They fight until one retreats or dies, for to show mercy is to show weakness. Fertile grassy plains and forests become lost memories as rains cease and desert hides the past.

Travelers, campfires casting shadows upon the head of an enigmatic cat statue sticking out of shifting sands before scavenged, broken pyramids, sleep restlessly under its unchanging gaze, more often than not waking before dawn seized by violent sense of loss. When the sun comes up over the timeless river to the east, they eat first meal and speculate what could have happened to the extraordinary people who created such wonders.

THREE

BALANCING WIDE-LEGGED IN THE BOW of a royal Egyptian long ship, the girl had the time of her life riding the rowers' lunging pulls through rolling sea swells. A trio of dolphins leaped out of the water alongside and she spun around with excitement. The front of the ship plunged, throwing a plume of cold water over the bow, drenching her. Squealing, she kicked off her sandals and jumped up and down in water streaming off the deck through gunwale drains.

Three ships, approaching from dead ahead since daylight, drew near finally. Amazed, she gaped at them. Four times the size of the Egyptian vessel, designed by her master and huge compared to Nile river boats, they had three masts and several billowed triangular sails instead of a single mast and one rectangular sail. Even more remarkable, they had no oars, none at all. As they gave way to pass to the west, light from the rising sun behind her brought their spectacular decorations to life. She shrieked, "Oh, how gorgeous!"

The first had twisting green vines sprouting white flowers with yellow centers painted stem to stern; the second, an enormous stylized red, green and yellow bird with its beak extended up the prow, body and wings stretched across the hull and tail feathers fanned over the stern; and the third, three leaping dolphins silhouetted against a yellow sun. Thrilled, she read aloud the name on the stern. "Dolphin Racer."

Close behind her, a man's voice. "My, you're up early this morning, Lady."

She whipped around and tangled her feet, only his strong arms keeping her from falling on her face. Flushed with embarrassment, she freed herself. He was tall with ebony skin and a classically handsome Egyptian face, yet she knew he must be the Kallistian Envoy, the only person onboard she did not know by sight. But he appeared no older than sixteen or seventeen and wore workman's clothes---heavy sandals strapped up the calves, a simple waist-skirt to just above the knees and a sleeveless, lightweight vest with no fasteners. His wide leather wristbands could have been an ornamentation, except they were the rugged type stoneworkers wore. His hair was close-cut like an Egyptian commoner, too. Even more confounding, numerous crisscrosses of scars were on his muscular torso and forearms as she had seen only on warriors, though never so many and certainly not on anyone so young. She caught herself staring and averted her eyes as befit her station to wait for him to speak again.

He was puzzled. She had read the name of the ship written in an old form of Kallistian no longer used. She and her father had been the guests of the King on Kefti for more than a year awaiting permission to open an embassy on Kalliste, but young girls did not study old languages and histories. Moreover, she behaved more as an undisciplined child than a privileged noblewoman did. Her wraparound dress was common, the sandals cheaply made and coming apart from wet and she did not wear the face paint upper crust Egyptian girls used. More notably, she did not wear a wig, perhaps because her hair was such thick, fine brunette, though unevenly cut and frazzled rather than expertly braided. She seemed much younger than they told him, too, but who else could she be? Again, he addressed her in Egyptian. "Do I have the honor of meeting the Ambassador's daughter?"

She lowered her head even more. "No. Her personal maid."

He meant to tease to put her more at ease. "Isn't a personal servant for the daughter of a prominent family usually a bent, old crone?"

She looked up sharply. "I'll have you know that I'm thirteen, going on fourteen!" She realized she had forgotten her place again, put her head back down and mumbled, "Sorry if that sounded rude, Master."

He snapped, "I'm no one's master!"

Could have fooled me, she thought. "I apologize if my humble presence offended you, sir. With permission, I will withdraw now."

He had her blocked in the point of the bow and did not move, instead placing a finger under her chin and forcing her head up. "What's your name?"

It was all she could do to stop herself biting his hand. "Maidservant."

He made a critical clucking sound. "No, little girl, not your job, your name."

She pushed the finger away. "The name and job are the same. Please do not presume me too stupid to know the difference. And don't call me little girl...Master."

He glared. "I'll have you know that you are addressing Envoy of the Temple of Light, on mission to accompany the Egyptian Ambassador and his daughter to Kalliste Island."

She crossed her arms and looked him up and down. "Oh, yes, come to think of it, someone did mention a dignitary would be traveling with us. By your fine clothes and impeccable manners, I should have realized at once that you are that very person and not simply an arrogant nitwit. I am so-o-o honored to be in your presence." With a wide flourish of the hand, she bowed deeply and remained down.

The neck of her wet, ill-fitted dress puckered, and he saw her bare back covered with red welts and dark bruises. Examining her closer, he noted more on her arms and legs skillfully hidden with blended dabs of Egyptian makeup paint. Moreover, she held herself stiffly and trembled slightly, doubtless expecting him to strike her. He cleared his throat. "I've acted like a pompous ass, Miss Maidservant. Please forgive me."

No one had ever apologized to her before. She looked up with one eye closed and tongue stuck out the corner of her mouth, a peculiar way she had of showing surprise, and did not know what to say.

Just then, two soldiers trotted across deck unfurling a length of scarlet fabric mounted on long poles. They positioned either side of a large private pavilion in the stern and shaded the entrance. Lord Hariset, Egyptian Royal Ambassador, emerged and walked to the bow, the soldiers alongside carefully keeping him shaded. He stopped just beyond the wet part of the deck and waited for the Kallistian to come to him. "What manner of ships were those that passed, boy? They had no oars."

"They're an invention of a Temple Priest, Lord. He spent a lot of time developing them."

The Ambassador made a determined effort not to look impressed though both knew such ships would revolutionize trade and travel. "May I be permitted to examine them?"

"Since an exception has been made for Egypt to establish an embassy on our island," the Kallistian answered smoothly, "I'm certain the Head Priest will consider your request seriously."

The non-answer irritated the Ambassador, but he let it go and peered ahead at four more ships approaching from the north with the usual complements of oarsmen. "The Keftiu Empire is fortunate to have the commerce of Kalliste supporting it, but Egypt thinks it strange we had not heard of your island until last year. I found it particularly irritating during our stay on Kefti that whenever I asked how that is possible, everyone gave vague answers, laughed and changed the subject. Can you shed any light on the matter?"

The Kallistian nodded. "It is just that Kalliste is such a humble island, Lord, that no one paid it any mind until the southern port of Eao blossomed almost overnight into a trade center. The route between Eao Harbor and the capital on Kefti has long been the main trade artery within the Empire but of no importance to anyone else, so there is no mystery, none at all, that others paid it no attention." He laughed. "What did you think of the royal court of the king? The palace is splendid, is it not?"

Hariset glared, wanting to strangle him. "It wasn't the scale one expects of a first rate power. I was surprised to hear you have never seen the great pyramids. The previous Pharaoh spent a lifetime restoring them. He replaced hundreds of broken stone blocks, some bigger than houses, then had the whole thing completely encased in white plaster. They were in amazing disrepair, but now, they're more magnificent than anything someone like you can imagine."

The young man nodded. "Your captain told me that the same Pharaoh had the head of your most sacred monument, a great lion statue, re-sculpted into his likeness. It certainly takes a special person to think of ways to improve ancient wonders."

The Ambassador thought the comment a thinly veiled insult and made his more blatant. "Being near the sea all the time makes people smell like fish, don't you think? Then again, I suppose one becomes accustomed, living on islands and all."

A young woman emerged from the pavilion. A woven white gown clung to her supple bronze body in a manner that suggested lewd destinations for onlookers to rest their gazes. A long black wig, expertly cut and combed, framed an exceptionally beautiful face, made up and painted to accent her intelligent, sensuous eyes. She walked to the bow, every move nuanced to hold attention. Then she spotted Maidservant, and the illusion shattered. She wagged a twelve-inch gold scepter chained to a matching bracelet on her right wrist. "Useless creature! Attend me!"

Maidservant ran, jumped over her mistress' shadow and carefully positioned exactly three paces behind and to the side.

"Idiot! Why are you soaking wet? Where are your sandals? Strike the pose I taught you!"

Clumsily, Maidservant did her best to look haughty, but mainly, she looked ridiculous, especially after her mistress started forward and she did not notice her stop to fix a loose wig pin. She walked past her. Fortunately, though, her mistress' eyes had latched onto the Kallistian and did not notice her scrambling back into place.

"Ah, Seydi," Hariset declared. "You grow more radiant every day."

She showed no sign she heard him, going straight to the Kallistian and staring up at him with very bold eyes. "Please, tell me living on Kalliste will not be as boring as my time on Kefti. Tell me it will not be as dreary. Tell me diversions exist that I might find...exciting."

Paying her no attention whatever, the Kallistian turned from her to the Ambassador. "Your daughter is fortunate to have been chosen to attend the Temple of Light."

Hariset bristled. "She was recommended by no less than King Ermiticus, himself!"

Although he smiled, the Kallistian's response was anything but agreeable. "While the Head Priest certainly has deep abiding respect for the King's opinion, she has sole authority over Kalliste."

Suddenly, Seydi struck Maidservant a stinging blow on the arm with the scepter. "Stupid toad! Your dirty feet are on my shadow again. Since you can't pay attention, go scrub the deck in our quarters again."

Hariset wanted to ask why the Head Priest could ignore the king, but the Kallistian irritated him too much at the moment. "I have private matters to discuss with my daughter. Go tell the captain to set up a table and food on deck for us. I'll talk to you later."

***

IT WAS LATE WHEN MAIDSERVANT CREPT OUT to retrieve her sandals and stopped, amazed by myriads of lights in the distance reflecting brilliantly on the water. Then she hurried to the bow to get a better look and did not notice the Kallistian in the shadows. He said, "We're outside Eao Harbor."

Not understanding why, she was glad he was there. "How come the lights go so far up into the sky?"

"The upper part of Eao is on the side of the mountain."

"Is it as tall as the Great Pyramid?"

"It is higher than clouds. Much of the time, you can't see the top."

She thought he exaggerated. She pointed to the left where raging fires burned on top of a high tower that seemed to rise out of the sea. "What's that?"

"The Southern Lighthouse. It is on the outer jetty and warns ships to stand off until daylight. There are three jetties across the harbor with staggered ways through them for defense. They say that Kalli planned their construction personally."

Her master would reward her for anything she found out about Kalli, but, for some reason, she felt a twinge of guilt getting information from him. "Who is Kalli?"

"Founder and first Head Priest of the Temple. Until recently, we didn't speak of her to outsiders."

"Why?"

"If you don't mind, allow me to tell you more about Kalliste. There are four lighthouses."

She was disappointed and relieved at the same time, adding to the confusion growing in her. "I bet this one is oldest."

"Uh, yes, but how did you know?"

She smiled in the darkness. "You told my master that the shipping lane between Eao Harbor and Kefti is the main trade route, so it stands to reason this would be first. Strange, though, that so many ships traveled from a harbor too puny to be noticed by anyone until last year."

He wanted to see her face better, for although he had the ability to see in the dark, she kept her head down and all that hair hid her face. Two long, mournful sounds carried across the harbor. "In addition to lighthouses, huge horns are blown every hour. We have a lot of fog around the island."

"Hope our quarters aren't close to them. I'm a light sleeper."

He hid his surprise. "Surely, you're not planning to go ashore?"

"I told you. I take care of Mistress Seydi."

He hesitated then pointed to a line of lights in the darkness above the city. "That's the avenue where your master and mistress will stay temporarily. The horns can't be heard that far up. Under normal circumstances, they are only loud outward from the island, not inward."

Immediately, she replied, "Then there must be some sort of mechanism for turning them. Are they mounted on swivels or such?"

There was certainly more to this girl than first impressions indicated. He bent closer. "Yes, they're inside shell-shaped structures that float in pools of water and easily turned."

She knew she should stop carelessly showing off, but impressing him felt good. "You're Egyptian heritage, aren't you?"

He tensed, but she did not notice. "Why do you think so?"

"People in the Keftiu Empire are mostly brown-skinned like me; not black, like you."

"There are black people scattered in all the lands around the sea."

"Yes, but the way you pronounce words is different than Kallistians I encountered on Keftiu, and when my master bragged about the pyramids, I got the distinct impression you've seen them. That's why I asked if your mountain is as tall as the Great Pyramid. Anyone who had not seen it would have asked how high it is." She waited for a response but he said nothing so she baited him using the name of an Egyptian feline deity. "What's wrong, Bastet got hold of your tongue?"

He laughed. "I didn't ask because there is no structure on earth as high as our mountain, but please allow me to ask a question. How is it you could read the name of the Kallistian ship this afternoon?"

Caught by surprise, she blurted, "Female slaves aren't permitted to read."

Now, he was surprised. "Surely, you're not a slave?"

She did not understand why he asked such an obvious thing. "What else would a servant be?"

"But slaves are not allowed on Kalliste."

"Who does the work?"

He sighed and changed the subject. "Are your parents in Egypt with you?"

She was very flustered. "No. My family died when I was...ouch!" She doubled over holding her head.

He grabbed her. "What's wrong?"

It was hard to speak. "Bug bite. All right in a minute. My mother is a cook in my master's house. Don't know about my father."

"But you just said they died."

She held tightly to him. "Please, I don't want to talk about it."

He rubbed her temples until she recovered. Then, in the kindest voice he could manage, he asked, "Does Seydi beat you?"

She was not offended in the least. "Only when I misbehave."

"Often?"

She was sleepy and yawned. "It's not important."

"But…"

She shushed him. "She can do whatever she wants. She owns me."

She woke up hot, stiff and aching from sleeping on the hard deck, yet when she remembered she was under the Kallistian's cloak, she smiled. He had put her down and covered her. Then she realized she had not asked his name. What must he think of her? She poked her head out, momentarily blinded by sunlight. Then she saw him perched in the bow peering down at the water intently. He raised his left arm and the ship turned that direction. She had not even noticed they were moving. What time was it, anyway? She jumped up, planning to run to her duties, then forgot everything except the breathtaking spectacle of the island.

The lighthouse, five stories of polished white stone, loomed over her. The harbor was enormous, its blue-green water bustling with ships from all over the world. The jetties curved out toward the sea with countless warehouses and docks crowding them. On shore, the buildings of Eao City were every gorgeous color imaginable and set among adorning trees and abundant flowering plants. Then, there was the mountain, filling the sky with an ascending majesty of greens on the lower elevations and blended bands of blues and purples upward until disappearing into high tumbling clouds that cast dancing shadows and sunlight patches across the earth below---a wondrous kaleidoscope created by gods, surely. For an instant, the clouds parted, and she glimpsed three silver lines that had to be the great aqueducts the Kallistian described last night. Then neck pain forced her to stop looking up, and she found her master next to her, bent back, also looking up at the mountain. Lest she disturb him, she bowed and waited.

Hariset had spent what amounted to several lifetimes researching stories about this island and concluded Kalli probably concocted them to conceal her true final hiding place. Now, however, he knew he had been wrong. He forced his full attention to the Kallistian in the bow. "So, boy, this is the humble island everyone sailed by for hundreds of years without noticing?"

He jumped down and bowed "Yes, Lord. This is Eao, the main port."

Hariset looked at the docks and lines of warehouses on the jetties. "Strange, don't you think, a landmark so prominent isn't on any maps except ones made recently? Moreover, I did not see this mountain on the horizon last evening. What's your explanation?"

"Clouds often obscure it."

"The sky ahead was crystal clear."

"Maybe the sun was in your eyes."

"The sun wasn't a factor as we approached from due south."

"Sometimes, sea mists create haze along the horizon that melds sea and sky into unbroken blue."

Seydi ran out of the pavilion, stopping their conversation. "Where's that worthless girl? Attend me! Attend me!"

Maidservant tripped on the cloak and fell. Before she could get up, Seydi was there. "Your appearance is atrocious! You will stay onboard until dark then find the way to our quarters yourself. Don't make that face at me. And don't whine about being afraid of the dark, either. You will have my makeup and breakfast ready when I wake up in the morning if you know what's good for you. Now get out of my sight!" She whacked Maidservant on the ear with the scepter as she ran past. "Father, I swear that girl is worth less than a pile of dung."

Quietly, the Kallistian asked, "Did you sleep well, Lady Seydi?"

Remembering his insolence the day before, she turned her back and glared at the island, its wonders insufficient to combat her dark mood.

Hariset blocked the gangway. "I'm unaccustomed to such ill treatment!"

The Kallistian did his best to be polite. "Things are done differently here, Lord. There are no government officials. Members of the Temple take care of everything."

"How does anything function?"

"That can only be judged after you go ashore."

"But there is no one but you to greet me? Who's your superior? You must answer to someone."

"I answer to the Head Priest."

"Everyone can't answer to one person. If that's the case, you're in charge of Kallistian diplomacy."

"Yes, under direction of the Head Priest."

Hariset scowled. "I'll go ashore, but this insult will be noted when I talk to the Council. However, I am not comfortable with my men not taking weapons. I plan to file a complaint about that, too."

But now, the Kallistian blocked the gangway. "There is another matter. Your daughter's maid doesn't have permission go beyond the port's public trading areas. Only you and your daughter were granted access to the rest of the island."

"Surely, no one expects Seydi to be without a servant."

"She will be a Temple Prospect, and they aren't allowed servants of any kind."

This was news to Hariset so he did not respond immediately as it messed up his plans. "There are private circumstances that make it necessary for the girl to accompany us. I'm certain the Head Priest will give permission when I explain, but for now, since you are in charge of diplomacy, please make an exception."

The Kallistian took a deep breath. "Very well, but the Head Priest will not be happy."

"By the mouth of Osiris, I said I'd talk to her, didn't I?"

***

BARTERED AT DIZZYING RATES, goods from all over the world crowded the port trading zone. Sailors' pidgin was the common language of trade, although many others added to the cacophonous noise in the area. Hariset wondered if the wealth of Kalliste could possibly be overestimated. It was astounding.

They wound through narrow streets lined by inns, bars and businesses catering to a large port's clientele before arriving at a high stone archway with a huge set of artificial bull's horns extending over buildings either side. A jovial man in a neat green tunic came from a booth. "Fair weather, Envoy."

Envoy introduced Lord Hariset and Lady Seydi. "This man is from the Temple. He's in charge of assisting visitors who start to stray out of the port area."

They exchanged niceties then continued to a wide avenue paved with translucent milky tiles. Each was a perfect three feet square. Hariset bent and ran his hand across one. "What manner of material is this? I've never seen anything like it."

Envoy shook his head. "No one knows. By all accounts, the roads were here when the first settlers arrived and found an empty island devastated by long ago earthquakes and eruptions."

Hariset accepted the explanation. "Egypt has forgotten more than it remembers, also." He looked up at the mountain. "Is it active?"

"Occasional smoke and tremors, but it hasn't erupted since resettling the island."

"How long ago was that?"

"There are no records, sorry to say."

Hariset looked around. Fine stone and stucco buildings, some high as six stories, lined every street he looked down with no less affluent areas apparent. Nearly all had exteriors of bright colors. Bulls' horns adorned roofs and doorways, yet he suspected they did not have any more religious significance than the many murals of other animals he saw in houses. People carried knives, but as tools, not weapons, and no other arms. On Kefti, they had a powerful navy and soldiers everywhere on the island, but he saw no military here at all. There were no fortifications around the cities, either, making him doubly sure someone here had great power. Yet, he sensed none, and it made him uneasy.

The Kallistian interrupted his musings. "The Head Priest requests that you stay with your daughter in the House of Kalli since your embassy in Cadisum City and her quarters in Prospect Village are not quite ready. The building was supposedly the first on the island and not very comfortable, I'm afraid."

Hariset had decided to refrain from asking questions about Kalli until accepted into the community, but the Kallistian was so casual mentioning her that he changed his mind. "Was Kalli a king?"

"She founded the Temple and was first Head Priest. Not much is known about her other than a few hand-me-down stories."

"Surely the Temple has records of someone so important."

He shook his head. "Kalli destroyed everything about her before she died, even statues and likenesses painted on buildings. She was remarkably thorough."

"But surely, others recorded information about her after her death."

"You would think so, but there is nothing. I realize it sounds odd, but it is true."

He spoke so openly Hariset chanced a question about something else. "Why is access to the inner island restricted? Almost makes one think you're hiding something."

The Kallistian gestured around. "You can go anywhere you like except Temple properties, though there's nothing hidden there, either. I'm sure your daughter will tell you all about them."

"Then why are restrictions necessary?"

"It was one of Kalli's rules and has been mindlessly enforced ever since. Rhea, the new Head Priest, wants to change all the outmoded practices, but some on the Council object strongly. Allowing Egypt to establish an embassy is a case in point."

"I'm surprised that merchants in the towns stand for being segregated. It must cost them dearly."

"Yes, that is an astute observation, and another thing I think Rhea will change soon."

They arrived at a market next to a park where people relaxed around a gigantic octopus fountain casting mists from its eight arms. Seydi confronted him. "Boy, I'm not overjoyed wandering hot streets all day."

Unfazed, he responded politely. "Once your studies begin, you'll be required to run everywhere."

Seydi looked askance at him. "So they told me. All the more reason not to endure a long boring walk today. The goal is to arrive at one's destination, not take a lifetime getting there, is it not?"

He surprised them by apologizing. "I will arrange transport at once, and food and drink while you wait." He nodded to two buildings, one painted with delicate blue fish and the other bold yellow birds. "Yellow is for men to refresh, blue for ladies. Use any of the cups on shelves inside to drink. They are spotlessly clean."

A generous lunch laid out on rich linens beneath two olive trees next to the fountain greeted their return, but the Ambassador had other business first. "The toilets have hot and cold running water. How is such a thing done? I saw no one heating water."

The Kallistian smiled. "Aqueducts and pipes bring water down the mountain. Some of the springs have very hot water. Nearly all homes have running water, as well, although one small city on the north side of the mountain doesn't have hot. Soon, you'll wonder how you ever lived without it."

Seydi spoke before Hariset asked another tiresome question about plumbing. "Do you always leave gold cups in public places, or is it just to impress us?"

"The Council presents a gold cup to every islander at age ten. People leave them in public places they frequent. Others may use them, provided they leave them washed in soap and hot water."

Seydi thought he did not understand her point. "What keeps someone from taking them?"

He shook his head. "It is not a problem. Everybody has one."

Reddening, Seydi glared at him as if he was the world's greatest fool. "But they are worth a fortune. What would be the punishment if somebody stole them?"

He shrugged. "Whatever the Head Priest decides, but please, I'm keeping you from lunch. Sadly, I must sail at dawn tomorrow to pick up new Temple Prospects. I will leave you now to go make preparations. I will stop by tonight with additional staff for the house, though likely it will be long after you retire. The bearers will be here in a few minutes, but take all the time in the park you want. I look forward to seeing you when I return. May good health be yours always."

MAIDSERVANT THE GOD

Hariset lounged and ate with Seydi while watching families in the park. Everyone appeared so carefree and unconcerned about the dangers of the outside world that he would have laughed if he could have shaken feelings that it was all an elaborate trap.

FOUR

THE BOOK OF MAIDSERVANT: THE WOMAN IN A TOMB

FROM ACROSS THE HARBOR, the lighthouse cast herky-jerky shadows on the dark dock, playing tricks with Maidservant's imagination. Before leaving Egypt, servants had told her awful stories about young girls abducted in ports, smuggled onto ships and never seen again. Shivering, she pulled her patched cloak tighter around her neck even though the night was humid and warm, picked up the blanket tied into a bag to carry her meager possessions and crept across the gangway.

As she started away from the ship, a man detached from the shadows and pressed something into her hand. Terrified, she took it then ran away fast as she could toward the nearest lighted area, the exact opposite way she had watched the Kallistian take her master and mistress that morning. Looking back over her shoulder and imagining someone behind her frequently, she darted through several intersections before stopping out of breath next to a lit curtained window to examine what he had given her. It was a small scroll written in common Egyptian script giving directions to the house. She laughed aloud because she had told him she could not read. What a tricky so-and-so.

From inside the building came a gruff voice. "Who's out there? Go away or I'm letting the dog out!"

She dropped the scroll and ran around turn after turn until finding herself in an alley lined with well-lit buildings full of music, singing and laughter. Drunken sailors burst out a doorway. She tried to pass, but one grabbed her arm and spoke the sailors' pidgin she had learned shopping for her mistress in the markets of Kefti. "Look, fellows, a fresh one! Want to come away with Saggius, darling?" Too scared to scream, she knocked his hands off and ran. He yelled, "Got no meat on you, anyway, you scrawny chicken! Not worth a nibble, much less a bite!" The others laughed and added coarse insults. She zigzagged through alleys with no idea of direction until calming down enough to work out the way the Kallistian had gone.

Eventually, she arrived at an intersection lit by big oil pots on poles. The left way was through a high arch with a giant set of bull's horns above it. As she looked around in confusion, a sleepy man stepped out of a small kiosk across the road, pointed through the arch and spoke to her in perfect Egyptian. "Go this way, miss. Turn right on the big white avenue and follow it all the way through town and up the mountain. The house you seek is on the right past the last intersection, directly across from a high hill."

Too afraid to say anything, she nodded and ran the way he said. Unlike the dark port area, the neighborhoods along the wide avenue were mostly residential with bright oil lamps mounted on buildings and poles as well as light streaming from open windows and doors. Unfortunately, though, it was crowded with people strolling, socializing and lounging on benches in front of numerous small bars and eateries on the ground floors of houses. Since strangers were a rarity, conversations stopped and stares followed when she passed.

Self-consciously, she avoided eye contact, walked fast and did not respond to greetings, but the buildings were amazing colors with intricate stencils around windows and doorways. Inside, gorgeous murals of sea life, animals, flowers, people and landscapes kept demanding her attention. It was not surprising she plowed headlong into a family and fell, tearing her dress where the right knee struck a carved toy pulled by a small boy.

The father and mother helped her up while children ran circles around them asking why she dressed so strangely and wore a cloak in summer. More people gathered and, after she did not answer their questions, assumed she did not understand then discussed why the Temple allowed a vagabond out of the dock area. Motioning she was all right, she pulled away and turned at the next intersection to get out of their sight, and the next, and another, then could not find the right combination back to the white avenue.

Throbbing pain in her knee finally demanded her to stop and examine the wound. It bled and needed tending, but these streets were also crowded and several curious people seemed on the verge of coming to offer assistance so she wiped it off and hurried on. She kept her head down and lost track of time. Exhausted, she could not keep going much longer. Sweat ran into her eyes, stinging and blurring them. Then she hurried around yet another corner, the city noise went away and cold air made her shiver.

At first, she could only stare at the vast misty plaza illuminated by line after line of tall lamps stretching far as she could see. Strangely, the first thing she noticed was that none of the lights flickered. Then she realized no one else was in the great space but her, which frightened more than the crowds of strangers had. She turned to go back and faced a large, glowing, pale blue lake enclosed by a low glossy-black stone wall a few feet away. Hovering just above the water at the lake's center, an enormous luminescent white statue of a woman had its arms stretched out toward her. All around the lake, the rows of lights continued out of sight in every direction.

Was she having a fit, was that it? She slapped herself in the face a few times, but nothing changed.

Blubbering quietly, she followed the wall while staring into the distance for anything different. After a while, she realized the statue continued facing her no matter how far she went. Consternated, she walked along a row of pole lights away from the lake. At the fifth one, she looked back. The lake was a few feet from her, same as before. She set down the bag and limped past two more poles. The bag and lake were still a few feet away. Deciding it must be a fit after all, she kicked the bag then sat dejectedly on the wall to wait for it to run its course.

Glumly, she stared at the statue and eventually noticed an almost invisible vertical line beneath it. She shaded her eyes from the water's glare and saw that the statue set upon an almost transparent pedestal. So much for magically hanging in the air. More importantly, it had something written on it. Leaning on one hand over the wall far as she dared, she continued shading her eyes with the other hand and made out five lines of the same ancient symbols as the documents she had stolen from Pharaoh's Library.

O Guardian,
Standing eternal against Gathering Darkness.
Protecting the path into the Garden of Light.
Rallying good to combat evil.
Heed the summons of your faithful servant.

Just more highfalutin nonsense, she thought, pushing back to get off the wall, but her hand slipped and she tumbled headlong into the water. Unable to swim, she thrashed and lunged for the top of the wall, but her arms were too short and the wet cloak weighted her down. In less than a minute, she sank into the light of the lake.

* * *

IN PITCH DARKNESS, MAIDSERVANT GAGGED, retched and gasped cold air darts that pricked the inside of her throat. The hard surface under her was painfully cold, so she curled up in a tight ball and wrapped arms around her legs, but it did not help. She sat up flapping arms against her chest and screamed.

A tiny light appeared about six feet away. Out of heavy shadow, the extremely white face of a young woman emerged. She was belligerent. "You're going to clean up that stinking mess, aren't you?"

Maidservant stared then prostrated in wet and vomit. She began praying in Egyptian. "O, great and mysterious Hathor, judge me worthy to pass through the gates of the afterlife. Forgive me for…"

"What are you babbling about?"

The woman had spoken Kallistian previously, but the last was a very proper form of Egyptian. Maidservant sat up and wiped puke off her face. "Uh, I thought I should pray for you to allow me into the afterlife."

The woman stuck out her tongue and made a loud raspberry. "That's rich. The original Hathor was a demon created from cows and a real mean bitch of a woman. I don't know how they made the current one, but the Egyptian gods are usually the evilest abominations around. But, surely, you already know that, don't you?"

She was confused. "Uh, is this part of a test, Great Hathor?" Bright light flared around the woman, dazzling her eyes. Then as they adjusted, her mouth formed a big, gaping O with her tongue stuck out the corner.

The woman lay upon a low stone platform with her head propped up on one hand. Her bare white shoulders and bluish feet protruded from a burial shroud tucked under the arms and wrapped loosely around the body. White-gold hair cascaded and made a thick pile of silver on the floor. Suddenly, she sat up and turned to face Maidservant. "Close that disgusting yap of yours before I put a big fly in it. How did you get here?"

Maidservant could not find words. The woman's body was the source of the light and her green eyes were positively luminous. Who could this be except Kalli?

"Answer me, you little imp!"

She stammered the first thing that came to mind. "Aren't y-your feet c-c-cold? I'm freezing."

"What did you expect, barging into my tomb and rolling around wet on the floor?"

Maidservant looked left, right, up and down. She jerked around. It was a claustrophobic space constructed of coarse limestone blocks with no openings. She let out a mournful cry.

In the blink of an eye, the woman snatched Maidservant around the waist and deposited her sitting on the hard bed so close their hips pressed together. Then the woman's eyes were only inches away, staring intently into hers.

Maidservant wailed, "It's not fair that I died so young. My whole life was nothing then I'm dead. Other people got to have something in life, but not me. It's not…ouch!"

The woman had given her a hard twisting pinch on the upper thigh. "Stop caterwauling."

A glowing blue and green orb emblazoned on the woman's right inside wrist caught Maidservant's attention and held her mesmerized. She saw images of sunny blue skies above tall forests and fields of tall swaying grass. Crystalline lakes with jumping fish and long-legged birds. Rolling hills of flowers and fruit trees. Jagged blue mountains with mysterious white peaks. Green river valleys and oceans. Rivers and deserts. Wondrous animals and strange people and…!

The woman shook her. "Is your mind working at all? I asked, who are you?"

"Stop, and I'll tell you!" She took a deep breath. "Before I died, I was…ouch! Why do you keep pinching me?"

"A riddle. Does a dead person feel pain or are you too dimwitted to figure it out?"

Maidservant stared at the darkening bruises on her leg. "I'm not dead?"

"Not yet."

"But I fell into the water and drown."

"No, you didn't. Who are you?"

"Maidservant. A slave. I…!"

The woman had her by the shoulders staring fiercely into her eyes again. Then she released her so hard Maidservant barely managed not to tumble off the end of the bed. "Why did someone waste time making something so useless? Or do you have some sort of hidden special purpose?"

Bewildered, Maidservant scratched her head. "Uh, I don't think I have a purpose other than being a maid. I started off in the kitchen and can cook, but…!"

The woman grabbed her and brought their foreheads together with a loud thud. She held her nearly a minute. "Your mind is a muddled mess. I can't even tell your age. You stink, too." She shoved her away.

Maidservant braced this time, but almost fell off the bed anyway. "You could just ask how old I am! I'll be thirteen soon."

"And I'll be twenty-six." She reached behind her and, from nowhere, produced a tray with a tall amphora of hot wine and two double-handled mugs. She set the tray on Maidservant's lap and sloshed wine into the mugs, splashing her lap. "This will warm you up."

Maid-Servant's dress was torn, wet and ruined, but she was angered by the wine stain nonetheless. She crossed her arms defiantly. "Go to hell. I'm not doing anything you say."

The woman gripped the back of her head and forced down the whole mug. Then she thrust another in her hands, slopping wine on her again, but this time Maidservant did not notice because the woman spoke incantations of submission so fast they sounded like buzzing bees to her.

Now, she could not stop talking and drinking. She even told about her other life and the attacks did not come, although she felt them struggling powerfully to reach her. She was very afraid. She had said too much. Then again, it felt good to tell someone.

"So," the woman asked, "in this other life of yours, your father was a scribe in Pharaoh's Library?"

"Yes, Lady, but as I keep telling you, none of it is real."

"What happened next?"

The words came out of her as if they had lives of their own. "He was accused of stealing secret histories and they sentenced the whole family to die---father, mother, two older brothers, the twin sister whose soul I share and me." She bit blood from her lower lip trying not to speak the next words but they came out. "But, as you can see, I was spared."

The woman stared critically. "Valuable boys executed and a useless little girl forgiven. Identical girls and only one killed. What can you do that they couldn't?"

She yelled. "I told you! None of it happened!"

"Could it be someone fancied you for perverse reasons?"

"No! It's because of my gift." Her hands flew over her mouth.

The woman leaned so close that her cold breath stung Maidservant's face. "Tell me about it."

Deep inside, the darkness grew stronger with every question she answered. "Father gambled and was not good with money. Our house was small considering his position. Sister and I had to play in the same room he taught lessons to our brothers. Though we didn't intend it, we learned to read and write before they did just by overhearing."

"How old were you?"

Sorrow tugged her face down. "Five. Father said the gods blessed his daughters and such abilities should not be wasted, even though a royal scribe squandering Pharaoh's time teaching females, even in his own family, was strictly forbidden." She stopped, staring at nothing.

"What happened?"

"Father got a new boss who wanted his job for a son. He forced Father to work at night deciphering obscure old documents that only gifted scribes could read. He tried his best but was not very talented, sorry to say. The boss complained about his lack of production to the Chief Scribe and requested a disciplinary review of his work." She smiled in spite of tears and remorse.

"What's so amusing?"

"Father guessed what he planned and sneaked sister and me into the library to help him. Hardly anyone was around at night so it was easy to bring stuff to us in a small storeroom. Father held back the results until the review. The Chief Scribe was impressed and promoted Father, giving him access to the most sacred secrets and histories, which greatly improved his pay and status, though basically the job was the same, only with much more expected." She sighed. "He couldn't do it, of course, so sister and I spent years helping until… until…" She gestured futilely.

"Continue."

She stared down into the wine, seeing the past. "Father shouldn't have trusted us, especially me, because he warned all the time not to look at any documents but those he brought, but I was bored with the stuff he gave us and sneaked other things in to read. One night, a Scholar of Amon---in my real life he's my master, Lord Hariset---witnessed me coming out of a secret area with old scrolls. Irate, he said he would report Father for allowing his children to play in the Library, but after I begged and showed I understood them, he went to Father and said how brilliant I was, female or not. Then he became a good friend to my family, helping us with money from time to time."

The woman poured more wine. "Exactly what was so special about you understanding those particular scrolls?"

"They were accounts copied long ago by scribes from walls of ruins in a forgotten foreign land and stored in hope they might be understood someday. I took them to read to my sister because they were the kind of romantic stories she liked. She was not good as me with languages."

"So you figured out how to read them on your own?"

"That is my gift."

"How old were you when this happened?"

"Ten."

She stared at the girl with more interest. "Go on."

"The Chief Scribe was killed in a robbery. Father got his job and no longer had to do the work himself. Money and ambition changed him. He said we must not read and study anymore then hired a special instructor to teach us household duties and how to be good wives so he could negotiate husbands that would raise our family's status even more. We did not want to stop learning and complained. He punished us severely. Sister gave in, but I sneaked away to ask the Scholar of Amon for help."

She hesitated, desperate not to continue, but the words flowed out of her. "It surprised me how upset the news made him. He offered Father a large sum of money to allow us to live and study with him, but Father accused him of impure motives and forbade us seeing him ever again. A few nights later, soldiers came and arrested us for stealing documents from Pharaoh and selling them. After that, everything is confused in my head. I remember mother crying and sister clinging to me while my brothers beat Father and us, insisting we confess and say they were not involved. Father did tell the jailers, but no one listened." She stopped, staring at nothing.

"Why did they let you live?"

"Before dawn the day of execution, men came and clubbed our parents and brothers unconscious." Pain erupted in her head, causing white flashes in her eyes and roaring in her ears, but she went on. "They smelled sour, like old beer. One had a patched eye and jagged scar splitting his face. He carried sister and me in fat sweaty arms to another cell and threw us on the floor. He gave us a scroll, took out a big knife and said he wouldn't gut whoever read it. It was one I had that night in the Library. When sister realized, she went crazy and yelled me to keep my mouth shut. Then we fought until the man held us apart and said five more minutes then we both die. That's why...that's when..." She began shaking violently and striking her head with fists. "Dark! Dark! No! Let me go! Don't put me in there! Let me go!"

The woman grabbed her hands and spoke quietly. "Obey your master. Forget I forced you to talk. Obey him. Close your eyes and forget. Obey him."

She sagged into the woman's cold embrace for a while before sitting up confused.

The woman handed her a full mug of wine. "You promised to tell me your earliest memories of your new life with your master before you dozed off."

She took a big gulp and smacked her lips. "Not much to tell. I woke up one morning on the floor of a big kitchen cupboard chock full of expensive food and wares. No idea where I was. The staff laughed when I asked and said Maidservant is having another fit. I asked, 'Who?' 'Maidservant,' they said, as if it was a big joke. Then one named Cook-Servant started crying and said she was my mother and tried to hug me, but I hit her in the eye---two times." She stuck up two fingers accompanied by a drunken, cockeyed smile. "After that, they kept me bound and tied to a big whetstone until a healer whipped the delusions out of me." She sighed and held out the mug for topping off.

"You don't really believe your other life is a lie, do you?"

She flinched but answered honestly. "What I believe is that it doesn't matter what I believe."

"Did you ever ask your master about it?"

"I didn't know who my master was until a whole year later when he returned from the south with a new adopted daughter---an orphaned niece. He looked exactly like the Scholar of Amon and I said so to Cook-Servant, but she summoned the healer again and he made me understand it was my madness getting me into trouble again." She smiled, but it was tragic to see. "In the end, everything turned out for the best because he favored me with a better job, which I didn't want to jeopardize, so no, I never asked."

"What is your job?"

She spoke with pride. "I am his daughter's personal maid, and although she was snooty about someone my age serving someone as mature and high in status as her, Master told her it was because she's so exceptionally brilliant and everyone except me was so exceptionally not." She snickered. "He made her take me everywhere, too, even Pharaoh's Library when he arranged her to be schooled there. Drove her crazy having me around all the time, let me tell you. She always has lots of boyfriends."

"I didn't think royal scribes were allowed to teach girls."

She was surprised the woman knew that. "The old Pharaohs didn't, but exceptions are made now---for a price." She seemed confused for a moment. "My master has more wealth than just about everyone, I guess."

"Do you perform any personal favors or duties for Lord Hariset?"

"Oh, no, Lady. In fact, Mistress Seydi punishes me if I disturb him with my presence without summons. I hardly ever see him, except when he..." She stopped herself and yawned, hoping the woman did not notice.

"You started to say when you dream about him, didn't you?"

Her eyes filled with fright. "How do you know that?"

"It is not uncommon, sorry to say. Tell me about it."

She hesitated then went on. "Cook-Servant took me to a sage-healer because I screamed so much in my sleep, but it didn't help, though since leaving Egypt I haven't done it as often. I think the change in environment made a difference for some reason."

"Stop beating around the bush and tell me the dreams you have of him."

Maidservant stared into the darkest corner of the room expecting something to leap out to keep her from telling, but nothing did. She took a deep breath. "I go to bed. I dream he calls me to come to him, and when I don't, his shadow comes to me."

"Have you ever gone to him?"

"No. I'm too afraid."

"Do you remember anything about the visits?"

"He talks to me. I talk back. I never remember details. Pretty weird, huh?"

"You are much stronger than you seem. Never go to him or ask for his help in any way. Understand?"

She nodded and the woman put a cold arm around her shoulders. In spite of the cold, the woman holding her felt good. She experienced feelings she had all but forgotten as she went to sleep.

The woman gazed down at her and mused aloud. "A half-remade creature of darkness is going to save us? If I had that idiot seer here, I would strangle her. No wonder she insisted so many of the visions from this time were difficult to see." She considered for a moment then produced a dagger out of the air, slit a forefinger and dripped blood into an amphora of water. After sealing it with wax, she placed it next to Maidservant and slid away from her. "As you came, you will go, and as you go, you will forget."

***

MAIDSERVANT BROKE THE SURFACE OF PITCH BLACK WATER choking for air and tangled in clothes. She started under again but strong hands pulled her out and pounded her back while she coughed and threw up volumes of filthy water and wine. Then the sodden cloak flew off and a big dry one wrapped around her. "Can you walk?"

It was her Kallistian, of course. She took a brave step but the injured knee gave way. He swept her up, grabbed the blanket-bag and started away. She squirmed around in his arms and pointed to a blue-green amphora on the wall. "Don't forget my medicine!"

He put it in her bag. "Strange, I didn't see that."

She said nothing, staring aghast at the grime-streaked statue of a sailor at the center of a dark lake, listing as if it might topple over any minute. By the light of large roaring bonfires, shadowy figures with great hammers worked, breaking and removing paving stones. A jumble of buildings ringed the plaza, which was big but certainly not endless. He carried her past lines of broken posts that might have once held lights. She passed out.

Quiet sounds of lapping water and soft conversation stroked her awake. Warm, snug and experiencing sensations of weightlessness, she half-opened her eyes. Large oil lamps mounted on high stanchions cast moving light patterns on a sky blue vaulted ceiling painted with graceful clouds and colorful birds. She sighed, rolled onto her side and saw she was on a pile of luxurious pillows next to a big steaming pool. Exotic scenes of undersea creatures covered the walls. She closed her eyes and sighed again, happy to be having a good dream. Then she burped up sour wine, choked a little and sat bolt upright coughing. She had nothing on but a short cloth around the waist. It was not a dream. She grabbed a pillow to her chest and looked around frantically.

Two young women, perhaps sixteen or seventeen, wearing the same waist wrap as her but with no apparent concern about nakedness, sat a few feet away dangling feet in the water. The closest, a medium-sized girl plain in every way, picked up a large bowl from a tray, reached it out to her and spoke Kallistian slowly and loudly. "Drink...this. You'll...feel...better."

Maidservant's mouth was dry and icky so she accepted and took two big gulps. It was wine. She made a face and almost threw up.

"Oh, you don't drink wine?" She gave her another bowl with water, waited until she drank then pointed to herself and pronounced, "Air-i-a."

Maidservant nodded and repeated, "Aria." Then she gave a traditional Kallistian greeting. "Fair weather. I am Maidservant."

Aria laughed. "He didn't tell us you speak Kallistian. You must think me a real dunce."

Maidservant shrugged. "He doesn't know. We only spoke Egyptian."

She raised an eyebrow. "Well, this certainly makes it easier. Allow me to introduce my friend, Cytheria. We're Prospects at the Temple."

The other girl, all blondness and blue eyes, leaned around her, gave a tiny wave and smile as warm as it was dazzling. "Hi-ya. Please call me Cythe, Maidservant."

Speechless, Maidservant could only stare. There could not be a more beautiful creature anywhere in the world.

Aria, accustomed to dealing with Cythe's effect on people, whipped off the wrap and cannonballed into the water, splashing them. Cythe threw her wrap at her friend and performed an extremely clumsy belly flop that had to hurt. Furious splashing and dunking ensued, and they called Maidservant to join them, but she was too embarrassed until they carefully stopped paying attention.

Slowly, she slid to the water, stuck her feet in and soon was in all the way, but stayed in one spot with just her head above water and the wrap clutched around her. She worried because they were members of the Temple and she, a slave, was in the water with them. Then another terrible thought occurred. They had undressed her and seen all the welts, scars and bruises. What must they think? Then she realized her knee did not hurt, reached down and felt a new scar. How was that possible?

When they said it was time to get out and showed where her clothes were, she discovered someone had done a decent job cleaning her dress. Aria pointed to the tear, which was expertly mended, and informed that Cythe did it. When Maidservant thanked her, she blushed and seemed embarrassed. Carrying her blanket-bag, Maidservant trailed them from the pool into another room.

The Kallistian sat at a low table laden with fruit, cheese, fish, olive paste, loaves and wine. Aria and Cythe ran back, pulled Maidservant to a bench across from him and made her sit between them. Speaking Egyptian, he inquired, "Did the bath help you feel better?"

Aria, very mannerly sipping wine, laughed. "She speaks Kallistian better than you do, dunderhead."

Stuffing bread in her mouth, Cythe was hard to understand. "Can't believe you ended up in that old plaza, Maidservant, though at night Eao streets are confusing, even for me, and I grew up near there."

He asked, "Weren't the directions I sent you any help?"

Maidservant put a hand over her mouth to hide her amusement. "Do you mean the scroll a man gave me? You must have forgotten that I can't read. The man at the gate was helpful, though. Thank you."

He was concerned. "Then how did you wander way out to the west side and get past barricades across the entrances to the plaza with no one seeing you? Priest Atlas' crews work day and night constructing the new park."

She was warm all over seeing him, but wished he would not ask so many questions. "Maybe I hit my head or something. I don't remember. Sorry"

Aria grabbed Maidservant's arm with exaggerated concern. "They say that pool has no bottom and anyone falling in gets sucked down into a netherworld and never seen again. You are so lucky."

Cythe elbowed Maidservant to turn her way. "That's an old wives' tale, but it is true that statues placed on that pedestal crumble after just a few years. I witnessed it several times growing up. Impurity in the water, maybe."

Aria shook Maidservant's arm, making her turn back. "I heard that, too. Let us know right away if your skin starts itching, burning or flaking off."

Wine dribbled down Cythe's chin as she tried not to laugh. "Yeah, that's how the dreaded molting disease starts. Quick, check your arms. Any splotches, rashes or rot?"

Dismayed, Maidservant stuck them out. "Not yet."

They burst out laughing and Envoy leaned across the table. "Don't pay attention to them. The water won't harm you, though it's true anything set on the pedestals where statues of Kalli once stood decays very quickly."

This was news to Aria. "Has anyone tried replacing the pedestals? Maybe there is some sort of corrosive in them."

He shook his head. "They can't be moved and are indestructible---same as the avenues."

Cythe nodded. "You should be a teacher, Envoy. You'd be good at it."

Maidservant asked, "What happened to Kalli's statues?"

He answered, "Supposedly, she destroyed them."

"Why would she do that?"

He smiled. "Uh, I think we'd better change the subject. This is getting into Temple history and we're not supposed to discuss it with nonmembers."

Aria made a face. "Ah, come on, Envoy, don't be an officious fuddy-duddy. How can her knowing possibly hurt anything?"

He shrugged. "Yeah, I know, but rules are rules. For what it's worth, the Head Priest will likely change them soon."

Maidservant expressed another concern. "Is your name Envoy? I thought it was just a title."

"The name and job are the same. Funny, huh?" They exchanged private smiles only they understood as he refilled her wine.

Watching them, Cythe showed growing concern. "It's getting really late. Shouldn't we be going?"

Envoy asked Maidservant, "Should I arrange transport? It is a steep road and will take about an hour walking."

She did not want to hurry. "I can see more walking."

Cythe frowned. "There's not much to see at night."

Aria grinned. "Yeah, except for the moon, the stars, the lights and colors of the town. The view of the harbor from higher up is pretty, too. Actually, all of it is kind of romantic, don't you think, Cythe?"

Giving her a warning stare, Cythe tapped Maidservant's arm, making her look away from Envoy. "Wait until you see the House of Kalli. It's enormous, but nearly all the space is an interior courtyard with a river running down the middle. You have to cross a bridge to get to the bedrooms. It is really something. Wait until you see the big statues."

Aria responded critically. "The river is more like a canal and keeps the place uncomfortably dank. The courtyard is a ridiculously huge room with no purpose other than being a pain to clean, especially since there is a big opening over the bridge that lets in weather and dust. The statues are monstrosities. Otherwise, there are two small bedroom suites, a garden maze of ugly hedges and olive trees."

Cythe commented, "I guess some of us grew up accustomed to the finer things in life and some of us have pedestrian tastes, huh? You left out the outlook over Eao City and the cottage. I thought you liked staying there."

Aria reddened. "Open mouth, insert feet. I didn't mean it the way it came out, Cythe. I'm just tired."

Cythe spoke to Maidservant. "Aria and I are tasked to keep the House of Kalli clean. We live in the cottage when classes don't require we stay at the Temple."

Maidservant was speechless. They did the same kind of work as her. They shared baths and expensive meals with her. They treated her as an equal. What were they going to say when they found out? Without really intending to, she blurted, "I'm a slave!"

Cythe nodded. "Yeah, we know. I think it is terrible to own people. If you don't mind, I want to hear all about it after you're settled."

"Me, too," Aria added.

Quietly, Envoy said, "We'd best be on our way."

FIVE

THE BOOK OF MAIDSERVANT: TESI-RA AND CZN-TANTH

ARIA AND CYTHE, SWEEPING THE FLOOR of the House of Kalli's courtyard, stopped to listen to the shouts echoing down the hall from Seydi's quarters. Aria threw her broom down to go stop it, but Cythe pulled her back. "We were told not to interfere."

Aria shook free. "I'm not going to stand here doing nothing while she abuses Maidservant. This new Prospect must be a monster!"

Ambassador Hariset emerged from the hall next to Seydi's and smoothed the folds of his extravagant tunic. "The only abuse the maid suffers is from excessive tickling, not that it's any of your business. Why are you girls eavesdropping on private matters that do not concern you, anyway? Go sweep the other side of the canal until we leave, and don't let me catch you doing this again." He watched until they were well away before going to Seydi's rooms.

She had Maidservant on the floor, making her roll back and forth by twisting her hair one way then the other. Hariset closed the door. "Can't you find a quieter way to torment her?"

"The little twerp came in just before dawn stinking of wine and went to bed rather than attending me. Do you know how long makeup and a wig takes without help? Well, do you?"

He was not sympathetic. "Perhaps you should reconsider your aversion to anyone seeing you without paint smeared all over your face. It will likely be an issue with the school, anyway."

The response was quick and hot. "Then you'd better come up with a reason they accept, hadn't you? The Master forbade me showing my face to anyone but him. If you don't like it, tell him…if you dare."

He did not believe her, but both knew he would not bother the Master with such a trivial matter. He shrugged. "The girl was drinking?"

Seydi lied easily. "I think she developed an appetite for it while we were on Kefti, which means bars and sailors and such, though I can't understand how even the commonest people could stand to be near her."

Hariset chuckled. "About time she developed a personality."

She kicked Maidservant's hands reaching to free her hair. "Surely you did not come to my quarters to discuss this useless worm. What do you want?"

"Those two Prospects in the courtyard heard you. The pretty one asked too many questions when she brought breakfast, too. They are probably spying for the Head Priest, so have care around them."

Seydi sneered. "Those servants are Prospects? You must be joking."

"You might do well to make friends with them. They can give you pointers."

"I don't need anything from the likes of them."

He did not hide his amusement. "Apparently, a certain amount of servitude is required of Temple students, especially Prospects. Have you ever used a broom?"

She bridled. "I hope you don't think I'm going to be anyone's servant. I'm not going to be friends with the people who clean my toilet, either."

"We must do whatever necessary for the mission. I called on the merchant in the big house across the way. He told me quite a bit about the Temple school. Seems that it…"

"Does it really matter?" she interrupted. "On Kefti you said our forces could crush the king's navy in a day, so why are you waiting? This masquerade is so tiresome. It's making me ill, kowtowing to weak–minded idiots as if they actually matter."

He answered sharply. "How many times do I have to say it? First, we must find out what abilities the Priests possess and if Kalli left any ancient documents of power hidden here, which is why you'll abide by their rules, even if it means scrubbing floors on your hands and knees and swabbing out toilets."

Her expression darkened dangerously. "I've heard those ridiculous stories about hidden temples filled with forgotten magic until I want to puke. Why would they have wanted to leave anything behind, and if they did, do you really think it could have survived for thousands of years? You do not need to preach and prod me to do my duty, either. I will play the role of spoiled rich daughter to perfection. Just see that you do your part as well, daddy dearest."

"Very well, but be careful not to harm the girl excessively. She's important to gathering information, too."

"This ugly insect---important?" She bent down, slapped Maidservant's face several times then drew back to kick her.

"Enough!"

Seydi froze wearing a perfect expression of innocence. "Oh, I've upset you, haven't I? How selfish of me, acting as if I can do whatever I want. Do you know why I do it? Because I can!" She kicked Maidservant in the stomach.

"If mistreating her interferes with the mission, you will answer for it, mark my words." He returned to his rooms.

Seydi shrieked. She kicked over a chair. She smashed a vase. She jerked Maidservant up from the floor by the hair and slung her into the hallway against the wall. She twisted her arm behind her back, marched her on tiptoes into the courtyard and to the wide canal. She held her teetering at the edge.

Directly across from them, Cythe and Aria watched in stunned silence. Seydi knew they were there, but acted surprised. She waved, gave them a big smile and let Maidservant fall into the water. "Hi. I'm Seydi. Looking forward to our classes together. I'm sure we'll be best of friends."

Aria yelled, "Help her! She can't swim!"

Seydi shrugged. "True, but then she can't do anything, can she? Well, you probably need to get back to your sweeping, and I have to get dressed." She turned to go.

Aria called after her. "What about Maidservant?"

Seydi answered over her shoulder. "Oh, I suppose I do not mind if you save her, but if you'd rather not bother, I do not mind that, either. Ta-ta."

Cythe and Aria looked down at Maidservant on her back between them as Aria's anger spilled out. "I say we drag her out here and throw her painted butt in the water!"

Maidservant shook her head. "You mustn't get into trouble over me. Already one of you has been injured."

Dripping wet from jumping in to get her, Cythe cocked her elbow, looking where she scraped her arm on the edge pushing Maidservant out of the canal. "It's nothing."

"It's bleeding, Lady."

Cythe bent down to her. "Use our names. How do you feel?"

Maidservant sat up and tilted her head side-to-side, trying to get water out of her ears. "Seems I've been wet since I arrived."

They grabbed her under the arms and lifted her up. That was when they heard a loud sniff behind them.

Hariset was a few feet away leering at Cythe's lightweight work tunic plastered to her skin with little left to the imagination. "A proper young lady does not display herself so disrespectfully in public. What do you have to say for yourself?" Aria started to reply hotly but he cut her off. "I'll not listen to a common thug who threatens my daughter. Both of you get out of my sight until you are better mannered and dressed in a way that doesn't show a lack of virtue."

Aria followed Cythe running down the third hallway to the rear door into the garden maze. Counting steps, they ran down a wide pathway between thick, high hedges, glanced back to insure no one watched then leaped sideways, disappearing through the shrub onto another path with the small garden cottage at the end. When they were inside with backs against the barred door, Aria took Cythe's hand. "I couldn't stand his sleazy eyes all over you."

She pulled away and headed for the bedroom. "I'm accustomed to it."

Aria went after her. "We should ask Priests DoSo and Leto to find you other duties. You're not safe around him."

"I can take care of myself. Anyway, Priests shouldn't be bothered with the petty concerns of Prospects. It's best we go about our business unless something important happens."

"We should tell the Council how they treat Maidservant, too."

Cythe faced her. "No, this won't do at all, Aria. Criticizing the Ambassador or his daughter will call Rhea's judgment into question. Don't forget, she argued the Council to open the island to him. The Scholars and other political enemies will use it to undermine her authority even further. We can't be responsible for that."

"But we have to do something!"

Cythe sighed and put her arms around her. "Listen. In a few days, the Ambassador will move to his new embassy in Cadi-sum and likely we'll never see him again. Seydi will go to Prospect Village and not have time for more mischief. As for Maidservant, she will either go live at the embassy in Cadi-sum or return to Egypt. All we have to do is make the best of this situation for a little while and it will resolve itself."

Aria went and stared out the small window next to the front door. "Why can't I reason things through as quickly as all of you? I try, but just can't do it. I'm pretty sure Athy and Arty don't think I'm going to survive probation. Have they said anything to you about it?"

They had, but Cythe refused to believe that Aria, the most important person in her life, might have to leave the Temple, not to mention the pain it would cause Aria to know their harsh opinions. She denied it with a smile no one ever questioned then suggested, "How about we get drunk and sing songs this evening?" Aria nodded, but seemed only half-listening, so Cythe tried to bait her into giving one of her characteristic acerbic comebacks. "We'd better leave for Cadi-sum soon or we'll miss the Head Priest introducing Seydi to the Temple."

Aria said nothing as she went to the cupboard to get their Prospect uniforms.

***

ALL RANKS OF TEMPLE MEMBERS--Priests, Initiates, Scholars and Prospects---packed the tiered amphitheater. It was a raucous crowd rife with arguments and shouting. No one paid much attention when Head Priest Rhea, grossly overweight with a lumbering limp, entered from the rear without ceremony. Ignoring the disorder, she negotiated the steep steps sideways down, her gruff booming voice and guffaws ratcheting up the noise. Her progress was painstakingly slow, especially since she seemed determined to speak to everyone she passed. Following after her were the Council Priests, two women and a man, remarkably trim, fit and beautiful to behold in the jade tunics of their office. First came Leto, characteristically unkempt, uncompromising and ill-disposed. Next was Selene, pale, impatient and mysterious. Last came Atlas, massive, strong and affable.

The room was stifling hot and Rhea's big tent of a dress was soon drenched with sweat, yet the wide smile never left her face, not even with Scholars shouting complaints and grievances while Priests and Initiates---split into two political groups---yelled for and against her leadership. For the most part, the Prospects engaged in noisy horseplay, although a few of the seniors joined in yelling about politics.

Hariset, seated in the first row in front of the low stage next to Seydi, could not believe the chaos or that the sweating whale of a woman was the powerful protector of Kalliste. Looking back over his shoulder, he studied the Council Priests, dwelling longest on Leto because she seemed to have more self-assurance and toughness. She was definitely the most feared, gauging by the reactions of people when she neared them, yet he sensed nothing any more special about her abilities than the others, who seemed to have none. He was perplexed.

A full thirty minutes passed before the Head Priest grunted up the steps onto stage and plopped down in an oversized chair shoddily reinforced to support her weight. Four Prospects ran from the side of the stage with a long table and set it before her. Then Atlas and Leto sat either side of her. Selene had stopped to talk to Hariset, delaying the meeting even longer, until Leto called irritably for her to take her place.

Hariset whispered behind his hand to Seydi. "These Priests have symbols of power on their wrists same as other Kalli cults I've read about."

Seydi feigned a cough then kept her hand in front of her mouth. "On the way in, I saw two Priests with the crossed axes on their chests."

He nodded. "Then they'll all have them. They're only worn by groups Kalli led personally."

Seydi snickered. "The Head Priest is a cow. Was her injury caused by carrying all that weight, do you think?"

He appreciated her nastiness when not directed at him. "In the past, Head Priests in some of Kalli's societies maimed themselves to be more like her. That could be what this is, though in these modern times it would be unusual."

Seydi stared and barely remembered to keep her voice quiet. "Kalli was lame? You must be kidding."

"In the Master's library are references to her being gravely injured in a battle but nothing about the details. Perhaps you'll learn about it in your studies."

Seydi held her hand over her mouth again. "Selene just glanced this way again. I think her interest in you is more than commerce."

He nodded. "It will be useful."

Without warning, every Scholar in the room jumped up shouting and stomping feet. Leto ordered them to take their seats but they persisted until Rhea declared the meeting postponed. The Scholars, singing a song of solidarity, waited until most of the crowd exited then marched out of the building together.

Meanwhile, Leto came to the edge of the stage and asked Hariset and Seydi to stay as though nothing unusual had occurred.

The Head Priest had her fingers locked on her big belly apparently taking a nap while Atlas just seemed bored. Selene, on the other hand, showed growing anger with Leto, demanding to know why Hariset brought Maidservant to Kalliste without permission.

He, a perfect picture of contrition, turned to Seydi and gazed an unspoken communication which she answered with a brave nod. Then he explained, "Maidservant was the daughter of two of my household servants. During infancy, she suffered fevers that left her slow-witted and ill in the head. Her parents wanted to send her away so as not to embarrass me, but I thought she would benefit staying with them. I made a place for her in the kitchen working for the head cook, a kindly old woman who helped look after her. Doctors said the girl would improve, but her condition became worse every year and they could not understand why."

He choked slightly with emotion. "When I adopted Seydi, she discovered the parents resented the extra work caring for the girl caused and were cruelly abusive. You may judge me harsh, but I could not tolerate mistreating a sick child and banished them to labor on one of my farms. The cook became her de facto mother and Seydi a big sister."

Beaming fatherly pride, he gazed down at his daughter, who returned love with adoring eyes. It was an emotional, heartwarming scene.

Selene pushed long black hair back from her face. "Did the poor thing's health improve with removal of the parents, Hariset?"

"Oh yes. She has learned to plod through each day on her own, and now only occasionally suffers fits. Unfortunately, though, we were careless on Kefti, because she began sneaking out to bars at night, drinking and getting into mischief. Once we realized, we nipped it in the bud, of course."

Only Leto was not sympathetic. "What do these fits entail?"

"She injures herself and blames it on accidents or accuses poor Seydi of mistreating her. She suffers delusions, too. It sounds worse than it is nowadays. None of it keeps her from duties."

Leto drummed the table with her fingers. "Explain why she disembarked alone at night and wandered streets willy-nilly peering into people's houses and making a nuisance of herself."

"New environs confuse and agitate her. I thought she would benefit remaining on the ship an additional day to get used to the change. But music from the bars lured her off the ship. By incredibly good fortune, Envoy happened upon her and brought her home, but she had gotten wine somewhere. Poor Seydi, though it tore at her heart, sobered her up in the canal until she could go to bed without being sick. I am sorry for the trouble it caused."

Seydi, playing shy eye catch games with Atlas by looking away whenever he glanced her way, spoke up suddenly. "Dear Father is taking too much blame. I should have been stricter and watched her closer. I should have waited on the ship with her rather than giving into my excitement to see your beautiful island firsthand."

Rhea opened her eyes. "The girl may stay on the island."

Caught by surprise, Leto fumed. "She can't live with Seydi at the Temple. The Ambassador, regardless of good intentions, won't have time to care for her. The best course is for her to return to Egypt where she can be looked after properly."

Rhea cracked her knuckles. "Have the wax removed from your ears, Leto. I just said she will stay. We can work out the details another day. Anything else?"

Noting how much it pleased Selene to see Leto put in her place, Hariset stood and bowed. "Thank you for your consideration, Head Priest. She has ample kitchen experience. I wonder, might it not rattle the cages of those ungrateful Scholars if she worked at the Temple? I've never seen such reprehensible displays of rudeness as I witnessed today."

Atlas objected. "Employing an outsider would be a direct threat to the Scholars very existence, Head Priest. It will stir them up even more."

Selene agreed. "It's imperative nothing else be done to provoke them."

Leto glared and said nothing.

Rhea obviously liked Hariset's suggestion. "It would be a charity given her condition. Surely, no one can argue that point."

Atlas and Selene did, and strongly.

Rhea stopped them. "I'll think about it and let you know my decision. In the meantime, Selene can help the Ambassador settle into the Embassy. Are we finished?"

Leto pounced. "Shouldn't the Ambassador submit to the Challenge before he's allowed to live among us?"

Selene jumped up. "You are so petty and trite."

Leto looked her up and down. "Your pasty face is breaking out in big red splotches. Did coming out of your lair in daytime make you ill?"

"At least I bathe and change clothes regularly. You make my eyes water."

Rhea laughed, slobber flying from her thick lips. "Heed and improve, you two. Heed and improve."

Atlas was a bureaucrat. "I must point out that the Challenge is required by law unless we vote exception, Head Priest. Recall that Envoy submitted to it when he asked to join us."

Selene replied sharply. "Only because he claimed to have served Kalli in the City of Bulls and no one believed it."

Rhea pounded the table. "Do not discuss that here. Having visitors drink the elixir to determine if they are members of Corruption is no longer necessary and you know it, Leto."

Leto taunted Hariset. "Surely, a big strapping man like you is not afraid of tasting a Priest's blood."

Seydi had taken hold of Hariset's hand, squeezing to get his attention, but he ignored her. "I don't have a clue what you are talking about, but give it to me. For that matter, give it to Seydi. Give it to the whole damned crew that brought us here. Don't forget the maid. I certainly don't want Priest Leto so frightened that she can't sleep."

Leto went red with anger, but before she could respond, Rhea took charge. "Each of you vote and otherwise keep your yaps shut."

Leto struck the table with her palm. "Yes!"

Selene struck just as loudly. "No!"

Atlas shrugged. "Abstain."

Rhea turned to Hariset. "Abstain. You don't have to take it."

Hariset threw his hands up. "After all this, I insist!"

Giving Leto a hard look, Rhea popped open the green emerald setting of a heavy gold ring, revealing a compartment. She held out the forefinger of the other hand and Atlas jabbed it with the tip of a dagger. She filled the compartment with blood.

Meanwhile, Selene went to a cabinet and returned with a bowl of dark wine. Rhea dumped the blood in, whispered an incantation and pushed the bowl to Leto, who handed it down to Hariset. "One small sip will suffice."

Hariset took a big gulp and set the bowl on the stage at her feet, ignoring that she had her hands out to take it back. Leto returned to the table without it. After a minute passed, Rhea pushed herself up out of the chair. "Welcome to Kalliste, Ambassador Hariset."

He bowed. "I am honored to be here."

***

IN A PUBLIC TOILET, HARISET THREW UP as much as he could, but it was not soon enough. The blood attacked his system as they walked along the white avenue back to Eao, forcing him to stop on a high bridge over a steaming hot river that roared through a steep ravine down the mountain. He pretended to admire the view while concentrating all his power to fight off the attack. Then he locked arms with Seydi and somehow finished the journey back to the House of Kalli before sprawling and convulsing face down in the big room.

Maidservant, setting a table for midday meal next to the canal, came running. "Is the master ill, Mistress? Has he been injured?"

Seydi greeted her with a blow to the face with the scepter, sending the surprised girl to the floor with nose spurting blood. "You're too stupid to help anyone. Be quiet or I'll squeeze your heart until it bursts." She bent over Hariset. "Fool! You deserve to die."

He shoved her away, twisted up off the floor then staggered and swayed as he struggled to remain standing. "I...will...endure...it."

She was amazed. "It's not possible!"

"I...told you...I...will endure."

"Even if you can, so what? What if they had given it to me? You endangered ME!"

"You think...this mission...has no...risks? Now, they won't... suspect either of us. They won't...watch us...so closely."

"What if you were wrong? They would have killed me, too."

"I knew...I could do...it. Not...first time."

Seydi regarded him with increasing suspicion and fear. She backed away a step. "The Challenge of Kalli's blood has always been certain death for us."

Hariset forced himself to stand straighter. "A thousand years of Kalli's blood passing through so many people dilutes her legacy. If you had real power...enough to be feared...you'd have recognized that."

She shook a fist. "You dare question my power!"

He backhanded her across the face, twisting her completely around.

She attacked with the scepter. "You're going to pay for that!"

He grabbed her by the neck with a hand suddenly heavy and bestial, lifted her into the air and squeezed. She lashed out with long black claws, raking flesh off his arm, but he did not flinch and the wounds healed instantly.

Meanwhile, her face turned red then purple. "You had best behave, Czn-tanth. You've become so enamored of your rank and protections given by Shelitine that you do not know the Master's right hand even when it holds your life by the neck."

He dropped her in a heap next to Maidservant and spat on her. "If you hurt the girl in front of those Kallistians again, jeopardize this mission or go to Shelitine or the Master behind my back, it will be your last act on this earth. Is that clear?"

Seydi made her voice work, but could not keep it from trembling. "Lord Tesi-Ra, Lord Destroyer, First of the Six? It is you, isn't it? But why are you cloaked from me?"

"Because I do not trust you, Czn-tanth."

"But Great Lord, I was concerned that..."

"Shut up! This Head Priest cannot possibly be as weak as she seems, nor can she believe the One Master no longer poses threat to this island. And now we hear Envoy came to them making preposterous claims of longevity, yet the Head Priest accepts him with no other explanations. Your main task will be to discover his secrets. Meanwhile, I will use the girl to find the truth about the power of the Head Priest and Council. Do you have any objections?"

She shook her head vigorously. "Your will be done, Lord."

He put a hand on Maidservant's head and said an incantation to make her forget all that had just transpired then left them alone in the big room.

Seydi, known as Lady Czn-tanth in the ranks of Corruption and Lady Wither to its uninitiated followers, was the youngest and most feared Blood Daughter of the One Master, but at the moment, she was simply glad to be alive. She let out a long sigh of relief, sat up and slapped Maidservant to vent frustration for allowing someone so powerful to catch her unaware.

SIX

THE BOOK OF MAIDSERVANT: ATHY AND ARTY

CYTHE, RESPLENDENT IN A YELLOW PROSPECT'S TUNIC, came around the corner of the garden house, the only access into its small backyard closed in by high hedges and canopied by mature olive trees that held in heat and made the area particularly stifling. She yelled back over her shoulder. "I found her."

Maidservant, stooped over a big overflowing tripod tub up to her elbows in soapy water, had hoped they would not think to look for her here. After she routinely reported to her master that Cythe and Aria were bringing their mentors, Initiates Athy and Arty, to meet her, he surprised her by already knowing much about them and threatening punishment if she did not discover something new and useful. After thinking about it, she decided avoiding the meeting altogether would result in less grief than having to report she did not find out anything, which seemed likely to her. She rinsed her hands under a leaking terracotta spigot sticking out of the wall and studied the newcomers nervously while Cythe introduced them.

Athy and Arty were very different in appearance. Athy had neat, shoulder length brown hair tied back loosely, penetrating brown eyes and a perfect profile enhanced by dark tanned porcelain skin. Arty had short curly red hair sticking out every which way, a pale boyish face overburdened with freckles and slightly crooked nose poking out sharply between mischievous green eyes.

Yet, in every other regard, they were amazingly alike. Both wore Initiates' blue tunics exactly the same fit and size. They were exceptionally willowy, athletic and graceful. They seemed to share thoughts and always know what the other was about to say. Moreover, although they appeared the same age as Cythe and Aria, they gave the impression of being much older.

Never had Maidservant seen two people more self-assured. She was intimidated and in awe of them. No wonder her master had so much interest.

Cythe pointed to the big pile of clothes on a blanket. "Why do you have so much laundry? Didn't you do it a couple of days ago?"

Maidservant forced her voice to work. "Master Hariset sends his clothes for me to do until he finds a satisfactory cleaning service in Cadi-sum and Mistress Seydi is moving to the Temple in two days. She wants everything rewashed and pressed, Lady."

Cythe sighed. "I've been telling you for weeks to use my name."

Maidservant was not comfortable addressing people casually, so she nodded agreement without planning to do it. However, this time, Cythe insisted Maidservant say her name and planted a big smacking kiss on her cheek after she did it. Surprised, Maidservant gaped with one eye closed and tip of her tongue sticking out.

Aria hipped Cythe out of the way. "How can you be so darn cute? Now you have to say my name. I'm going to stand here until you do it."

How she wished they would leave her alone. "Aria."

Aria pointed to the redhead then the girl with calculating eyes. "Arty. Athy."

Maidservant repeated after her then her face scrunched up. "All of you have such short, unusual names. Are you from the same place or related in some way?"

Arty shoved Aria aside and grinned down at her, freckles moving everywhere on her face. "Here's the skinny. We got drunk one night and started making up nicknames for each other, most of them unmentionable because everyone but me has such dirty mouths. Then we started using some of them amongst ourselves..."

Athy slid in front of her. "...and now no one uses our real names anymore."

Arty pushed her away. "Heck, shorter names are more distinctive and memorable than our real ones, anyway."

Cythe struck an exaggerated pose, head turned to the side and nose high in the air. "Maidservant, however could you think I am related to such common girls of the streets as these?"

When they stopped laughing, shoving and insulting, Arty went back to Maidservant, who watched their shenanigans with no clue how to act. "What other work haven't you finished?"

Maidservant thought it was criticism for not having everything done, especially since she had gone back to bed for an extra hour after Seydi left for the Temple, so she made excuses, natural for someone used to frequent punishment. "The rain made a mess in the big room last night and the toilets are dirty because I decided to tidy Mistress Seydi's rooms and do the wash first, but I didn't realize how much there was or I would have started two hours before daylight instead of one."

Athy replied quietly that Arty had not meant it as a complaint then shocked her by divvying the work up. "I'll mop the big room. Cythe and Arty, help Maidservant with the wash. Don't waste time doing Seydi's clothes, just refold them." Seeing distress on Maidservant's face, she added, "Don't worry, Selene took her and the Ambassador to a town on the north side of the island and won't return until tomorrow evening. She'll be too busy moving to notice." She nodded to Aria. "Give the toilets a royal cleaning then come help me in the big room."

Cythe clapped her hands. "First, group hug!"

They mobbed around Maidservant, hugged the air out of her then spun around and around, upsetting the tub and making everyone so dizzy they fell down in the mud.

Laughing, Athy said, "Darn, Maidservant, guess we'll have to wash some of Seydi's clothes after all."

Maidservant felt as if she might to throw up. "You shouldn't do my work. I can handle it."

"Shush," Cythe said. "We'll be done in no time then can have some fun."

"Wait, guess who this is?" Aria stuck her lower lip out pouting, made circles around her eyes with thumbs and forefingers and imitated Seydi perfectly. "I always have to do the toilets. Really I do. It is so unfair. Really it is."

Maidservant had not heard her do it before and nearly choked trying not to laugh.

Cythe looked fabulous even with mud splashed on her face. "Hey, Aria, what did Seydi say when she heard Kalli's lessons about humility?"

Aria struggled up off the ground and sashayed around the corner of the house swaying her muddy backside outrageously. "Humility does not apply to me. That is why I get to wear fancy makeup, even if other Prospects are not allowed."

When Leto had informed Seydi that Prospects must conform to an appearance code, she requested an audience with the full Council to explain why she could not comply. Then, in Rhea's house, she told them a story in monotone, not changing her dour expression a single time.

"My mother believed it improper to appear in public without formal makeup and a wig, but I considered it outmoded thinking, especially as braided hair was the new fashion. She insisted, I resisted, we argued and she forbade me leaving the house without complying, but I did anyway. Mostly, because I resented her spending days on end in bedchambers claiming all sorts of maladies with servants catering to her every whim while requiring me to do all her work running the house. We stopped speaking to each other for the longest time. Then she died."

She caught a solidary tear running down her face on the tip of a long blue fingernail and flicked it away.

"After the funeral, Father said I would be sent away because she suffered so much hiding her illness so that I would not worry and all I did was complain. I cried my eyes out and vowed to be the best daughter in the world to make it up to him, but he said go pack and get out. Hoping to change his mind, I got up extra early to prepare his breakfast next morning, but when I took it to his study, he was still in the big chair where I'd last seen him, dead from grief and poison by his own hand."

She caught another tear and flicked it.

"Crushed and alone, I took to my bed no longer wanting to live, but just before I wasted away to nothing, Mother appeared in a dream and said I must represent the family now. You will think it silly, but I pledged never again would I allow anyone to see me without makeup and wigged. I am sorry, but I will not break my vow to my dead mother. So now you know." She left.

Leto commented that more likely Seydi poisoned her parents, making Rhea laugh. Selene and Atlas expressed disapproval that Leto would suggest such a thing. Then Leto insisted the story was ridiculous and they must consider that most of the males, as well as many females, sniffed after Seydi like love-starved puppies, causing Rhea to laugh again. Lastly, she opined, "Remove the makeup and solve the problem. I vote no exception."

Then Rhea surprised and upset all of them by declaring there would be no vote. She would make the decision after discussing it with Hariset.

Next day at the embassy, the Ambassador explained that when he first met his niece, he found her propped up in bed with paint smeared all over her face and wearing one of her mother's wigs that sagged over her forehead to the eyebrows. And, while his brother had good income, he had no reserves and left the poor girl destitute. What could he do but settle the family debts and adopt her? Also, he realized Seydi's discomfort speaking likely made the story sound farfetched, if not outright contrived, but please consider that even he had never seen her without makeup and wig.

Rhea granted the exception and told the Council to focus on more important matters when they tried to argue.

Arty wiped sweat out of her eyes and took one of Hariset's tunics from Maidservant to wring out. "Seydi fabricated that story about her mother, didn't she?"

"I did not know her mother."

On her other side, Cythe was skeptical. "You apply and remove her makeup. You care for the wigs. You must see her face, so the story is hooey."

Maidservant did not understand why, but nothing frightened her more than Seydi's unmade face. She could not stand thinking how it looked, much less talking about it with others. Fortunately, she knew a sure way to change any subject with them. "Slaves don't count."

To end the awkward silence, Arty held one of the Ambassador's tunics up. "He casts quite a striking figure, don't you think, Cythe?"

"I don't care for him."

"Well, he's causing quite a stir in Cadi-sum with the female Priests. Rumors abound about him and Selene."

Cythe looked away so Arty would not see her expression. "I used to think she was so wise."

Arty lifted the hem and peered inside. "Tell me, Maidservant, have you ever seen him naked?"

She dropped the soap, splashing herself in the face.

Arty laughed. "Come on. Surely, you've seen his dingle dangle at least once, huh?"

"Lady!" Maidservant, having just fished the soap out, dropped it and splashed herself again.

Cythe took one of Seydi's fine robes from the pile, dried off Maidservant's face and threw it on the muddy ground. "By the way, Arty's not a lady, so use her name."

Maidservant, worried about the robe being ruined, mumbled, "Yes, Lady."

"Yow!" Cythe slapped the water with both hands and stamped her feet in the mud, sending it flying everywhere. Then she went to her knees in a fit of giggles. Arty stared at her a moment then splashed down on her backside. She and Cythe pointed at each other, laughing hysterically.

Looking back and forth at them, Maidservant burst out laughing and sat down between them, setting off a frenzy of slinging mud and splashing.

***

MAIDSERVANT LEANED ON THE TOP RAIL of the white bridge staring down into the deep, clear water of the canal, which halved the huge room exactly. It flowed from the north wall to the south at varying speeds. There was no water outside the building, and Cythe and Aria, who swam in it frequently, insisted the tiled sides and bottom had no openings. She asked her master about it, and he said there had to be some, but they might be cleverly concealed, not surprising considering the Kallistians' plumbing expertise. When she tried to discuss it more, he told her to stop wasting his time.

She looked around. What was taking them so long? They had gone to the garden house to clean up and see if Athy and Arty could wear any of Cythe or Aria's clothes. She had ruined her dress, too, and they told her to go put on a clean one as if she was rich as they were. She had four dresses when she came to the island. Now, she had two.

Finally, Arty, wearing a work tunic too big and obviously belonging to Aria, came out of the garden hallway. Maidservant glanced down at her dress, embarrassed by its cheapness and amount of wear.

Arty trotted onto the bridge. "How do you like the House of Kalli? Interesting, isn't it?"

Maidservant hated the dark, gloomy place. The walls were enormous gray stone blocks that seemed to absorb light. Making matters worse, sunlight shining through the ceiling opening never reached the north and south ends, leaving them in constant darkness. The ceiling, supported by nothing but the perimeter walls, was approximately five stories high. Her master said that without columns and such a huge opening in the center, he could not figure how it stayed up, especially with so many tremors shaking the island, causing her to worry constantly it would fall on her.

Arty, not the most patient person, fidgeted and reminded herself the girl had mental problems. "Uh, I bet you were surprised by how big it is."

Maidservant had paced it for her master. Absurdly enormous for no reason, the big room was approximately four hundred feet long and two hundred and thirty feet wide. A set of double doors with two huge sets of shuttered windows either side were equally spaced across the front wall and provided five of the six ways into the building. Walking from the front doors directly across the bridge took one to the back wall and three narrow hallways. Two went to small, mediocre bedroom suites that had no openings to the outside and the third to the back door into the garden maze. Nothing about the place made sense.

Arty tried asking a more specific question. "What do you think of the statues? Amazing, aren't they?"

Massive and hideous, especially viewed by torchlight, each stood on a heavy high pedestal. In the southeast corner, a red bull with flaring nostrils and hooking horns charged. In the southwest, a green cat with amber eyes and long curved tooth jutting down each side of its jaw stood poised to attack. In the northwest, a reclining golden lion outstretched its front legs like the Sphinx, but the head raised up in a ferocious snarl. An empty obsidian pedestal with a broken top where once set a Kalli statue occupied the northeast corner. It was the most attractive one, far as Maidservant was concerned.

Arty's face was red. "How about the floors? Striking, huh?"

Big tiles of the same type as the avenues divided the room into four rectangles of color matched to the statues---green and yellow on the front side of the canal, red and black to the rear. The colored sections met precisely at the center of the ends of the bridge. Nothing about it was special.

Arty's patience ran out just as the others joined them. She declared, "I bet you don't have anything this impressive where you are from."

Maidservant, in spite of everything else, was a proud Egyptian. Words spilled out of her. "We have thousands of monuments and buildings decorated with depictions of gods, legendary creatures and fantastic events, Lady. Several lifetimes would not be enough to see all of them, especially as artisans add more every day. Nowhere else in the world is there so many incredible sights and beauty as in Egypt."

That was the first time anyone heard Maidservant speak more than a few simple words, and they turned Arty's smile upside-down. "You...you don't like it at all, do you?"

Maidservant wanted to say something improve the situation. "It's all right, I guess."

Arty turned to Athy. "Race me to a statue."

Athy smiled. "We just got cleaned up."

Never one to stay upset long, Arty grinned. "Yeah, wouldn't do for us to get into trouble after the last warning Atlas gave us, either. No point racing, anyway, since I always win."

Athy pushed her. "Name a wager."

"Two cases of Leto's best wine and dinner at Kosto's Tavern. I mean the good one in Eao, not his crap place in Cadi-sum where you like to eat. I'll even let you pick which statue, long as it's not the bull." She raised her right arm, pulled down the sleeve hole and showed Maidservant a big jagged scar from the armpit down her side. "Zigged. Should've zagged."

Maidservant started to ask what she was doing with a bull, but Athy made a big, exasperated noise. "Do you have to show your little boo-boo and tell your zigzag joke to everyone you meet? You act like being too fat and slow to get out of the way is something to brag about."

Arty made a face. "Four cases of wine and no limit on the price of the dinners."

"Deal! You think I will choose the green cat and you can use those enormous thighs to advantage on hills, don't you, lizard breath? Well, I pick the yellow lion!" Athy took off across bridge, Arty no more than a stride behind.

"Take some water!" Cythe yelled then turned to the others. "Quick, let's go to the other side to watch."

When Athy and Arty were about halfway to the statue, a loud whoosh sounded and the yellow area expanded at incredible speed, spreading over the canal and black area to Maidservant's right. Then the three perimeter walls north of the bridge receded out of sight. At the same time, Athy and Arty became distant specks angling away from them toward the corner. Always analytical no matter what she faced, Maidservant's mind raced, trying to reason out how everything could move different directions at the same time without something breaking. Then she looked up and saw the ceiling over the area had risen out of sight and gave up trying to figure it out.

Suddenly, the building shook violently and the yellow area blurred. Then a vast desert baking under a blazing sun in a cloudless sky stretched before her. Maidservant walked out a few steps, knelt and burrowed an arm into sand up to her elbow. It was hot deeper down, exactly as desert should be at midafternoon in summer. She turned and looked at the room's south areas. The red bull and green cat were garish with all that light shining on them. The white bridge, the canal and ceiling from the middle of the bridge southward were unchanged. The two hallways to the bedrooms were still there, but the hallway to the back garden and the doors and windows on the front were solid block wall. Dumfounded, she went to Cythe. "Lady, what's happening?"

Cythe took her hands and fixed those incredible blue eyes upon hers, making it impossible to think about anything else. "I have decided to break a rule and tell you about my life. I was born on a tiny island in a poor fishing village. When I was seven, because they had more children than means, my parents traded me for two mended nets and pieces of a salvaged boat."

She laughed without humor. "They took me far away to another island where people spoke a language I couldn't understand, but the elder saw to it that I was not mistreated, which was often the case with outsider girls. By the time I was nine, there were already discussions of betrothal because the area had lost so many females in raids and I was pretty with a reputation for working hard. The competition for me became crazy, especially from a nearby island. A man, whose offer for me was insufficient, led raiders to take me by force. While they butchered and burned the village, I escaped into the sea on a door ripped off a burning hut. A Kallistian ship found me all but dead. It was Envoy, and he brought me to Eao, where a new family loved and cared for me until last year when the Temple chose me Prospect. The only possession I've had my whole life is my name. Call me Cytheria if you are determined to keep distance between us. Call me Cythe if you wish to be friends. Nothing else will suffice. Understand?"

Maidservant was not used to feeling so much emotion, because she, more than anyone, understood the importance of names. "If I slip, Cythe, don't get mad. This is new for me."

Cythe kissed her cheek then went to Aria and hugged her. "Stop blubbering, you."

"Why didn't you tell me you had it so bad? I didn't know about Envoy, either. When I think of the things I've said to you, I…"

Cythe's smile always made things better. "I am thankful for every step I've taken in my life because they brought me here, Aria, so be happy about them, not sad."

She turned back to Maidservant. "Now, about the House of Kalli. Athy and Arty did not show you this without the Head Priest wanting you to see it. However, under no circumstances, ask them questions about it, especially Athy. She will tell you what they want you to know and nothing more. Understand?"

Her tone frightened Maidservant a little. "Uh, may I still ask you and Aria questions?"

That brought back the smile. "Of course."

"Do you know why Kalli destroyed her statues?"

"Just a guess. I think it was because people had begun to worship her as a god, and it made her angry."

That made no sense to Maidservant. "Why would that make anyone angry? I sure as heck wouldn't mind being a god."

Cythe smiled. "And I can't imagine anything worse. Kalli teaches us that all people possess the powers and abilities attributed to gods, but, except in rare instances, they are not developed."

"So, if you develop them enough, you can be a god. Right?"

She shook her head. "I swear, you ask a lot of questions. Let's talk about something else and leave philosophy for another day."

Aria quipped, "Five hundredth Lesson of Kalli: If you're overcome by need to worship a god, find a rock with a shape that pleases you, carve a nice stand and write compelling stories about it to gather followers."

Cythe shoved her. "Maidservant, you will have to learn to sift facts from fiction whenever Aria tells you anything."

Aria laughed. "She understands me so well."

Hot wind blew clouds of fine dust from the desert. Sneezing, Cythe said, "Here they come. I swear, even if Athy and Arty are stronger than everyone else, they tempt fate too much sometimes."

Aria shaded her eyes with both hands and squinted. "I can't see anything."

Maidservant saw nothing but hazy dust. "How can you see, Cythe?"

She mumbled something and a vision of Athy and Arty running in a sandstorm materialized in front of them. Aria jumped straight up. "Cythe!"

The vision vanished and Cythe pinched her nose to stop it running. "Dorry, Maiddervant, but you'll have to pretend dat didn't happen. Remember, don't ask them questions."

Aria pulled an elegant handkerchief from her tunic and gave it to her. "If you keep holding your nose like that, your head is going to explode."

Cythe handled the handkerchief as if it was a piece of art. "Are you dure?"

"Yes, I'm dure. Blow your dose, please."

The desert disappeared and everything in the room rushed back into place as Athy and Arty ran back across the floor to them. Caked in dirt and sunburned, they paced around the others, stretching and catching breath. Then Arty knelt to examine her cracked, bleeding feet. "For a while, thought you might catch up, Athy."

Bending forward, Athy shook an amazing amount of sand out of her hair. "In your dreams. I was first as always."

Arty scooped sweat-soaked sand from inside the waist of her tunic and threw it on her. "I was a step ahead the whole way."

Aria asked, "Did you reach the statue?"

Athy looked at her critically. "It takes much longer to go that far. If Arty hadn't slowed us down, we could have done much better, though."

Arty laughed. "What a liar!"

Athy tugged the tunic off her shoulders and let it drop. "Stupid storm got sand absolutely everywhere." She took three running steps and dived into the canal. Not bothering to undress, Arty hit the water a split second behind her.

Maidservant could barely hold her tongue when they climbed out. The sunburn and blisters were gone. In fact, except for Athy's dirty tunic on the floor and layer of dust on everything, there was no evidence it happened. Athy saw the questions on her face. "Something bothering you?"

Maidservant caught Cythe's warning glance. "There's no place like this in Egypt, that's for sure."

Athy knelt down to her. "If you run from the bridge directly toward a statue, that area expands and changes. You can walk to the statues from the bridge or run from anywhere else in the room and nothing happens. To change it back, you run a direct line from the corner toward the bridge, something very few people can do with an area expanded because you have nothing to judge directions. If you can't get back, you'll die. Until now, the Head Priests have allowed no one other than a few Temple members inside this building, so don't do anything stupid. Understand?"

Maidservant nodded, wondering why the Head Priest wanted her to know all this. It made absolutely no sense.

***

CYTHE AND MAIDSERVANT PREPARED SUPPER in the cottage while the others laid out a picnic in the maze using two of Seydi's dresses as blankets. The meal was simple but hearty, and they drank ample amounts of robust wine and water flavored with fruit to wash it down.

Just before sunset Cythe ran back to the cottage and returned with a small olive tree in a pot. They led Maidservant to a T-intersection. Cythe said, "Aria and I thought this would be a good place, but you have to be careful not to land on it when you use the shortcut."

Maidservant did not understand what she meant so Aria took her hand and jumped back and forth through the hedge several times. Then Maidservant did it herself until Cythe stopped her. "It's getting dark and we must plant the tree."

Athy nodded to Cythe, who cupped her hands and whispered something. A glowing globe hovered over them, lighting the area. Cythe clapped her hands with excitement. "I just learned to do that."

Maidservant did her best to hide amazement, at the same time noticing Aria's hurt expression after Athy gave her yet another critical glance. What was going on between them?

After planting, they joined hands in a semi-circle around Maidservant and the tree. Athy said, "This tree is to welcome our new friend, Maidservant, to Kalliste. Let us remain friends forever."

"Forever," the others repeated, beaming at Maidservant, who was more than a little surprised to have tears in her eyes.

"To close the ceremony," Athy announced solemnly, "I'll honor our new friend by reciting ancient words of power known only to Initiates and Priests of the Temple." The others looked at each other with surprise.

Maidservant, in spite of badly pronounced words, recognized the passage from the base of the white statue of Kalli above the pale lake, which distressed her because she had convinced herself that the confused recollections from that night were not real. Then someone put an arm around her shoulders and she remembered a cold pale woman holding her close and staring with strange green eyes. Arty asked if she was all right and she managed to say yes. Then Athy said she and Arty had to go because of early classes and everyone kidded and made small talk until they actually did go.

Aria and Cythe bundled the remaining wine and led Maidservant through the maze to the overlook. It was a clear night with a big full moon. Eao City stood out in stark detail and the harbor glistened. Boats, jetties and the lighthouse seemed almost close enough to touch. They drank too much and jabbered about silly things like boys and serious things like life at the Temple and nasty things like Seydi until Cythe and Aria stumbled off to the cottage and she to her little room off the hallway to Seydi's suite.

Maidservant could not sleep. The drop of medicine she took every night made her head pound even when she did not have too much wine. Moreover, she felt guilty even thinking about telling her master everything that happened because it betrayed her new friends' trust. Then she thought of something else and sat up. Wouldn't he just say it was a fit? She had no way to prove it except by running toward a statue and probably ending up trapped in some strange place. She remembered the invisibility pill and Mousey. He certainly would not try to save her. Then again, if she did not tell him and he found out, he would be really angry, but how was he to know unless she gave him reasons to pry secrets out of her head? She lay back down. She would tell him later if necessary.

SEVEN

MAIDSERVANT BURST OUT THE BACK of the House of Kalli running full speed. In spite of not being able to see in predawn darkness, she counted steps and jumped sideways through the shortcut over her little tree. Aria and Cythe kept an oil lamp burning in the tiny window next to the door of the garden house for her and, in less than half a minute, she bounced up and down next to their bed. "Time to get up, sleepyheads!"

Cythe groaned. "It's too early. Crawl in beside me and sleep a little while."

Aria, behind her facing the wall, rolled over and lifted her head. "Pipe down, will you?"

Maidservant could not contain her excitement. "I go to the Temple, today!"

Aria was a grouch in the morning even when she had enough sleep. "For mercy's sake, the Head Priest is giving you a job cleaning, cooking and waiting tables, and the Scholars will do everything they can to make you miserable, not that the place is any great shakes even when everything is perfect."

A crushed expression replaced Maidservant's big smile. Cythe sat up and hugged her. "That was mean, Aria."

Aria struggled up onto her knees. "Sorry, Maidservant. I'm sure everything will be fine."

The smile was back instantly. "Then get dressed and let's go already."

The day was dreary and threatening rain as Cythe led them up the road past the hill with the merchant's house. They turned left into dark woods, pausing to create a light before hurrying along a series of rugged trails across the southern slope of the mountain. Maidservant half-ran to keep up, wondering why her friends did not have a problem with all the roots, rises and dips that impeded her.

Cythe pointed left down a steep craggy slope. "We're going west, parallel to the avenue that runs between Eao and Cadi-sum. Most people are afraid to use this shortcut. I'll make you a map if you feel brave enough to try it; otherwise, you can use the road." Maidservant assumed people worried about getting lost, not a problem for her as she remembered every step of the way.

They turned onto a wide path with less foliage overhead, letting in enough light for Cythe to extinguish the globe. Soon, the powerful roar of water drowned out conversation. Ahead, the trail disappeared into billowing fog. Cythe shouted, "We have to cross Boiling River on a rope bridge. Stay close behind Aria and hold the ropes tight. I'll be right behind you, so don't worry."

Before she had a chance to think about it, they plunged into dense steam onto a slick, three-plank-wide, swaying footbridge with rope handholds. The heat and noise were incredible. Without meaning to, Maidservant pushed Aria in the back with her head to go faster while staring down through wide cracks in the boards wondering how far below the water was. When they reached the other side, she cupped her hands around her mouth. "I'll never go this way!"

Wrapped in fog, they hopped down wet rock steps cut into a high bank onto a muddy white tile avenue. It was wider than others she had seen. Cythe explained, "This is Temple Avenue, but everyone calls it First Test, as in First Test of the Day. You'll see why in a minute."

The way was steep and took them up out of the fog quickly. Maidservant stopped dead in her tracks. The avenue bent straight up the mountain at an extremely steep angle and cut so deep into the stone face that black glassy walls twenty feet high closed it in on the sides.

Cythe nudged her to go. "This is the only way to the Temple plateau, and there's no way off the road until you reach it. You will see narrow passages through the rock on the right, but they're for draining water off the avenue into Boiling River. They're very dangerous and people have fallen in, so don't go exploring."

The avenue was wet and treacherously slick. Maidservant's feet went out from under her several times, so they took her arms. Cythe said, "This afternoon, I'll make you a pair of sandals that'll grip the road better. It'll make a big difference."

Maidservant's legs had cramps. "Why is it so steep?"

Aria responded with bitterness. "Like everything else at the Temple, it is designed to make students give up. That's why most Prospects don't last through the first year. Then, of those who do, only a few become Initiates and even fewer become Priests. I can live with that, but the judging is inconsistent, arbitrary and dependent on who likes you and whether their standards are fair or audacious."

That was when Maidservant understood her problem with Athy.

Cythe spoke before Aria said anything else. "Don't treat Scholars with more respect than Priests because they're older. They are failed Prospects kept on because they possess a skill useful to the Temple. Mostly, they spend their lives studying in hopes someday they might be reconsidered for promotion, but it seldom happens."

"Yeah," Aria added, "so it doesn't take a genius to see why the older they get, the nastier they get."

Cythe shot her a look but did not say anything.

Something bothered Maidservant. "How can Scholars be older than Priests and Initiates if they come to the Temple as Prospects?"

Cythe shook her head. "I can only tell you that a person's age is a subject you must never ask about, no matter what. Is that clear?"

She did not understand at all, but agreed.

Aria tried to lighten the mood. "And you must ignore rumors that Head Priest Rhea disabled herself so she could live at the Temple and not have to climb First Test every day. No truth to it at all."

Cythe answered, "Don't fill her head with nonsense!"

Once started, Aria was difficult to stop. "Yep, they claim she did it to be like Kalli, who they say could go up and down First Test faster than anyone else in spite of an old leg wound. Can you imagine her hopping on the other one and passing everybody? I'd give a lot to see that, let me tell you."

Cythe did her best to sound angry. "Have respect! No one knows for sure that Kalli had a disability."

Aria grinned. "Rhea, on the other hand, is so fat that it takes six strong bearers to carry her specially made chair up First Test. Gosh, think what would happen if they dropped her. She'd roll down the avenue all the way to Cadi-sum and demolish the arena or a whole neighborhood, maybe. Why, it'd be a catastrophe, a tragedy, an absolute devastation. Might even wipe out most of the town's population."

Cythe stopped and confronted Aria over Maidservant. "If you continue with this, I swear I'll not speak to you for a week."

Maidservant hoped Aria would say something else because she was so darn funny, but both had their mouths clamped shut, snickers escaping the corners. In the end, as usual, Cythe laughed first.

Suddenly, they moved Maidservant to the right shoulder close to the black glass wall. Cythe whispered, "Don't turn around, but Leto and Selene are coming." She had not looked back and Maidservant wondered how she knew.

Magnificent in jade tunics, the two Council Priests ran by effortlessly. Maidservant knew from descriptions that the stern woman who gave her a disapproving look was Leto and the pale pretty woman with long black hair, Selene. The latter called out to them. "Fair weather, Prospects."

In accord, Aria and Cythe answered, "Good health!"

Three melodious tones echoed off the avenue walls from the Temple and Cythe explained that they strike three huge obelisks behind Leto's building one hour before class start, at midday and class end.

Aria responded critically. "Once they were inscribed with ancient words of power, but the Priests teach us that Kalli obliterated them before she died. Call me skeptical, but I think they made that up to cover their lazy butts for allowing the Temple to fall into such a state of ruin and ignorance."

Cythe whispered urgently. "We'll get into trouble if Maidservant slips and says some of these things. What's the matter with you?"

No one spoke again until Cythe said, "Our class is coming. San-zeus and Daedalus are with Atlas. They must be teaching us today."

Atlas, jade tunic stressing over moving masses of muscles, was the biggest person Maidservant had ever seen. The men either side of him had Priests' green tunics with gold trim. San-zeus was tall, lean and handsome with noble bearing, while Daedalus was gawky with big feet and a goofy face. The Prospects followed in three lines. Maidservant hid her smile when Seydi huffed and puffed by at the rear.

Cythe and Aria waited until all of them passed before calling out. "Fair weather, class."

Atlas yelled back over his shoulder. "Hope your morning stroll isn't too tiring."

The class laughed. Cythe laughed, too, but Aria reddened and tried to pull Maidservant along faster. "We're being criticized."

Cythe replied irritably. "Slow down, she can't do any better."

"He'll only remember that I...well, you know."

Cythe ignored it. "Maidservant, remember those big ships you saw coming here? Daedalus designed them. I hope to know him better someday."

Aria rolled her eyes. "You're getting all worked up over silly Daedalus again? You don't even notice San-zeus, the handsomest stud at the Temple, who has the hots for you, by the way."

"Looks aren't everything."

"Not if you have them. Do you know what I'd give to look like you?"

Cythe stared wistfully. "I'd trade with you if I could. You know I would. The thing I want most in the world is to be as respected for my intelligence as Daedalus."

"You probably will be. You're the smartest student in our class. I think you may even be smarter than Athy when she was a Prospect."

Cythe was surprised. "Thanks, even if it is not true. You know, if I had to go through life stupid, I'd ask someone to put an arrow through my heart and be done with it."

Aria laughed. "Yeah, like either of us is brave enough to sacrifice ourselves for anything. I don't understand you sometimes."

"Yeah, I know."

With no warning, no prescience, nothing, Athy and Arty were beside them. Athy yelled, "Hi, Cythe! Hi, Princess! Hi, Maidservant!"

Arty tugged her sleeve and pointed up the avenue. "We can pass the new class before they reach the top if we turn it on. Atlas will have a hissy fit if we go in front of him again." Off they flew.

Maidservant asked Aria, "Why does Athy call you Princess? Is it another nickname you made up?"

Aria made a sour face. "Bug Juice! Forget about it."

Cythe shook her head. "She's going to find out anyway. Better if one of us tells her." Getting no response, she continued. "You see, Maidservant, Aria's just a plain girl with a crap personality, surly disposition and incredible talent for saying inappropriate things. She has terrible taste, too."

Aria stuck her tongue out. "She can see that by whom my best friend is, Miss Fish Guts of the Islands."

Cythe made a face. "When she first arrived at the Temple, she nagged and whined until I agreed to hang out with her. The only reason anyone associates with her is she buys wine and meals for everyone. She's filthy rich, you see, because she's Princess Ariadne, only child of King Ermiticus and Queen Malidia of the whole darned Keftiu Empire."

Maidservant's eyes bugged out and legs stopped working, pulling them to a stop. She had been inside their fabulous palace and now was in the presence of their daughter. She tried to bow, but couldn't with them holding her arms. "Oh, Lady, I didn't realize, or I would never have presumed to…"

Aria knelt in front of her. "Double bug juice to all that! Treat me the same as everyone else and forget that royal stuff. It doesn't mean anything here, anyway. Let's just be friends. Can you do that? Well, can you?"

Maidservant wrinkled her forehead thinking then gave a big nod. "Yes, I'll make allowances for your shortcomings like everyone else if you buy me expensive wine and meals, too."

Laughing, Cythe danced around red-faced Aria. "Maidservant zinged you! Too much!"

They reached the top of First Test and passed through a big stone archway. In spite of the warnings, Maidservant was shocked. The buildings, deteriorated by damp, mold and slapdash repairs of myriads of cracks from tremors, stood in no particular order around a dismal garden square called Main Court. Crumbling, uneven stone walks crisscrossed the entire area haphazardly, many terminating at no particular destination. Untended shrubs, brush and weeds were rampant. A heavy canopy of low-limbed trees cast dreary pall over it all.

Grandly, Aria announced, "The Temple of Light."

Cythe led past an algae-choked pond with a cracked, muck-encrusted emerald pedestal jutting out of murky water. "A Kalli statue was here. You can imagine how pretty this once was."

Aria could not help herself. "If you try really, really hard."

Maidservant spotted a new two-story building painted with red and blue sea creatures set back in the trees. Aria patted her stomach and belched. "Gets you right here, doesn't it? That's Rhea's new residence. We call it Jellyfish House because a big one over the front door looks like a portrait of her."

Cythe had enough. "Give it a rest. Fun is fun, but sheesh, you don't know when to stop. Maidservant, don't let the Priests hear you call it that."

Aria started to speak, reconsidered then stalked away. "I'll have lunch with you if I can get permission to talk by then, Maidservant. Good luck."

Cythe mumbled something then took Maidservant all the way across Main Court. Situated behind the middle of three identical three-story buildings, the obelisks were fifty feet high and each the color of a statue in the House of Kalli. A low wooden stage stood at the exact spot where a fourth obelisk would have formed a rectangle with the others, and Maidservant wondered if there might be a black base under it. Fine lines of text, infuriatingly blurred, covered their sides.

As they hurried back across Main Court, people rushed in all directions. Maidservant noticed heads turning when Cythe passed, and how well she ignored them. They stopped before a low, sagging L-shaped building at the westernmost edge of the grounds.

Cythe explained, "The baths are in the long side. Kitchens and dining rooms, the short. A terrace in the rear looks out over Cadi-Sum City. It's the best place on the island to watch sunsets and is always crowded after school."

She checked to make sure no one was close enough to hear. "Priest DoSo was one of the few Scholars to earn promotion. Give her tons of respect, do exactly as she says and try not to let her upset you too much. Eventually, she will warm to you. I'll come have lunch if I can get away. Otherwise, Aria and I will wait for you at the top of First Test and walk you back to the House of Kalli this evening."

***

MAIDSERVANT STOOD IN THE MIDDLE OF A LARGE KITCHEN before a big, middle-aged woman with a broad shiny face, numerous worry scowls and eyes separated by too much nose. She had a distracting habit of wringing her red, knobby hands so hard while she talked it seemed she might pull off the fingers. "You understand Kallistian, don't you?"

Maidservant was afraid and did not like her. She felt certain the woman was a bully with a mean streak. She nodded.

DoSo threw up her hands. "I don't see how a pissant girl with fewer abilities than a slug can replace a Prospect and a Scholar, but it's not my place to question how the Head Priest assigns help." She jabbed directions with a forefinger nail chewed ragged. "That hall goes to the baths. That one to the dining rooms. The swinging door, to the small kitchen. The big door next to the sinks, out to the terrace. Keep it closed when you're not serving outside or flies and mice get in. The big hall without a door is the way you came in from Main Court. Think you can remember any of that?"

Maidservant nodded.

DoSo grabbed a heavy wooden tray off the counter. "Can't wait for the likes of you to try carrying this full. Just have to make more trips, I guess. She slammed the tray down, making Maidservant jump, and picked up a big square board with a cord tied through holes in two corners. "This is a map of the grounds, each building labeled with the name of the Priest in charge, but since you're too ignorant to read I had to go to the trouble of having a different color put on each building. Match them to the colors on the trays so you know where to take them." She dropped the cord over Maidservant's head and the heavy board banged painfully against her chest. "This way you'll have both hands free to lift. Do you understand anything I've told you?"

The cord cut into her neck, and it was all she could do not to burst into tears. She nodded.

"You're not mute, are you?"

She shook her head.

DoSo made an exasperated noise and hit the counter, causing Maidservant to jump again. "Just see that you don't bother the classes when you make deliveries. There are places to leave and pick up trays, usually small tables in the halls; otherwise, use common sense, if you have any." She went over and whispered something to two Prospects on the other side of the room giving Maidservant spiteful glances. Suddenly, she whipped around. "Why are you still standing there? Report to Initiate Kore in the small kitchen!"

Initiate Kore had a surly attitude and dark features exacerbated by wavy black hair hanging so close around her face that she frequently pushed it out of her eyes. Without a word, she pointed to seven trays laden with drinks and food. Each had a bit of cloth with a Priest's name and a smudge of color. Then she left Maidservant and joined the others in the big kitchen. Her remarks carried through the swinging door. "Mother, you're too much. I almost peed myself when I saw that board around her stupid neck."

DoSo laughed. "A little weakling like her won't last the day."

Maidservant slapped herself to make the tears go away, removed the board and jammed it in a waste bin, making certain it stuck out so that cow, DoSo, and her calf, Kore, would be sure to see it. Colors next to names on the board did not match colors next to names on the trays, nor were the names on the right buildings. She had already seen that the buildings had a Priest's name on small signs at the entrances and remembered them.

She went to the trays and selected one for Selene, surmising Council members should be first. Straining with all her might, she lifted it onto her shoulder, kicked the swinging door open and rushed past DoSo and the others to Main Court, stopping their whispering and giggling.

But now, she encountered more problems. People, mostly older ones in gray tunics trimmed in gold who had to be Scholars, kept stepping in the way so that she had to dodge, sometimes even off the walks. Her legs wobbled and arms ached, but she felt amazingly stronger of late.

Selene's was at the left end of the three-story buildings. The middle one with the obelisks belonged to Leto. She had not seen the name on the other, but it did not take a genius to figure out it was Atlas. She would go back another way to see more buildings. After three or four trips, she would know them all. The only question was whether she could last to the end of the day.

Two Scholars, an elderly man and young woman, stood inside the drab entryway of Selene's building. They stopped talking and gave nasty looks as she went down the hall to leave the tray. Through the doorway, she saw Selene behind a podium saying that inner peace required concentration, meditation and self-discipline. Maidservant thought it sounded like high-minded nonsense that should be obvious to anyone.

The next tray went to Leto, conducting class from the stage in the obelisks' courtyard. Maidservant spotted a small table near the red obelisk and tiptoed to it. As she set the tray down, she scanned the old lines of text, so enticingly close to readable. She looked higher and higher then realized Leto had stopped talking. To her chagrin, the whole class had turned to watch her. She stumbled backwards, almost falling. Laughter chased her around the building but it was Leto's glare that most concerned her. Why did the Council Priest hate her so much?

The rest of the day was nonstop work. She missed her meal waiting for Cythe and Aria, but they did not come. After DoSo that morning, not another person spoke to her. By day's end, she hated the people at the Temple, but then Cythe and Aria were at the top of First Test and said how sorry they were for lunch and how much they had worried about her. Long as she had them, she reckoned she could stand anything. But two weeks later, Rhea ordered them to move back to Prospects' Village so Aria had more time for studies, leaving her alone at night.

Over the following weeks, Maidservant's appetite dwindled until each day she consumed nothing but a few nibbles from the trays, increasing amounts of wine and a drop of her medicine at bedtime. She had always been thin, but now, she became gaunt. Yet, she had so much energy she could not sleep, staring up at the ceiling drenched in sweat with her mind going a mile a minute.

The big room in the House of Kalli was a huge expanse of dark, creepy space, but it never occurred to her to be afraid of it. Then one night, while drinking wine at a small table next to the canal, she began imagining someone lurking and watching from just beyond the edges of the light cast by four torches she had placed around the table. It did not bother her much at first, but as more days passed, the feelings grew stronger until she ran across the big room with a torch when she came from work and stayed in her room. Wine she stole from the kitchen storerooms helped immensely.

***

HER MASTER'S SHADOW HAD NOT VISITED HER for so long that when finally it did, she was not ready. Sprawled across her bed in drunken stupor, sudden jabbing pains made her sit bolt upright. "I'm here, Master!"

"What kept you? Make your report."

She struggled to put thoughts together. "The classes don't seem to teach much, but I heard advanced classes conducted on the third floors of the Council Priests' buildings do. I tried to go see, but they are restricted and Scholars guard the stairs. I heard of a Temple library in Cadi-sum. Perhaps it houses Kalli documents. There is a place the Temple calls the Amber Area higher up the mountain, but only specially chosen Initiates and Priests may go into it. I hear it is just for training, but it doesn't make sense it would be limited if that is the case."

"All this time and that's all you have? I've been inside the Cadi-sum library. It's little more than a study hall for those idiot Scholars. You didn't mention the obelisks. Your mistress says they have inscriptions obscured by Kalli. Can you verify that?"

"I examined them and some sort of magic has made them unreadable. I've never seen anything like it."

"They might have copies of the text hidden somewhere. Find a way to get into the top floors of the Council buildings and look for secret rooms. Surely, you have more information. Think!"

"Uh, the Temple performs magic by reciting Eirycian verses, but it is weak because they recite by rote, don't understand what they're saying and don't pronounce words correctly."

Now she had his attention. "How can you tell all that without understanding it?"

Her hand flew over her mouth. She fought down her fear. "Because I have an ear for languages and the speakers are inconsistent with pronunciations."

"Hmm, perhaps you are justifying your existence somewhat. Anything else?"

"The colors of the obelisks match the floor colors in the House of Kalli, and I think there might have been a fourth obelisk, a black one."

"Is that important?"

"I don't know, yet."

"Don't waste time with extraneous conjecture. What about those friends of yours? Is there anything I should know?"

Maidservant stared into the darkness, not wanting to betray them.

"Why are you hesitating?"

"Uh, I was trying to…uh, thinking that maybe…!" Her arms twisted up behind her so painfully the joints felt as if they might pop apart. "Aria is the daughter of the Keftiu king and queen!"

He released her. "Well, well. Guess that explains how something so homely and untalented got into the Temple. Why didn't you tell me right away? Is it because you think they really are your friends? Surely, you don't think they like you."

That made her angry and she could not hide it.

He laughed. "Are you so foolish that you believe Temple Initiates and Prospects want to be friends with a little nobody such as you?"

She had asked herself the same question hundreds of times and already thought he was probably right, but hearing it hurt worse than twisted arms. She shook her head. She did not want to discuss it.

He laughed. "They are using you to find out more about your mistress and me, that's all. You must be careful with them and never forget they are the enemy. I will make allowance for your inexperience this time, but it had better not happen again. Now, hold still. I must reinforce your ability to withstand the Head Priest's scrutiny. Selene says she will summon you to meet her soon."

A few nights later, Seydi showed up at the House of Kalli and announced the Head Priest would send for Maidservant tomorrow and that she would spend the night to help her prepare. Sitting at her dressing table with Maidservant kneeling on the floor across from her, she fingered the gold scepter absentmindedly as she talked. "Wear one of the new Temple work tunics I brought. From now on, you are to wear them to work."

Maidservant could not hold back her delight about new dresses. "Yes, Mistress."

"Answer her questions politely with no hesitation."

"Yes, Mistress."

"Don't speak unless spoken to first."

"Yes, Mistress."

"Praise your master and mistress at every opportunity."

"Yes, Mistress."

"You're the ugliest, most useless creature in the world."

"Yes, Mistress."

She laughed. "Crawl over here on your belly, my little worm, and kiss my feet." But when Maidservant reached her, Seydi struck her a sharp blow on the shoulder blade with the scepter to see if she showed anything other than utter submission. Maidservant did not flinch, disappointing her. "I want you to remember when you dropped my makeup jar after I came to live with your master. Do you recall it?"

Seydi had whipped her with thorny boughs. Maidservant shuddered. "Yes."

"Pull down your dress and show my favorite shoulder." She ran fingers across the scars. "Embarrass us tomorrow, and I'll make the other shoulder match it. Would you like that? No? Then crawl back to your room. I can't stand looking at your ugly face any longer."

Next morning, Maidservant waited for Seydi to eat breakfast and was late leaving. She wore one of the new tunics and carried the other rolled up in her cloak to protect it from steady drizzle. She wished she could ask Cythe or Aria what to expect, but they were on the other side of the island studying plants. Athy and Arty were in the Amber Area finishing the Tenth Test of Kalli, whatever that was. The swinging bridge over Boiling River was foggier than usual and First Test very slick, but she made way without any trouble, even marveling how easy it had become.

DoSo and Kore ran by just before she reached the top and Kore called back. "Why are you carrying your cloak? It's raining, you stupid clod."

***

TRITIUS, THE TEMPLE'S HIGHEST RANKED SCHOLAR, caused a stir bringing word personally that the Head Priest wanted Maidservant. While she hurried to the baths to change tunics, DoSo, Kore and the others knotted around him, whispering. She was back in three minutes, expecting to accompany him, but Kore was alone with a large tray loaded with wine amphorae, plates of food and brimming bowls of hot soup. "Take this to Atlas. It's on the way."

Maidservant glared. It was not close to being on the way. They wanted her to mess up her clothes or argue and be late. She shouldered the tray and hurried through Main Court, carefully avoiding dripping trees and mud puddles. Fortunately, there were few people about and she made the delivery, but then a surly Scholar told her no one ordered it and to take it back. She left him yelling to do as he said. Trying to make up lost time, she passed too close to a Scholar and she bumped her into a deep puddle. Then, while she squatted to clean her sandal, another Scholar stomped mud at her, but it missed. She jumped up and ran the rest of the way.

Dark clouds threatened downpour by the time she bound up the wide stone steps of Jellyfish House and used a silver ball hanging from the jamb to knock. An old Scholar opened a small viewing port in the ornate carved door, peered down then shut it as the rain started. She waited then knocked again. The Scholar opened the door a crack and stared down disapprovingly. "What do you want?"

"The Head Priest sent for me."

"Wait. I have to check the list." As he closed the door, Maidservant shoved inside, nearly bowling him over. He stared hatefully for long seconds then pointed through a wide arched opening. "You are late. Get in there, now!" Dripping wet, she looked around for a way to dry herself. Suddenly, the Scholar shoved her through the doorway.

The Head Priest, wearing a voluminous lime robe with big yellow flowers, sat facing her behind a large table and making symbols with a brush onto a piece of white cloth. Leto and Selene watched over her shoulders. Across the table at a respectful distance, Seydi stood waiting with her back to the entrance. Quietly, Maidservant went to stand three paces farther away than her mistress did. As no one paid her the slightest attention, she looked around.

If colors made noise, the room would have deafened her. Red carpets with black and brown flowers covered the floor. Blue tapestries with stylized pink, blue and green birds hung across the back of the room. Uneven shelves filled with bric-a-brac, vases and carvings filled the right wall. The left wall was bright yellow with a full-sized statue of Rhea standing before it, girth and features interpreted to more pleasing conclusions and proportions than the original.

Set in a line along the front of the Head Priest's table were four exquisite statuettes about fourteen inches high. One was an obsidian obelisk. The other three were Kalli statues. One was white, a perfect replica of the statue above the pale lake. The second was obsidian, arms straight out pointing a white staff held at one end. The third was emerald, staring down at a tablet held on upturned hands. All had broken, jagged bottoms mounted onto little wooden pedestals painstakingly carved and fitted to each one. She thought they must be replicas of the missing Kalli statues, which confirmed her theory about the black obelisk. Then again, why would they go to the trouble to have replicas show the damaged bottoms so exactly? It made no sense unless...

Leto broke into her thoughts. "I will not ask you again!"

Seydi had turned around glaring, but Maidservant's gaze went over her shoulder to the Head Priest, whose image appeared out of focus slightly. She stammered, "Sorry, L-Lady. Did you ask something?"

Leto had fire in her eyes. "My title is Council Priest! Face us, Prospect. Let her answer on her own."

The Head Priest's appearance became normal when she spoke. "Come around the table and tell me how old you are."

Maidservant was amazed not to feel afraid as she went to stand next to her. "I am thirteen, Head Priest." She had a feeling similar to when her master looked into her, but Rhea's probing was subtler. Then Rhea hugged her with ample arms into a bosom even more ample. It was surprisingly pleasant in spite of strong body odor. When she released her to go back to her place, Maidservant was sorry.

Leto's piercing eyes followed her every move. "Could you tell what's wrong with her?"

Rhea shrugged one shoulder. "It is as Hariset said. Poor child."

Selene complimented Seydi for her efforts to help her. Seydi was appropriately humble.

Rhea looked sidelong at Leto, waiting impatiently. "Aren't you the one who said allowing this girl to work here would unravel the fabric of our universe? So much for your highly touted insight and wisdom, huh?"

Leto's face tightened. "We're handling it, but it's causing all sorts of difficulties with the Scholars and Priests who support them. You still haven't decided where she is to live, either."

Seydi had been waiting for the right chance to offer Tesi-Ra's idea. "Couldn't she live with me at Prospects' Village or in the Temple Baths? That would allow me to keep a closer eye on her and not be in the way of the Scholars."

Rhea drummed the table louder, staring up at the ceiling as if pondering solutions. "Allowing her to live on the Temple grounds would cause even more ruckus. What to do, what to do?"

Leto could tell she had already decided the matter. "As I keep saying, send her back to Egypt."

Rhea brightened. "Oh, I know. She can remain in the House of Kalli and be responsible for its upkeep in addition to the Temple job. I will have more torches placed in the big room to make it homey. Assign some Prospects to light them after school so she does not have to return to such a dark house. Have them do some of the cleaning, too. Come to think of it, designate Maidservant officially as Caretaker so she can earn a little pocket money."

This was too much for Leto. "I couldn't believe you allowed anyone to stay there at all, and now you propose her to use it as a residence. It is too dangerous for someone without powerful abilities. What if..?"

Rhea shushed her. "She already knows how to avoid the dangers of the place. I had Athy and Arty show her."

Leto looked at Rhea with disbelief.

Selene asked, "What dangers are you talking about?"

Now, Leto looked at her with surprise.

Rhea ignored them and addressed Maidservant. "They told me you can't swim."

"No, I can't."

Rhea nodded. "You should learn soon as possible, but in the meantime, do as Athy said and be careful not to fall into the canal and drown."

Leto started to say more, but Rhea hit her leg and gave a warning look.

Selene noticed but was used to Rhea doing outlandish, petty things. "That Caretaker job belongs to Cythe. What will she say?"

Rhea had already discussed it with her. "She has hands full helping Aria with studies. Neither of them has time for anything else. She won't mind."

Selene brought up another matter. "What about the Scholars? Having more Caretaker jobs is one of their top demands. When they find out you are giving one to Maidservant, it will cause more trouble."

Rhea spoke without raising her voice. "Marko."

Instantly, the old Scholar appeared in the doorway. "Yes, Head Priest?"

"Be sure to tell Tritius the girl will not only have the Caretaker position and work in the kitchens, she will also help clean my house every afternoon. That will afford her status equal to yours as a member of my personal staff. I will listen to the formal complaints next week. Now, scurry back around the corner where I can't see you, please."

Rhea gave them a big smile. "Isn't it nice how we can work our problems out if we simply listen to one another? Selene, ask Hariset if he has any objections tonight when you go to bed, and let me know." She noticed Maidservant staring aghast. "Want to say something?"

Crushed, she answered the only thing she could. "Thank you, Head Priest."

Rhea beamed. "You are very welcome. Run along back to DoSo, dear."

Maidservant made it out of Jellyfish House before bursting out crying. In the downpour, no one noticed.

EIGHT

THE BOOK OF MAIDSERVANT: KALLI'S FINAL TEST

C YTHE AND ARIA KEPT PROMISING TO COME STAY in the garden house soon as they could get away, but so much time passed that she gave up hope it would ever happen. She seldom saw Athy and Arty, even at the Temple. Prospects did some of the cleaning every evening, as well as refilling and lighting all the new torches provided by the Head Priest, but they were usually gone before she returned, not that anyone talked to her. Her master's shadow had not visited since the decision for her to live in the House of Kalli, and when she asked Seydi about it, she said that he was too busy to waste time with her. Then she heard a comment on the terrace between two male Priests that one of them should try to renew his relationship with Selene while the Ambassador was away in Egypt and knew Seydi had lied to her again. As for Envoy, no one knew when he would return. If she had money, she might have gone shopping so she could at least talk to strangers, but Leto gave it to Seydi for her.

***

THE FINAL TEST OF KALLI BEGAN ON A NIGHT indistinguishable from any other. Maidservant sat on her bed drinking wine when wind whooshed down the hall, flapping the door curtain. This had never happened before and she ran out to look.

Gusts whipped the new torches providing a light corridor from the front entrance across the bridge to the hallways. Thinking a freak storm must be blowing through the ceiling and front openings, she went to the bridge and looked up at the sky, but saw only blackness. That was strange, because usually stars or island lights reflecting off clouds were visible, regardless of weather. She plodded back to look out the rear entrance before going to bed.

She held the heavy door open a long time, staring into a warm, still night at trees and hedges bathed in light from an almost full moon. All the while, cold wind blew from the hallway behind her, billowing the gown and raising goose bumps on her legs. She had not suffered delusions this strong since her master's house in Egypt. Heartsick, she returned inside, slouched down in the hallway and watched her imagination wreak havoc in the big room.

Winds howled, churning waves in the canal so big that she heard them hitting the south wall. When most of the torches were out, she got up and walked slowly back to her room. She sat on the bed and whispered prayers to Hathor and Isis for it to end, but they did not hear her. It continued until first light shined through the ceiling. Relieved she had not hurt herself, she went to work.

On the second night, Maidservant's hands shook when she put the daily drop of medicine in her fourth cup of wine because, for more than an hour, she heard the noise of wind blowing through big trees. She stopped the cup at her lips, wondering if perhaps the medicine had something to do with setting off this latest bout of illness. She tried to dump it into the water basin but could not make her hands obey. She yelled, "Pour it out, dummy!" Then she yelled back, "No! Drink it!" and gulped it down. Numb, she stared into the empty cup for a while then plodded out to see what was going on.

The sounds came from the green area on the other side of the canal. The wind was not violent like the previous night, so she went out and crossed the bridge, vaguely thinking it might help to confront her delusions, but when she stepped onto the green floor, hundreds of tiny shadows skittered out of the darkness and swirled into the air. Screaming, she fled back to her room and cowered under the blanket until daylight.

She took a torch from a stand and walked to the bridge, looking everywhere for leaves, but found nothing. Dejected, she walked to the front entrance, threw the torch down and went to work still wearing the same wine-stained tunic from the previous day.

On knees, scrubbing the floor in the small kitchen, Maidservant shouted at her reflection in the container of water that it was weak, ugly and stupid then threw up on it. Appalled, Kore chased her outside to dump the mess. A short time later, while juicing fruit, she got into a nonsensical argument with herself about whether she should have poured out a cup of wine or not. Kore sent her to sort the big supply cupboard then found her sitting on a storage jar drinking a jug of wine. Kore reported it to DoSo, who immediately went to the Head Priest to complain. "She's out of her mind and stays drunk most of the time. I've about had it."

Rhea shrugged. "Like I told you yesterday, and the day before, keep an eye on her and make sure she doesn't harm herself. As for the wine, you are a big powerful Priest, Kore is an Initiate and she is an unfortunate young girl. Surely you can deal with it."

As far as DoSo was concerned, the more the girl drank, the better chance of her getting into so much trouble the Head Priest would have to remove her, so she continued to argue. "I don't know the last time she had a bath or changed clothes. What a stench, and working with food, too. What if she hurts herself, or worse, makes someone sick?"

Rhea regarded her coolly. "Then you and Kore will be demoted. Anything else?" DoSo stormed out of Jellyfish House, slamming the big door behind her. Rhea spoke to the empty house. "It will be over all too soon, DoSo."

On the third night, Maidservant staggered down First Test from work, climbed the bank and took the shortcut. In spite of darkness and heavy fog, she skipped onto the swinging bridge not bothering to use the side ropes and even stopped halfway to pull an amphorae of wine out of a bag slung over her shoulder. Then she lurched along the trails in complete darkness drinking, but still made good time.

At the front door, she threw the empty amphora into the green area and watched it smash to bits. She followed the torch stands to the bridge, pulled out an amphora of Atlas' wine, took a swig and dropped it into the canal. "Ugh! What sweet, girly wine you drink, Ast-lax...Ats-la...Atlas!" Giggling, she leaned against the rails, nearly fell through them into the water then somehow made it to bed before she passed out.

The noise of driving rain woke her, but a pounding head, desert-dry mouth and spinning room kept her from getting farther than propping up against the wall. Then lightning flashed down the hall and illuminated the door curtain, followed by rumbling thunder that shook the bed. Very afraid, she whispered, "It's not real."

The sounds of downpour intensified and she heard trickling water. Stupidly, she had closed the cover of the lamp, so she scooted to the edge of the bed and put her feet on the floor. It was wet. She nearly knocked the table over franticly fumbling to open the lamp.

Horrified, she saw water streaming in from the hall. The door curtain was sopping wet. She stuck her head out and glimpsed water running down the hall walls when another flash of lightning and a resounding boom of thunder came from the big room. She stumbled back to her bed and pulled the damp blanket over her head.

At daybreak, she tried to ignore the dripping door curtain, crept out and witnessed the last of the water streaming off the floor into the canal. Strong wind blew from the black area, drying everything. She ran to a wet spot and put her hands on it. She patted it on her face. In wonder, she whispered, "It isn't me. It's real."

She walked to the bridge and tried to make sense of it all. She could not, of course, but now she could deal with it. Feeling better than she had in weeks, she started across the floor to work then stopped dead. Enormous wet paw prints crossed the floor, coming from the darkness of the green area and disappearing into the darkness of the yellow. Screaming, she ran outside and vowed never to go inside the House of Kalli again.

That night, she considered sleeping in the woods, but that seemed a place monster cats would hunt. Having nowhere else, she worked up all her courage and dashed from the avenue into the maze to the garden house. She slept inside the bedroom clothes cupboard with the doors closed. The next six nights she used the bed, and that was where Seydi found her. After punishing her severely on the back and stomach, she warned, "If he can't find you, there will be hell to pay for both of us."

Maidservant knew her master had not returned and looked up from the floor as she rubbed spit on the welts. "I'm not going back."

Seydi took her by nape of the neck and marched her into the House of Kalli to the bedrooms. When she saw how damp and unkempt everything was, she flew into another rage and punished her again. Then she gave her another warning and left her cowering in the corner of her little room. Maidservant counted to a hundred then ran back to the garden house fast as her legs could carry her.

Two weeks later, Maidservant hurried across Main Court with a tray of dirty dishes balanced on each hand, deftly dodged a Scholar who tried to hip her and cursed him in Egyptian, which, it turned out, he understood. He gave chase, but changing classes helped her lose him. Continuing to look back over her shoulder, she did not notice Seydi, who knocked the trays from her hands and tripped her to the ground.

Seydi spoke loudly so everyone heard. "Father said to tell you he won't tolerate your bad behavior in the Eao bars any longer. Next time you are not in your room when he looks in, he will send you back to Egypt." She bent close over her. "You don't know what that really means, do you, worm?"

A vivid image flashed in Maidservant's mind. She was on her back looking up into nighttime from a dank, tight place at huge shadowy creatures staring down with red eyes and touching her with black, cold hands. It terrified her too much to speak.

Seydi laughed. "That is what will happen if you move a muscle or utter a sound before midday bells. Use the time to figure out how to ask Father and me forgiveness for your disobedience."

Maidservant lay across the busy walk afraid to move. Two Scholars and several new Prospects made a game of jumping and landing close to her face until Athy and Cythe arrived. Athy told her to get up, but she would not answer or move. Athy left aggravated, but Cythe missed a class sitting on the ground next to her to keep everyone away. When midday came, Maidservant ran away without a single word to her. Back in the kitchens, Kore and DoSo scolded her for neglecting morning duties while smirking at the others because the story of her behavior with sailors had spread through the classrooms like wildfire.

***

MAIDSERVANT, SOBER FOR THE FIRST TIME IN WEEKS, expected to die that night. She gathered her possessions from the garden house and walked the dark maze from memory with eyes closed rather than using the shortcut to prove to the gods she was brave and worthy to enter afterlife, but as she approached the back of the House of Kalli, pulsing light made her open them. Next to the entrance was a single Eirycian word: BEWARE. She jerked the door open, banging it against the wall, and shouted down the hallway. "No shit!"

Not letting herself look at the dark areas, she went to her room, straightened the musty bed and strewed wildflowers from the woods around it. She put on her clean tunic, extinguished the lamp and lay on the bed watching dim torchlight shadows dance on the moldy door curtain. Eventually, gentle canal sounds and crackling torches lulled her into an exhausted stupor.

Heavy padded footfalls from the big room, somewhat remindful of Mousey and friends scurrying around her lying on the floor of the cupboard, grew louder then faded away. Soaked in sweat, almost too scared to breathe, she listened as the sounds passed by several more times. Then, at the loudest, they stopped suddenly. Something blocked the light into the hallway. She bit blood from her fist to keep quiet. She heard the curtain moving. She imagined a huge head poking into the room, jaws salivating as they opened wide to eat her. Then a loud snort and a warm, sticky substance showered her.

Maidservant opened her eyes. Flickering light shined on the curtain again. She started to sit up but the pillow block stuck to her face and hair. In a furious flurry of motion, she yanked it free, leaped off the bed and slung the pillow into the curtain. She stepped out of her clothes, grabbed up the washbasin and slammed it down on the table repeatedly, shouting curses at the top of her lungs. She kicked over the table, ripped down the curtain and marched resolutely out to the big room.

Glaring one way then the other into the darkness, she followed the torches to the canal, sat down and plunged her feet into the cold water. Dipping the bowl full, she poured it over her head and bathed for the first time in weeks. Next, she stretched out on the floor next to the canal and sang bawdy sailors' songs in pidgin until the sky turned gray. She got up and shook fists all around. "Dying isn't worse than being sick and afraid all the time! Dying isn't worse than being alone all the time! Dying isn't worse than living with no friends!

Dying isn't worse than not having my real life and family! Dying isn't worse than anything else I do, so leave me the hell alone if you know what's good for you!"

At work that afternoon, Kore yelled at her for being too slow and Maidservant threw a bowl of fruit at her. When DoSo came storming in from the other room, it was all she could do to not yell back and throw something at her, too. DoSo realized it and simply yelled a threat before hurrying away to see the Head Priest. "You'll stay out of the wine if you know what's good for you!"

Straightaway, Maidservant went to the cupboard, filled a sack will the best wines and left early. At the House of Kalli, she chased away the Prospects before they finished filling and lighting the torches. When night fell, she lurched back and forth across the bridge, singing so loudly her voice cracked. She opened the last amphora, one of Leto's prized wines, and took a long drink. "At least you're good for something, you ugly camel butt!"

After that, she lost track of everything until she was in her room staring dumfounded at the medicine bottle, empty finally. She smashed it against the wall, glad she no longer had to take the awful stuff. She shook fists in the air again. "Nobody's going to tell me what to do anymore!"

A woman's voice boomed from the big room. "If you are sufficient, come to me."

It was a refined accent, somewhat like Aria's. Steady bright light shined down the hallway. She grabbed the washbasin and staggered out to the big room to bash whoever was dumb enough to bother her.

The light came from the black corner. The statues at the south end were shadowy, but the golden lion in the other north corner positively gleamed. It was strange seeing all of them at the same time.

"If you are sufficient, come to me."

The voice came from the black corner, too. Was someone hiding beside the pedestal? It was impossible to tell with all that light. She started toward it, but only went a few steps, because when she stepped from the red floor to the black, she ran into something invisible and solid as a wall. Amazed, she walked back and forth feeling it.

"If you are sufficient, come to me."

Angry, she backed away then ran at it full speed, knocking herself silly to the floor. That made her angrier, especially as the washbasin had broken. She got up, took her upper right leg under the knee with both hands, pulled it off the floor and tried to push it forward. "Ugh!" Then she did the left. "Ugh!" She made no progress at all. Furious, she kept at it and soon was soaked in sweat. She was still in the same spot, too. Feeling sick to the stomach from the wine, she bent over, hands on knees, catching her breath.

"If you are sufficient, come to me."

She yelled back. "I can't do it!"

"If you are sufficient, come to me."

"It's too hard!"

"If you are sufficient, come to me."

She shook a fist. "If you want to see me so bad, you come to me!"

The building rumbled and shook. Her first thought was the mountain shaking the island, but then crashes and clattering came from the front side of the room. The entire front wall moved toward the canal, knocking torch stands over and tumbling them. The doors and windows were gone. She spun around. All the walls were moving in toward the bridge. The three back hallways were gone, too. The ceiling was coming down, the opening no longer square but a round, closing iris. With no way out of the room, she dashed to the bridge.

She watched the canal growing shorter while the width remained the same. Why didn't it overflow? She leaned out and could no longer see the tiled bottom. Okay, it was getting deeper, but how could four walls come together at the same time the ceiling they supported came down? It was too incredible to comprehend, so she sat back against a post and watched the big statues rumbling toward her. She thought they would stop before they crushed her, but prayed just in case.

It was remarkably fast. The walls pushed most of the torch stands and tables and chairs into the canal then everything stopped when the ceiling touched the haunches of the great bull, which were slightly higher than the head of the golden lion and tail of the green cat. The new room had the pool and bridge at the center and statues jutting out over the water from three corners. The voice, which had been silent while the room rearranged, boomed a last time. "You are sufficient."

***

MAIDSERVANT LOOKED BETWEEN FINGERS into the bright light as she walked slowly from the bridge to the pedestal. No one was there. Most of the light came from the top so she wedged against the wall and climbed up onto it, careful of the jags, cracks and sharp edges. Shielding eyes, she squatted, carefully noting the pattern of damage until something moving on the bridge caught her eye.

A woman with long blond hair, pale shoulders and a dirty shroud tucked under the arms leaned over the rails staring down into the water. Then she limped to the other side and looked down again. Maidservant shivered, for surely, this was Kalli. She tried to make her voice big, but it came out small and squeaky. "May I help you with something?"

The woman looked around, missed seeing Maidservant the first time then found her in the light. "Ah, the bothersome girl. Why are you up there?"

"Lady?"

"Answer me."

Her tone rankled Maidservant. "How did you get in here?"

"Come down and stop being annoying. We need to talk."

"I don't think I'm coming down until you answer me. Is there a secret door out of here?"

"Get down this minute!"

Maidservant put hands on her hips. "I don't think so."

The woman snapped her fingers. "Remember our last meeting. Now!"

Maidservant jerked backwards, eyes widening with fear and surprise. Then she gawked in disbelief.

"Close your yap or I'll put a bug in it; not a fly this time, but a big juicy dung beetle."

"You tried to kill me!"

"You're spouting nonsense."

Maidservant stretched up on tiptoes, pointing and shaking her fist as breathless words tumbled one over another. "You lured me asleep and threw me into cold filthy water to die. You did it, you know you did, and you might as well fess up. I would've drown but for Envoy. Then he treated me like a helpless child because you made it so I couldn't remember anything." Her voice trailed off then started again. "What a mean thing to do! I'm most certainly not doing anything you tell me. I'm Caretaker of this place and you can get your butt out!"

"Come down."

"No!"

"Perhaps a dose of humility is what you need."

Maidservant took a deep breath to let fly another tirade but something nuzzled her backside. She spun around. A cat. Huge. Green. Amber eyes. Drooling lips. An enormous curved fang each side of a maw of sharp teeth. She took three running steps off the pedestal and landed in the water with a huge splash. She thrashed to the surface.

The woman yanked her out by the hair, deposited her roughly on her backside and stared down with a self-satisfied smile. "Changed your mind, I see."

Maidservant kicked her feet. "You made me lose my sandals."

"You can get more."

She blubbered. "Cythe made them for me. They were a present. Only present anyone gave me my whole life. I rubbed oil and tallow on them every week. Oh!"

The woman dived over the bridge rail and left almost no disturbance on the surface as she disappeared into the water while the shroud floated down onto the bridge. An instant later, she shot out of the canal at tremendous velocity, grabbed the top rail with one hand and pulled up over it. She tossed the wet sandals between Maidservant's legs. "There you go."

Except for the crooked right leg, she was every bit as beautiful as Cythe. Symbols of crossed double-axes above her left breast and a blue-green orb on her wrist glowed radiantly. She wrapped in the shroud and dried her hair by running fingers through it a few times. That was when it occurred to Maidservant that she could not have reached her from the bridge to pull her out of the canal, yet here she sat.

The woman gestured to the debris in the water. "Never a good idea to put stuff in this room."

Maidservant nodded glumly.

The woman sat down with feet hanging off the bridge. She motioned Maidservant to sit beside her, handed her a big cup of wine and had one for herself. "I am a representation of Kalli."

"What does that mean?"

"It means I'm not Kalli, but I do represent her."

"Okay, if you say so."

"Tell me what's happening at the Temple."

As before, Maidservant could not stop talking, only this time the words came faster and faster.

The woman stopped her. "How can you possibly fast-speak? No one develops that ability this quickly, especially without instruction. If the Corruption notices the changes in you, they will break you apart to find out why. We certainly can't have that."

Maidservant was frightened. "Break me apart?"

The woman put a hand on the side of Maidservant's head. "Forget what I said about anyone hurting you." She waited about half a minute. "I can't believe you passed the tests of wind and water and stayed in the House of Kalli after the cat."

Maidservant stared, realization turning to anger. She jumped up and threw the empty cup down, peppering the woman with flying shards. "I should have known you'd be involved!"

"Oh, piffle. Don't see any gnaw marks on you."

"No thanks to you!"

"Calm down, will you? I think you were exceptionally brave to come back after seeing paw prints on the floor."

"I ran away," Maidservant admitted sullenly, "but my master made me come back because his shadow couldn't find me."

That seemed to concern her. "What about when the cat came to your room. You overcame your fears, didn't you?"

"I peed my bed and fainted, probably because I was too afraid to breathe."

The woman was perplexed. "Yet, you reached the pedestal. You certainly don't look that strong."

Upsetting her felt good. "I tried, but couldn't do it. Then I yelled it to come to me and this happened."

Exasperated, the woman stood and looked down on her. "Hundreds of the strongest, brightest people who ever lived have passed through the Temple, yet, someone like you was chosen."

Maidservant jumped up and faced her. "I didn't ask for this!"

"What would you say if I told you there was no cat?"

"Don't play games with me. It was in my room and on top of the pedestal a few minutes ago."

"I didn't see it."

"Sorry to hear you're blind. If I still had a cup, I'd give it to you to beg the streets."

The woman handed her another cup of wine. "Don't break this one. You certainly have a mouth on you."

"I'm tired of being messed about!"

"The cat came from your own imagination."

"It touched me! Next, you will say I imagined the wind and storms. I got wet!"

"The House of Kalli has abilities built into it. Don't suppose you know the difference between magic and science, do you?"

The condescending way she acted aggravated Maidservant. "My guess is that the same ancients who constructed the indestructible white avenues built the House of Kalli using science that we don't understand anymore, so most people would call it magic. Big whoop-de-do."

The woman was startled. "So you think people long ago could do things that present day people cannot. Does that seem sensible to you?"

"Yes, of course. Civilizations do not progress in straight timelines. I've certainly read about enough of them to know that."

"That muddled mind certainly keeps anyone from suspecting how intelligent you are. How are you doing with First Test?"

"Uh, it was difficult at first, but I walk up it easily now. I don't have any problem with the rope bridge shortcut through the woods, either."

"From now on, you will run up and down First Test, but only in darkness or you'll be seen by the Watchers. Moreover, you will run around Kalli's big room every night and try to set your mind free to wander and wonder while doing it."

Maidservant had heard Watchers mentioned at the Temple, knew they worked for Leto and expected to learn about them soon. She had heard about meditating and solving problems while performing demanding physical activities, especially running. However, she was skeptical it worked and running around the big room was impossible. She mentioned the canal was in the way.

The woman shrugged. "Keep trying to jump over it until you do it."

She laughed. "No one can jump that far no matter how many times they try. Besides, I can't swim."

"If you are truly the one Alicia saw, you must be able to jump the canal when the time comes."

"Who's Alicia? Where did she see me? When the time comes for what?"

The woman dropped a necklace over Maidservant's head. "Find someone special to give this. Until then, don't show it to anyone and don't take it off."

Maidservant stared down, running her fingers over a fine gold chain with a tiny orb of blue and green crystal, same as the one on the woman's wrist. It was beautiful.

"I could never give this away." Then Maidservant looked up, suspicious suddenly. "It's not going to make me do evil things, is it?"

"Save the jokes for someone else. Daylight will be here soon. The house only obeys you, now, so you must put the room back the way it was. To command the black area, stand on a black tile, face the pedestal and tell it what you want it to do. Then jump onto the bridge quickly. Go on, try it."

Feeling more than a little ridiculous, Maidservant stepped onto the black floor and looked back to ask what she should say, but the woman was gone. She looked at the pedestal. "Uh, go back the way it was before?"

The building shook and rumbled as it changed. Maidservant sat down on the bridge and began planning how she would show all this to her master and speculated what he would give her as reward.

She woke up with a terrible headache and no idea why she was on the bridge. A sealed medicine jar was next to her and she could not understand how since she remembered emptying and breaking it. Then she spotted furniture and torch stands in the canal. She hit herself in the face. "What have you done now, you little idiot?"

NINE

NORTHWESTERLY BREEZES TEMPERED HEAT and sweetened air with a heady scent of blooming flowers that invited appreciation of amazing views down across Eao City to the harbor, but Athy and Arty set too fast a pace for anyone to enjoy them. Aria and Cythe followed with Maidservant behind them, jogging to keep up. Heads turned as they passed because of Cythe and the Temple tunics.

Carping about San-zeus' reputation as a lady's man, Aria said, "Why do so many girls throw themselves at him? He is more arrogant and self-absorbed than Ambassador Hariset, if that's possible."

The conversation had started with Arty making a favorable comment about San-zeus, so she defended him. "If you knew him better, you'd see how charming and thoughtful he is."

Athy glanced back at the others with a knowing look and raised eyebrows. Then she smirked at Arty but said nothing.

Arty's face reddened. "What are you insinuating?"

Athy could not have looked more surprised. "Well, I wasn't going to say anything, but if you weren't in line to make Priest and have a vote to select the next Council member, he wouldn't be so enthusiastically pursuing your...uh, favor."

Arty shoved Athy off the road. "You keep it up and you're really going to get it!"

Athy trotted back alongside her. "No, you're missing the point. San-zeus is going to get it."

Arty exclaimed, "As if!"

As everyone laughed, Athy spun around, walking backwards down the hill without slowing the pace. "Hey, Maidservant, hard to believe you haven't been to town since you came. Eao is practically on your doorstep."

Cythe looked back over her shoulder. "We'll have to take you to Cadi-sum next time. I love all the fountains and flower gardens there."

After ignoring her for months, yesterday they proposed she go work with them in Eao today and paid no attention when she said she should do her job at the Temple. Dully, she replied, "I'm forbidden to go there. Leto thinks it will make too much trouble with the Scholars."

Cythe's face fell. "Sorry, I didn't know."

Maidservant shrugged. "Yeah. Well, we haven't talked in a while."

Aria tried to make things better. "On the other hand, Eao is not so full of gossipy Temple members that we have to be concerned that everything we do is discussed all over the place."

Arty jumped around, matching Athy's backward strides. "What do you have in mind, an afternoon of forbidden pleasures in a bawdy house?"

Cythe spoke in a deep breathy voice she often employed to tell dirty jokes after drinking too much. "Alas, Destiny holds higher purpose for Princess Aria than for mere mortals, so she must always prepare, PREPARE!"

They stopped, shoving each other and saying prepare in deep voices, except for Maidservant, who watched quietly and smiled when she thought someone noticed.

A short while later, they entered a busy intersection and Maidservant finally said something that was not coaxed out of her because she wanted to hurry the day along. "Wouldn't it be faster to turn here then take Dolphin Avenue down to the baths' north entrance?"

Athy halted the party. "Whoa! Are you sure?"

Maidservant realized by their expressions she had made a mistake and wished she could take the words back. Her reply was reluctant. "Yes."

Arty scratched her head. "Cythe, you grew up here. Is she right?"

"I'm not sure. My neighborhood is farther south and west and we went to the baths from that direction."

Athy shrugged. "What the heck, better ways are not learned until tried."

A short time later, Arty looked back over her shoulder and asked the question Maidservant knew would come. "If you haven't been in Eao since you came to Kalliste, how come you know the streets so well?"

She hesitated too long, making it seem she searched for an answer. "Envoy brought us this way from the baths the night I came. He mentioned he lives in this area and that it is a less busy thoroughfare to the House of Kalli. Remember, Cythe and Aria?"

Aria shrugged. "Too much wine, and who was paying attention anyway? Right, Cythe?"

Cythe was busy gawking at Maidservant. "Envoy told where he lives? When he visited where I grew up, he always led me to believe he lived in

Cadi-sum. I didn't find out differently until I joined the Temple. I can't believe that he…uh…"

Aria laughed. "Watch out, Cythe's jealous."

Cythe's face turned scarlet. "You promised!"

"When did you say it was a secret? Not once, never! Besides, everyone can tell just by looking at you."

Cythe wagged a finger. "From now on, you'd better check your wine for mashed bugs."

Aria sneered. "They'll go up your nose if I find any!"

"I'll pull them out and make you eat them!"

Aria chortled. "Next day, you'll get them back with extra sauce. Hey, Maidservant, tell her about your conquest of Envoy. She needs some pointers."

Maidservant cried, "I've never conquested anyone!"

After a bout of telling each other to get conquested, Athy became serious. "Truth be known, when I came to the Temple, I followed Envoy around like a cat looking for a leg to rub against. All of us have worn his patience thin with attention at one time or another, haven't we, Arty?"

Arty ignored her. "Ah, there's Dolphin Avenue, and unless I'm mistaken, Eao Baths down at the end." She glanced back. "This is definitely the shortest way."

The baths echoed with clamorous noise. Politely not checking out the mostly naked bathers too obviously, the girls hurried down a narrow hall into a small room and changed into plain work tunics. Then they went to a big changing room with piles of wet drying wraps strewn everywhere. They scooped them up and went down another hall into a central courtyard where three Prospects washed them in big tubs and hung them on lines. They helped until an hour after midday when the crowds thinned out and Athy said they could go.

Arty looked at the water longingly. "Do we have time to bathe before we change?"

Athy started removing her clothes. "Great idea. I feel kind of grimy after handling those dirty towels."

Arty, noticing Maidservant standing and staring blankly, gave her tunic a playful tug. "Get 'em off!"

Maidservant clutched the garment to her, burst out crying and bolted for the changing room. Mystified, Arty stared after her. "What did I do?"

Cythe ran after her. "She'll be all right in a minute."

Athy turned to Aria. "Any idea what's wrong with her?"

"Probably afraid you'll see all the scars and bruises. She hides the ones on her arms and legs with makeup, but her back and shoulders are a mess. Cythe and I pretend not to notice and she's learned to relax around us, but I think she'd die of embarrassment if anyone else saw them."

Arty nodded. "After she destroyed the furnishings in the House of Kalli, we should not be surprised she still hurts herself. I feel sorry for her, but…"

Aria interrupted with darts in her voice. "Mostly, it is from Seydi beating her with that golden rod of hers."

Athy thought Aria directed the retort at Arty and replied strongly. "Must I tell you again that Rhea judged Seydi acceptable? I don't like her, either, but we must be careful not to allow Maidservant's accusations damage a Prospect's reputation without any evidence. Face it, the poor girl is known to hurt herself and lie, especially about Seydi."

Arty agreed. "Like that shortcut this morning. Do you really believe she would remember when you and Cythe don't? Give me a break."

Aria knew she should apologize and shut up. She also knew she would not. "If you'd seen Seydi throw Maidservant into the canal then stand watching her drown, you'd not be so quick to take her side."

Athy's jaw tightened slightly. "Cythe told me about the incident and I confronted Seydi. She knows she overreacted, but it was out of concern for Maidservant's well-being, not malice. She even spoke highly of you and Cythe for going out of your way to befriend the girl."

Aria grew louder. "You saw what Seydi did to Maidservant in Main Court and just walked away and left her."

Athy's patience stretched as far as it would go. "Actually, I complained to the Head Priest and she ordered me to stay out of it, which is something an Initiate should not disclose to a Prospect. Now, why don't we agree to help Maidservant deal with her difficulties and leave it at that?"

Arty tried to give Aria more time to think before it was too late. "Yes, working together is the best way to help someone with challenges like hers."

Aria persisted. "Well, I certainly know the truth even if Seydi has you fooled."

Arty moved between them to stop Athy from reacting. "Ah, here they come. We'd better change. I hope this lunch Cythe's promised us is a good one. I'm starving."

***

CYTHE TOOK THEM INTO AN AREA OF NARROW STREETS, stopping finally before the whitewashed walls of a large two-story house decorated with paintings of flowering trees. Real ones shaded a side garden with intricately carved benches and a gurgling fountain. A sign beside the door proclaimed: Plinius the Goldsmith.

A step up from the street went into an oversized room with long tables displaying gold and bronze jewelry. Four artisans worked behind a low counter at the rear. Suddenly, from a side doorway, appeared a man with a round full face, boundless energy and jovial personality. His bare brown belly hung prominently over a fine kilt that reached to just above his knees. Dozens of jangling chains and bracelets adorned his neck, arms and ankles. He swept Cythe up in his arms. "There's my beauty!"

"Plinius, my father," Cythe introduced. A woman raced down stairs and out a short hall on the other side of the room. Cythe ran and hugged her. "My mother, Denear." Squealing with excitement, a four-year-old in a sack dress tore down the same stairs and jumped into Cythe's arms. "My sister, Erran."

Cythe took her friends upstairs to her bedroom. For such a wealthy house, the furnishings were simple: narrow bed with rag mattress, decorated wooden storage box with a cushion top and shelves on a sidewall for clothes.

The murals were another matter. V formations of red birds commingled with yellow stars on a blue ceiling. Luscious green vines with blue flowers covered the wall behind the bed. Tears in her eyes, Cythe pointed to it. "They had it painted for my first birthday here." She pointed out a single, tiny yellow flower above the pillow block. "Plinius added this one before I went to the Temple and said it was so I would always be with them."

During the meal, Erran began crawling onto Maidservant's lap then sliding off. Maidservant was very awkward with the energetic little girl but had not stopped smiling once. Denear asked the obvious. "Haven't you been around children before?" When Maidservant shook her head, she said, "Well, you've certainly found one who likes you."

Plinius told story after story about Cythe growing up, laughing almost nonstop. "What a pain. From six-year-old boys to married old men who should know better, every male in the area found no end of excuses to visit the shop or hang around out front in the street. Got so crowded sometimes, we considered moving before we finally palmed her off to the Temple. Much better now."

Denear tittered. "Tell them about Gurney the Baker. He brought us so many cakes that Plinius gained twenty pounds. The fool thought Cythe ate them. Can you imagine? Look at her."

Plinius held his stomach. "Proves you don't have to be over-smart to be a great baker."

"Stop telling those stories!" cried Cythe. "They'll torment me with them."

It was over too soon, and when they left the house, Maidservant did not understand why Cythe apologized to the others. "I'm sorry. It was selfish. I didn't realize until we were there. I hope you didn't find it hurtful." Then she saw the stoic Athy and fiery Arty were teary.

Athy shook her head. "No, we enjoyed it. No one can fault you for making as many memories with them while you can."

What a nice thing to say, Maidservant thought, not yet knowing the implications in her words.

***

ON THEIR WAY TO A CAFÉ TO DRINK WINE, they passed a barricade across the left way of an intersection. Arty pointed. "Remember that, Maidservant?"

She had never seen it before. "No."

Arty looked at the others as if she had proved something. "This is the entrance to the old plaza where you fell in the water."

"Give it a rest," Aria said sharply. "She was lost and confused."

There was an edge to Arty's reply, too. "Whatever you say, Princess."

Cythe wore a very sad expression. "It's almost ready to open. Let's go see."

Trailing them, Maidservant hardly recognized the place. Intricate mosaics of birds and sea creatures had replaced the paving blocks. Colorful stone buildings identified by signs as restrooms and concessions ringed the area. The broken remains of the seafarer statue lay next to the dark lake. A knot of men stood nearby engaged in discussion. Then Arty said, "Envoy and Atlas."

Athy said, "Thought Atlas would be at the Temple this afternoon or I wouldn't have come here. He has surely noticed our uniforms, so let's put the best face on it and go pay respects. Likely to be bad tidings so have care what you say."

Atlas spoke as they approached. "I assume you Temple members have urgent business in Eao since this is a class day."

Athy gave her friendliest smile. "Good health, Council Priest. We volunteered for extra duty at the Eao Baths since it is a city holiday."

He smiled back, but it did not reflect in his voice. "And you finished early and are hurrying back to the Temple? Very commendable."

The plaza was very much the wrong way back to the Temple so Athy did not answer the question. "Good thing we started extra early because it was an unusually busy morning. Children everywhere, making the biggest messes imaginable, but business dropped off after midday because everyone went to the harbor to watch the boat races. As much as you like sports, surprised you're not there."

Atlas did not take the bait. "Why are you and Arty wasting time doing work that should be left to Prospects?"

Envoy leaned close to him and spoke quietly, but everyone heard. "Perhaps you would allow me to deal with this so more of your precious time is not wasted?"

However, Atlas pointed to Maidservant, staring at the grimy pedestal jutting out of the murky pool. "What is that one doing here?"

Cythe had a powerful ability to charm and few were immune. She used it on Atlas. "It was my idea. After your inspiring class about improving character through good deeds and hard work, I suggested to Athy that this unfortunate girl might benefit from working with us. Did I understand the lesson correctly? Did I do okay?"

It seemed to him that he could fall into her blue eyes, bask in the sunlight rippling through her golden hair and hear music and taste honey in every syllable she uttered. Mesmerized, he smiled as though intoxicated. "Why, you are wonderful. Was her work satisfactory?"

Barely hiding a smirk, Arty replied, "She did well scrubbing soap with dirty children before placing them in the basin to be wrung out and hung to dry."

Cythe nearly laughed, which would have broken the spell, but Atlas did not notice. "That's wonderful, too."

Envoy elbowed Arty in the ribs and pulled Cythe away. "The Council Priest needs to finish giving instructions to the project foremen and doesn't need your silliness distracting them. Come with me and I'll give you a quick tour on the way out."

The girls kept their heads down to hide snickering. Atlas thought it was out of respect for him and wished them a good day. Envoy led to a bubbling drinking fountain on the perimeter and gathered them around. "Atlas is a good man. You should not disrespect him."

Arty's freckles spread around a wide grin. "He's so vain we can't help ourselves."

"Yeah," Aria chimed in, "did you notice how he flexes his chest and strikes poses when Cythe is around?"

Envoy grabbed her to stop an imitation because Atlas' gaze had followed Cythe. Then he leaned around Athy to look at Maidservant, who kept moving so someone was always between them. "I hear the Head Priest gave permission for you work at the Temple."

She muttered, "Uh-huh."

Athy motioned the others. "Let's go check out the new mosaics while these two talk."

Arty followed, but Cythe lagged, not wanting to leave them alone, causing Aria to quip, "I'd rather stay with Cythe to watch Envoy and Maidservant play hide and seek." Amidst giggling and whispers, Athy ushered them away.

Envoy stared and Maidservant fidgeted until finally she blurted, "You promised to come see me first thing when you returned."

"I intended to, but the Head Priest sent me to help Atlas finish the plaza. We've been working night and day"

"Don't give me that. I only live ten minutes away." He did not answer, which upset her more. "Guess you don't feel you have to explain to someone like me, huh?"

He took her arm. "What's wrong with you? Has something happened?"

She pulled free. "You don't want to be seen with me because you heard about the fits and me going to the harbor bars. That's it, isn't it?"

He had no idea what she meant but asked a stupid question rather than stating his belief in her. "Surely, those things aren't true, are they?" Then he compounded the mistake by not going after her when she ran from the plaza.

Alone with Athy at a cafe, Envoy shook his head. "I had planned to tell her that the gap between our ages will close then we can determine what our relationship is. Meanwhile, I'll make certain no one bothers her ever again."

She put a hand on his arm. "Don't you think the Head Priest will be upset if you tell Maidservant about long life, and aren't you concerned she'll resent you---all of us, for that matter---if she knows the truth? What about later, when she grows old?"

"There are ways to deal with that."

"Not unless you can bestow long life. You can't do that, can you?"

"Not the way you mean."

She looked at him sharply. "What other way is there?"

He turned away.

She stared at him in ways that communicated much more than she dared say. "Why didn't you tell her then?"

"She thought I'd stayed away because I'd heard about her fits and misbehaving in bars. What is she talking about?"

She took a deep breath. "I did not want to be the one to tell you."

"Out with it, and don't try to spare my feelings."

She took a long sip of wine. "She steals, drinks too much and sneaks down to Sailor's Row. She babbles nonsense one minute, is disrespectful and rude the next. Hurts herself then blames Seydi for it. She even smashed the furnishings in the House of Kalli and threw them into the canal."

He showed no reaction whatever. "Why hasn't Rhea done anything about it?"

"That's what everyone wants to know. Leto even demanded Rhea send Maidservant from the island after tearing up the House of Kalli, but she refused then replaced everything. She has even forbade DoSo and Kore disciplining her."

Envoy nodded slowly. "Perhaps she senses something special about her, same as I do."

"What about her do you think is so special?"

"When she came here, she could speak our language better than most Priests and Scholars who teach it, but when she arrived on Kefti from Egypt with the Ambassador, she only knew a few words. No one taught her. I verified that personally. I am certain she can read and write several other languages, too. She is unusually intelligent, quick-witted and not impaired in the least when I've been with her."

Athy was concerned. "Rhea's argument for her working at the Temple was that she wouldn't understand anything she heard. Shouldn't you tell her?"

"I did. She said it is no problem and to keep it to myself."

Athy was silent for long seconds. "So, you like her for her mind? Is that all?"

He laughed. "For now, yes. Of all the people I've met, she is the most unique and interesting."

That hurt Athy though she did not show it. "You're the second person today who argued on her behalf."

"Who was the other?"

"Aria."

He nodded. "There's something special about her, too. You don't give her enough credit."

"There are too many good people in the world for a spot at the Temple to be taken by someone because of who her parents are." She stood from the table. "I just remembered, I'm supposed to have dinner with Arty in Cadisum. I'll stay over a night next week, if that's okay."

They hugged good-bye and went separate ways, full of thoughts and questions about each other, the Head Priest and Maidservant.

TEN

THE BOOK OF MAIDSERVANT: THE WORM TURNS

MAIDSERVANT HAD A PLAN TO GET BACK AT SEYDI for humiliating and hurting her, but was jittery from several days not drinking wine and extremely nervous now the time was upon her. In spite of waiting for him, she jumped when her master's shadow called out, spilling a full cup of fruit water on her bed. Then, instead of answering immediately, she cursed and tried to sop it up with the blanket before it soaked the bedding. "I'm sorry, Master. I spilled something."

"You've become more trouble than you're worth, indulging personal needs rather than obeying me and gathering information. I will dismiss you from service tonight unless you convince me otherwise."

Nothing to lose, Maidservant took a deep breath and plunged straight into her plan. "I have not been going to bars but staying late in the Temple kitchens because crowds gather on the terrace after work to drink. Waiting on tables, I hear many important things. Mistress Seydi knows this because she is there with one of her men friends nearly every evening, recovering from working so hard spying out information for you, I suppose. I told her I would be staying in the Garden House a few days because of leaks in the big house, but her attention was on San-zeus, so it must be my fault she didn't remember. After all, she would never tell you a lie, would she? Her loyalty to you is unquestionable, isn't it? She always takes your orders without complaint or comment, doesn't she? So if she claims I shirk duty, it has to be true, doesn't it? You let Master down, you bad girl! Bad! Bad! Bad!"

"Not a subtle performance, but you made your point. Stop hitting yourself."

"I'm sorry, Master, but my life has no value if you do not trust me. Serving you is everything to me. It's all I live for."

He did not say anything for a time. "Why did you destroy the furniture? You know they consider that old building some kind of holy relic. It caused no end of uproar, especially with Leto. Your mistress says you even ruined clothes she left there."

"I was angry because they said I could not stay with you at the embassy and upset that you stopped coming to visit me, but it was the damp that damaged Seydi's clothes, not me. I must admit, though, I wish I had thought of it first."

He chuckled, liking her this way. "Didn't she tell you I had to return to Egypt to review troops?"

That was the question she wanted him to ask. "No, Master."

"She says you are still under the illusion those Temple girls are your friends and stopped gathering information in case it harms them. Is that true?"

"No, Master. I try to tell her things, but she always tells me to stop bothering her or come back when she's not busy. To be honest, I can't find when that is."

"Tell me what you have so that I might judge."

She presented concise details of information eavesdropped in the baths and dining rooms. She summarized everything gleaned from Aria and Cythe. She told of documents left on Rhea's big table and animosities between the Head Priest and Council. She noted that Athy and Arty attended many private Council meetings, as well as Priests San-zeus, Daedalus, DoSo, Posei and Eos, who, in her humble opinion, were most likely to have powerful abilities.

His anger erupted. "Why can't that scheming little harpy learn these things? I'm going to wring her neck. What about Envoy?"

"He had a successful trip recruiting a new Prospect class and now works full time helping Atlas complete the new plaza before leaving again."

"Selene says Athy and Arty will be the next Priests and that Athy will be Head Priest one day. I told Seydi to get closer to them, but she hasn't done it. Do you know why?"

"It is because they can't stand her."

It sounded as though he hit something. "Then it falls to you to provide information about them. Do you have any more surprises?"

"The Head Priest ordered the ships we saw coming here, the ones you asked permission to examine, destroyed."

"Why in thunder would she do that? They were revolutionary, priceless!"

"I don't know why, but I heard Atlas report it done."

"These people are crazy. If you can, get me the name of the Priest who designed them. I'll try to keep him alive to serve us."

"He is Daedalus. I also heard the Head Priest speak of something called the *Tablets of Guidance*. They may be some of the ancient documents you seek or hold a clue to their whereabouts."

"Excellent. Search Rhea's house tomorrow. No one will be there. She's having lunch in Cadi-sum with Selene and the Senior Scholars to iron out differences, as if there's a chance of that."

"I'll do my best, Master."

"Where is your mistress spending her nights? Do you know?"

"Mostly, she stays at Priest San-zeus' house in Cadi-sum but has begun sneaking around to see Council Priest Atlas, who is so jealous of San-zeus that rumors are whispered he may harm him."

"I've seen her leading San-zeus around by the nose. Atlas is news, but can't say I'm surprised. You've done good work."

"Thank you, Master."

"In spite of your shortcomings, you are proving valuable. You're eager to serve and bear up well under Seydi's abuse. Keep it up, and perhaps I will arrange for you to replace her someday. Would you like that?"

Maidservant was stunned. "If it pleases you, Master."

"We'll see. I hear Selene returning. Be a good girl and remember the things I want you to do. Forget the rest. Duty always. Go to sleep."

For the first time ever, she did not fall asleep at his command. Instead, she stared up at the ceiling fighting to fend off the confusion and forgetfulness that always followed his visits. Suddenly, Seydi's unmade face swooped down to make her obey, but instead of cowering and begging it to go away, she leaped off the bed to run in the big room.

Running was a compulsion that started the night after she destroyed the furniture. She had fallen into a fitful sleep and had a strange dream of running naked in the big room. Exhilarated with wild energy surging through her, she sprinted out of torchlight into darkness, yet could see the way ahead. Reaching the black pedestal corner, she turned and glided along the back wall to the canal and jumped with no hesitation.

Then came the terrifying realization that she really was in the dark water, but she did not panic. She kicked, splashed arms furiously and managed to climb out on the yellow side, only to jump up and start running again. She turned at the golden lion, sped along the front wall, noting the big windows and doors had shuttered and locked. Passed the line of torch stands into the green area. She turned at the emerald cat, jumped into the canal and discovered she could not swim back, only ahead. Emotionally and physically spent, she lay on the red floor gasping and trying to figure out when the dream had become reality for a long time.

That first night, she was able to walk dejectedly past the bull to her room after one time around, but from then on, she ran and swam farther each night until reaching one hour before daylight when the windows and doors flew open. Then she dressed and ran to work, sandals strapped together over her shoulder. She ran home after dark each evening. When she was not running, she craved speeding along forest trails, bounding across Boiling River footbridge and up and down First Test. Eventually, she ran with eyes half-closed, awareness skimming the way ahead for the best places to step. Then she began reciting memorized stories to the rhythm of her footfalls. It was addictive. She never wanted to stop.

ELEVEN

THE BOOK OF MAIDSERVANT: ELBOWS AND BUZZING EARS

RHEA SLOUCHED OVER HER BIG TABLE, practicing fast-speaking ancient text she had memorized for spells. Maidservant, confounded to even know what fast-speak was, went through the motions of dusting, removing objects from shelves and putting them back while concentrating to follow Rhea's mangled recitations. She lost track of her hands. A vase tumbled. She twisted around to catch it, lost balance and fell on it. She cried out.

Two Scholars ran into the room. Tritius, Senior Scholar of Administrative Affairs, barked at Marko, Caretaker of the Head Priest's Residence. "She's getting blood on the rug! Didn't I tell you to keep a close eye on the little idiot?"

Marko grabbed Maidservant under the arms, pulled her to sitting then made her hold the dirty dust rag against the gash on her right elbow. Rhea came around the table, creaking loudly as she used it for support. "Leave her to me, Marko."

Tritius, acquiescent and superior at the same time, stroked his bushy gray beard and amended the Head Priest's instruction, something he did often because he knew it irritated her. "As the Head Priest said, Marko, clean up the glass while I take this clumsy girl outside to punish her."

Rhea pointed to the foyer. "Take Marko and shoo, Tritius."

He bristled. "Head Priest?"

"Take Marko for a walk and discuss how fortunate you are to live on such a beautiful island and work for such a fine Head Priest. Don't bother hurrying back. I will discipline the girl."

She waited until the outside door slammed then squatted, rocked and sat down on her heavy butt with a loud grunt. She struggled to pull her legs into a crisscross, only managing it by keeping the knees high off the floor. She shook with deep, rumbling laughter. "Bet that was a sight you'll never forget."

Incredulous, Maidservant was afraid to reply.

Rhea grabbed her injured arm in a big hand and examined the long shard embedded in the elbow. With care and skill that did not seem possible by such short, pudgy fingers, she worked it free. "Hurts, huh?"

Maidservant realized that she was bleeding on the Head Priest's dress and tried to pull her arm away.

"Don't worry about the dang dress. Don't like it much, anyway. Makes me look fat. Or is it the other way round?" She guffawed, the fat around her middle heaving, and clamped a hand around the wound, squeezing until Maidservant saw an expanding dark frame closing around her vision.

Rhea realized and spoke soft words. "There, there, just think of removing a sun-warmed honeycomb from a tree hollow. Um, feel how sticky the honey makes your fingers. Put a piece in your mouth. Ah, so sweet." She let go of the arm and pulled Maidservant into her bosom. "You'll feel better in a moment."

Maidservant had felt the honeycomb in her hand and tasted honey in her mouth. The sweetness spread through her, taking away the dizziness and pain. Rhea released her, and she marveled at the healed wound.

Rhea thrust an enormous elbow out, showing a big ugly scar. "Did that climbing the mountain when I was a Prospect, same time I banged up my leg. Never was particularly graceful. Got it from Ma, who used to trip and drop things all the time. We young'uns nearly starved to death because she could never get supper to the table without dumping it on the floor." She laughed then stopped abruptly, staring at Maidservant. "Well, are you going to hold your elbow up to mine or not? We've got to compare wounds."

Maidservant held up her arm. It looked like a twig beside a mighty hardwood tree.

Rhea said, "You know, girl, everyone laughs at me, too, and I'm the big mucky-muck around here. Don't let it get you down so much."

Maidservant could not stop the tears.

"Made any friends since you came here?"

"A few."

"Ah, you can talk. At the Temple? In town?"

"Cythe and Aria. I met Cythe's family in Eao, too. They have a little girl, Erran. She likes me, I think."

"Life is worthless without friends, even if you're the Head Priest. Besides, you never know when you may need someone to help you out of a tight scrape or maybe save your life. I think you should remember that."

It seemed as if she expected an answer so Maidservant nodded. "I will, Head Priest."

Gently, Rhea took Maidservant's head in her big hands and looked into her eyes. "Now, because you've pleased me, I'll share a tidbit of Kalli's wisdom. Only Head Priests get to know this one, so listen carefully. When you think enemies are close, beware most the humblest person in a crowded room; or, put the other way round, when among enemies, be careful to be the humblest person in a crowded room. Kalli was wise, don't you think?"

Maidservant swallowed hard and nodded.

"Now, you know everything you need to be Head Priest someday. Not much, is it?" She released her and motioned to a red curtained alcove in the corner. "Get your broom and sweep the pieces of the vase into a little pile here in front of me. Quickly, now."

Rhea cupped hands over the pile and fast-spoke verses so jumbled and mispronounced that all Maidservant could decipher was part of a phrase about Kalli departing the City of Bulls. Then Rhea switched to verses about Kalli establishing the Temple of Light thousands of years ago, which she recited better.

A small whirlwind of yellow light manifested under her hands, sucking the pieces into it. Then smoke, swirling fire and a bright flash. Rhea wiped sooty hands on her dress and leaned forward, studying the vase on the floor between them. "What do you think? Did I get the color right?"

Maidservant, with tongue stuck out the corner of her mouth, wondered what to say because the vase was lopsided and much duller green. "Uh, it has a more modern aspect than before, I believe."

Rhea poked it with a finger, making it rock. "A bit unstable."

"This shade of green is more interesting, though."

Rhea beamed. "Why then, it is better, isn't it? Quick, put it back on the shelf before someone comes in who prefers vases that just set there unable to move." When Maidservant returned, she sighed. "Leto and Selene will be here shortly. It wouldn't do for them to see me like this. Afraid you'll have to help me up."

Maidservant was a very little girl and Rhea a very big woman. In the end, the Head Priest had to roll onto her stomach, push up to her knees and pull up on the table while Maidservant tugged, huffed and puffed, not really helping much. Then Rhea leaned on a very bent Maidservant and went to her small room to change. She was barely back behind the table before Leto showed up, more officious and severe than usual. "Tritius told me the girl has been into mischief again."

Rhea regarded Maidservant. "You'll do better after my stern lecture, won't you, girl?"

Maidservant tried not to smile but failed. "Yes, Head Priest."

Leto snapped, "Then leave us!"

Maidservant ran from the room, but lingered in the foyer to listen.

Rhea said, "Before Selene comes, I have an errand for you. Go see Ambassador Hariset and..."

Leto interrupted, "Girl, I told you to get out!"

Heart pounding, Maidservant ran from the house.

***

MAIDSERVANT HAD JUST FINISHED putting the small kitchen in order when DoSo and Kore came in. It was already dark and late for them to be there. Kore was positively livid, obviously held in check by her mother. They just stood staring until Maidservant could stand it no longer. "Have I done something wrong?"

DoSo sounded bitter. "The Head Priest ordered me to tell you that as of today you are a ward of the Temple."

She had no idea what that was.

DoSo rolled her eyes. "You no longer answer to Prospect Seydi and the Ambassador, but to the Head Priest and me for everything. Did that get through that thick skull of yours?"

"Do you mean that my master sold me to the Temple?"

DoSo drummed fingers on the counter. "He gave you to us for nothing. Ask me, he got the best of the deal. From this moment forward, you will not leave the protected areas of the island. That means no more lollygagging with sailors and hanging out in bars, or you will face discipline. What do you have to say to that?"

Anger helped her regain some of her composure. "I have never been in one, anyway."

The red on DoSo's face deepened as she eyed Kore before continuing. "You have been given the new rank of Worker, which is lowest in the Temple. When duties require, the Head Priest says you will make deliveries to the restricted classes of the Council Priests rather than leaving trays for Scholars to take. Moreover, you will make deliveries to special classes in the Amber Area whenever necessary. The Watchers have added you to the list of those allowed in."

Kore threw a full tray to the floor.

Always a Priest before a mother, DoSo did her duty. "Initiate Kore, the Head Priest listened to objections and made her ruling. Be respectful of the decision."

Kore stamped a foot. "Why does this worthless, no rank wretch get to see the Amber Area? It's not right and you know it. I've half a mind to quit the Temple!" She stormed out.

DoSo hesitated, cursed Maidservant then went after her.

Dazed, Maidservant whispered the question she had been afraid to ask. "Does this mean I'm not a slave anymore?"

***

HARISET HAD AGREED TO MEET SEYDI on Boiling River Bridge in hopes that a public place would force her to behave. He looked both ways to make certain no one passing on the avenue could hear before responding to her protestations. "Nothing has changed except the Priests no longer feel guilty having a slave working for them. The whole thing is silly if you'll stop a minute and think rationally about it. She does our bidding same as before."

"But she belonged to me!"

He set his voice to soothe and persuade. "The Scholars had the Head Priest in a corner, slowing down work and demanding an increase in their numbers. She countered by creating the Worker rank, supposedly to do menial work and leave Scholars to teach and do admin. They assume it is the first step to get rid of Scholars altogether, which is a good thing for us because they're ripe for rebellion."

"None of this has anything to do with you giving away my property!"

He maintained calm only with great effort. "What could I do but agree when the Head Priest asked for her? Besides, as I've pointed out already, it does not alter our mission one iota."

"I won't have it!"

"You can still torment her when it's inconvenient to find insects to pull the wings off."

Two Initiates approached, forcing her to lower her voice. "Funny, I am sure, but then you don't see how she's changed, do you? Her status as a slave helped keep her manageable. You always threaten me with your great power, so why don't you use it to see her for what she is---a conniving little liar."

The two Initiates trotted across the bridge carrying purchases from Eao and shouted greetings, which Hariset returned with a smile and wave. "Good health to you." He glanced both ways along the avenue before turning back to her.

Meanwhile, Seydi realized with dismay that they would be alone on this stretch of road when the Initiates turned onto Temple Avenue. She decided she must bide time and acted contrite. "I'm sorry, Lord. It's just that I long so much for you to show these fools what real power is." She raked her nails across a forearm, cutting blood trails, and something dark and slavering pushed out of the shadows cloaking her then faded away fast as it had come.

In spite of his hatred for her, the malevolence appealed to him. "It will not be much longer. Have you made any progress with Envoy?"

"He's away on another tiresome trip. As soon as I can be alone with him a few hours, I'll uncover the symbol on his wrist and you can identify him."

"Selene says new Priests will be named soon and he's to play a part in the ceremony, though I can't imagine what. If it's true, he won't be gone long. You'll have your opportunity then."

"You'll be sure to tell the Master about my contributions, won't you?"

Hariset glared. "Just make certain that Envoy doesn't see through your childish games. I suspect he may be a famous person of history, so care must be taken."

This set her off again. "You think that ignorant boy could possibly possess that much power? I'll rip his heart out and present it to you if it will give you the courage to stop finding excuses to delay the attack." She turned to go then realized she should have checked the avenue for people again.

Responsible for most of the catastrophes to befall mankind for seven centuries, Tesi-Ra's power slammed Seydi against the side of the bridge and filled her with threatening visions of unending suffering, pain, wretchedness, mutilation and torture. "Ambition makes you careless, Czn-tanth. One more act of disobedience and I'll burn you eternally in the fires of the Master's realm."

He released her to collapse on the bridge, but immediately she got to her knees. "Show me more, Lord. Please, more. I'll do anything you want."

He stared down at her, disgusted. "Get control of yourself. If you understood the devious ways of Kalli better, you would be urging even greater caution dealing with these Priests."

She fought against the hungering needs churning in her. "They seem so weak. Couldn't Kalliste simply be a diversion from another location?"

"No, this is the right place, but with the smell of a very elaborate trap. Several times in the past, Kalli almost destroyed us when she seemed in a hopeless position. You do understand that whether the girl is a slave or not, nothing has changed?"

She nodded. "I'm sorry I overreacted. If you permit, I'll visit her this evening to insure she still understands her responsibilities."

People streamed onto Eao Avenue from First Test, showing that the class day had ended. "Yes, that is prudent. I have to meet Selene in Cadi-sum."

A group of Prospects ran by going toward Eao and Seydi hurried to join them, calling back over her shoulder, "Have a good evening, Father."

***

MAIDSERVANT STOOD SILENTLY ACROSS THE TABLE waiting for Seydi to finish eating so she could clear the dishes. She had been shocked to find her sitting at a table next to the stream reading a lesson by torchlight. Seydi asked, "Aren't you afraid, staying here alone? This place gives me the creeps."

Maidservant could not imagine Seydi fearing anything. "Not so much now, Mistress."

"You probably like it because I'm not here."

"Oh, no, Mistress. I miss you."

She picked up the tablet. "Come look at this. I can't make sense of it." Maidservant reached, and she drew it away. Seydi's eyes narrowed. "What's wrong? Don't you want to help me?"

"Sorry, Mistress." She reached again.

The scepter struck sharply on the back of her hand. "I don't like you standing on my left side." Holding the hand, Maidservant started to the other side, but Seydi jumped up, pushed her down on her face and straddled her. "Your dirty feet were on my shadow again."

"But Mistress, the torches make shadows all around the table."

Seydi jammed her knees into Maidservant's back then sat on her. She beat the side of her head with the scepter until she could not raise her swollen hands to stop the blows. Seydi leaned close to her ear. "Never learn, do you, slave?"

Maidservant tried to buck her off.

Seydi gave her a wet kiss on the neck and blew on it, enjoying how Maidservant stiffened with anger. "I love my little slave ever so much, even if she connives to take my place." She kissed and blew her neck on the other side. "But she'd better watch out. Soon, the day will come when her master looks for his little protégé and discovers me weeping and pointing to parts of her strewn everywhere. Oh, Great Lord, I will cry out, how could those awful Priests have done such a thing to my little sister?" She laughed hysterically.

"I'll tell him you threatened me."

Seydi bit blood from her ear. "You've said that to me so many times, and every time I explain that the One Master gave me skills no one suspects, not even your precious master. Then I make you forget what I did and leave you believing you hurt yourself. It is so much fun." She began fast-speaking.

Outraged, Maidservant tried to roll her off. "I'm not your slave!"

Surprised, Seydi sat back. "It'll be easier if you give in. You'd know that if you weren't so stupid." She reared back and struck Maidservant with the scepter repeatedly. "Submit! Submit! Submit!"

Maidservant came to on the floor of her room. She tried to lift her head and everything tilted and spun. Unable to see clearly, she reached under the bed, pulled out the medicine jar and fumbled the top off. She took a swallow and blacked out again.

Voices.

It took a few seconds to recognize one of them was hers.

"I'm sorry, Master. Please say that again."

"Get on the bed where you belong!"

She pulled up onto the bed. The room kept moving after she rested her head on the pillow block. "I don't feel so good."

"Have you been drinking?"

"Not that much."

"I've warned you to be more careful. Now tell me---what transpired in the house of the Head Priest after you cut your arm? Did she heal you?"

"Scar."

"What?"

"My elbow."

He was silent a few seconds. "Selene said she saw no signs of the broken vase when she arrived. What happened to it?"

"Smoke. Fire. Poof!"

"You're drunk again, aren't you?"

"Buzzing ears."

"Buzzing what?"

"Ears."

"If you don't pull yourself together, I'm coming over there to rip a report out of your head!"

Maidservant could not make her mouth say the right words. She had the medicine clutched to her chest like a talisman. She remembered a warning it would damage her if she took than a drop a day, but she had already taken much more and it made her feel better.

"Report!"

Desperate, she gulped down half the jar and gasped. Burning radiated through her, but the jumble in her head cleared.

"I told you to stop drinking!"

"It was water, Master. Sorry, I was sound asleep and confused when you came. I have good news. The Head Priest granted me access to all the restricted areas. Tomorrow, I will go to Selene's third floor class then Leto's and Atlas' the day after. Then I'll visit the Amber Area."

"Excellent. What of Seydi's visit?"

"Haven't seen her since the Temple baths two days ago with Atlas."

"She told me she would visit you tonight."

"Oh! She was here."

He made an exasperated sound. "If I find you this way again, I will punish you severely."

She stared intently at her thumb, trying to stop the room see-sawing. "The Head Priest has a list of four hundred eighty-four Priests living other places. A notation said Phoebe, a former Head Priest, is in charge of the largest group on another island, but then I saw another document that says Phoebe led the Temple two hundred years ago. I see lots of dates and times that don't make sense."

"You don't need to be concerned about all that now. I will explain later. Were you able to make a copy of the information?"

She almost said it was in her head but caught herself. "Yes, I have it here."

He chuckled. "The Master will certainly support your ascension when I tell him all you've done. The entire Council of Six will embrace you as well, but you must control your behavior. All this drinking will waste your usefulness if you keep it up. Read me the locations, names of people in charge and numbers assigned and I'll jot it down. Then I'll take a boat before daylight and arrange the extermination of the outposts before we attack Keftiu and Kalliste."

TWELVE

THE BOOK OF MAIDSERVANT: THE BREAKING OF CYTHE

S
O SHAKY SHE COULD HARDLY HOLD THE BRUSHES, Maidservant painted layers of makeup over the left side of her face to conceal the welts and bruises, but the right side was so swollen all she could do was pin her hair forward over it. Taking a last look in the mirror, she moaned, "Why can't I remember what I did?"

She made her way to the Temple late then accomplished little in the kitchens but getting in the way. Everyone assumed she was drunk and stayed clear of her until mid-morning when she knocked over a full wine amphora. Fed up, Kore ordered her to take a tray to the third floor of Selene's building, hoping that the Council Priest witnessed her despicable condition and disciplined her.

Climbing the stairs to the second floor, Maidservant's heart pounded in her ears like a mallet striking a hollow tree. She weaved down the long hall to a burly, middle-aged Scholar seated behind a table. With a huge sigh of relief, she rested the tray on the corner of the table and nodded across the way to a heavy red door. "I have a delivery for the Council Priest."

His heavy gold rings flashed in sunlight streaming through a window behind him as he jabbed a finger at the tray. "Get that off my table and identify yourself!"

Everything went out of focus when she jerked the tray up then she was not sure whether she had answered him or not. "Worker Maidservant with a delivery for Priest Selene." He stared, waiting to see what she would do, so she wobbled to the door and tried to pull it open with a couple of fingers but could not. She looked back. "Will you help me, please?"

He got up and came around the table, but instead of helping, continued down the hall, whistling merrily. She mumbled a curse from an old kingdom named Sumer for winged guardians to rip out his innards for sacrifice then set the tray on the table noisily, hoping he would return to take issue so she could hit him with a wine jug, but he disappeared into a room. Anger gave her strength to scoot the table across the hall, hold the door open on her hip and carry the tray through.

No apparent source provided the dim light in the stairwell. Somehow, she labored up four long flights of steep stairs connected by switchback landings, confounding her as the building was three stories high on the outside and she had climbed two floors before this. Then she stepped through a curtained stone archway into a nighttime wonderland.

Directly across from her, a huge three-quarters moon in a starry sky beamed through massive floor-to-ceiling windows. To the left and right far as she could see, hundreds of lights penetrated the room's darkness rather than illuminating it. Arrayed in mesmerizing patterns and displays of every color and configuration, some lights were static, but most fluctuated and moved in all sorts of ways.

Two figures in gray hooded robes detached from a nearby group gathered before a sparkling waterfall of lights and came to her. They uncovered their heads, and there stood Arty, grinning. "Hi, Maidservant. Welcome to Moonlight. Causing quite a stir, having you here." She hooked a thumb at her companion, who had a manner and bearing suggesting she was older, although in appearance she was not. "Priest Metys, my teacher and mentor."

Metys looked no older than Arty. She bowed slightly. "My daughter has spoken of you. Well met."

Maidservant looked back and forth between them, not certain she had heard correctly. Arty realized her dilemma. "She is Athy's mother."

Maidservant remembered the warning never to question age and returned the bow best she could with the heavy tray and confusion pounding in her head. "Honored to meet you."

Metys smiled and spoke to Arty. "Not at all what I expected."

They stood awkwardly trying to make small talk until Arty mercifully indicated a faraway group of lights. "That's Selene. Give the tray to Tatum, Senior Scholar in Moonlight. Look around all you want, but be very quiet so as not to disturb anyone."

Maidservant went across the exceptionally smooth stone floor, marveling and gaping at fabulous lights until, as she veered around three Initiates meditating under a rotating triangle of blue globes, she heard Arty and Metys talking about her. She stopped and looked back. They were a long ways off and walking the other way. How could she possibly hear them?

Metys said, "She's hurt, a head injury. Do you know what happened?"

Maidservant felt Arty reaching out to her, same as her master did, only it was clumsy and weak. "Sorry, it's too far for me, but she's known to have fits and hurt herself. Imagine that's what it is."

Metys replied sharply. "Her injuries are serious. I wonder that she can function. She's hidden it with her hair. You should have realized before we spoke to her. You spend too much time with your bow and not enough developing other skills."

"May I go make certain she's okay?"

"No. We were told to leave her alone unless something..."

Apparently, they had moved too far away. She continued walking toward Selene. Ever since waking up on the bridge, her abilities had improved, but she had not realized the extent.

Nausea forced her to set the tray on a low wall to rest. Nearby, people sat in a circle staring up at a wavering bar of violet while chanting about Kalli going to a land called Omeni or something like that, but they made such gibberish of the verses she could not understand more.

At another stop, a Priest crouched under a dim yellow orb reciting disjointed fragments over a wounded owl. It was about Kalli making a king stop a war, a daughter's marriage, a baby son, someone dying and another war. Suddenly, the owl screeched and flapped up off the floor. The Priest caught it and declared, "These verses work well with healing abilities. After the break, we'll see who has them and can use these words. Laleni, you may stop now." Standing a short distance away, a pretty girl dropped her arms and the orb winked out.

After that, Maidservant lost track of everything until reaching Selene. She had her back arched and arms straight out to the sides, staring up at the vertex of an upside-down, slowly revolving spiral cone of pulsing multicolored lights. The scene was beautiful beyond words. Maidservant briefly forgot the weight of the tray as she marveled at the outermost lights passing by. Then someone pushed her.

The tray penetrated the spiral, which ripped it from her hands and flung it and contents across the room at tremendous velocity. Everything crashed into one of the huge windows then the broken pieces showered down on the floor. Meanwhile, all the big windows flickered and vanished.

Meanwhile, Maidservant, thrown sideways down, struck her head on a bench. A pasty-skinned Scholar with a wild white beard and mustache jerked her up and around. He shook her, snapping her head forward and back. He seemed to be yelling but she only heard strange gurgling and roaring. Then she threw up on him and he shoved her away.

Slender arms radiating light caught her. Sweet-scented breath felt warm on her face. Kallistian words formed in her mind: "Metys, there's been a bad accident." Then she heard ancient Eirycian words whispered with almost perfect pronunciation. "White light, bright light, take away the night." She closed her eyes to shut out sudden harsh brightness then could not find a way back to it.

MAIDSERVANT THE GOD

***

CYTHE SLEPT SLOUCHED OVER IN ONE OF THE CHAIRS from the big room next to her bed. Maidservant tried to call out, but it was very weak. Cythe awoke instantly, jumped up and threw her arms around Maidservant. "Oh, thank goodness. It's been four days. We didn't think you...you..."

"Please do not jar me. My head."

Cythe pulled away carefully, relieved because Selene and Metys had insisted Maidservant would die if moved from Moonlight and their care. Yet, Rhea inexplicably ordered her taken to the House of Kalli and looked after by Cythe and Aria solely. It was such an irrational decision that many openly speculated the Head Priest had decided to let the girl die rather than admit she made mistakes creating the Worker rank and giving access to secret areas. The Scholars considered her impending death a victory and had been celebrating openly.

Cythe smiled down at her. "Do you remember what happened?"

"No."

"I'll tell you the details later. Main thing now is to rest." She kissed her cheek.

Even that slight contact caused bright flashes in her vision. "Please stop touching me."

Relief turned to concern. "Oops, sorry. Maybe Selene and Metys will know medicine to make you feel better."

It took her a few seconds. "I have medicine. Under the bed."

Cythe got onto her knees, reached around and found the unsealed, dirty jar. She sniffed the narrow mouth and made a sour face. "There's still something in it, but I'm not giving you this stuff. We'll wait for Selene and see what she says."

Maidservant grabbed it from her hands, sucked it empty and began shaking so hard the bed knocked the wall. Cythe started to go for help but Maidservant gasped she wanted water. She held the jug to her lips expecting a sip, but Maidservant gulped down all of it and fell into deep sleep. Carelessly concerned for her friend, Cythe picked up the medicine jar, stuck the tip of her pinkie in and touched it to her tongue. Energy burned her insides. She fell to the floor, paralyzed.

She became amazingly aware of every square inch of the small room then became part of it. It spread rapidly into the hallway, the big room, the canal, all aspects of the bridge, up the walls, over the pedestals and statues. It sped across the ceiling, through the opening onto the roof and down the exterior walls. She was on all paths of the maze, inside the garden house and the House of Kalli simultaneously.

For an instant, she thought that was everything, then plunged down level after level of secret areas beneath the site. At the bottom she found a room filled with strange apparatuses clustered around a small raised platform. She rushed up four steps onto it and knew that continuing to stand here would show her all the building's memories. Fascinated, she awaited them eagerly.

Suddenly, she knew the building had been located somewhere else. She witnessed demons and servants of demons celebrating final victory over the building's creators, the Eirycians. She watched demons in the maze, the garden house and big room mangling, mutilating and devouring them. The building's intense grief and frustration that it could not defend them without someone giving commands overwhelmed her with grief.

She fought to break away but could not. In subsequent lifetimes, the site became a center for making people into despicable demons or remaking them into even more monstrous beings for the foulest purposes imaginable. On and on the memories continued until the building suffered something she could only associate with a series of emotional breakdowns. Then everything went black and it released her.

Cythe, pure, virtuous and gentle as anyone who ever lived, had never considered the lessons about Corruption were literally true. She believed, as did most at the Temple, that they were stories created to make everyone work hard and choose righteous paths in their lives. She could not face such a horrible reality. Cythe, so wondrous and full of potential, came undone.

***

LATE AFTERNOON, THE HOTTEST PART OF A STIFLING DAY, especially with a fat sun in a hazy sky. Cythe sat beside Maidservant on a bench in the shade of olive trees at the maze overlook staring glumly at Eao while her friend, propped against a tree, kept glancing at her warily, suspecting she was about to ask the question again. Cythe tried to act nonchalant, stretching legs and hitching her tunic up around her thighs to cool off. "If I didn't have to stand, I'd remove this."

Maidservant, who wanted to keep her talking about other things, stretched her legs out and wiggled toes, which reached about halfway down Cythe's shins. "It's not fair I'm so short."

"Maybe you'll grow; then again, maybe you'll always be less than a pee crock high."

Maidservant forced a laugh then quickly went to another subject before Cythe said more. "Have you done something to yourself? You look incredible." It was exactly the wrong thing.

Cythe faced her, unusually serious. "I've changed, and not for the better. Where did you get the medicine? You have to tell me."

Maidservant looked away. "I told you that I don't remember."

"We have to discuss this, Maidservant."

She shook her head.

Cythe started crying. "I tasted the tiniest amount imaginable. I didn't think it could possibly affect me, but it did. My mind is cloudy. I feel stupid. I'm really scared, Maidservant."

Maidservant could not stand seeing her this way and gave in. "The medicine was on the wall when Envoy pulled me out of the lake in the plaza. Somehow, I knew it was for me."

"How could you just know it was for you?"

"I have no idea, and if you ask a hundred times, I'll still not know. I tried to stop taking it but couldn't. When I used it all and smashed the jar, I woke up next morning holding a new one in my hand. Now you can see how crazy I am, huh?"

Cythe shook her head. "You simply don't understand how important this is. Aria and I were told this morning we've been chosen for Initiation."

"Boy, I bet Athy and Arty are shocked---about Aria, I mean. What did Athy say?"

"Will you please stop trying to change the subject? We'll be given an elixir to improve our abilities, but it affects each person differently and not always for the better." She tried to find words to help her unfortunate friend understand better. "For instance, a disease may be cured, or it might worsen, or even cause death."

Maidservant held up a hand to stop her. "Elixir is just a fancy way of saying Priest's blood, isn't it? It allows you to live longer, but in some instances has side effects. That about sum it up?"

Cythe was surprised. "Yes, except that some bloodlines are much stronger than others and it takes a Priest with special abilities to extend life more than a few dozen years. Rhea is the only one at the Temple who can do it."

Maidservant cocked her head. "Darn. Guess that explains the age discrepancies and probably the real reason the Scholars are upset with her. She refuses to share elixir with them. Am I right?"

Cythe could not believe this was the same Maidservant. "I suppose you know about long sleep, too."

"I pretend I don't, but it's the most discussed subject at the Temple."

"I can't believe people talk so openly around you. It's our closest kept secret."

"Yes, but then no one thinks I have as much sense as a piece of furniture, but I do. I have feelings, too."

"Are you angry with me for some reason?"

"I'm just sick of being interrogated. Are you done?"

"Sorry, but I don't have any choice. After they administer the elixir, they will take us to a vault under Leto's building for our first long sleep, but I dare not do it without knowing what I've already had. It may hurt or kill me. That's why I have to tell them."

Maidservant sat straight up. "I thought you'd already told and were asking these questions for them."

"I'd never do that without talking to you first. We're friends."

"You mustn't tell, Cythe."

"What are you so upset about? They can probably reverse the damage your elixir is doing to us. Where on earth did you get it?"

"I don't know, but it's making me stronger and better."

She patted Maidservant's leg. "You poor thing, don't you see? The elixir must be responsible for you hurting yourself and the bizarre ways you act. You'll thank me when you're better."

Maidservant began to panic. "I was this way long before the elixir, but that's not the point. If I can't tell where I got it, they'll look into me deeper and discover the real reason my master brought me here."

"You're scaring me."

"Just promise not to tell them."

Cythe shook her head. "It's for your own good."

"Why do you think the Head Priest is so certain Corruption no longer exists, Cythe?"

"She can sense their presence in the world. All Head Priests have had that ability to protect us."

Maidservant was harsh. "No one at the Temple would realize if they shared a bench with someone working for Corruption. Take my word for it."

Cythe held out her right hand. "This is the Head Priest." She held out the left. "This is you. Who do I believe?" She raised the right hand over her head. "Is that too complicated, or should I draw a diagram?"

Angry, Maidservant jabbed a finger at Cythe's bundle of lessons under the bench. "Show me what you're studying and I'll prove who's right."

Cythe practically threw the bundle at her. Maidservant pulled out a large piece of cloth with row upon row of tiny red symbols painted on it. "Why do you have this?"

"It is ancient text I copied. When I learn to say it properly, I will be able to do better with light magic. Oh wait, you know all about that because you blundered into some of it at Selene's, didn't you?" She stopped, suddenly ashamed of herself. "Sorry. Let's stop this, okay?"

But Maidservant glared. "This is not even ancient text. It's the oldest form of the Kallistian language. She began reading.

...in my dream last night, again I witnessed the Head Priest abandon the Temple to the flames of Corruption to take the four generators to the Chosen in the House of Kalli, yet, only one of them survives long sleep, and it is the Head Priest. Shadows and mists continue to obscure all my visions of this subject. I have no explanation for this discrepancy, nor will I ever, no matter

how many stupid times you make me dream about this because you're pigheaded and determined to have your way. Well, no more! I demand that you grant Alicia, most exalted Seer and abused servant who ever lived, a final request. When you jump into the fires of the mountain, burn and scream in agony for all eternity, you bitch, and never bother me again.

Cythe ran. Maidservant jumped on her back. Holding her down, she recited verbatim the words of submission Seydi had used on her, not understanding how and why she knew such a foul spell but realizing its purpose. Then, guilty and appalled by what she had done, Maidservant helped her back to the bench. "I'm so sorry, Cythe. How do you feel?"

Cythe did a slow double take then stretched her legs and hitched the tunic up around her thighs. "It's so hot. If I didn't have to stand, I'd take this off."

THIRTEEN

THE BOOK OF MAIDSERVANT: EDDIES IN THE STREAM

SECLUDED BY TREES growing against the upper part of Jellyfish House, Rhea watched Main Court from a lounging couch on her bedroom's second floor balcony. She perked up when Maidservant came out of a building with a heavy tray balanced on each hand. "Hmm, she certainly looks chipper in spite of it being little more than a week since you thought she was good as dead."

Selene, crowded on a small divan next to Leto, was defensive. "It was a good diagnosis. I can't account for her recovery."

Leto's cold stare followed Maidservant. "Better that you were right. She's less than useless, and nothing but trouble."

Rhea clucked disapprovingly. "I know your heart isn't as hard as your words, Leto, but I don't like hearing them just the same." She coughed, grimacing and holding her chest.

She had made it clear she wanted no fuss about her illness so Selene continued. "Metys and I believe Cythe knows more about her recovery than she's telling."

Leto was snide. "You and Metys would rather look for excuses than admit you made a mistake."

Selene shrugged off the insult. "Cythe's overall performance is suffering, too. She insists nothing's wrong. I think we should submit her to an examination. Something's going on."

Rhea dismissed the notion with a wave of the hand. "I have to examine her at Initiation. That'll suffice."

Selene disagreed. "With respect, it needs to be sooner."

Rhea frowned. "You will leave those girls alone. Tell Metys that goes for her, too." She switched subjects. "Do either of you happen to know what the secret is that Envoy has planned for the Priests' ceremony?"

Leto could not help smiling because just mentioning the subject put life in the Head Priest's tired eyes. "It's something to do with the test of the bull that he says will challenge Athy's and Arty's abilities, but he's cagy with details. Couldn't get more out of him."

Selene, in spite of having just been dressed down, was not about to sulk and let Leto curry all the favor. "Hariset brought a special gift for you from Egypt. He asked if he can attend the Council meeting in Eao this afternoon to present it."

Rhea agreed immediately and wanted to ask more about it, but something in Main Court caught her eye. "Drat! DoSo and Posei are coming for the meeting already. Selene, will you be a dear and run downstairs while Leto helps me dress?" She waited until they were alone. "Do you sense anything different about her?"

Leto shrugged. "Seems as inconsequential as ever."

"You'd be well advised to stop letting petty dislikes cloud your abilities to see what's going on under your nose. Next time I ask, I expect a better answer."

She had caught Leto by surprise. "What do you mean?"

"Exactly what I said. Get me the brown dress with yellow flowers and the red and orange beads for my hair. That should keep everyone's attention away from my condition."

***

MAIDSERVANT ARRIVED ON THE THIRD FLOOR of Atlas' building after climbing the same number of extra stairs as Selene's. It was another huge room with high walls, but exposed to the sky except for one small area where rows of thick red columns supported a peaked tiled roof. A big pool of water occupied most of one end where people performed all sorts of spectacular dives off two high towers. Otherwise, sports and physical activities took place everywhere she looked, pretty much what anyone would expect from Atlas. It might have been amazing had she not already seen so many other wonders. She did not even bother delivering the tray before hurrying back downstairs, eager to see Leto's building.

At first, it was even more disappointing. After climbing but a single flight of stairs, she emerged on a rickety landing a few feet above the floor of a depressing shadowy room less than half the size the building suggested from outside. It had no windows with light provided by rows of dim yellowy globes hanging from a low, beamed ceiling. Nine huge square tables with four high chairs on each side took up nearly all the floor space. Two Priests called Watchers wore red robes with big hoods over their heads and sat perfectly motionless above each table. Why, she could not fathom, because they were dark and empty. Two minutes dragged by, so still and quiet the room might as well have been a painting. It made her nervous.

Leaving the tray on the landing, she tiptoed down narrow wooden steps so creaky she expected a challenge, but no one seemed to notice. Hardly daring to breathe, she moved toward the two closest tables, thinking this was another waste of time until she crossed a black line on the floor.

Spectacular light images of different parts of the island shined over each table. She did not recognize all the areas, yet she realized that pushing the tables together would show the entire island. Intrigued, she moved to the corner of nearest table then just stood there, astounded.

Viewed from high in the sky, Eao and its harbor had sunlight sparkling off a gently rolling sea. Ships moved across the water. People, little more than specks, went about their business. She slipped around the corner of the table to where the town began and followed the big avenue up to the House of Kalli, thinking it would be interesting to see from above, but encountered an anomaly. A perfect square of green mists obscured the site. Then the entire table changed.

As though seen from the top a tall mast, the view was workmen offloading a ship on Eao dock. The image fluttered to a close-up of a woman and two children shopping in a crowded waterfront market. Then the view spun at extreme velocity back into the sky over Eao. Suffering vertigo, Maidservant almost pitched headlong onto the table but saved herself by looking away and focusing on a light over a high dais at the back of the room. It had not been there previously. Leto sat beneath the light behind a small table. She motioned her to come.

Leto rolled a gold vial on a long chain between thumb and forefinger as she appraised the girl then directed her into a hard chair across the table. "Why are you snooping?"

"I brought your lunch and could not decide which of those big tables to leave it on."

"Then you really are an idiot."

Maidservant would never have dared insult anyone in a high position a few months earlier, but now, she could not stop herself. "No one's called me an idiot for at least two hours. That something they teach in Priest's school?"

Reddening, Leto leaned across the table. "You want to play games? Where did you get that expensive necklace you're wearing? Let me see it."

Maidservant had discovered it around her neck after she destroyed the furnishings in the House of Kalli and it was her most prized possession. She thought she must have stolen it in the baths so was careful to keep it hidden. Instinctively, she felt for it under her tunic before realizing Leto could not possibly see it, yet she had a smug expression and her hand out. She did not intend to be so loud. "No!"

Leto took her hand back. "You must have done something special in the bars to earn something so precious."

Maidservant hated her. "From what I hear, you're not one with experience to judge such matters."

Leto went to her feet so forcibly she knocked the chair off the dais behind her. "I can snap your neck with a thought if I've a mind to, girl!"

Maidservant stood on the chair rung so she was tall enough to look Leto in the eyes. "You're a big powerful Council Priest and I'm a defenseless servant. My, you're so brave."

"Get out!"

***

HARISET CAME ONTO STAGE with a small yellow-brown monkey perched on his arm, its expressive black face and big soulful eyes an instant hit with the crowd. Rhea reached out to the creature and it wrapped a little pink hand around one of her pudgy fingers then gazed around the room making cute eh-eh-eh noises.

The crowd erupted with laughter, frightening the animal, and it jumped to the floor, restrained from running away by a long tether fastened to Hariset's arm. The little creature looked back at him then executed a perfect back flip in place. The crowd went wild.

Selene, seated next to Rhea, picked a bunch of grapes from a bowl and tossed them to Hariset. The monkey scampered up his body onto his arm, deftly plucked a grape and popped it into its mouth. Then it flung its arms around his neck, chewing and staring unblinkingly at the Head Priest.

She laughed so hard tears ran down her cheeks. "Does it have a name?"

"That's to be your pleasure," he replied. "I have dozens more animals on the way, if others want them for pets."

Atlas boomed over the noise. "I could construct a habitat for them in the new Eao Plaza. With your permission, Head Priest, I can have it ready for grand opening."

The crowd cheered and Rhea beamed. "Put announcements in all the towns and have murals of monkeys painted in the public baths, but not too close to pictures of Priests. I don't want captions to be necessary so people can tell which is which."

Hariset joined Seydi waiting in an alley outside the meeting hall. He still had the monkey on his arm and held it out to her. "I told Rhea you'd take it to her house this evening."

The little creature instinctively reached out but she swatted it to the ground and kicked it against a wall. "Keep that vile thing away from me!"

Hariset spoke through clenched teeth. "This one isn't sick like the others. Besides, our blood makes us immune to their disease."

She was adamant. "I don't care! They make my skin crawl."

He pressed the tether into her hand. "You need to get back in the good graces of the Head Priest after mistreating the girl in plain sight of everyone at the Temple. Now, do as I say."

"Oh, very well." She reached down for the animal but it drew back, hissing and baring teeth.

"Sure you're not related?" Hariset walked away.

"Very funny, I am sure," Seydi said under her breath, waiting until he turned the corner before snatching the monkey up by the scruff of the neck and glaring into its face. Immediately, it was too terrified to move.

***

HARISET'S SHADOW WOULD NOT STOP ASKING QUESTIONS about her injuries, expressing suspicions that Seydi was responsible and growing frustrated that she could not remember. Finally, he ordered her to report, although he showed little interest until she mentioned the Watchers. "I don't understand that kind of power."

"Me, either, Master, but the point is, the Watchers can see everything happening on Kalliste."

"If that's truly the case, we must be more careful. We are fortunate they have not discovered us. Can they see through roofs into buildings? Can they see activities at night?"

"Their abilities are more like birds high up in the sky that can zoom down close to the ground or peek into open windows and doorways. They can't see through walls and roofs or in the dark. Cythe told me they used to make people on passing ships unable to see the island and steer around it."

"Hmm, more pieces of the puzzle in place. That proves they still know some old magic, at least. Tell me more about the Watchers' room."

She described what she had seen. "Perhaps the extra chairs mean it took more Watchers to keep the island hidden, or maybe more are needed for some tasks than others."

"Do you think these Watchers have powers to protect the island against attack?"

"I don't know, but I heard Leto threaten to snap someone's neck with a thought. I'm not sure she meant it literally, though."

"Did she now? I think I'll prepare a small skirmish to test their mettle so we'll know once and for all what they can do. Anything else?"

"There's a stone wall across the back of the Watchers' room that doesn't match the rest of building. I suspect it hides a secret area. Besides, Leto would never tolerate having less space than Selene."

"Nose around and find a way inside. Meanwhile, I'll ply Selene for information, but she still shows reluctance to discuss the Temple's deepest secrets. When are you going to the Amber Area? It may have hidden weapons and warriors."

"I'll visit soon as I can, but searching Leto's is impossible with the Watchers always there."

"Hmm, wouldn't do for you to get caught and tip our hand now we're almost ready. Hold off until I work out a few things. I'll let you know when."

"Thank you, Master. Cythe said when Athy and Arty become Priests, she and Aria will take their Initiate positions. They have to long sleep in vaults underneath Leto's building to prove they're worthy."

"Found out about the sleep on your own, eh? Good for you. Your information is excellent, things I tasked your mistress to gather, incidentally. A large sleep area might spell trouble. Hundreds of powerful Priests may be kept there, ready to be summoned. If you find nothing suspicious in the Amber Area, we'll concentrate the attack on the vaults and kill everyone before they can be resurrected."

Without thinking, she blurted, "But Cythe and Aria will be there!"

He surprised her. "Oh, very well. You've earned the right to claim rewards. If possible, I will spare and present them to you as spoils. The pretty one has potential, but I see no use for the royal frump except maybe for sale to a collector. Anybody else you fancy? Generally, you should look for people with unique abilities that you can put to use. You can get rid of them if they don't live up to your expectations."

"Uh, can I have Athy and Arty?"

He laughed. "Good choices. You learn fast. After our little test, the Priests will be suspicious of us, so just do your job and be extra careful. Now, forget this conversation and be a good girl. Sleep deep, my little servant."

She closed her eyes until she felt him leave then jumped off the bed and went to the big room to run and swim, all the while thinking of other rewards she might be able to get from him when they took the island.

FOURTEEN

WISHING SHE HAD TAKEN THE MAIN TRAIL around the other side of Prospect Village instead of the little used back way, which was a steep path winding up the mountain through brush and scrub that provided scant shade, Maidservant set the heavy basket down and wiped sweat out of her eyes. Up ahead, a hip-high, badly eroded, rock wall crossed the trail and disappeared into the brush both directions. Wondering if something so humble could be the boundary for the Amber Area, she jumped over and continued onward.

After another ten minutes of the same steep terrain, she had about decided to turn back when she reached a high ridge that ran around an enormous, bowl-shaped grassy meadow. Full of all sorts of huge animals she did not recognize, most of them grazed on the flat bottomland this side of a lazy, meandering stream. On the far side, completely incongruous to the surroundings, thirty-six small white buildings with pitched blue tile roofs stood in a square of precise rows.

She studied the animals for any that might like the taste of small girl then moved down through the tall grass. Carefully skirting a herd of brown and black-flecked antelope and another comprised of strange beasts with huge twisting horns, she was relieved they paid no attention to her. It took longer to reach the stream than she had estimated though it proved well worth the effort because the water was cool and good to drink. Then she waded across to the buildings.

Made of the same material as the avenues and floors in the House of Kalli, she could see no difference one building from another. Each had a single slab door on the north facing with a small niche window either side. She could not budge any of the doors. She jumped, grabbed one of the niches and pulled up to look in, but saw only darkness and smelled dank odors. Frustrated, she decided to move on in hopes of finding at least one thing of importance to tell her master. She turned east, the direction that should intersect the main trail.

She found a plateau with trees and marshes teeming with birds. They were glorious to behold, but of no import to her mission. The sun was directly overhead now, and the basket heavier with every step. She decided to see where one more path led then find a shady spot to have lunch.

She went a little higher up the mountain and arrived at a pretty area of rolling hills, fruit trees and no animals of any kind, which struck her odd. She wandered a few minutes then crouched to drink from a sparkling, sandy spring. Suddenly, she sensed something behind her, jumped up and around, banging into Arty, wearing a blindfold. "You scared me near to death! What are you doing?"

Arty pulled the cloth off her face, held up a short curved bow fitted with an arrow and laughed. "Almost shot you before I realized you weren't Athy."

Maidservant noted the bag of arrows hanging from her belt. "You're running around blindfolded shooting at each other? Are you crazy?"

Arty closed her eyes tight, spun around and hit a distant sapling dead center. "The hard bit is dodging arrows, especially Athy's. She's a dead shot."

Finally, something that would interest her master. "Where is she?"

Athy whispered in her ear. "You have to be careful or someone will creep up behind you and slit your throat."

Maidservant twisted around. "That's not funny!"

Athy had her blindfold off. "Can't tell you how glad I am to see you so well. Besides, it's boring, trying to teach Arty the correct way to use a bow."

Arty made a rude noise. "Tell her who won Atlas' last match, who's ranked first in our class and whose name is on top of the Wall of Merit. Is it you? No, me, that's who!"

Athy shrugged. "Only because of gusty wind when my turn came."

Arty jumped in the air. "The only wind that day came out of your butt and smelled bad!"

Athy whipped an arrow from her bag, fired it high into the air and watched it come down in a tall tree on a low hill farther up the trail. She stuck her tongue out at Arty. "Let's see you do that."

Arty ran a few steps toward the hill then turned and taunted. "Do what? Hit the top of a big tree from a hundred feet away? I'm so-o-o-o impressed."

Athy pointed her back to the tree, where the arrow caromed limb-to-limb down, a greenish-red fruit half up the shaft. It dropped to the ground with a heavy thud. "My lunch."

Arty drew and fired an arrow so fast Maidservant barely had time to gasp before it cut a fruit from a low limb, dropping it next to the other one. "Big deal. My lunch."

Athy wagged a finger. "Anyone can shoot unripe mela fruit from the low limbs and lose an arrow, but who can pick one from the top of the tree where the sun makes them sweetest, juiciest and most delectable, then have the arrow not get caught in limbs and deliver it to the ground? No one named Arty, I wager."

"Spiders up your nose! Make one lucky shot then act as if you did it intentionally. What a faker! Bet you can't do it again."

Athy sighed as if the whole matter was a bothersome waste of time. "A case of Priest's wine?"

"Two!"

Athy pulled an arrow from the bag, fitted and fired so quickly Maidservant could not follow her hands. Again, it arced high, came down in the tree and carried a mela to the ground. Athy smacked her lips. "That one is bigger than the first, which means it'll be even sweeter. Your lunch, Maidservant."

Arty's freckles were crimson. She fired an arrow exactly as Athy had, but it passed clean through the fruit and stuck in a high limb. She tried another with the same result.

Athy held her bow by the ends over her head gyrating hips and turning in a circle. "Arty can't do it! Arty can't do it!"

Arty stepped in front of her. "One more time, only not so fast that I can't see what you're doing. There's a trick."

Athy, never taking eyes from Arty, used slow, exaggerated movements to take out an arrow and fit it onto her bow. Then she stopped and lectured. "Handling an arrow properly is an art, not at all like a boxing or wrestling match. You must use finesse, grasp it gently with respect instead of pinching the life out of it with clumsy fingers. Draw the bow gracefully instead of employing herky-jerky motions. If you will kindly point out a replacement for that sour piece of crap mela you shot, I'll get it for you and save you the embarrassment of failing again."

Arty grabbed Athy's arrow off the bow. "You're so full of it! How do you stop the arrow from going through the fruit?"

"Oh, come on. Some of us can hit little targets when the wind stops blowing in tournaments that mean nothing, while others hone useful skills and dine on delicious fruit."

Arty aimed and adjusted for considerable time then shot Athy's arrow. It came down perfectly into the top of the tree but passed through the fruit and stuck in the tree trunk. Frustrated, she fired another arrow and missed the entire tree.

Athy shook her head. "It'd be faster for you to climb the tree and pluck fruit with your hand."

She tried another shot. Then another.

Athy dropped her bag of arrows on the ground next to Arty's, put an arm around Maidservant and led her up the trail. "Let's go get our mela off the ground and have lunch while she practices. I don't think we need to worry about fruit-laden arrows falling out of the tree on us."

Maidservant called back over her shoulder. "Bye, Arty."

She did not answer.

Maidservant whispered, "She's really pissed."

Athy laughed as an arrow deflected off a branch and snapped in two. "Oh, yeah."

"How long will she keep trying?"

Athy whispered back. "Until she does it."

"What if she can't?"

"Then we'll have to bury her with that bow clutched in her hands. She's as stubborn as I am. That's one of the reasons I like her so much."

***

MAIDSERVANT WATCHED ATHY pulling arrows from the fruit. "Uh, what's that little disk on the shaft?"

Athy glanced back at Arty sitting on the ground stringing her bow looser. "Shh, she can hear like you can't believe. Has eyes like a hawk, too." She ran her fingers down the shaft and the disk closed into it. She thumped the tip and it sprang open. "Neat, huh?"

"She's going to be so angry."

Athy choked a laugh. "I knew she'd go crazy after two shots. I'll be nice and leave them here so when she comes to gather arrows she'll understand. Probably be no more than an hour or two unless she stops to think about it, then it might be all night."

Maidservant snickered. "If you don't mind, I'll go eat somewhere she can't find me. Point the way to the main trail, please."

Athy glanced back at Arty. "Uh, maybe I'd better go with you so you don't get lost. Where are you taking all that stuff, anyway? The only Priests' classes were down near the main entrance and they should be done by now. How did you miss them?"

"I came the back way."

"Through the meadows with animals? That can be very dangerous if you wander into the wrong one. I don't understand why no one told you when they sent you."

Maidservant was sheepish. "Well, it was a slow morning, DoSo is out and Kore acted a bigger pain in the butt than usual, so I fibbed that the Head Priest wanted me at Jellyfish House. Hope you don't think I normally shirk my duty."

"I can't be around Kore more than a few minutes without wanting to slap her face, but that doesn't excuse lying to your boss." Athy raised the basket cloth. "On the other hand, you have cheese, bread and meat, and those are Leto's best wines, aren't they? Tell you what---just this once, I'll help you get rid of the evidence. I know a great picnic spot. What do you say?"

"I would like that very much, but shouldn't we ask Arty to join us?"

"Nah. She's learning a valuable lesson. Besides, she'll hog the wine."

Lounging next to a shady spring, Maidservant spotted something moving through tall grass toward the water. Athy twisted to look then shrugged. "Probably elephants."

Maidservant laughed.

"What's funny?"

"You said elephants."

"Yeah, they get into everything if you don't keep a close eye on them."

Maidservant scratched her head. "Uh, the only elephants I know are big as houses and can knock over trees."

Athy stopped eating. "Must be talking about different things. Our elephants have long noses, big ears, stout legs, skinny tails and short bristly hair. Same thing you mean?"

Maidservant giggled. "Yes, Athy, and big as houses."

"Really? One behind you is big as any I've seen."

A tiny elephant, two feet high at most, stood cocking its head, waving its trunk and hoofing the ground. Maidservant squealed. "Oh, how cute! Look at the tiny tusks!"

"No, don't give it food!" It was too late. Athy shook her head. "Now, they'll never leave."

The elephant jammed fruit into its mouth, raised its trunk and tooted, sending Maidservant into fits of giggling. Seven more of the creatures out of the grass. Athy tried shooing them away, but they came back, rocked side-to-side and watched every bite the girls took. When Athy prevented Maidservant giving them anything, they all began tooting, little high pitched noises that kept Maidservant in stitches.

Finally, Athy uttered an expletive and tossed food, causing a mini stampede and head butting, except for the first elephant, which remained apart from the others. Maidservant gave him more fruit and none of the others challenged while he took his time eating. With a note of respect, Athy observed, "Leader of the pack."

Maidservant poured wine in a bowl and pushed it to him. He tasted then slurped it up greedily. Boldly, he wrapped his trunk around Maidservant's wrist, wanting more. She poured another portion and rubbed his ears while he drank. When it was gone, he brushed against her like a cat. She let out a yell. "Ouch! Rough."

Athy burst out laughing. "I think you've made a friend for life. Say, do these things really grow so big in Egypt? Maybe someday the Temple will send me there and I'll see for myself."

Maidservant, feeling the wine, answered, "Maybe I'll go with you."

Athy regarded her with quiet surprise. "Well, no one can predict the future, that's for sure."

Basket clacking against her leg and the elephant following close by her heels like a dog, Maidservant trotted to keep up with Athy crossing a log bridge and around a large outcrop of boulders where acrid smoke curled out of fissures. She wrinkled her nose. "Ugh! What's that?"

"Smoke from fires inside the mountain. You can see them if you climb to the top and look down into it."

"Is that the place Kalli died?"

Athy looked at her curiously. "Yes. Don't take offense, but I don't understand why Rhea let you into the Amber Area. What did she say to you?"

She squatted to rub the elephant's ears. "Haven't seen her since I returned to work. DoSo told me I'd been given permission and didn't say why."

"It's very dangerous here. I'll answer questions if I can."

The wine made Maidservant bold and careless. "Why don't the birds and animals leave the areas they're in?"

Athy hid her surprise. "Most people ask why so many strange animals are in the Amber Area, not why they don't leave."

Maidservant pushed the elephant over onto its side. "I think mine is the more obvious question. They should be all over the island, especially the birds. They don't even go to other parts of the Amber Area. I think that is very strange."

Athy nodded slowly. "No one knows why. Some animals move around several areas, but most stay in one. If you stand on the other side of the old wall and offer food to them, they will not cross. If you carry an animal out, it dies and shrivels up into something unrecognizable, so don't try to take your elephant home. Ask something else, and I promise to give a better answer."

Maidservant thought a few seconds. "What keeps townspeople out? Do they die and shrivel into something unrecognizable if they go in?"

Athy pursed her lips. "No one can find this place without permission. I can't explain why."

Maidservant tickled the elephant under the legs, making it shiver. "But islanders hike mountain trails."

Athy tensed slightly. "How do you know that?"

Maidservant rubbed the elephant's tummy, making its stubby legs kick. "Denear mentioned she was in a hiking club when Cythe took us for lunch. Remember?"

Athy sighed. "I do now. You'll just have to accept no one can pass through the Amber Area and reach the top of the mountain without Temple permission."

"I bet the Watchers keep it hidden."

Athy frowned. "Let's talk about something else, shall we?"

The elephant had gotten up, running circles around Maidservant and she missed the change in Athy. "Okay. The Amber Area got its name because it shines golden at night. Is that right?"

"How can you possibly know that? It can't be seen except out to sea. Oh, you saw it when you came here with Envoy, didn't you?"

She nodded. "Actually, he told me lights reflecting down off clouds caused the golden glow on the side of the mountain, but now I think the Amber Area glows on its own because of where I remember seeing it, which accounts for the name, too. That's right, isn't it?"

Athy looked up at smoke curling lazily from the top of the mountain and took a deep breath. "I think when Envoy expresses an opinion about someone, I should take more heed."

Maidservant did not hear because the elephant butted her legs, nearly causing her to fall. He had twigs curled in his trunk and when she took them, he trotted off to get more. Something else occurred to her. "What are the little houses with blue roofs in the bowl-shaped meadow?"

"That's Hidden Meadow, but there are no buildings anywhere in the Amber Area. You must mean Prospects' Village. None of those have blue roofs, though."

Maidservant had never seen Prospects' Village before today, but that surely was not what she meant. She started to explain further but finally noticed the look Athy gave her. The elephant butted again and she accepted more sticks while thinking how to extricate herself from the situation. She said, "Thanks, Hari."

"Hari?"

Maidservant grinned. "Short for Hariset. What do you think?"

Athy tousled her hair. "I think it's getting late. We'll take the main trail back to the Temple."

It was not far. They passed through a narrow opening in the low wall and Hari stopped, trumpeting plaintively after them. Maidservant ran back, gave him a last piece of fruit and a hug good-bye.

They found Arty sitting next to the trail carving an evil-looking caricature of Leto into a tree trunk. She tossed Athy's arrow bag to her. "You are too smart for words. Useful little gizmo, though. I kept one, if you don't mind."

Athy shrugged and said nothing.

Arty took her arm and walked along with her. "Okay, I overdid the bragging a mite. Was there anything else?"

Athy hugged her. "Truth be told, I can't beat you with a bow without using other abilities. Tell anyone I said that, and I'll swear you're a liar, though."

Arty pointed to Maidservant. "I have a witness."

Maidservant shook her head. "I wasn't listening."

Athy reached into a pouch and handed Arty a full amphora of wine.

Arty grinned. "Heritage wine. At least, Leto is good at raising grapes."

Maidservant could have sworn Athy drank all her wine. She would certainly be more careful around her in the future.

The setting sun painted crimson and orange on darkening blue sky. Maidservant walked between the Temple's most powerful Initiates, grinning up at one then the other, the whole time sifting through the events of the day and preparing a report for her master. Athy returned her smiles and exchanged banter with Arty while mulling over everything the strange little Egyptian girl had said and done. Arty acted her usual competitive, half-serious self, though she sensed unease between her companions and wondered why this inconsequential girl concerned Athy so much.

FIFTEEN

DOUBLE GATES FLEW OPEN IN THE HIGH WALL connecting the tips of the crescent-shaped Cadi-sum stadium. The packed crowd, expecting the Head Priest to emerge, cheered then fell silent when a giant bull, a black mass of sinewy rage like none they had ever seen, exploded into the arena. It ran around the field, bellowing and crashing horns into the wooden wall barriers.

Two Priests, a man and a woman, clad in nothing but short ceremonial kilts tied up between the legs and body oil, sprinted across the field. The bull charged, viciously hooking horns and missing by the narrowest margins when they skirted past either side. Furious, it tore great chunks out of the ground turning to give chase showing extraordinary speed then slammed into the barrier a scant second after they scrambled over it into the stands. The crowd roared approval.

Another pair of Priests sped at the animal, but this time it was cannier and caught an arm with a horn tip. The Priest spun free and redeemed herself by smacking the bull on the rump, but the slight delay nearly cost her life, because just as she reached for the top of the wall with her good arm, it smashed the wooden barrier from under her feet. Fortunately, her fast-thinking partner, sitting on the wall, caught her with his legs and flipped over backwards, throwing her into the ecstatic crowd.

Maidservant, squeezed on a narrow bench between Cythe and Aria, felt sick to her stomach when the bull gored the Priest, especially after waiting so long for the ceremony to begin in the hot sun, but then Aria chased away all other thoughts when she grabbed her and pointed. "There he is! Tell Cythe!"

Standing before the double gates, tall, proud and glistening, Envoy could have been mistaken for the statue of a god. As the crowd became aware of him, noise abated until they heard only the buzz of flies and bees around food and drinks. Even the bull grew quiet, looking around for the reason everything changed until it spotted the new adversary. It snorted and shook its head, throwing off globs of slobber while plowing a furrow in the ground with a heavy front hoof. Nervous laughter and whispers rippled through the crowd as anticipation grew.

Envoy raised arms straight over his head. Athy and Arty vaulted over the fence in perfect unison, landing either side. They pointed across the arena and bowed to Rhea, somehow seated unnoticed at the rail where the Priests pulled up out of the ring. Surprised, the crowd cheered wildly. Then everyone heard her in spite of the noise. "Initiates, your bull is without equal. Now, the people will judge whether you are worthy of Priesthood. Begin."

Athy and Arty trotted opposite ways around the wall, confusing the bull, which looked one way then the other. Arms still above his head, Envoy waited then trotted across the field whooping. The bull charged him. With incredible bursts of speed, Athy and Arty veered to center arena and performed flips across the back of the bull as Envoy flipped from head to tail. From the stands, it appeared they must surely collide, yet all landed going away at full runs. The bull tumbled trying to stop then sat in a dust cloud, watching its tormentors come together on the far side of the arena where its charge began.

Rhea stood to offer congratulations, but Athy, Arty and Envoy joined hands and jogged in a line toward the animal again, inciting another charge. This time, Envoy and Athy swerved either side as Arty flipped into a handstand on the horns. Furious, the bull's head jerked up, catapulting her over its back, where Envoy and Athy caught her. The bull made a half-hearted attempt to pursue, but they outran it. Then they leaped over the wood barrier and came down sitting on the high wall facing Rhea. The arena erupted with cheers.

Maidservant, gaping with tongue out, had not moved since seeing Envoy. Suddenly, a fly flew into her mouth and she sputtered and gagged. Pounding her back, Cythe and Aria kept asking if she was all right, but she did not hear them because the incident triggered a memory: a shrouded woman in a tomb telling her to close her mouth before she swallowed a fly. The woman gave her wine and asked questions about her other life. She held her in cold embrace as she fell asleep. Then Maidservant woke up in putrid black water drowning. It was real and she knew it was real without any doubt. She screamed, but no one heard in the bedlam, not even Cythe and Aria, cheering and wiping fly pieces and spit from her lips.

After the show, Cythe led Maidservant by the hand through the milling crowd. "Most people are waiting to see the boxing matches. They are hugely popular but Aria and I don't care for them. If you want to go back, Athy and Arty will make room for you. Today they have a special bench down in front with the Head Priest."

Maidservant, looking longingly at a queue in front of a beer vendor, shook her head. "I don't care to see people hurting each other."

Walking beside her, Aria made them laugh. "Yeah, it'd be dull after watching an expert catch flies in her mouth."

They found Athy cradling the bull's huge head in her arms and reciting a calming spell while Arty and Envoy bathed it with warm scented water. Arty knelt to examine a hind leg. "A bad bruise. I'll heal it."

Envoy lobbed a jar of ointment to her. "Use this. It's faster."

Arty dabbed some on. "Amazing. These concoctions of yours could make us rich if you'd share what's in them."

Arty asked if anyone wanted to pet the bull. Cythe and Aria accepted eagerly, but no amount of coaxing could get Maidservant inside the pen with those horns. Not only that, their nakedness embarrassed her and she was afraid they would notice if she got too close, but when they finished, Athy went to Maidservant, who obviously could not decide where to look. Fortunately, everyone was too polite to mention it. "We are happy that Rhea gave you permission to visit Cadi-sum finally. Tomorrow, we would like you to go with us to climb to the top of the mountain. You can see where Kalli died as well as the fire inside. It is a long climb but we will help you. Envoy's going, too."

She was going to say yes before the mention of Envoy. "I have to clean the House of Kalli after neglecting it today."

Aria broke in. "Maidservant, it's a great honor to be asked to share private time with Initiates ascending to Priesthood. Of course you'll go."

Athy accepted that as the answer. "Great. It will be an experience you'll remember the rest of your life."

Cythe whispered a warning. "Here comes Seydi with San-zeus and his entourage. Hey, what's with Seydi?"

Her tunic was long and loose rather than short and tight. Muted greens with no outline highlighted her eyes, rendering them vulnerable instead of aggressively sensual. Her cheeks had the usual blush, but the shading softened rather than being suggestive. Most unusual, the wig was not black, sleek and fashionable but long, brown and somewhat unkempt, very much like Maidservant's hair.

As the group milled looking at the bull, Seydi maneuvered close to Envoy and backed into him, separating them from the others when she turned around. "Oh, I am ever so clumsy."

He bowed. "I hope you are well, Prospect Seydi."

She looked down his scarred chest, wet her lips and said, "I want to compliment your magnificent performance."

"You're too kind."

She glanced to make sure everyone watched them then took his arm, hung on it and sighed up at his face with sweet breath that blended with her perfume to devastating effect "The others don't like the new way I look. Does it please you?"

He studied her for long seconds. "Is something different?"

She fought to keep the smile on her face as she gripped him harder and pressed more of herself against him. "I have a wonderful idea. Will you bend down so that I might whisper it to you?"

He took a half step back, leaving her hanging on him at a very precarious angle. "Oh, I've gotten body oil on your clothes."

She had to let go to regain her balance. "San-zeus asked that I invite you to his house tomorrow for a party to celebrate the Priest Naming Festival. Simply everyone who matters will be there." She lowered her voice to a whisper "More importantly, you and I can sneak away to…!"

He left her batting eyes at nothing and went to San-zeus. "I must decline your generous invitation to attend your party for I have another commitment tomorrow."

San-zeus, accustomed to Temple members of lesser rank kowtowing to his every whim, showed displeasure with a dark scowl that usually brought instant reconsideration. When he did not receive it, he pressed. "I assume your business must be of critical nature?"

Envoy, known for being soft spoken, replied loudly. "Yes. I promised to accompany Seydi's maid on a hike up the mountain."

Athy broke in before San-zeus reacted. "Envoy will have his little jokes. Actually, Arty and I invited him to spend Second Day of Priest Naming with us. We're meditating at Kalli's place of sacrifice. The maid's only along to carry food and prepare lunch."

San-zeus considered what to do. Rumors suggested Envoy possessed powerful abilities though no one had actually seen them. The Head Priest treated him with deference, but then again, she was a buffoon. That Envoy insulted him intentionally by expressing preference for the company of that degenerate female he had no doubt, but Envoy also had scars of a warrior and showed no concern for San-zeus' formidable abilities. San-zeus simply had too much to lose if he challenged and failed, so he laughed it off. "Had me going, Envoy. Very droll sense of humor."

Everyone had moved closer around them except Maidservant, deeply embarrassed. Suddenly, Seydi was next to her, pointing at Maidservant's feet, planted squarely in her shadow. Then she doubled her over with a punch in the stomach.

Looking over the crowd, Envoy witnessed the attack but gave no sign as he took San-zeus' arm in the traditional gesture of friendship. "Might I have the honor to supply all the wine for your party to make amends for my poor joke? I found some amazing vintages on the way to the far northlands."

San-zeus appreciated such an expensive gesture but also took it as a sign that he was right about Envoy's overblown status. He wished he could reconsider taking him down a few pegs, but now the others would think it unwarranted. Athy might even come to his defense, which would mean the months spent pursuing Arty's support would be for naught. He showed his best smile. "Thank you so much! Please, may I be first to congratulate you and our new Priests for the show this afternoon."

Just then, a small cloud crossed in front of the sun, casting a patch of shade over them, and Envoy pointed up to it. "And thank you, San-zeus, for a brief respite from the heat."

Everyone laughed and applauded. Envoy bowed politely and pointed up again as the cloud moved on. "Ah, shadows can be so unpredictable. We must go clean up. Cythe, Aria and Maidservant, will you assist us, please? Have a great party, San-zeus."

Seydi had pulled back to hit Maidservant again then stopped as she saw an expression of amazement on her face. She followed her stare to the ground and found a single shadow---Maidservant's. They gaped at one another then Maidservant ran after the others, leaving Seydi twisting in circles and looking back over her shoulder. When San-zeus called asking what was wrong, she ran away before anyone noticed.

Nothing Hariset said could keep Seydi seated at his table in the embassy garden. She jumped up again. "That little twerp is not going to make a fool of me and get away with it. Use your power to fix this. Now!"

He enjoyed watching her squirm. "Surely you don't think she's capable of doing this. Tell me what happened so I can determine who possesses such great power."

She kicked the ground. "You call this great power? Find out who did it and I will teach them a lesson they won't soon forget!"

"Calm down."

She sagged back into the chair. "I've done nothing to deserve such a hateful personal attack."

"You're acting like a child of common blood."

She made a rude blowing noise.

He grabbed her around the neck and choked until she agreed to recount the details. When she finished, he laughed at her. "So, you failed to entice Envoy but the maid has him sniffing after her? Now, I understand your frumpy clothes and cheap wig. Perhaps the Master overestimated your worth when he shared blood with you. Maybe he would be happier with the maid, too."

Seydi came at him flailing nails but he pushed her back into the chair with nothing more than a look. He drew symbols in the air with his hand. Blue fire ignited around her ankles and burned slowly up her body until it engulfed her to the neck. She screamed but no sound escaped her lips. She could not lose consciousness, no matter how hard she tried. It seemed hours to her though less than half a minute elapsed before he stopped and held out a goblet of water. She gulped it down, noting nothing whatever wrong with her skin though intense pain lingered.

Waiting for her to recover, Hariset stared out at ships moving across the most beautiful bay in the world with no appreciation. Finally, he asked, "You will do as I say?"

She croaked, "Yes, my Lord. It's just that I'm upset."

He nodded. "You still have your shadow, but no one near you can see it. Do you understand the significance?"

She shook her head.

"It requires a great deal of power to make something invisible to even a single person. More importantly, the spell must be recast on every new person the subject meets, which means the caster has to be nearby at all times. Does that tell you enough to figure it out?"

She looked around the empty garden. "With respect, that can't be right, can it? There's no one here."

He chuckled. "You are the caster."

"But I don't know anything about this kind of magic."

"It is an old Egyptian magic that is embedded in someone's subconscious and triggered by a mannerism or whatnot. I've read about it but never come across it until now. Interesting, don't you think?"

Seydi started out of the chair again. "Get it out of me! Get it out, now!"

He pushed her back with another look. "It's Envoy, of course. Too bad Theia isn't with us. At her great age, she can sense abilities that should no longer exist. It would certainly be helpful to know what we're facing with him."

Seydi struggled to raise her hand then wiggled two fingers. "Please, Lord, will you get his evil out of me?"

"Finally, you asked properly." He snapped his fingers and her shadow reappeared. "Child's play."

She hid resentment behind grateful eyes. "Thank you."

He poured wine for her. "Yesterday, I set the plan in motion to test their defenses, but it will take a few weeks to get everyone here."

"At last!"

He relished her youthful excitement and wished he could feel such things again. "I've decided to have Atlas killed during the test run rather than waiting until we take the island. It'll make the final battle much easier."

Surprised, she sat up straighter. "Do I have a part?"

"Yes, you are vital, but we'll have to discuss details later. I've got to give the girl instructions then go meet Selene."

***

ENVOY, ARTY AND ATHY WALKED ABREAST through the wet grass of Hidden Meadow with Maidservant and Hari trotting behind. They were at the very place Maidservant found the little houses with blue roofs but there was no evidence of them anywhere. Dismayed, she refused to believe she had imagined them, a complete change from how she reacted to such things a few months earlier.

It took two hours to climb into the clouds. Maidservant was not sure what she expected, but was disappointed they were no more than common fog. Not long after emerging into bright sunlight, they passed under two enormous aqueducts supported by tall stone pillars. Condensation rained down on them. The others were oblivious to being wet, but the cool altitude and stiff winds made Maidservant shiver so much her teeth chattered. Arty called a brief halt, reached into a pack and tossed her a blanket. "Wrap this around you until we start climbing."

Athy eyed Maidservant. "You're keeping up remarkably well. Have you been doing something to improve your strength and endurance?"

Maidservant knelt to Hari and teased with a piece of fruit to make him trumpet. They had laughed before, but now they waited for an answer. She stood up, stretched and groaned. "I have tried hard not to slow you down but my legs feel so heavy and stiff I can hardly move them."

Athy nodded to Hari. "Then he shouldn't go any farther. It will be too dangerous if you can't look after him."

Maidservant responded sharper than she should have. "He doesn't need looking after. He's way more surefooted than he appears."

Athy shrugged. "I'm just saying that it would be better if he waits here."

"He can do what he wants," Maidservant insisted, "and what he wants is to be with me. He will feel bad if I make him go away."

"That may have been true when you first met him, but now he approaches every passerby and performs for food. That's why he didn't come with us until you coaxed with some."

Arty interceded. "Ah, come on, Athy. Hari will know if it gets too hard for him. Animals are smart that way. What do you say, Maidservant? If he wants to stop, you'll let him, won't you?"

She agreed and they looked to Athy to compromise, but she was aggravated at Arty for butting in and started up the trail. After a few seconds, Arty and Envoy followed with Maidservant and Hari close behind.

They arrived at the bottom of a rubble-littered, v-shaped gorge with wind roaring down it. Arty walked back to Maidservant. "Steps used to go to the top, but an earthquake destroyed them. There is a doozy of a drop-off to negotiate up ahead. Hope you are not afraid of heights."

Then it happened. Envoy asked Athy and Arty to go in front, went to Maidservant and put an arm around her back. "I'll help you and Hari."

She was flustered. "We don't need help."

He bent down, looked into her eyes and spoke from the heart. "Please, I want to. Okay?"

She could not think straight. Last night, her master ordered her to get information about Envoy, but if she discovered something and tried to withhold it, he would know. Yet, she would not betray him, no matter what, so she had resolved to keep her distance and concentrate finding out something important about Athy and Arty. "Okay."

Arty paused and looked back before following Athy out of sight around a turn. "Maidservant, don't look down when you get up here and you'll be fine."

The outer half of the turn had collapsed down the cliff face, leaving a jagged ledge. Scrub grew along the edge and that helped, but Maidservant could not stop glancing down at roiling gray clouds that seemed far away now. Then they were past it, climbing inside a steeper notch with even more rubble than the lower part, but posts connected by heavy rope led the rest of the way up. Envoy went on the opposite side from Maidservant so he could keep an arm around her shoulders. She used the rope to pull herself up. Hari trotted at her heels, slipping and sliding but not having much difficulty.

Already at the top with Athy, Arty burst out laughing. "Maidservant, any man who walks hunched over like that just to hold onto you deserves something special. So, what are you going to give him?"

Maidservant stopped and looked up just as Envoy let go to move around a small boulder lodged against one of the posts. Hari ran into the back of her legs and she fell backwards onto him. A rockslide tumbled them down the slope, across the ledge and through the scrub. Envoy caught her by the ankle. Hanging headfirst down, she watched Little Hari disappear into the clouds, his frightened trumpeting carried up to her on wind.

Athy and Arty clung to her. Envoy stood just below, keeping them safe. Arty kept saying she was to blame for making stupid jokes at such a dangerous time, Hari was such a special pet and that she was sorry. Athy kept looking at her with those deep brown eyes that saw everything, said it was just an accident, no one was to blame and how sorry she was.

Suddenly, Maidservant could stand no more. She flailed and kicked until they let go. "Little creatures die! That's what we do! We don't matter! So shut up about it!" She took Envoy's arm, pulled it around her back and resumed climbing. A stunned Athy and Arty followed.

The plateau was hostile and otherworldly. Viewed from their vantage point, its shiny rock surface could be mistaken for a body of water rippling around islands of huge boulders. Gusty westerly winds blew almost constantly here, carrying acrid steam and smoke from fissures up a distant steep black slope. At its base, ruins of what appeared to be a small temple stood. Arty spoke in a hushed, reverent voice. "That's where Kalli addressed the Priests before climbing up to jump in the mountain's mouth."

Envoy said, "We'll have to postpone seeing it. Here comes Daedalus."

The Priest, careful to avoid rocks running, tripped over nothing when he arrived. Jocular with twinkling eyes and a quick laugh, he also had a missing front tooth, long, wind-tangled blond hair and herky-jerky mannerisms. "Good health, Envoy, Athy, Arty and Maidservant. How peculiar to see you here, but doesn't matter, not important. Stick to the subject, D. Where are the others, Envoy?"

Envoy took Daedalus' arm to stop him jumping around. "Fair weather, my friend, if such a thing is possible in this place. This is the second day of Athy's and Arty's Priest Naming. Remember?"

"Oh! I was supposed to go to San-zeus' party. Marked it on the calendar I lost last week." He leaned close to the girls and spoke conspiratorially. "Don't let on, but I threw it away so I wouldn't have to tell an outright lie why I'm not there. Hey, Arty, if you tire of playing politics with San-zeus, you might want to give science a try, if you know what I mean." He gave a lecherous wink, causing Athy to laugh and Arty to turn red. Daedalus took off running back the way he came. "Follow me, everyone, I have something amazing to show you!"

At the westernmost point of the plateau near the edge of the cliff, two small lean-tos rested against the leeward side of a low stone windbreak. Two Initiates crouched over a protected campfire dabbing hot wax from a bronze pot onto two large kite-shaped contraptions tied by the corners to stakes. They looked up, expecting introductions, but Daedalus motioned to keep working. "When Hera and Icarus finish, if ever they do, I'll be ready to go."

Hera, well known for being humorless and speaking her mind, expressed her annoyance in a nasal monotone. "Another set of hands would make it faster by a third; or, in your case, Daedalus, a fourth or fifth, perhaps." Getting no response, she made a frustrated noise and resumed dabbing.

Envoy examined the kites. "Atlas said you're to wait until he comes to see your work for himself. Rhea has deep reservations about this."

Daedalus twisted half-around and back again. "Spare me the politicians, bureaucrats and Head Priest! After I succeed, they'll criticize me for taking so long and take all the credit, too. Oh well, humble scientists have no choice but to obey and explain, explain and explain. What time did you say that Atlas will be here?"

"Day after tomorrow. The ceremony, remember?"

He stomped around kicking rocks with his sandaled feet then hobbled back complaining that his toes hurt and it was Atlas' fault. "This is the first time in weeks the winds have been this calm. Who knows how long I'll have to wait for conditions this good again? Terribly inconsiderate, if you ask me. Downright rude, in fact."

Envoy made him stand still. "Must I remind that you were not expected to be here today? Are you sure it'll work?"

He grinned like a naughty little boy. "Well, in theory. Like everything else, can't tell for sure about something until you try it. Isn't that right, Arty?"

Arty grinned. "Keep it up and I'll teach you how to box."

Athy stood from examining one of the kites and regarded him with wonder. "Can you really do it?"

Daedalus snapped his fingers. "She figured it out just like that! Always the smart one. Keep saying you should work with me." He grinned. "Fringe benefits, too."

Arty danced in front of Athy, now having her turn with a red face. "What is it? What's he going to do?"

"If I'm not mistaken, he intends to fly."

After a few minutes explaining, Daedalus motioned them around the kite and untied it. Together, they lifted, carefully keeping it edgewise to the wind. Daedalus ducked under, slipped his arms into leather straps and got them to help him sidle close to the precipice. "The rest is downhill from here."

No one laughed but him. White-faced, Maidservant backed away while Envoy confronted Daedalus. "Surely you don't intend jumping off this cliff for your first flight?"

"Nothing to worry about," Daedalus insisted. "I plan to land in Main Court on Rhea's very doorstep. Imagine the commotion!"

Envoy shook his head. "This wouldn't have anything to do with her destroying your ships, would it?"

He smiled mischievously. "Of course it does. I want to see her hide this invention after everyone sees what it can do."

Meanwhile, Arty walked to the edge and leaned out, looking straight down. "I can see the Amber Area and the edge of the woods above the Temple through holes in the clouds. You know, this might be fun."

Athy pulled her back. "Assuming it works."

Behind them, Hera said, "Six tests, six crashes. Not going to get me on one of these things."

Icarus was next to her. "I volunteered, but Daedalus won't let me."

Hera stared at him in disbelief for a few seconds then grabbed and pulled him away a short distance, where they got into a passionate, whispered argument.

Envoy was concerned. "You've had six crashes?"

He shrugged. "Unmanned tests. Someone needs to be onboard for stability and the frame needed reinforcing. Ready to go now."

Hera came back. "Except now, it's too heavy unless the wind is so powerful you can't control it. D wanted me because I'm smart, but he doesn't listen to anything I say. Going to break his fool neck."

Envoy gave the kite a tug, pulling Daedalus sideways. "I can't sanction this. You must prove it works somewhere else, first. We'll help you pack your stuff and carry it down the mountain."

Daedalus looked heartbroken. "If it was anyone but you, I'd tell you what to do with your opinion. Guess I do tend to get a mite carried away. Say, do you know a place for tests in the Amber Area that is accessible to Rhea? I think she'd get a kick out of watching."

Envoy thought that was a great idea. "Athy and Arty know better than me." He turned to call them over.

Daedalus had watched the clouds below, gauged how long before powerful gusts roared up the cliff face and timed the jump perfectly, but instead of sailing out and down as expected, the kite shot twenty feet straight up then spun east across the plateau toward the volcano. Frantically, he slipped air, got the nose down and crashed in the temple ruins near a big fissure. The wreckage pinned him upside down with feet kicking in the air and head jammed sideways on the ground. When they reached him, he declared, "I told you it would fly!"

Staring at his holey undergarment, Athy commented, "An aspect of Daedalus I never before considered."

Arty was not to be outdone. "He puts his best side forward for science and comes up short."

Daedalus laughed. "Calm down, girls, there's plenty for both of you."

Hera squatted and peered into his face. "I've had it with this stupid project. You agree with me, don't you, Icarus?"

Icarus had other thoughts. "You could have flown all the way over the mountain if you'd not brought it down, D. You could have shown the Head Priest and been legendary!"

The wind grew stronger while they broke apart the kite to extricate Daedalus, who had ordered Icarus and Hera back to camp to make certain the other kite was secure. Then, just as they freed him, they heard Hera scream and looked up to see the other kite soaring over the plateau like a great red bird. In the harness beneath, Icarus kicked, yelled and cheered. Gaining altitude, he passed high overhead and they gave chase up the lava slope.

Nothing prepared Maidservant for the most frightening sight she ever experienced. The mountain's immense black caldron full of bubbling fire-brew was far below, but the heat and fumes were all but unendurable. She realized that without the wind, they could not stand here, and that thought jolted her to look up at Icarus.

Caught in eddies above the abyss, the hapless young man turned wide figure eights seeking crosscurrents of escape, each pattern slightly lower than the last. No one had spoken since arriving, but now Athy pronounced his sentence. "He will die shortly after dark unless the wind changes or he hastens the inevitable."

Hera screamed and fell to her knees sobbing. "Oh, Icarus, my Icarus. Is there nothing anyone can do? Is there no magic that can save you? No, no, no, this cannot be happening."

Athy and Arty knelt and put their arms around her. Then Athy recited: "And so, Kalli assembled the Priests upon the Plateau of Winds and they watched the sun sink into the sea."

Arty: "They watched twilight's arrival."

Athy: "They watched darkness consume light and stars multiply."

Arty: "She told them, I am not a god, but a woman with skills who has lived too long."

Athy, Arty and Hera: "Then Kalli the woman cast Kalli the god into the mountain, taking the first step to save the world from Corruption."

A long time later, a brief flash far below marked the passing of Icarus and Daedalus' latest marvelous invention.

Priests' lights illuminated Rhea and the Council in Main Court standing in front of the old pond. Daedalus, Hera, Envoy, Athy, Arty and Maidservant faced them in a loose semi-circle. Several people shared brief stories about Icarus then Rhea asked Athy to write a parable about his death without mentioning the volcano. Many people had emulated Kalli's death and she did not want to chance another spate of self-sacrifices.

It was over in less than ten minutes. Rhea asked Envoy and the Council to join her in Jellyfish House. Maidservant started to leave for the House of Kalli but Arty stopped her. Rhea had given permission for her to stay in the baths since it was well past midnight already.

On a bed of pillows next to the water, Maidservant could not sleep. She wished she could release the pain in her heart by crying, not for stupid Icarus, but Little Hari. She could not do it, of course. Running would help, but she dared not do that on the Temple grounds, so she swam slowly back and forth across the pool until daybreak.

***

ON THE THIRD DAY, PRIESTS CAME FROM ALL OVER THE ISLAND, straining capacity of the dining rooms and baths. The crowds were raucous, especially in the baths, splashing everyone who entered. In late afternoon, everyone rushed away to dress for the evening's festivities and the kitchen staff lamented they would not have time to get ready if they stayed to clean the facility. DoSo had departed hours before so Kore made the decision. "The dummy can stay and clean up. She doesn't deserve to attend, anyway."

Alone, Maidservant went to the terrace, took off the wet tunic---the same one she wore on the mountain---and draped it on the back of a chair to dry while she sat staring down at city lights until the obelisks announced the beginning of the parade. She tugged the damp garment back on and ran to meet Cythe and Aria, waiting for her at the top of First Test.

Priests' lights illuminated the avenue down through Cadi-sum to the stadium. Athy and Arty led the procession wearing pure white gowns. Overhead, a wheel of globes showered them with tiny sparkling lights. The Head Priest, carried in her ceremonial chair and awash in golden light, came next. Priests and Initiates followed in two stately lines, rainbows pulsing through their ranks. Then the Scholars and honored guests marched four abreast with torches alternating green and blue. Singing, dancing and drinking, Prospects trailed in a traditional unorganized, noisy mob. From the bottom of First Test to the stadium, cheering townspeople lined the road. Cythe, Aria and Maidservant drank all the way down and were in the last group squeezed onto the arena field.

Four Priests led singing of rollicking sailors' songs, each louder and bawdier than the last. Wine and beer fueled the festivities for adults while children had special mixes of honey and fruit juices. A chorus hummed an ancient melody that everyone sang. Then all the Priest lights and torches around the arena went out.

Light flared around a high platform and everyone saw Rhea close up standing between Athy and Arty. Rhea opened her tunic and Arty pulled it from her shoulders, exposing her to the waist. The double-axes above her left breast pulsed with energy. She took Athy's right wrist in her left hand and her voice reverberated the arena. "Union!"

A screech sounded from the night sky. Ten thousand people looked up. A beam lit a giant golden owl circling above the arena. It was the Kallistian symbol for wisdom, but it also had silver talons, their symbol for a warrior. The people applauded because it represented Athy so perfectly.

The great bird came down and flew circles just above the audience. People ducked and cried out with excitement and awe. Suddenly, it flew at Rhea and the new Priests from behind, talons raised to attack. Thousands shouted warnings. The creature disappeared in an explosion of golden light. The Head Priest held up Athy's arm and the symbol of the gold and silver owl emblazoned on her wrist glowed in the air above them for everyone to see.

Rhea took Arty's arm, bowed her head and waited silently until the crowd quietened. The light around the platform went out and a primal howl tore through the arena. Someone shouted, "The moon is falling! The moon is falling!"

It came down until half-filling the sky above the stadium. A shadow moved in front of it, a female hunter raising a bow. She aimed straight at them. An arrow of light flew at their faces. People shouted, ducked and dodged. Many fell over sideways or backwards into the laps of others. All was noise, confusion and turmoil. The lights came on. The moon was back in its place. Rhea held up Arty's arm, above them a shimmering gold bow fitted with a silver arrow turned slowly. A child's loud lament came from the upper gallery. "Mommy, I peed my pants."

From the other side, a burly voice answered, "So did I!"

Then colorful lights danced in the sky while the chorus performed traditional sing-alongs. People talked endlessly about the owl, wolf, bringing the moon down from the sky, wetting pants and the power of Rhea and the Temple of Light. Never had they been more certain of their futures.

Walking home along the beach, sharing an amphora of wine with Seydi, Hariset sniffed disdainfully. "Cheap parlor tricks."

Though she had been impressed, Seydi was quick to agree. "Totally boring, a letdown after all the talk how exciting it would be."

Hariset chuckled and passed the wine. "Lacked that certain flair, such as a grand altar of white marble and conducting random drawings to determine sacrifices. Nothing better than hot blood streaming across cool white marble to excite a crowd."

Seydi laughed, took a long drink and handed it back. "What else could be done to make it special?"

Hariset thought. "Well, this is always well received: sort out the fattest attendees, give them dull knives with broken points and have them fight to the death for a fabulous prize to the last one standing."

Seydi smiled with equal parts malevolence and mischief. "I would promise the winner a blissful night with the beautiful Seydi, although it might be too much for a common little heart to withstand."

He feigned dismay. "But surely, you wouldn't actually do it?"

She moved around him, acting out the words. "I'd sashay up to fatty all hot and bothered like I can hardly wait. Pucker to kiss then hesitate so he leans toward me with delicious fatty lips that I slice off with my razor sharp nails. Then I cast fatty onto your marble altar and carve a sculpture to present to the family as a memento."

Hariset hurled the empty amphora far out into the harbor. "A delicious presentation. Well done."

They laughed and made jokes until reaching the neighborhood around the stately homes of the Council Priests, where handsome Lord Ambassador Hariset bade his beautiful daughter, Prospect Seydi, a good night before they retired respectively to the houses of Selene and Atlas.

Cythe walked slightly in front of Maidservant, holding her hand and leading as a mother would a child. Aria had said she was sleepy and gone ahead, so Maidservant felt certain Cythe wanted to discuss something with her. Sure enough, Cythe stopped and held the oil lamp up between them, but Maidservant's appearance distracted her. "You shouldn't have worn dirty work clothes to the ceremony."

"No one noticed."

She hesitated. "You've changed so much."

"In what way?"

"Uh, you're more self-assured than you used to be. You act less like a mouse and more like a...a..."

"Rat?"

Cythe laughed, set the lamp down and threw her arms around Maidservant. "Don't be silly. I meant that you were timid and afraid of everything when you first came here."

"So should everyone be."

Cythe hugged tighter and cried over her back. "I keep having dreams that you did something to me, something that makes my head hurt all the time. I'm confused and not like I was. I know it makes no sense, but did you? Did you do something?"

"I'm not a Priest who messes with minds, Cythe."

Cythe let her go and rubbed tears away with the backs of her hands. "That's what Aria said. She thinks I'm just scared about...uh, things."

"What uh, things?"

"Don't make fun of me. We have to go away tomorrow."

Maidservant played dumb. "Where are you going, Cythe?"

"I'm not supposed to say."

"You know you're going to say it. Get it over with."

She nodded. "Tomorrow we're being initiated."

"Will there be a parade and ceremonies at Cadi-sum arena?"

Cythe missed the sarcasm. "Initiations are conducted in private at Jellyfish House. Oh, Maidservant, we may never see you again."

"Why's that, Cythe?"

"We have to go away, maybe a long time. When we return, you might be...uh...may be..."

"Just say dead, Cythe."

"I was going to say gone. You know about long sleep, then?"

Maidservant was tired of repeating this conversation. "Since I've been given an official position with the Temple, no one seems concerned about me knowing things any longer."

"I didn't realize. Uh, there's a favor I want to ask you."

"What?"

"Will you look in on my family from time to time? I can't ever go back to them. They will be made to forget me because when I return I'll be the same age while they…while you…you…"

"Grow old and die! But surely, you'll not be the same age forever, will you?"

"We grow older so slowly that it seems that way. The rate is different for each of us, though." Suddenly, she was confused then had a blank expression for a few seconds. "Uh, sorry, did you say you are a rat?"

Maidservant picked up the lamp and took Cythe's hand, leading her as a mother would a child. "Time for bed. Big day tomorrow."

SIXTEEN

THE BOOK OF MAIDSERVANT: DESOLATION

MAIDSERVANT SAT AT THE MAZE OUTLOOK staring down at Eao City under the same moon that illuminated it last night when she and Cythe walked home from the Priest Naming. Dejected and emotionally wrung out, she recalled the whirlwind of events that occurred since then.

She had tucked Cythe into bed with Aria and crawled into her usual place between them, but stayed above the covers because she did not want to undress. For a while, she wondered how it would feel entombed while everyone else continued his or her lives, then she remembered Samus Thoth's first sleep. It had seemed one night's sleep to him, not five years. It didn't sound too bad unless you left behind friends, family or loved ones who had normal life spans. That's when it finally hit her. Cythe kept trying to tell her, but she didn't really feel it until now. They were leaving her, would be young forever, and she was the friend left behind.

She smirked. At least, that's what they thought. If her master kept his word, they were going to be so surprised when they found out they owed their lives to her. Guilt washed over her, making her frown. Surely, they would understand she couldn't have done anything else, wouldn't they?

Craning her head up, she felt relieved that faint light showed through the shutters already. She eased out of bed and took a last look back, glad she would not have to see them again before they left. She started to go change clothes because DoSo and Kore would yell if she was dirty again then realized they would yell for not cleaning the kitchens, anyway. She took off her sandals, ran to the avenue and on to work.

At mid-morning, the Head Priest sent for her, and she assumed it was to perform some menial cleaning task. Strangely, the Scholars were not on duty, so she set the basket of rags and sponges down and peeked into the main room.

Backs to her, Leto, Aria and Cythe stood across the table from Rhea, who waved her inside. Leto glared so fiercely that she thought she had misunderstood. Then Rhea said, "Come stand beside me, Maidservant."

Leto blurted, "There's no precedent for this! The Council…"

"Can lump it," Rhea finished for her. "You know, Leto, there are times a Head Priest simply needs people to shut their yaps and not make a fuss. Cythe, Aria, I assume you have no problem with your friend witnessing your Initiation?"

Leto was more hardheaded than usual. "You should not allow her to see this. I don't understand why you keep favoring her, of all people."

Rhea replied so sharply the three girls jumped. "Shut up! I'll attend to her afterward so you are making a fuss for nothing. Understood?"

Leto nodded, but clearly did not agree.

Rhea motioned Aria to come around the table then took her head in hands and stared into her eyes. "Don't just stand there fuming, Leto, bring the wine."

Tight-jawed, Leto set two bowls in front of Rhea, who popped open her ring and carefully emptied half the compartment's contents into one of them. Leto swirled the bowl and presented it to Aria. "Drink all of it."

Rhea intoned, "Welcome, Initiate, to the Garden of Light. Welcome, Initiate, to the Path of Right. Your father and mother would be proud of you. You should have allowed me to invite them."

Aria shook her head, set the empty bowl down and went back to her place.

Rhea motioned Cythe to her and stared into her eyes so long that Leto had concerns. "Is something wrong?"

Rhea released Cythe and turned her ring over the bowl, but when Leto reached for it, she pushed her hands away. "I've had enough attitude. I'll do it myself."

Leto backed away and stared at Maidservant, obviously blaming her for the dressing-down, unnerving the girl to the point she only remotely heard Rhea. "Initiates, you may have a few minutes for goodbyes with your friend."

Cythe clung to her. "I'll miss you all my life."

Aria hugged them both. "You'll be in my heart forever."

Maidservant uttered not a word, more relieved seeing Leto leave the room than concerned about her friends following her. She would not let herself think about them, rendering her emotionally numb. That is why it took so long to notice Rhea holding the open ring out for her to see. It was still half-full of blood.

Rhea criticized. "I'm disappointed you didn't try to stop me giving Cythe more elixir, Maidservant. She already has more energy than she can manage, but you knew that, because if she's the moon, you're the sun."

She tried to run away, but Rhea said words that kept her legs from moving.

"In fact, you have so much energy that it should be consuming you like wildfire in dry brush since no one is sustaining you. How is that possible? Who gave it to you?"

Shrill noise assaulted Maidservant, and she put hands over her ears, but it was inside her head. It hurt, and she could think of nothing but wanting it to stop. Suddenly, it did.

Rhea slumped in the big chair, perspiration streaming down her face. "You don't have a clue what you just did, do you?"

Maidservant, more concerned for the Head Priest's well-being than her own, shook her head.

Rhea fast-spoke an ancient passage to force Maidservant to stop fighting her magic. It was her strongest ability. It had never failed---until now. Her breath came in heavy gasps. "It's for your own good."

Maidservant assisted her to sit up straight and stuffed pillows next to her for support. Then she went to the other side of the table. "I'm unworthy of your help, Head Priest."

"How about you just tell me where you got the elixir? I promise no one else need know."

Maidservant told her everything she remembered about falling in the water, the woman in the tomb and finding the medicine on the wall.

"Did this strange woman have a name?"

"She said she was not Kalli, but I think she was."

"You've described her exactly, but hundreds of Priests witnessed her passing and it was felt all over the world by everyone with powerful abilities."

"I still think she was Kalli."

Rhea stared at Maidservant for long seconds. "Have you encountered her since then?"

Maidservant replied in her most forthright manner. "No, Head Priest."

"That was a lie, wasn't it?"

Guilt showed plainly on her face. "Maybe."

Rhea responded with power that pushed Maidservant back several steps. "Perhaps I should just kill you."

Maidservant went slowly to her knees and clasped hands against her chest. "That may be best, I think."

"You're supposed to be terribly afraid and blurt out all your secrets, not agree with me."

"I'm sorry."

Rhea sighed. "When you first came to the Temple, I watched you every morning from my bedroom balcony. You were such an odd little thing, seldom speaking, darting out of everyone's way and bowing all the time. Then you began veering off walks and hopping suddenly for no apparent reason when you took the main way to and from the kitchens. You spilled food and wine and broke more than a few cups and plates. People laughed and ridiculed you, but you kept doing it. I thought you had an aberration or simply wanted attention. Then I went to look closer at the walk. When I came back to my room, I cried. It takes a lot to make me cry."

Maidservant looked most wretched. "I know it's silly to most people, but if I can avoid stepping on little creatures, I do it. They have a right to live, too. Fortunately, they migrated away from the walk."

Rhea smiled, remembering Leto's consternation when she ordered sweet water and crumbs sprinkled around the shrubs and trees every night to entice the ants to relocate. "Kalli teaches that the humblest acts of kindness are the best measures of worth, especially when they cause one hardship. I regret that so many misguided idiots felt entitled to pick on you. I expelled several Prospects and demoted a few Scholars before it stopped. Get up off your knees, please."

"You're not going to kill me?"

"Not today. Tell me why you're so glum."

Maidservant stood. "Cythe has always been good to me, and I was mean to her because I was afraid. I didn't even say anything when she left."

"How were you mean to her?"

"I can't say."

"What were you afraid of?"

"Everything."

After a long minute, she said, "Skedaddle back to work, Maidservant. I'll tell Leto that I made you forget the ceremony. Oh, please take a bath and put on clean clothes before you come to work tomorrow. You smell almost bad as she does."

Maidservant did not go to work but directly home, the loss of Cythe and Aria made worse by knowledge that soon Rhea would die, too. She did not know why, but now she could tell how sick the Head Priest really was. She plodded through the House of Kalli and out the back door through the maze to the Eao outlook.

***

IT WAS LATE WHEN MAIDSERVANT RETURNED to the House of Kalli and discovered Seydi stretched out next to the canal reading by torchlight. "Where have you been?"

"I had things on my mind and went to the outlook to think."

She jumped off the bench. "I don't want to hear about your stupid problems. Come, help me prepare for bed."

After setting out oils, perfumes and soaps, Maidservant helped Seydi undress then removed her wig and placed it on a stand. She scrubbed off the makeup and started to apply a special ointment to moisturize the skin, but

Seydi waved her away then stared over her shoulder using a hand mirror. "Am I attractive without my face painted, do you think?"

Maidservant had two dilemmas. She could not bear looking at Seydi's unmade face and anytime Seydi asked for her opinion, she usually ended up punished for answering wrong, so she chose words carefully. "You're beautiful either way, Mistress."

Seydi jumped up and put her face a few inches from Maidservant's. "Boo!"

Maidservant stumbled backwards, terrified. "Please, Mistress, stop."

Seydi laughed. "Maybe you can't look at me because I'm so beautiful and you're so ugly. That's right, isn't it?"

Maidservant nodded tiredly. "I guess, Mistress."

Seydi sat in the chair. "My head itches. Shave the stubble."

Maidservant hurried to the wardrobe, took out a leather box and removed two exceptionally sharp barber's knives. Using the smaller one, she expertly whisked away fuzz.

Seydi eyed her. "Your master visited here last night. Says you weren't in your bed again, but don't fret. You're his little darling now so he isn't angry, but, if I was you, I'd stay in my bed from now on. He's not one to trifle with. I thought he was, but he definitely isn't."

Maidservant was not sure how to deal with this Seydi. She acted as if they were confidants. "Uh, I already planned to stay in my room starting tonight."

"Wasting my time trying to be nice to you. Not even a thank you."

"Thank you, Mistress. You're always good to me."

"I try, but you make it hard. Still, it is better that we are friends now."

Maidservant scarcely breathed while rubbing scents and oils into Seydi's scalp. Then she knelt on the floor, dabbed water on her feet and legs and gently fanned soft cloths to cool them. She glanced up frequently, concerned she might be attacked, but Seydi appeared to be dozing until she mumbled, "Neck and shoulders, too, please."

Seydi never said please to her. Maidservant's heart missed a beat then she could not make her hands stop trembling while she put fragrance in a bowl of water and patted Seydi's neck and shoulders with a sponge. "Should I do your face, Mistress?"

"Umm, not tonight, thank you."

Maidservant tasted fear. "Are you ready for bed, Mistress? Should I prepare it for you?"

"Yes, that would be very nice."

Biting her lip so hard she had to swallow blood, Maidservant fluffed and smoothed the bed pad so it would not leave marks on Seydi's delicate skin then spritzed with scent and fanned to make it cooler.

Seydi spoke in a quiet, lazy way. "Do you think Envoy is a pig?"

Maidservant's throat constricted so she could hardly breathe. "I believe everyone regards him highly."

Seydi smiled, coy and pretty as a young girl could possibly be. "Not San-zeus. Calls him a pig all the time. Many others don't like him, either. However, I don't think he's a pig, even if he likes you more than he likes me. Why is that, do you think?"

Maidservant dared not answer.

Seydi stood out of the chair onto toes graceful as a dancer. She shrugged out of the robe and pirouetted naked around Maidservant. "I mean, look at me. Have you ever seen anyone else so finely constructed and proportioned? Such fine skin? So much allure?"

Maidservant wished she had the nerve to say Cythe. "No one, Mistress."

She wore an exaggerated pout. "How do you explain your boyfriend then?"

"I don't have a boyfriend, Mistress."

She twisted around, trying to look at her backside over her shoulder. "What do you have that I don't? Has my butt gotten too big, do you think? Could that be it?"

"Mistress, it is perfection."

"Then why does he want you!" she screamed then continued in the same calm, measured way. "I bet you discovered an exotic love-making spell in those dusty old scrolls and tablets you read all the time. Did you conjure a love enchantment that night with him on the ship? You can share your wicked little secrets with me. I won't tell anyone."

Maidservant blushed from the top of her head to the tips of her toes. "I don't know love-making secrets, and even if I did, I would never use them to trick him."

She twirled around Maidservant, stopped abruptly and poked a finger into her chest. "Yet, the high and mighty Tesi-Ra thinks you can get information from him that I can't. Hmm, you do have nice hair, but most of the time, it looks as if rats nest in it. Don't dare repeat it, but I'll even admit your ugly face has some potential." She laughed hysterically. "But you are not put together well enough to raise a man's desire, and you have less personality than a three-day-old mashed scarab. Yet, Envoy wants you. You know, maybe I was wrong. Given that he has such erroneous predilections, perhaps he really is a pig; but then, what does that make you? Oh, it's so obvious. You're pigs' slop!"

Seydi danced around her yelling pigs' slop repeatedly, and Maidservant was afraid to move. Then Seydi hugged her. "Oh, I've insulted you, haven't I? Please don't tell Tesi-Ra that I mistreated his little pet because he will be ever so angry after he ordered me to step aside and allow you to perform the conquest of the pig. Even ordered me to help you. So come, sit in the chair and let me attend you, Mistress."

Maidservant was too terrified to sit so Seydi shoved her down, took the sponge and dabbed water on her legs. "Mistress, did I mention that I saw you in Main Court today talking to the one who you insist is not a pig? Well, he stared after you a long time when you left. I think he likes you. Do you like him, too?"

Maidservant was surprised to find she was more angry than afraid. "Leave me alone."

"I just asked an innocent question. Do you like him?"

"He's nice to me."

"How precious. I suppose you know that he and San-zeus sail tomorrow with that ridiculous Daedalus to the northern islands for some bothersome reason."

"He asked me to see him off, but I told him no."

"Oh, but you must go." She placed a finger across Maidservant's lips to stop the reply. "After all, you can't take chances his mind wanders while visiting exotic lands, but your looks are a challenge." She backed away, tapping her chin with a finger. "What to do, what to do? Oh! I know! Your pretty hair is inharmonious with the ugly rest of you. I'll get the knives."

Maidservant jumped out of the chair. "No, Mistress, not my hair! Please, I'll do anything!"

Seydi pointed a finger and hissed. "My sweet little sister had best get her sweet little bottom back in the chair if she knows what's good for her sweet little neck."

***

SAN-ZEUS PACED AND FUMED at the bottom of the gangway, glancing frequently at Seydi and Envoy talking farther down the jetty. His irritation had ratcheted up because he should be able to hear them but could not for some reason. Perched on bales of cotton, Daedalus stared glumly into the harbor thinking about his destroyed ships and his irritation with the Head Priest. Two Senior Initiates, Hera and Didion, excited about their first trip off the island since joining the Temple, were on the boat deck, amused how upset San-zeus was about Envoy and Seydi being together.

Meanwhile, Envoy frowned. "But she seemed perfectly well yesterday when I spoke with her."

Seydi took his and. "One minute she's fine, the next she goes crazy and shaves her head for no reason. I shudder to think what she would have done had I not worried her friends leaving might upset her. Just considering the possibilities makes me lightheaded." She swooned into his arms.

Envoy kissed her hard on the lips then pulled her standing. "When I return, we should have dinner."

Pleasantly surprised, she looked toward the ship and sighed. "I will count the days until your return, but I suppose I must go say goodbye to that bothersome San-zeus now."

Envoy walked her to San-zeus then boarded and signaled the captain to cast off. San-zeus had to run and leap onto the vessel. He started after Envoy to give him a piece of his mind then noticed Seydi stamping feet, turning circles and shaking fists at the ground. He shouted, but the dock noise was too much for her to hear.

Envoy, on his way to the bow to pilot out of the harbor, called back to him. "Haven't you heard? She's prone to the same fits as her maid. Mind that you don't catch them."

Hariset had just concluded breakfast with three Senior Scholars in his secluded garden. Now, they would do anything he wanted, and all it cost were promises of position and wealth, because he told them Pharaoh planned to overthrow the Keftiu Empire. He picked up the documents they brought him and threw them on the ground. He needed nothing from them other than continuing to disrupt activities at the Temple.

Seydi rounded the corner and marched resolutely to the table. Irritated by the interruption, he waved her away. She jabbed a finger at the ground. Hariset's face clouded with annoyance then he mumbled a few words and her shadow reappeared. "I told you to leave him to the girl. Now get out of here and stop wasting my time."

Seydi kicked the heavy table so hard she knocked over drinks and broke two toes. Cursing and wincing, she hobbled away. Hariset salted her wounded pride with laughter.

SEVENTEEN

THE BOOK OF MAIDSERVANT: OTHER TIMES, OTHER PLACES

MAIDSERVANT STARED IN THE MIRROR at her shiny, shaved head. Could there be an uglier, more pathetic creature in the world? How could she face anyone this way? Seydi had said the words to make her forget, but they did not work this time; in fact, it was as if a door in her mind opened because she remembered every instance of Seydi mistreating her. She shouted the vilest Egyptian curse she knew, crashed the mirror into a corner and stormed into the big room to run off her anger.

She had gone nonstop for two hours, streaking naked through light and darkness, pivoting precisely at corners and leaping far as she could then swimming across the canal with a few strong strokes. Practically leaping out of the water, she was back to full speed in a few strides. She did everything with eyes closed now, fast-speaking her favorite romantic stories in original languages in time with the rhythmic padding of her bare feet. At the same time, her exquisite mind counted steps, keeping track of her exact location. Tonight, however, something different occurred. Passages from the Book of Thoth intruded her recitations until she gave in and recited them, thinking they would then go away.

She had said it hundreds of times trying unlock its power with nothing happening, but when she reached the section about Great Seth and King Ramond, she was there, seeing every vivid detail through the eyes of one of Ramond's warriors at the base of the hill. Moreover, she had his memories, experienced his fear and tasted the dust in his mouth as the great southern army approached; yet, at the same time, she ran, jumped and swam around the big room. It was frightening. It was exhilarating.

Great Seth appeared astride a monstrous horse with snapping maw and grasping claws in place of hooves. Sensing something amiss, his gaze locked upon her warrior. They both fought to keep Seth from taking possession of their life forces, but his attack was partly conquest, partly seduction that turned resistance to longing. Meanwhile, in the House of Kalli, Maidservant reached the canal, leaped and stretched into another dive, but this time, she crashed to the floor on the other side.

Moaning, she rolled onto her back and examined to see if anything was broken. Her wrist was badly sprained. Her bloody nose felt intact. She had a big egg on her forehead and a very sore chest.

She did not realize she was in the black area until green light from the empty pedestal filled the room suddenly. Grimacing, she pushed up with her elbows to sit. All the openings except the one over the bridge had closed. Otherwise, everything was the same. She managed to stand and, gripping the throbbing wrist, wobbled to the corner. Glowing white Eirycian text floated on the front of the pedestal.

Need to hide where no one can reach, escape certain doom?
Create a place no one can breach, create a tomb.
Stand on red, face the bull.
Four times say dead, four times say cruel.

Hurry onto the bridge fast as you can
Or your bones will be ground to sand.
Be prepared to sleep long
Or you will die, despairing and alone.

"Create a tomb? I don't think so, thank you very much." The light went out and she hobbled to the bridge where she was not surprised to find the woman waiting. "Why do you keep bothering me?"

"Ah, you remember, do you?"

"It's all mixed up in my head, but I know you tried to kill me."

The woman healed her then held out the spare tunic from a small chest in her room and the Cythe-made sandals from under the bed. She acted as if it was perfectly natural she could produce them from thin air. "Why are you running around with no clothes on? It is very off-putting as you're all skin and bones."

Maidservant glared. "Who said you could take my stuff?"

"Has a bald head become the new fashion or have you begun wearing those dreadful Egyptian wigs? Or is it because persistent parasites infested your hair and you had to shave it off? Whatever, you should learn to do it properly without cutting the scalp."

Maidservant grabbed the clothes from her. "I'm fed up with everyone messing with me. Especially you."

"Well, aren't you a snooty little Miss Sunshine?"

Maidservant started to curse her but had sudden recollection of the giant cat creeping up behind her, which made her even angrier because she could tell the woman caused her to think about it. "Leave me alone!"

"Have you, by any chance, recalled anything more about your previous life? Anything at all?"

"I wouldn't tell you if I had!"

Her demeanor hardened. "Then let's discuss how the spying and betraying your friends is going. You realize they're going to die, don't you?"

"Go climb back into your hole in the ground. I can't do anything to stop it." She started to walk away, but the room spun, blurred and dissolved, leaving her alone in a place of unending grayness with no up, down or anything. She took a tentative step and plunged downward into nothingness.

***

MAIDSERVANT KNEW IT WAS PREDAWN before she opened her eyes in another place, another time. Tired and sleepy, she yawned and looked up at the dazzling dome of stars stretched over the sacred land of the Horutep. A cool breeze carried familiar night smells and noises up to her from the ground far below. She felt at peace and proud of her ascension in rank, because she was also Raiku, a newly appointed Chief Cleric, honored to stand at summer solstice atop Benben Tower in the holy City of Pillars to greet the sun god when he blessed the land with the light of a new day. She brushed long fragrant hair from her face and mouthed a prayer to create harmony amongst gods, earth, heavens and people.

To her right, an incense lamp illuminated three clerics. She nodded and they began the ceremony, pointing to the glorious river of stars across the sky and chanting how the great river, the Life-Giver, mirrored its course across the homeland of the Horutep. Then they sang praises to the new god whose fabulous statue on the Plain of Monuments priests were dedicating this very morning by announcing his name to the people.

Raiku wished she could be on hand for such an auspicious occasion, but politics and rank required her presence here. As ceremony required, she turned and bowed to the holy Benben, a large pyramidal stone set on the very pinnacle of the tower just above her head, and Maidservant shared her awe of it. She also shared knowledge of old texts that claimed the unknown writing on its faces were holy messages from an ancient race called the Shining Ones, who existed even before the long ago Time of Myths. Once, the Horutep believed a former god named Kalli had given it to the people, but the new religion taught Kalli had practiced deception and ancestors of the Horutep took it back after she stole it.

Someone took Raiku's left hand. Surprised, she turned and gazed upon a wondrous woman with alabaster skin, white-blond hair and crystal green eyes.

Raiku trembled, for this was a god, and not just any god, but Kalli, if she believed the secret ancient drawings and documents available to privileged Clerics. They related how Kalli would return for retribution if the Horutep betrayed promises to follow her teachings. Of course, no one believed such a ridiculous story. Raiku had even laughed and made jokes. Now, however, she knew the truth and was powerless to resist, remaining hand-in-hand with Kalli until the rim of the eastern sky tinged rose.

Instantly, they were high in the sky speeding toward the western horizon. Sunlight, streaming across the land, overtook them from behind. As they passed over the Life-Giver, fishermen shouted prayers to them. The three golden pyramids, stars on earth, appeared over the horizon. Then they were over the Plain of Monuments, filled with people multitudinous, temples lofty and monuments magnificent, all awash in glorious golden light.

They stood between the stretched-out front legs of the silver-clad lion god, golden pyramids and temples reflected across its surface. Tremendously excited, Maidservant made the terrified Raiku speak. "Lady, I know this place, but not like this. Has Egypt become so grand since I left it?"

Shocked that Maidservant could make herself heard, Kalli replied, "You see as it was, girl, not as it is in your time. Now, be silent and give sway to the Chief Cleric. You are here to watch and learn, not participate."

Maidservant could not hold it in. "Only gods could have created such wonders!"

Kalli glared. "Men build structures. Some appear wondrous for a time. Then men destroy them. So ever has it been. So ever will it be."

Maidservant persisted. "How could mere men achieve all this?"

"I repeat, hold your tongue. Observe the fate of Raiku and her people and learn, for learn you must."

Time slipped. A procession of holy men paraded by. The leader brandished an ornate silver staff while the others clapped hands every other step and chanted warnings about the powers of the new god. Following in line, ten somnolent maidens in long white robes and wooden wigs painted silver carried cushions bearing curved, long-bladed knives.

Raiku looked up at the great lion's silver face and began a prayer of sacrifice, but Maidservant fought through her suffocating pride and reverence. "Must you have their blood, O Great One? Please, spare them."

Kalli grabbed the horrified Raiku and shouted into her face. "Are you stupid, girl, or do you simply seek to provoke me? That pile of rocks is not a god."

Maidservant's emotions were raw. "I'm sick and tired being called stupid. I know this story and gods are in it!"

Kalli threw Raiku against the statue, knocking the breath out of her. "Give this priest her mind back before I forget myself and kill you both. This existed ten thousand years before you were born, more time than your puny mind can grasp, so stop playing the fool and saying you know about it."

Maidservant twisted Raiku's face into defiance. "You should have said ten thousand season-cycles as would the Horutep, formerly known as the Obsi and, before that, the Mud Men. They built all these monuments to appease a god---you, Kalli. Samus, son of Thoth, oversaw construction after you abandoned them and made him a god in your place, so why do you persist standing here lying to my face?"

Astounded, Kalli gawked.

Maidservant put Raiku's hands on her hips and filled her voice with sarcasm. "Better close your mouth before I put a big juicy fly in it."

Kalli slammed Raiku to the ground and stood over her. "Other than me, only an evil creation of the One Master could know this story. I do not understand how you withstood my elixir and scrutiny, but your careless mouth has betrayed you. Use all your power to fight, though it will do little to delay your death!"

Raiku could scarcely breathe as crushing pressure on her increased. Something broke in her side and forced sorrowful tears from her eyes. More bones cracked. She began blacking out. Maidservant experienced the same. Both screamed.

***

MAIDSERVANT WAS ON HER BACK on the bridge in the House of Kalli holding her chest and gasping. The woman stood over her. "Why didn't you resist Kalli?"

"I did, not that anyone could tell."

The woman hesitated then knelt and put a hand on the injuries one after another. "Move your hands. Move them, I said. Stop being such a baby."

Healed, Maidservant twisted up to her feet. "You probably expect me to thank you for not mashing and breaking me anymore! Well, you can lick my dirty feet! You can lick Raiku's dirty feet, too! What gives you the right to treat people this way?"

"What are you ranting at me for? Kalli did this to you."

Maidservant looked at her askance. "Yeah, right. Go to hell."

The woman thrust a cup of wine into her hands. "This will help you feel better. Tell me, if you didn't learn those things from the Corruption, how can you possibly know them?"

Maidservant stared at the wine before taking a small sip then big gulps, emptying it. She wiped her mouth with the back of her hand and held it out for refilling. "You won't believe me, so what's the point?"

"I'll be the judge of that."

She downed a second cup, savoring the fuzzy feeling it made in her head. "Remember what I told you about my Master catching me in Pharaoh's Library? Well, he had long sought information about you from the scribes, but they..."

"You mean he sought information about Kalli, who died a long time ago. This is now. Remember?"

"Sure looked and sounded like you."

"It wasn't."

Maidservant downed half the wine. "Oh, suit yourself. The scribes insisted they never heard of Kalli, and my master couldn't use his power to break in because his master would know, so he arranged to have Mistress Seydi tutored in the Library to get me inside because I knew all the secret areas."

"You drink too much," the woman said, filling the cup. "How do you explain your familiarity with the place if your other life wasn't real?"

The question annoyed her. "I don't waste time thinking about that anymore, so please stop asking. Anyway, the Nile flood set a record that year, catching everyone by surprise, and the scribes and staff worked like crazy moving scrolls and documents out of basements. The secret areas were left guarded by a single captain, a famous hero, but Mistress Seydi can make people do things for her even if it might get them killed."

"So you and your mistress worked together to steal the documents?"

"Never would I work with her! I hate her! She...she's..." Maidservant screamed. "Go away! Leave me alone!"

The woman grabbed her arms. "Forget I asked about her, forget it." After a moment, she released her. "What did you find?"

She explained about the documents and what she kept for herself.

"You expect me to believe some unknown scribe unlocked the power of the Shining Ones then sealed it up again rather than using it?"

Maidservant shook her head. "He only deduced the meanings of a few symbols. He never understood that some had several meanings while others were markers or existed only to confuse. It was extremely difficult to figure out, let me tell you."

The woman regarded her critically. "I have enough problems believing that scrawny body of yours jumped over the canal, and now you claim to have accomplished something the smartest people who ever lived failed to do."

"Told you I have a gift, didn't I?"

She was skeptical. "Why didn't your master see through your deception if he's as powerful as you say?"

"He considers me so useless and weak that he hardly ever glances my way. In fact, he was so surprised when I gave him the damaged documents that he had fabric bought for me to make a new dress. Mistress Seydi burned it, though."

"Let's return to the subject, shall we? Was there uproar when the scribes discovered the storage areas had been violated?"

She shook her head. "I resealed the jars, remade labels and rubbed them with root pigments to look old. Then I sneaked the documents into a public room and hid them where my master could retrieve them. His position as an advisor to Pharaoh exempted him from searches."

"How did you move piles of documents inside the library without being discovered, and how did you get the ones you kept out?"

"I stole a cart and pushed it around picking up trash, work relegated to lowest level female slaves like me. Smuggling them out was easy. Mistress Seydi made the captain of the guard carry her study bag when they left together. I packed and unpacked it for her."

The woman shook her head. "I still can't believe you can read them. Will you recite some of it and tell me what it means?"

She was glad the woman had not asked how much she could recite. She selected a passage and made intentional mistakes when she said it.

"You know it that well? I'm surprised."

"Only because I liked that part and read it so many times."

"Do you feel anything when you say it?"

"I do not become powerful and full of magic, if that's what you mean. Although tonight, while running, when I recited the Seth and Ramond parts, suddenly I was there. Then Seth tried to possess a warrior through whose eyes I watched. That's why I hit the floor so hard. I had my eyes closed as you said. Does any of that make sense to you?"

The woman stared in wonder. "You can put your life spirit into a story but can't use the power of the words? I have never come across such a thing before. What did you do with the documents?"

"I burned them."

The woman grabbed her by the chin and peered into her eyes. "Did you really destroy all the stuff you kept from your master?"

"Yes."

She grabbed Maidservant's hands. "Close your eyes and don't open them until I let go or you'll die. Close them!"

Heart pounding, Maidservant squeezed her eyes shut and experienced falling into nothingness again.

***

Freezing cold, she could not get her eyes focused because dreary, diffused light and layers of thick frost glazed every surface, distorting perspective into a flat sameness. She squinted and blinked until her dry eyes adjusted then gasped at the size of the cylindrical passageway they were in. At least three hundred feet in diameter with massive X-shaped struts at precise intervals, it continued out of sight before and behind them. The floor was made of the same white tiles as the avenues on Kalliste, only bigger. Tall dark doorways lined the sides, again at equally spaced distances. The exactitude and symmetry made her strangely uneasy.

The cold was unrelenting. She hugged arms to her body and blew on her hands while looking around. She turned to the woman for help, only to see her limping away down the corridor. "Wait for me!"

She kept going. "We came in the wrong place and don't have much time."

Though the woman did not appear to hurry, Maidservant could not catch up. Her feet and legs lost feeling. Her hands and face burned with cold. She became addled and could no longer focus on the bare footprints in the frost.

Next she knew, arms guided her to sit as heat spread through her. Her backside was steamy wet. Then she could think again. The woman held her leaning in her lap. She pulled away and the cold attacked again. "I think you enjoy hurting me!"

"Had to see if you could do even the simplest things. Apparently not. Whatever did they do to make you so helpless?"

"What are you talking about?"

She shrugged. "Try to think of desert or anything else warm while fast-speaking the passage you memorized. With practice, you can recite in the back of your mind while doing other things. Even you should be able to do that much."

"I'm not doing it. It's probably just a trick to set me on fire."

"Then you'll have to hold onto me to stay warm." She led her to a solitary emerald floor tile and brushed ice off it with her toes. "Don't just stand there, help."

Maidservant scraped with the edge of her sandal until they had most of it cleared. "Why is this one green?"

"The colored ones are called platforms. Each corridor has a different color." She took her by the shoulders, positioned her on the tile facing down the corridor then stood in front and crouched. "Put your hands on my hips and do the same as me."

It looked ridiculous and Maidservant only made a token effort.

The woman spun around, kicked her ankles apart and pushed her down. She resumed her position and leaned forward. Ridges came out of the tile against the outsides of their feet and the platform began moving. Very quickly, they moved at tremendous speed, a glowing green tail of tiles behind them, furthermost fading back to white. Wind whipped them. Struts whooshed by. Ten minutes passed. "Blue corridor coming up! Lean with me in the turn!"

She glimpsed a blue light overhead then held on for dear life and squealed, certain she was about to go flying off, but the platform came half out of the floor sideways, allowing her to keep her feet planted. Then it turned blue.

The blue corridor was half as huge as the green one. Monotony set in as more than thirty minutes passed before the woman leaned back and brought them to a long, gliding stop. When they stepped off, the ridges slid back into the surface and frost glazed it instantly.

Faraway, crashing and wrenching noises reverberated then whooshing sounds followed by silence. The woman gestured around them. "When a section of corridor collapses, it is automatically sealed away from the rest of the building. Don't worry, it is reasonably safe." She pointed to a doorway on the right. A big blue square with gold symbols shined next to it. "Can you read it?"

"Seven thousand and two, B."

The woman attempted casual small talk as they walked. "Kalli used to zip through these corridors to see how fast she could go. Flew off once and slammed into a strut about twenty feet off the floor. Can you imagine how fast she had to be moving?"

Maidservant had heavy foreboding. "She came here a lot, did she?"

"Part of her was born here."

"What does that mean?"

"Think of it his way---you woke up in a cupboard in your master's house as daughter of his cook with memories of a previous life. Well, Kalli woke up in the Great Wheel of Nun, which is the name of this place, aware that she was Guardian of the legacy of the Eirycians, yet she retained vivid memories as a shaman's daughter."

The woman stopped at a blue platform segmented into four squares. She directed Maidservant onto one, she stood on another. They separated from the others. "The only way to enter rooms is riding a small platform. You can go into any of the rooms, but this is the only one I know that works."

When they crossed the threshold, lights illuminated across the ceiling and heat filled the room. They went to a line of waist-high pedestals along the back wall and the woman pressed buttons on one of them. A big square of light appeared on the wall and filled with a language unknown to Maidservant. The woman pressed another button. A second square appeared next to it with Egyptian symbols. "Nun's purpose is to record stories about people who changed history. All written languages are stored here, too. Choose one and it can be translated into any other you choose." She glanced at Maidservant, absorbed reading the story on the wall. "Are you listening?"

She nodded absently.

The woman took a deep breath. "The Wheel of Nun existed long before the Eirycians discovered it and figured out how to store power in a secret language." She touched a button and ancient Eirycian filled all four walls floor-to-ceiling. "These are the passages Kalli recited to create her spells. I want you to memorize as much as you can. If you don't like these stories, you can translate stories from other languages into the Eirycian words of power and learn them."

Finally, Maidservant understood and backed away, shaking her head.

"Some stories are only a few paragraphs. Others are several chapters or an entire book. Stories recorded in the words and thoughts of the subject are rarest and most powerful, so concentrate learning that type. Usually, you can't access stories in process, but there are exceptions. Ironically, the oldest story in this room is the Book of Thoth. Events prior to that are probably in the previous numbered room, but that is only speculation. The rooms after this one are unnumbered and empty, no equipment or anything."

Maidservant dropped to her knees. "This is everything my master seeks, absolutely everything. Are you planning to abandon me alone in this awful place? Is that why you're showing me all this?"

"You said in your other life you shared a soul with your twin sister?"

"Yes, but what does that have to do with this?"

"And you loved her, really loved her?"

"Half my heart still belongs to her."

"Then tell me her name."

"I can't remember it."

"Are you so certain you even had a sister? Perhaps, she's simply another fiction they created for you to hide behind."

Maidservant shook her head. "She was real and same as me."

"Are you sure? Maybe both girls you remember were you."

"No, and we were good girls, both of us."

"What was your name?"

Immediately, her expression blanked. "They said I'm nobody, will always be nobody and will never have a real name again. Someone else said I'm Maidservant, will always be Maidservant, and Maidservant is nobody." She began banging her head against a pedestal.

"Yet, you want to join them, don't you? You think your master will help you rise in rank and make you rich and powerful."

She shook her head. "I will always be least in any room with other people in it."

The woman dragged her up by the collar, saw guilt on her face and threw her across the room. "You're lying."

Maidservant jumped on a platform and rode it out the doorway but stopped just beyond the threshold. So much space, nowhere to hide. She went back into the room. "What of it? He says I can have my friends with me. They'll be safe and we'll spend the rest of our lives together."

"Darkness will corrupt you and everyone will suffer, which brings us full circle. Now, to answer your question: I'm not going to leave you here, but when you long sleep, you will find the way back often as you want."

Maidservant shook her head. "No one is ever going to put me in the ground alive, and I'll never come back here. If you think I will, you're crazier than I am."

"Unless you regenerate, the energy in you will burn through your sanity. To regenerate, you must long sleep."

Maidservant sagged to the floor. "Then I will die insane."

The woman started to comment more about it then reconsidered. "Kalli's Plan depends on fulfilling certain tasks. The seer said that person would pass the Final Test of Kalli, and here you are."

"I assumed it must be something like that, but if you think I'm the one to save your world then your world won't be saved. I don't care who wins. It's like the Mud Men said: it sounds like bogeymen and demons you're talking about, not real people."

"Yeah, it does. Have you ever seen any? Close your eyes and think seriously about it, why don't you?"

Maidservant got up slowly, went to the threshold and stared silently into the corridor.

They turned a corner and the platform changed to yellow. The woman looked back over her shoulder and spoke the first words since the blue room. "We'll be in the hub shortly. I'll show you the Shining Ones before we leave."

They entered an ancient ruined city under a black dome made to appear as night sky. She stopped in what once had been a market square. Four life-sized statues of a man, woman, boy and girl wearing odd-looking pants, boots and long jackets stood in a line holding hands and staring up into the dome where the man pointed.

Maidservant was surprised, but remembered not to mention gods. "They're so ordinary. I thought they would be giants gazing down at us."

The woman led to a panel on top of a podium and passed a hand over it. Chimes sounded in the dome and a blurry sphere materialized, nearly filling the entire space. She brought her hands together slowly and it became distinct blue, brown and green with shimmering gray-white patches over some parts.

Maidservant recognized it. "It is the picture on your wrist. Kalli has the same one, by the way. Quite a coincidence."

"It is the world upon which you live."

"But it is round. How is that possible?"

"Some of the stories in the blue room explain if you happen to read them, but today the lesson is history, not science. Do you see the small blue area on the right? That is the sea you sailed to Keftiu and Kalliste."

"Then what is the big sea to the side?"

"For now, concentrate on the smaller one. Below the sea is Egypt. The blue line is the Nile, or Life-Giver, depending on the age." She moved her hands and a green mass appeared on the big sea. "The land of the Eirycians before it was destroyed."

"If they had such incredible power, how is it they perished?"

"Some stories refer to sudden disaster. Others suggest they fought and destroyed themselves or lost to an invasion. Regardless, devastation was complete. It is unclear whether the One Master had anything to do with it or even existed then, but, regardless, he came to prominence in the dark times that followed and reigned unchecked until Kalli fell from the sky."

"Fell from the sky? What does that mean?"

"It is not important. Just know that either the Eirycians miscalculated or Nun malfunctioned, because by the time she opposed him, the Corruption was too entrenched and powerful to stop, in spite of many spectacular victories. Which brings us to the present."

Maidservant put a hand to her forehead. "That was thousands of years you just skimmed over."

"Which would you chose to be: a queen in a minority dedicated to keeping the rest of the world in a state of endless suffering or an average citizen in a world of relative equality and freedom?"

Maidservant thought the answer would irritate her, but she seemed to expect it. "Both sound good to me, but if I could pick, I'd be on top."

"Time to go."

They went to a small park where stood a little stone house with a blue tiled roof identical to the ones in Hidden Meadow. "What is that?"

The woman put a palm with spread fingers on the door and it opened into the wall. "A portal to another place. There are many in Nun's hub and recreation areas, but this is the only one I know that works. Remember its location so you know how to leave when you visit."

"I told you that won't happen." Maidservant followed her inside and glimpsed faded pictures of birds and trees before the tiny windows and door closed. The building hummed, vibrated and opened again. They emerged into a big u-shaped gorge full of pastel flowers growing out of tall grass. Though she had never been to this location, she recognized from the smoke they were on Kalliste just below the rim of the caldera.

The woman gestured around. "This is the Valley of Clouds. You can only get here using portals."

Maidservant had a disconcerting thought. "Are we still on the bridge with you making me imagine Nun and this place, or do they really exist? You could even make me imagine Raiku and that soldier watching Seth, huh?"

The woman gave a smug smile remindful of Leto. "You have a keen intellect, so you will figure it out soon without my help. By the way, if you transport into Eirycian stories, you suffer the same fates as people you inhabit, so be careful not to get killed." Before Maidservant could comment, she pointed to a second portal at the far end with roiling storm clouds filling the mouth of the gorge behind it. "That one takes you down the mountain."

As she looked, fast moving cloud streamers snaked through the gorge past them and out the east end. Then rushing clouds surged up and engulfed them. Deluging rain beat down. As fast as the storm came, it was gone, and so was the woman.

Ankle deep in water, Maidservant wrung out her tunic then wiped off with it before tugging it back on. She muttered, "This is real, all right. Very funny."

She splashed to the other portal and had no problem with the door. The inside was dank and moldy, but in a few seconds, she stepped out in Hidden Meadow. Noting which little house it was, she trudged up the hill past the grazing herds to the ridge and looked back. The buildings were gone, but she no longer had doubts they had been there. She lay down in warm grass and stared up at blue sky, acutely aware how inadequate she was to save the world, even if she changed her mind and tried.

EIGHTEEN

THE BOOK OF MAIDSERVANT: HARISET'S FEINT

HEAVY FOG GREETED EARLY WORKERS streaming out of Eao into the free trade area. Conversations were hushed so not to disturb sleeping neighbors, yet filled with the kind of good-natured jibes only friends of many years can utter without offense. People using the big avenue gate passed by the wharf designated for boats with special passengers and cargo. This morning, however, two large vessels with no markings had docked during the night without approval.

The Harbor Master, an officious man who took his job very seriously, asked a gathering crowd if anyone knew the whereabouts of six people assigned to nightshift just as flames erupted on the sterns of both vessels. He had a fire bell rung and designated people to form a bucket brigade. When he was satisfied everything was according to procedure, he led a party up the gangway of the nearest boat to see if anyone was onboard.

Tarpaulins flew back, revealing scores of warriors. They killed the boarding party and leaped onto the dock, killing everyone in sight. Then they swarmed into town, passed through the great horned gate and scattered, burning buildings and slaughtering anyone they encountered.

Meanwhile, in Cadi-sum harbor, another ship landed marauders different from the ones in Eao. Stealthy and efficient, they darted along dark streets toward the waterfront homes of the Council Priests, killing only when necessary until reaching their objectives.

Ordered by Hariset to be in the Watchers' room an hour before dawn, Maidservant was on her knees scrubbing the floor between the big tables when Senior Watcher Gallae on the Eao table announced ships were afire at the VIP dock. Maidservant craned her head up and witnessed Leto entering the room through the solid stone back wall. Carefully noting the spot, she crouched down and waited.

Senior Watcher Pierzi on the Cadi-sum table called out, "I have a docked ship on fire and a large force with torches gathering around your and Atlas' villas, Council Priest."

Leto hurried to the table and showed no concern her house was afire. "Use the obelisks to alert the island that we are under attack. Atlas and Selene should have these fools under control already. Where are they?" Then she called to the Eao table. "Gallae, report."

"Large numbers of workers are slain on the dock next to the burning ships, but I can't locate the raiders."

Leto rushed to the Eao table, which showed four views---one of burning ships and the others sweeping jetties and docks. She directed to show the town, where they saw numerous houses burning and gangs of warriors butchering people. Leto began a quick count of enemy, but suddenly, the picture went a-kilter and out of focus.

A hysterical Watcher had jumped from his chair. "Do something! Why isn't anyone doing anything?"

Leto mumbled an incantation and he fell unconscious. More Watchers arrived and she directed two to chairs at the Eao table. The picture righted and focused. Now, Athy, Arty and Envoy were on the avenue facing the attackers. Envoy directed his companions to use bows. Leto was dismayed. "What on earth does he think he's doing? Why isn't Athy giving the orders?"

Rhea, supported by two Watchers, appeared on the stairwell landing. "What's wrong, Leto?"

She did not look up. "Against all reason and good sense, Envoy, Athy and Arty are attacking the enemy with weapons rather than subduing them with spells."

The fastest anyone had seen Rhea move, she jumped the steps to the floor and rushed to the table. "I'm sure they have reasons."

Leto stared at her across the table with surprise. "He is unarmed and Athy and Arty do not have many arrows. They're in a hopeless situation."

Rhea took over. "Gallae, show us a close-up of the big warrior directing the others."

The view zoomed to attackers forming a rank behind shields then moved to a spindly female officer beside them giving orders while striking Athy and Arty's arrows away with a bloody saber.

Leto was flabbergasted. "How can she possibly do that?"

Quietly, Rhea ordered, "Closer, Gallae."

The warrior's leather breastplate ill-fitted and had loose and missing studs. The short-horned helm was too big and cleaved across the top so that her black hair stuck out.

Rhea said, "That is armor scavenged from someone killed in battle."

A deflected arrow struck her in the upper left arm. She flew into a rage and threw down the sword. She ripped a heavy torch post out of the ground, hoisted it over her head and broke it in two across her shoulders. After tossing the smaller piece away, she waved the other in one hand as though it weighed nothing. Then Gallae showed her contorted face with wild, reddish-black eyes and sharp-pointed teeth protruding from a bloody mouth.

Leto recoiled. "You said that the Corruption was gone from the world!"

Rhea sat down heavily in a chair brought for her. "These are mindless brutes driven by a lust for blood, which explains the burning ships. Their minders had them set afire because creatures like these are more vicious when they have no escape. Envoy, Athy and Arty understood what they're facing and knew they're not powerful enough to use magic against them. They're keeping the enemy from the townspeople until a Council Priest arrives, but it will take too long. Leto, you must go and avenge their noble sacrifices."

Maidservant was at the back wall when Rhea made the dire pronouncement. As Leto departed with most of the Watchers, she ducked down, ran back to the Eao table and hid behind a chair where Rhea could not see her watching the action.

The warriors, in a loosely formed four-by-four phalanx with swords and spears pointed between shields, waited for Envoy, running alone down the avenue toward them without weapons. The officer with the lamppost moved to meet him, but Envoy dodged past her, scooped the sword off the road and spun by a second time, cutting her throat. Then he pushed between two spears of the phalanx and shoved through the shields.

A furious melee ensued, the center two rows of the formation collapsed and Envoy, sword in either hand, emerged the other side backing away fast. In disarray, the remaining warriors went after him. Athy and Arty killed all of them with arrows before they reached him.

It had taken less than two minutes. Envoy, Athy and Arty gathered arrows and moved down the avenue to engage the next group.

Watcher Pierzi called from the Cadi-sum table. "A big force has massed around the House of Atlas."

Rhea---white-faced and visibly upset after watching Envoy---went to the other table just as a solitary figure, barely discernable in the shadows of Atlas' back garden, must have called out, because a dozen warriors rushed to attack. Dazzling spirals of lights spun out and sent them flying. Rhea sat down in another provided chair to watch.

Many of the downed warriors sprang up to attack again. More came around both sides of the house and joined them. Rhea said, "Selene cannot stand against so many." But then the attackers fell to the ground, rolling and slapping their bodies. Rhea had never seen anything like it.

Pierzi opened a close-up view of them. "They act as if they're on fire or attacked by swarms of vicious insects, but nothing is visible. It must be a spell of some kind. Look! Many have stopped moving. It is killing them. Head Priest, someone is in the shadows with Selene." The view jumped to a vague silhouette moving forward.

Rhea yelled, "Put it back on the dying attackers and give me control of the table! Now!" Then, soon as he complied, she ordered, "Take your Watchers to assist with Eao. Everyone else, help at the other tables and look for attackers on other parts of the island."

Just then, Leto's incredulous voice sounded from the Eao table. "We're moving down Eao Avenue into town. We passed several enemy dead on the road. Apparently Envoy and our Priests killed them before we began viewing them. Are they still alive?"

"Yes," Gallae answered, "and driving the raiders back toward the big gate. I suggest you take the west way to intercept them."

Meanwhile, Rhea watched Hariset move out of the shadows, pass effortlessly through Selene's spirals and take her hand. He shared power with her as they moved slowly toward the House of Atlas. Warriors thrashed to the ground and died everywhere they looked. Rhea made a clumsy attempt to shift to a close-up of their faces but only caught Selene's. Her mouth twisted terribly and her eyes were ravenous and wild.

Maidservant had scurried back to the wall when she heard Envoy was all right, but half her attention still followed the activities on the tables while she felt for the secret entrance. Then she stumbled through it, tangled her feet in a blanket Leto dropped and fell. The wall did not appear to exist from this side and she was afraid it might be gone, but she did not have time to wait or make sure, so she got up and looked around.

Except for light from the Watcher's area, it was dark, but she could see long rows of tall shelves in the distance. She hurried to them with high expectations, but they contained nothing except dust and disappointment. She forced herself to calm down and think.

Since Leto had appeared so quickly after the alarm, she must have been close to the wall. She backtracked, darting looks every direction until a glimmer of red light caught the corner of her eye, but it disappeared when she tried to look straight at it. She managed to follow it to a low arched opening and ducked through. Bright light illuminated, dazzling her and shining through the doorway across the dark room. Terrified, she looked at the Watchers and Rhea for reaction, but there was none.

She was inside a small dusty room lined with rickety shelves bent under the weight of documents so carelessly stacked that many had tumbled to the floor. Everywhere she touched, dust stirred, making her sneeze. A quick examination showed they were duplicates of lessons she had seen already, but now, her handprints were all over them. She pushed over several of the tallest stacks, causing a whole section to avalanche to the floor. Thinking how ticked off Leto would be, she grinned.

Then she examined a small bed, the only furniture in the room, set against the back wall, its rumpled bedcovers dirty and stinking. Just like Leto, she thought, with a nasty smirk. One of the legs seemed a little askew and, not really expecting anything, she squatted and turned it. A section of wall with shelves swung open, revealing another small room.

Lit by a dim overhead light, the walls were bare except for dust and smudges. A small wooden table set in the center with a single rickety chair. Haphazardly piled documents, topped by a thick bound tome with a shiny cover drew her nearer. Scrawled across the front in black Kallistian symbols was *Kalli's Tablets of Guidance*. Barely controlling her excitement, she reached for it then glimpsed red light again. She looked sidewise, moving her head back and forth, and made out a web of lines around the entire stack. She left quickly, disappointed almost to tears.

At the same time, Rhea fumed and fidgeted, waiting for Selene and Hariset to emerge from the House of Atlas. Finally, Hariset came out the back door with Seydi in his arms. Wrapped in torn bedclothes, she was bloody, bruised and battered. Rhea's first thoughts were how different she looked without a wig and that she really did wear makeup all the time, even in bed with a lover. She had thought it was a lie. Then, rather than placing Seydi carefully down as a loving father would, Hariset dumped her on the ground like a sack of grain. Surprised, Rhea laughed.

Leaving her alone in the back garden, Hariset started back to the house. An arrow struck him in the back shoulder. He faced two hulking warriors running from the side street, knocked down one and grabbed the other, twisting him apart so ferociously his body appeared to explode. The remaining warrior ran, Hariset in close pursuit.

Trying not to upchuck, Rhea glanced to see if anyone noticed her distress and found Maidservant standing across the corner from her, horrified by the scene. Quietly, she asked, "Did you know your master was so powerful?"

Maidservant nodded, then gasped and bolted toward the landing exit.

Two Watchers guarded the steps but Rhea yelled to let her pass. As soon as the door closed, she addressed the room. "No one is to know the true nature of this attack. Say it was pirates. If anyone tells you any different, bring him or her to me, please. Burn all the raiders' bodies except those in the House of Atlas. No one else is to go inside until I get there."

Atlas, strongest man in the world, was dead in the interior courtyard with thirty broken warriors around him. Rhea bade him farewell then went inside to the front of the house to see if Selene and Hariset were still outside on Atlas' private pier. They were, Hariset doing all the talking while Selene pretended to heal his wounds. Satisfied no one would interfere, she went to find the real reason she had come.

Seydi was still on the ground in the garden propped against a wall. Her nightclothes were bloody and torn, arms, legs and feet bleeding from long scratches and gouges. When she saw Rhea approaching, she scooped up handfuls of dirt and rubbed it over her head and face, something she had been doing for some time, because tears had caked mud under the eyes and around the mouth. She sobbed loudly, tried to get up and sagged back down, trembling like a frightened rabbit. "I couldn't do anything to help him, Head Priest."

Rhea pulled a bench over, put a comforting hand on her head and silently fast-spoke to relieve her anguish, but she continued grieving, unaffected. Rhea removed the hand and waited, glad for the sun finding its way through the mists to fight the chill that had been growing in her all morning.

Seydi wiped dirt away from her red eyes. "I loved him so much, Head Priest."

Rhea patted her head. "If it's not too painful, can you tell me what happened?"

"Someone lifted me from bed. I thought it was Atlas. Sometimes he...sometimes we..." She bit her lip, managing to blush in spite of the smeared makeup and dirt.

"I'm not easily embarrassed, poor thing. Please go on, tell your story, if you can."

Seydi nodded bravely. "Vile warriors carried me out of the room, but I screamed and fought until Atlas came."

"You say vile warriors as if they were beasts rather than men acting beastly. Which were they?"

Caught by surprise, Seydi stiffened. "I'm sure I don't understand what you mean, Head Priest. It was dark and confusing."

Rhea patted her shoulder then held it gently. "If you can, tell me how he died, dear girl."

"I can't talk about it. I just can't."

Rhea closed her eyes. "Allow me to speculate, then. Atlas ran out and saw you next to the fountain alone. As he approached, scores of warriors attacked from the shadows of the colonnade. He fought them in spite of being unable to summon all his great strength because of a potion given him earlier in the evening. He could have escaped but wouldn't leave you. Yet, in spite of all that, he prevailed until struck down from behind with a large stone. Just before being overcome, he looked up from the ground to see who his assailant was, and..."

Seydi jerked away from Rhea's hand and threw herself face down on the ground. "I beg you, Head Priest, leave me to my grief. Oh, Atlas, Atlas."

Rhea, though she wanted nothing more than to show her true self and kill Seydi, got up quietly. "It will get better in time, dear, but all you can do now is be thankful for your time together." She went back into the house and threw up in a corner. Then she ordered the house burned.

***

THE MEETING SPUN OUT OF RHEA'S CONTROL after she proposed that DoSo replace Atlas on the Council. She had expected quick confirmation but dozens of Priests jumped up shouting for San-zeus, and, when she tried to quieten them, more joined in until San-zeus reestablished order with a slight wave of the hand, bringing jeers aimed at the Head Priest.

San-zeus spoke in a mocking manner. "Surely, we're allowed to vote for a new Council Priest rather than having one dictated, Head Priest."

He was technically right, though custom had long been to accept the Head Priest's nomination, so Rhea swallowed her anger and allowed a vote, not thinking he had a chance. To her chagrin, he won by a narrow margin. She had no choice but to invite him to take a seat at the table, but after strutting to the stage, he turned to address the audience rather than exchanging traditional greetings with the other Council members. Holding her temper in check, Rhea gave him unbidden approval to speak to save face. "Go ahead, San-zeus, we're listening."

He walked across the stage and back, letting anticipation build while making eye contact with as many in the audience as possible. "Good friends, which is best, hiding like mice in a hole or establishing ourselves as rightful leaders of the world by using our powers freely to win respect and support of people everywhere? The answer is obvious to you and me. Why can't the Head Priest and Council see it?"

Rhea harrumphed. "Cut to the chase. What you really want is for us to masquerade as gods and rule. Haven't you learned anything from Kalli's lessons?"

He spread his arms wide to the audience. "Kalli lived long ago. The world has changed in ways she could not have foreseen. The Corruption is no more."

Rhea clapped loudly. "Must I remind everyone that these are the very methods employed by Corruption to control people? Do not forget that Kalli said..."

San-zeus erupted, "Whatever the hell you and Leto claim! Does anyone else find it troubling the Head Priest withholds power and knowledge from the Priests and Initiates, doling it out to the Council and Watchers because she will not allow us protect ourselves? How much longer must we be ruled by the half-baked ideas of someone who has been dead for longer than any of us has lived?"

Rhea struck the tabletop a loud blow with a heavy stick she sometimes used as a cane. "Those matters are not for public discussion. Meeting adjourned!"

San-zeus yelled back, "But I'm not finished!"

Rhea stood, and the room fell silent as everyone felt the power behind her warning stare. "You are, unless you wish to defy my order to shut up and get out of my sight."

San-zeus knew it was not a bluff. He exchanged glares with her as he departed.

***

MAIDSERVANT HAD AVOIDED SEYDI SINCE THE HAIR INCIDENT, but had no choice, approaching her lounging in the baths the moment she was alone. She knelt, offering a cup of wine. "I have important information for my master. I thought he would come after the attack, but he hasn't. Will you ask if he has time tonight?"

Seydi did not look at her. "Give it to me."

"He will have questions that I need to explain."

"Then you'll have to wait. The Head Priest sent him with San-zeus to set up a perimeter of ships around the island."

"Why would she send him?"

"Who can explain anything that fat cow does? She's crazier than you are."

"How long it will be?"

"Weeks, months, how do I know? I'm never going to get off this infernal island. Now, go away. Being near you makes me feel sick."

A few days later, in the kitchens before daylight, Maidservant carried a big bowl of hot wine out to the terrace, sat on a table with her feet on a bench and stared down over the wall at the Cadi-sum lights, diffused by morning mists. At least, she thought, hugging the bowl to her chest for warmth, her master being away gave her more time to decide about all the stuff he and the woman said she had to do. Suddenly, she sensed someone behind her, surprised she knew who it was. "I watched you fighting from the Watchers' room. I thought you would be killed."

"It wasn't pirates that attacked the island. It was the Corruption."

She did not turn around. "Yes, I saw them."

"Soon their armies will come."

"I know."

"I want you to let me send you away. Later, I'll join you and we'll find somewhere to live away from all this, if you want."

Her heart pounded so hard it hurt her chest. "You can't stay behind. You'll die if you do."

"I must do all I can to help them, but if the island is overcome, I won't be killed."

He sounded incredibly nonchalant and confident about risking his life. She had to tell him. "I can't explain, except to say you may not want anything to do with me when you know everything about me."

"I know enough. No matter what happens, I pledge that I will protect you for the rest of your life."

She felt that he meant it. "I think someone may try to prevent me leaving."

"Until the Corruption comes in force, no one can stop me getting you off the island, but do not delay longer than necessary."

She kept thinking of her master and hesitating then twisted around to say yes, but he was gone. Head spinning, she slid off the table and started for the kitchen.

The door flew open. It was Kore. "I heard voices. Who were you talking to out here in the dark?"

She walked past her. "I just finished praying for your good health, same as I do every morning."

NINETEEN

MAIDSERVANT SMILED FOR THE FIRST TIME IN WEEKS as she led Erran by the hand into the new Eao plaza to join Plinius and Denear, who had gone ahead with neighbors, but it was so crowded she realized finding them would only be by accident. She did not care, for the little girl was an adorable chatterbox and always made her feel good.

Rhea had moved up the plaza's opening to get people's minds off the attack and opposition to her leadership. Envoy and DoSo, popular with the islanders, were in charge of festivities. It was a grand affair with free food, wine and all sorts of entertainment, most notably the monkeys.

Seydi had ordered Maidservant to listen for critical comments about the Head Priest, but in spite of a Scholars' strike that began the week before, no one talked politics that she heard. Her master was not going to be pleased when he returned, but she smiled because she would be gone before then.

Erran begged to see the monkeys, so Maidservant pushed and weaved through the crush to the big cages next to the lake. It took a long time, but was worth it seeing Erran squeal and mimic the animals. Other kids joined her, and soon everyone around them laughed except Maidservant, who had spotted Envoy on the other side of the lake talking to DoSo and Kore. Finally, he saw her, waved and began making his way around the water to them. All at once, Erran cried out, jumped into Maidservant's arms and held up a forefinger with a bloody gash. "Monkeys bite!"

A kind man gave Maidservant a cloth dampened from a water skin. "Wrap it until you can get her to a fountain and clean it properly. The poor little creatures are frightened and biting anyone who gets too close."

Maidservant pulled up on the cage and saw Envoy stopped by a group of Priests. It looked as if he would not get away for a while. Then a monkey leaped at her but she avoided it by jumping down. Disappointed that she would have to wait to tell him she was ready to go, she tugged Erran away to find water.

After washing the tiny gash and putting kisses on it, Maidservant pilfered some honey and fruit for Erran, a cup of wine for herself and returned to the house to wait for Plinius and Denear. Dark when they came home, she declined sharing a meal and ran back to the plaza, but Envoy had gone. She fought the impulse to look for his house and made her way home with frequent stops to refill the cup with wine taken from uncleared tables at sidewalk cafes and bars.

***

No one had seen Rhea outside Jellyfish House since Sans-zeus joined the Council, fueling rumors that she was in bad health. Although it was true, the primary reason she stayed in was due to exhausting all her energy using an ability only she possessed---watching enemy forces gathering around the Temple's far-flung settlements.

Meanwhile, the day-to-day routine was a shambles with the Scholars on strike, so it was not surprising that an early morning message sent by the main Eao health clinic did not reach the Council. Then, shortly before midnight, an Initiate brought word that Priest Ella, Eao's chief healer, and both Initiates working with her, were sick and needed assistance with a large number of patients. Leto, on duty with the Watchers, sent three healing Priests. Next morning, the junior team member burst into Jellyfish House unannounced. Rhea was asleep on a couch while Leto attended to business at the table. She glanced up. "How are Ella and the other Priests faring?"

Stemming blood from his nose, he sagged to the floor. "They're dead. Plague. Help me, please."

By nightfall, he was dead and frantic pleas came from all parts of the island. The Temple dispatched healers to every town and forbade all other travel including closing the ports, but they could do nothing but comfort the sick and burn the dead. As Eao was hardest hit, Selene and Metys set up an emergency hospital in the Baths, though it functioned more as a lab trying to isolate the cause rather than place of healing. Two horrific weeks passed. Hundreds were dead. Hundreds more were seriously ill.

Maidservant folded clean cloths and put them on the bottom of the monkey's cage, being careful not to excite the animal because she did not want to miss any of an intense argument between Rhea and Leto about whether to send Priests to protect outlying settlements.

Rhea was emphatic. "It will do no good."

"But we can't just abandon them!"

Rhea suffered a coughing fit. "Even if our people get through to them, they'll simply spread disease. I've decided to stop watching activities around them and use what strength I have left to search for the cause of the sickness. The answer should be in Eao, since it suffers most. Help me up."

"If people see you like this, it'll destroy their faith in us. I will go."

"No, this requires my abilities. Besides, I don't think their faith in us can get any worse. I'll need a nap before I leave. You go finish your work with the Watchers. Send someone to wake me in two hours."

Maidservant worked until the Head Priest's breathing became regular then tiptoed next to the couch, set her cleaning basket down and reached into it for something.

Rhea's eyes popped open. "What are you doing?"

Maidservant fished out her medicine jar. "This is the elixir Cythe tasted. Will it help you?"

Rhea took the jar, looked at it then handed it back. "It's too dangerous. It might kill me."

Maidservant looked her straight in the eyes. "You're going to die soon, regardless, and you're too weak to do anything but fall on your face the way you are."

Rhea stared for a few seconds then laughed. "Even you can tell that, huh? Well, Cythe continues sleeping normally in spite of the amounts of energy surging through her, and I certainly have no need to worry about long-term effects. Tell you what, wet the tip of a finger and touch it lightly to my tongue. Let's see what happens."

Maidservant did as told then stood terrified when Rhea's face contorted before she went perfectly still, eyes fixed and staring up at the ceiling.

Maidservant reached to check pulse in her neck, but someone grabbed her from behind, snatched the jar from her hand and pinned her face down on the floor. She twisted her head and saw Leto standing on her as she bent over Rhea. She yelled, "Get off me!"

Leto stomped her in the back as Rhea gasped and sat up. "Leave the girl alone. She's helping."

Leto rocked her weight on Maidservant, hurting her. "How can this worthless little troublemaker help anyone?"

Maidservant twisted and rolled, toppling Leto to the floor. She grabbed the jar from her hand. Leto sprang up and tried to take it back. Maidservant kicked her in the shin. "It's mine, you witch!"

Rhea guffawed like her old self. "Her elixir gave me a blast of energy the likes I've never felt before, though it burns like fire. Summon carriers. I don't know how long I have or what will happen when it wears off."

Instead of obeying, Leto shouted at Maidservant. "Where did someone like you get elixir?"

Rhea spoke powerfully. "Leave her alone and do as I said."

Leto was determined to have her way and grabbed for Maidservant. "I'll make her tell."

Rhea hipped her, knocking her down. "Soon as I'm dressed, I'd better see six strong Priests out front with great big smiles because they're so happy to carry my fat butt to Eao. Do you think you can behave like a Council Priest long enough to get that done?"

Leto hurried away after exchanging glares with Maidservant.

Rhea sighed. "Deep down, she's really a good person."

Maidservant gave her a very sour look. "Must take a lot of practice to hide being mean and nasty from you all the time."

Rhea let out a long breath. "Run along back to the kitchens, but don't tell anyone what I'm doing. Mustn't get hopes up."

That evening, while the crew did final cleaning of the big kitchen, a recent Prospect named Carnae ran in flushed with excitement. "Everyone's saying the Head Priest set the new zoo afire! She's killing all the monkeys, even those given as pets. She's gone mad!"

DoSo, sitting at a table working on accounts, stood, picked up a cleaning bowl full of water and poured it over his head. "You'll show proper respect for the Head Priest or I'll have you sent packing. Anything else you want to say before you clean the floor?" Too afraid to speak, he shook his head and took the brush she thrust at him.

Everyone laughed except Maidservant, who had stopped washing dishes and watched with face frozen in shocked disbelief. Suddenly, she ran across the room into the hall to Main Court. DoSo yelled, but she kept going.

People milled outside Temple buildings, jabbering and pointing at plumes of smoke in the darkening sky over Eao. In all the confusion and excitement, no one noticed the crazy girl from the kitchens running by them so fast that when she passed through the gate at the top of First Test, she left the ground and landed far down the avenue. Two Initiates, coming up from Cadi-sum, were too busy staring at each other and being in love to take note who she was and how incredibly fast she went by.

At the bottom of the hill, she turned left onto the avenue to Eao and crossed Boiling River Bridge. It was then she remembered a prayer to Thoth that her father inscribed on the wall next to a small shrine in his office. The darkness inside her demanded she punish herself, but she ignored it and whispered the prayer repeatedly as she passed through the westernmost suburbs. The few people on the streets gave her hard looks seeing a Temple tunic but scurried away from her.

Plinius and Denear's street was empty. She stopped in front of their house. The entrance had a big black X painted next to it. Then she realized every house on the street had one. For a long time, she could not go inside.

The stillness in the gloomy front room was ominous. Jewelry lay scattered on the tables, a fortune for the taking, but it meant nothing now. A mild, putrid odor from her past permeated the room's still air and made her shiver, but she could not quite remember what it was. Then she heard a soft sob.

In Cythe's room, slumped on the box seat staring at Erran's body---small, bloody and horrible---Denear was dying. She managed one whisper. "Made them leave until I was ready to go with her."

Maidservant pulled her onto the bed next to her daughter and cradled her head while she moaned and bled from every orifice. It was soon over.

Numb, she stared at Cythe's solitary yellow flower on the wall above the pillow block until she was able to make her eyes go to the thing that had been Little Erran. Her arm from the elbow to the wrist was mottled black. The small hand was solid black. The tiny shriveled finger with the bite was blackest of all.

She got up and stared out the window at the cold stars. "They didn't tell me this would happen."

***

THE HEAD PRIEST, SHUT AWAY for more than a week after stemming the epidemic, was accessible only to Leto until summoning Maidservant. The girl found her sitting on a couch alone. She motioned Maidservant to sit on the floor in front of her. "You look worse than I do."

She sat and said nothing.

"I heard you carried the daughter of Plinius from her house to the pyre in Eao Plaza and insisted putting her in the fire yourself. Weren't you afraid, especially as you had diseased blood all over you?"

She shook her head. "I waited until they brought Denear and burned them together. Plinius died the day before. I promised Cythe I would take care of her family, and now I killed them."

Startled, Rhea held out her arms. "You mustn't say things like that. Come, I'll take away some of the anguish."

"No."

"You said something when you put the child on the pyre. Were you praying?"

"I just said good-bye and how sorry I was."

"They said you didn't cry."

"No, I never do after someone dies."

"You've experienced it before, then?"

She nodded. "I heard people at the plaza say the life spirit goes to a better place. Is it true?"

Rhea's eyes became wet and glimmering. "Old stories say that virtuous spirits return to the place of creation, a palace in the heavens so immense that a glorious city thrives in its center courtyard and grand corridors, hundreds of times wider than Kalliste's white avenues, radiate all directions from it and form enormous circles around it. Countless rooms filled with all the knowledge of the earth and heavens line every corridor. The spirits study, converse and pass time in self-fulfilling ways until they are ready to be reborn to better lives than they departed. Some call it the Great Wheel of Life. Think of it whenever you're saddened by death, and you will feel better."

Doleful, Maidservant shook her head and stood. "I've been to the place you mean. It has a different name than you know. The city is in ruins. The corridors are cold and icy. All the rooms except one are dark and empty. Anyone who goes there will be alone and lost forever." She left Rhea staring after her, shocked.

TWENTY

THE BOOK OF MAIDSERVANT: SHATTERED

RHEA CAME STRAIGHT TO THE POINT. "I want to name you Head Priest in a few days."

Leto showed deep concern, but not about being Head Priest. "I had no idea your illness had progressed so far."

"Keep it to yourself and do not treat me any differently, even in private. I do not want anyone's pity."

"As you wish. Have you told Selene?"

"We'll discuss her in due course. As you are aware, the Head Priest must carry out the details of Kalli's Plan. I'm concerned you will not do it."

Leto responded hotly. "Haven't I dedicated my life to serving you and Kalli? Why would you say such a thing?"

"Phoebe was the most stringent follower and teacher of Kalli's lessons when she and I were Priests; yet, after she knew all of Kalli's plan, she abandoned the Head Priest position and asked to have her memories cleansed."

Leto's jaw set hard. "And to think, I always respected her. Everyone must face the challenges of duty without hesitation."

"Do not be so hasty to judge. For me, dying is easier than completing the plan."

"Surely, you exaggerate. Tell me what Kalli requires, and I will do it."

Rhea watched her closely. "Until now, I thought I would take the plan to fruition. I regret giving you the burden. Mostly, you must insure the Corruption kills or enslaves all Kalli's followers."

Leto was aghast. "Why would Kalli want this?"

"Our sacrifice at precisely the right time sets events in motion that lead to annihilation of most of Corruption's forces."

"How can that be true? Once the Temple is gone, there will be no one to oppose them."

"As safeguard against capture, that is all Head Priests know."

Leto shook her head emphatically. "I'm sorry, but I think your illness may be affecting your thinking. I'm going to summon Selene and San-zeus to discuss this before going any further."

"You can't do that. Selene and Sans-zeus have allied with Ambassador Hariset, who is either one of the six dark lords or a high general of one of their armies, which means Seydi and Maidservant are spies."

Leto regarded her in amazement. "Why haven't you done something about them?"

"They are vital to the plan, especially Maidservant. From here on, the biggest challenge for the Head Priest is to stand back and let pieces fall into place without interfering. Think you can do it?"

Fast-speaking a spell of protection, Leto bolted for the door, but Rhea stopped her with a more powerful incantation. She came back, dropped to her knees and put her head on Rhea's lap. Rhea said, "Sorry to do this, Leto, but there is no one else."

***

RHEA'S SNORING EMBARRASSED SAN-ZEUS AND SELENE, while the idiot servant girl standing next to a small table gaping at them also irritated San-zeus. "Leave us, you little trollop."

Leto's voice came from nowhere in particular. "The Head Priest says she will stay."

It took a few seconds before they spotted her sitting cross-legged with head bowed in a shadowy corner. San-zeus bristled. "An outsider can't be party to Council business. You know that."

Leto responded in fast-speak. "The Head Priest says the meeting will be conducted in fast-speak. The girl will stay."

Selene butted in. "We don't need her. I can take care of Rhea's needs."

Leto fast-spoke. "The Head Priest says it is decided and to use fast-speak as instructed."

"I still object," San-zeus replied sharply. "She finally calls a Council meeting then insults us with this charade."

DoSo came in. Not knowing what to make of the strained circumstances, she mumbled, "Fair weather," but no one replied except Leto, who told her to use fast-speak only.

Rhea moaned. Maidservant hurried to her with a sponge and dribbled water onto her lips.

Meanwhile, Leto, eyes closed, walked slowly across the room toward them. "The Head Priest says when her strength returns, she will make known her decisions concerning a great danger we face."

San-zeus did not use fast-speak. "Surely, those are decisions to be made with the Council, so why is DoSo here?"

Leto answered, "The Head Priest says you will listen. DoSo will stay. The girl will stay. You will use fast-speak or get out."

San-zeus' face turned angry red, but he used fast-speak. "I was elected by the people! I demand…!"

Leto stopped in front of him. "The Head Priest says it is time for all of you to learn her rule over the Keftiu Empire is as absolute as her rule over the Temple. You have what she gives you, nothing more."

San-zeus was furious. "Now, she claims power over the king, too! Who does she think she is?"

Rhea sat up. DoSo jumped to assist, but she waved her away and gestured for Maidservant, who arranged pillows around her for support then scurried back to her table. Rhea said, "The king and queen of Keftiu are Priests of the Temple and subservient to the Head Priest. Always, it has been so."

San-zeus sputtered. "And you live here in this ridiculous house without servants, soldiers or advisors, while they have palaces, armies and riches?"

Rhea was unusually calm. "Let's talk about important matters, shall we? Today, you are going to find out what you've gotten yourself into, but until I tell you, keep your mouth shut." She fished something out of a pocket and motioned Selene to take it. "I made this for you."

Selene stared down at a tiny, perfectly rendered statue of herself. It had gorgeous colors and minute details. She stammered, "It…it's beautiful, but why?"

Rhea shushed her and instructed everyone to sit on the floor. San-zeus made a point to be last then shoved in closer than Leto.

Meanwhile, Maidservant's thoughts spun because her master had been with San-zeus, which meant he returned already. In addition, the Head Priest was an expert making statues and pottery, so the shabby restoration of the vase had been a ruse to get closer to her, which could only mean she knew about her from the beginning.

Rhea asked, "How's Ambassador Hariset, Selene?"

"Hiding in the Embassy is not easy for him. He said to thank you and that he will pay for new clinics as well as compensate families for losses, if you think it will help."

Rhea shrugged. "Just tell him to stay out of sight until the islanders finish grieving. Now, to business at hand. As of today, DoSo is appointed to the Council."

San-zeus did a double take. "But there are no vacancies!"

She ignored him. "I will name a new Head Priest and take the unprecedented step of sharing power, not just with her, but the entire Council. Any objections, San-zeus?"

He gave a slight bow. "You are wise as always, Head Priest."

Her expression showed her opinion of him. "But first, I must inform you that the forces of Corruption have destroyed all our outposts. Next, they will subjugate the Keftiu Empire and come here."

San-zeus demanded, "How can you possibly know all that?"

Rhea mouthed an incantation and their settlement on Ge Island headed by Priest Phoebe materialized on the wall next to her statue. It showed demon warriors swarming around burning buildings. At the center of the hubbub was an area the warriors carefully avoided. A brawny giant in silver armor sat watching six small black creatures with darting eyes, long limbs and membranous hands and feet sort heavy tablets into two piles. One, others of their kind carted to a waiting ship. The other, they smashed and dumped into the sea. The images vanished.

Rhea explained with no emotion. "The small creatures are imps that conduct day-to-day business in the One Master's realm. The titan is probably Kronos, one of his six ruling lords."

San-zeus, rather than appalled or fearful, was incensed. "Head Priests have had this power since Kalli's time and not used it? What's wrong with you people?"

"Since the time of Kalli, abilities have passed through the line of Head Priests solely for the purpose of guiding her plan to conclusion." Then she motioned to Maidservant. "Bring a wet cloth and hold it on the back of my neck until we finish." She waved the others into a tighter circle. "Join hands and open your minds to me or this will take all night."

Soon, Maidservant realized without physical contact, keeping up with the Head Priest's fast-speak would be impossible for her, but she did not have time to consider the implications of that fact until later.

Leto took Selene's hands. "I know you're disappointed, but I hope I can count on your support." Selene nodded and Leto went to DoSo. "Your rise from Scholar to Council Priest has been one of the most remarkable achievements in the history of the Temple. Congratulations."

DoSo beamed. "I am honored to serve you, Head Priest."

San-zeus hugged DoSo then engaged Selene in intense whispered conversation, avoiding contact with Leto. Meanwhile, Rhea gave her green ring to Leto and directed Maidservant to wrap and place the statues from the table in a bag for her, but when the girl ran back from the closet with cloths and a bag, Leto snatched them from her hands and did it herself. Then she told the others, "We'll reconvene in the Watchers' room and let Rhea rest."

Rhea waited until they were alone then motioned Maidservant close and took her hands. "I take it that you did not know your master had returned. The news upset you."

She did not sound convincing. "No, I am glad he is back safely."

"Do you ever wish you were still in Egypt?"

She shook her head. "No. I would be married off and raising babies by now."

"You are not old enough for that, surely."

"I know I look younger, but I am close to fifteen. Don't know the exact day, but soon."

"I thought you said you were thirteen."

"That was when I came. It's been nearly two years."

Rhea spoke quietly, but deliberately. "Actually, it doesn't matter how long it has been. You've not aged one iota since the first time I laid eyes on you. Do you even know how old you really are?"

"No, you're wrong!" Suddenly, she could not breathe. She pulled away from Rhea, clutched at her throat and toppled onto her side. Her face turned blue.

Dispassionately drumming fingers on a tray, Rhea watched. "Wish we had more time for you to lie there choking, but we don't. All you have to do to escape the reaction is concentrate on things you hold dear, be they good or evil; otherwise, you won't recover until you pass out."

Maidservant only heard part of what she said, but it was enough. She thought of bright sunlight, blue-green sea and dolphins leaping. Beautiful ships riding high swells. Talking into the night with Envoy. The island. Envoy. Saved from drowning. Envoy. The Eao baths. Envoy! Envoy! She gasped, buried her head in her arms and sobbed.

Rhea waited a few minutes then raised Maidservant's head with a foot. "A visitor is coming across Main Court to see me. Go stand next to your table and do not say a word until he is gone, no matter what happens. We'll talk more afterward."

If Envoy was surprised or distressed seeing Maidservant crying quietly at the end the couch, he gave no sign. "You sent for me, Head Priest?"

"I'm dying and need a favor."

He showed no reaction. "Of course."

"It's vital that you tell me who you are and how much power you have."

He glanced at Maidservant then back to Rhea, who nodded that it was all right. "I am a child of Kalli, not of her body, but of her blood, with no one between us."

She shook her head. "Knowledge I possess from the time of her death says no direct descendants remained except four Priests who long since died without furthering the bloodline."

"She thought me dead for countless generations by then."

"Surely, you're not sticking to that ridiculous story about the City of Bulls, are you? It would make you an age beyond reason and belief."

"Actually, I lived longer before the City of Bulls than since."

Her eyes widened. "That's impossible. Other than Kalli and the One Master, no one could have sustained you so long."

"I sustain myself, but won't say more about it."

Rhea considered the claims preposterous, yet all her senses said that he spoke truly. Regardless, she had no choice but to continue. "Why did you stop serving Kalli and keep her from knowing you were alive? Did you continue fighting Corruption?"

"She was amazing and wondrous, but also infuriating, arrogant and uncompromising. We had many disagreements and parted on unfriendly terms. I faked death then did not use detectable abilities for many lifetimes before assuming another powerful persona to fight our enemies, a pattern I've followed to this day." He glanced over at Maidservant, staring at him with wonder, amazement and emotion.

Instantly, Rhea recognized their feelings for each other and almost lost her composure. She coughed until she recovered. "Are there any names I might know?"

He bent to her ear and whispered. She grabbed him and stared into his eyes. They remained that way for a couple of minutes then he stepped back. "You ask too much of me."

Rhea half-stood off the couch. "You must not interfere! Think what's at stake! There's no other choice and you know it!"

"But I can't..."

She sagged into his arms. There was a brilliant flash of light. A slender young woman with long red hair remained in her place. Envoy placed her on the couch. "I'm honored to have known you, Rhea, for truly, you are one of the most remarkable people I ever encountered."

Maidservant was beside him. "W-what happened? Who's that?"

"Rhea was cloaked to hide her abilities."

He did not look at her and fear twisted her stomach. She had trouble getting words out. "I have to leave today. My master has returned."

He hesitated, and she knew before he spoke. "You have to stay here."

"No, please. I will be different. I promise."

"That has nothing to do with it."

"You said we would be together! You said you would protect me forever!"

He turned away and left her.

She screamed after him. "Liar!"

***

"I HAVE WAITED FOR YOU EVERY NIGHT since you returned, Master."

"Leto ordered a group of Priests to stay with me at the embassy until the islanders calm down, though Selene says their real mission is to spy on me.

We don't have much time before they come back. Apparently, the Head Priest has known about us from the beginning."

"Yes, she all but told me that before she died."

"Any idea why she hasn't done anything?"

"No, unless it is a trap, but there is none that I can see."

"This makes no sense."

She told him about Rhea changing appearance.

"I surely didn't detect that she was cloaked. San-zeus and Selene don't know about it, but then again, Leto took care of the body. These Head Priests certainly keep their secrets."

She told him about finding the book and the red aura trap. "I'm sorry, Master, but I thought I'd better leave it alone."

"You did the right thing, but retrieve it the moment the attack begins. You'll have to be fast because that building will be the first destroyed."

"Master, just before Rhea died, she said I had not aged since coming to Kalliste. That can't be right, can it?"

"Of course not. Sometimes, people become delusional when they face death. Anything else?"

"Why didn't you tell me the monkey sickness would kill people? There was a little girl in Eao I liked. I feel bad she died so horribly."

"Hmm, I think I'll begin your transformation now. It'll answer most of your questions. Besides, it's only right you be able to savor victory properly with the rest of us. You'll have a few unpleasant weeks while your body purges that goody-goody garbage we stuffed inside you then I can finish the process."

He said words she did not understand then she could not speak.

"Just give it time, and stop tearing yourself up about the dead girl. Soon, you can get all of them you want. Now, go to sleep. Long days ahead."

During subsequent days, Maidservant developed deep eye circles, face tics and stopped frequently to stare at her hands as if forgetting their purpose. Then one day, while washing dishes in the small kitchen, she started imagining gruesome ways people could die until Kore yelled at her to get away. She was shocked to discover she had moved up against her from behind. A little while later, she did the same thing to one of the Prospects then kept doing it to other people, no matter how much they shouted, threatened and shoved her away.

***

ATHY'S VOICE CARRIED ACROSS THE TERRACE. "Can you imagine praying to San-Zeus or DoSo? It's so ridiculous."

Arty persisted. "You're missing the point. San-zeus is right. The Corruption uses religion to gather support and so should we. After we drive them away from Kalliste, the real war will be for the hearts and minds of the people. Giving them gods to believe in and good examples to follow are the best ways."

Athy looked at the sun sinking into the sea, turning rivers, lakes and mists of Cadi-sum shades of coral, then she nudged Envoy. "Don't just sit there like a lump, argue with her or something."

He had his eyes closed to the world. "It doesn't matter."

Everyone was on edge and the comment irritated Athy. "Of course it matters. What's wrong with you?"

Maidservant ran out of the building and brought food and wine to their table, not noticing who they were. She put the tray down and turned away.

Arty called her back. "Hey, Maidservant, aren't you going to speak? Haven't seen you for a while."

Her eyes were dark and haunted. "Leto restricted me to the kitchens and terrace. I can't go anywhere else except the road to work and back. Sorry, I have to go before I'm punished again."

Athy turned to Envoy. "Did she tell you about this?"

He took a cup of wine off the tray without opening his eyes. "We haven't spoken since Rhea died."

Arty was concerned. "Judging by her appearance, she took it hard, especially after losing the little girl and Cythe and Aria going away."

No one said anything else until Envoy opened his eyes to the gathering twilight. "I'm leaving Kalliste in a few hours."

Athy nodded. "Is Leto sending you on a mission?"

He stood. "No. I quit the Temple. I'm leaving and not coming back. I thought of asking you to go, but knew you would refuse. Having you as friends has been one of the best things in my life. Goodbye."

Shocked, Athy and Arty watched him walk around the corner into Main Court. Arty grabbed Athy. "What just happened?"

A table of Priests nearby heard. One said, "Coward," and the others agreed. Athy and Arty did not defend him. Then Athy turned and saw Maidservant's tragic expression.

TWENTY-ONE

THE BOOK OF MAIDSERVANT: DEMONS AND THE DEAD SISTERS

REPORTS OF ATTACKS POURED IN from all parts of the Empire before black ships surrounded Kalliste, isolating it from the rest of the world. For reasons not apparent at first, they remained carefully over the horizon out of sight. The people assumed the Temple prevented them coming closer and were unconcerned until the third week when Leto ordered the harbor cities evacuated to temporary camps higher up the mountain. Many people objected or ignored her until she sent Priests to force compliance, which took another week. Resentment, fear and unrest were rampant as a second month of blockade dragged to conclusion.

Prominent merchants, confident they could bribe their way past the blockade, hatched a plan to escape with families and friends. They sneaked into Eao, loaded four ships with enormous wealth and embarked at night in dense fog. The lead ship did not make it out of the harbor, floundering on rocks beside the dark lighthouse. The other ships did not stop to help them and few people survived the shipwreck. However, as it turned out, they had better deaths than the remaining three ships.

Leto paced around the Eao table, watching black ships close around the third Kallistian vessel as its two companions burned in the background. Volleys of arrows and spears, many streaking fire, came from all sides. At the last, a small group of men and women threw their children into fire rather than have them fall into the clutches of the terrible creatures swarming over the sides.

She hit the table in frustration, causing the image to jitter. "Those ships should be much farther away by now. They held them until the sun burned off enough fog for us to witness the slaughter. DoSo, have all boats except those in the two main harbors destroyed then post our best Priests to stand watch over them. If anyone else tries to leave, I want them stopped, no matter what it takes."

DoSo was flabbergasted. "With respect, Head Priest. Kallistians are the greatest sailors in the world. It is only natural they would rather take their chances at sea."

"They must stay here! How many times do I have to tell you?"

"With respect, don't you think you should explain your actions to the people, especially why you didn't send for the Kefti navy?"

Leto hit the table so hard it blacked out and several Watchers ran to assist reestablishing images. She took a deep breath and moved close to DoSo so no one else could hear. "Please join me in the back. It's time I explained what Kalli really expects the two of us to do."

Mystified, DoSo followed her. "Don't you mean the four of us?"

At dawn a few days later, the flagship of the Kefti Royal Navy drifted into Cadi-sum harbor. Everyone was dead except the captain, who was chained, mutilated and kept alive by a ghastly spell long enough to describe the destruction of Kefti. Panic swept the island. Then the Scholars, directed by Hariset, intensified the spread of rumors that the attackers were actually agents of Pharaoh, sent to free them from the Temple's oppressive yoke. They promised generous rewards from the Egyptians for everyone who supported the overthrow.

Leto warned the Scholars if they did not stop stirring up trouble, she would arrest the lot of them. Hariset called her bluff by having Tritius lead the Scholars to reoccupy the central part of Eao. The second part of the plan was to send messengers to entice people back to their homes to greet the liberators when they came ashore, but Leto stationed Priests around Eao and bottled them up inside. After another tense two weeks passed, DoSo lamented, "What are they waiting for?" To which Leto answered, "For us to implode, but they will come now that it has not happened."

The baths and dining rooms had begun operating twenty-four hours a day when the siege began. The staff, including Maidservant, stayed in the facility, sleeping in the baths. To help the regulars handle the extra work, Leto assigned more Prospects, including Seydi, who surprised everyone by volunteering for kitchen duty. She worked hard and uttered not a single complaint. In fact, she seldom spoke except to ask how to do something, astonishing Maidservant and raising her suspicions.

It was a cool, foggy daybreak, the terrace quarter full with overflow from the dining rooms. Booming chants rolled up the mountain from Cadi-sum, sending everyone rushing to the safety wall to listen and speculate what it was. Only Maidservant recognized the Eirycian verses and hung back, deducing the Council must be using the harbor horns to repel an attack. Yet, no one had sounded alarm with the obelisks, so she vacillated, wondering whether she should go to the Watchers' building or wait to make certain it was the attack. Then Seydi, carrying a tray of dirty dishes, passed behind her and whispered, "Not today."

Meanwhile, Tesi-Ra, unaffected by the powerful chants reverberating off buildings, sat in the Embassy garden. Antwah, Senior General of his armies, and Grayduk, General-in-Chief of the One Master's Navy, were with him, fending off the magic well enough not to be gravely injured, though the strain showed on their faces. Rolling and thrashing on the ground next to the table, Marine Bowman Second Class Ladikoo of Grayduk's personal staff had no defense against the Priests' magic.

Tesi-Ra refilled the cups with wine. "They are driving everyone on your ships mad, General. I warned you not to do anything until I gave the word. Any idea how many you've lost so far?"

Grayduk picked up his wine and studied the intricate gold inlay. "I thought all of Kalli's power gone from the world. It was a reasonable assumption, I think you'll agree."

Ladikoo convulsed and rolled into a table leg, sloshing wine on the table linen. Annoyed, Tesi-Ra reached down and snapped his thick neck like a piece of rotten driftwood. "If Antwah disobeyed me with a rash stunt such as this, he would be dead on the ground next to that sorry excuse for a warrior you brought."

Grayduk was not intimidated. "The One Master gave command of his forces to you with understanding it would only be a short while. This has gone on too long. Give the signal to attack or I am ordering withdrawal."

Tesi-Ra shrugged. "Then attack tomorrow at dawn, but follow the plan I gave you. Let's not have another made-up-as-you-go fiasco solely to maximize Shelitine and your percentages of the spoils."

Glaring, Grayduk leaned across the table. "I used her navy because it happens to be deployed outside this harbor. Besides, anything is better than wasting ships and men in unprecedented numbers as your plan dictates. The Master will be infuriated."

Tesi-Ra had enough. "You fragmented Shelitine's forces and stationed them at the mouths of all the harbors in order to claim spoils, demonstrating weak planning and double-dealing favoritism. Tomorrow, you will use my plan exactly, or I will charge you with treason and carry out the sentence myself. Of course, Shelitine will claim I did not have justification, but the rest of the Council will disagree."

Grayduk spoke with anger. "Shelitine has the Master's ear. He will punish you severely."

"You'll be dead and I will have just finished eradicating Kalli's last stronghold. I'll take those odds any day."

Grayduk jumped to his feet. "I'll do as you say, but you're taking responsibility for the losses!"

"If Kalli is still alive or has hidden armies ready to pounce, we'll need men ashore, not aboard ships. Moreover, if you want to give me all the credit for the victory, fine by me. Just make certain you do not make mistakes tomorrow or you might as well kill yourself. Dismissed."

As soon as Grayduk disappeared in the fog toward the harbor, Antwah cleared his throat. "I can arrange an accident when he comes ashore, if it pleases you, Lord."

He knew Antwah would find a way to use the incident against him. He shook his head and pointed to the dead soldier. "Drag him inside and wait for me. I want to be alone to think over the plans for tomorrow."

Tesi-Ra stretched his long legs and slouched down in the chair, savoring the solitude of fog and darkness. He had no concern about the battle plans at this point. His main worry was his ongoing struggle with Shelitine. She had long plotted to move Czn-tanth up to contend for the next vacancy on the Council, giving her the deciding vote against him. However, her plan hinged on Czn-tanth receiving a large amount of credit for the success of this mission. Well, she was in for a rude surprise, because he had laid groundwork to acclaim Maidservant as sole hero in this venture, dealing Czn-tanth a political setback that would allow him time to find someone more suitable for the next vacancy.

In the confusion after the botched attack, Scholars sneaked out of Eao to the mountain encampments, told people the Priests had defeated the enemy and they could return to their homes. As night wore toward next morning, long lines of torches wound down the mountain and night breezes carried jubilant sounds of spontaneous celebrations far out to sea to hundreds of silently approaching ships filled with grotesque beings for whom music, hope and joy no longer had meaning.

***

NEXT MORNING, MAIDSERVANT, SEYDI AND A PROSPECT named Judi worked like mad in the big kitchen preparing trays for five impatient Priests waiting to take them to the Watchers. Maidservant and Judi finished the food while Seydi went to the small kitchen to mix more fruit water. One of the Priests decided they wanted fragrance tea, too, and Maidservant ran to tell Seydi, who she found mixing fine powder into the drinks. "What's that?"

"An energy additive Priest Celeste said to use."

"They want an urn of tea, too."

Seydi handed her the additive. "Just a little in each one, or we'll not have enough. I'll get the tea."

A short time later, a surly Priest named Keyser stormed in, barked orders for three meals packed for travel then griped about Council Priest DoSo waking him early to go to the east side of the island. As they scrambled to put everything together, he started to leave and Judi called after him. "Could you wait a moment and take it back? We're very short-staffed."

He was indignant. "Do I look like a lowly kitchen servant to you girls?"

Seydi stuck two fingers in her nostrils and flipped them at him, a very rude insult. He stomped away down the hall to Main Court. "Celeste will hear of this!"

Adding the powder to the drinks, Maidservant whispered, "You shouldn't insult Priests, Mistress. You'll get in trouble."

Seydi laughed, spat into a jug of fruit water then held it out for Judi and Maidservant to do the same. They had a good laugh over it. When Keyser's bundles were ready, Seydi took them because Judi was all but out on her feet. Judi commented effusively how nice and not stuck-up at all Seydi was once you knew her, but Maidservant barely heard, staring after Seydi with growing apprehension.

At that same moment, Selene, standing watch at the Cadi-sum horns with three Priests, read a note brought by messenger. Her house was just up the street. She found Hariset sprawled on a couch in the dining room. "A hot bath sounds divine."

He surprised her with anger. "Why didn't you tell me Rhea shared power with the Council before she died?"

"I assumed San-zeus told you."

"You're lying. This morning you used new abilities against our forces, too. I thought we had an understanding."

"I'm sorry, but I had no choice with Leto standing over me. Besides, I think the terms of our deal needs renegotiation now that we have so much power. We can come to agreement in the bath, don't you think?" She left a trail of clothes down the hall to her ornate bedroom with a sunken pool.

He went after her.

Huddled together at the end of Eao's outermost jetty next to the dark lighthouse, Athy and Arty shivered, watching with bleary eyes as dawn brightened the fog. The rhythmic sloshing of the sea against rocks and ship wreckage had made staying awake difficult all night. Arty yawned. "I'm cold. I'm wet. I'm bored. I wish something would happen."

Athy reached out from under the blankets for a water skin and pulled a long drink, shivering as it ran down her raw throat. "Just be glad it's quiet and the wind is picking up. Maybe today the fog will lift and we can see something."

With no warning, Arty tossed aside the blankets, jumped up and leaned sideways to the sea. "Do you hear that?"

In an instant, Athy was next to her. After a few seconds, she shook her head.

Arty whispered. "A creaking noise, way out."

Athy listened, shook her head again. "Still hear it?"

"Yeah."

"Can you tell the direction?"

She moved her head back and forth then pointed, arm ramrod straight. "Dead on."

Athy fitted an arrow in her bow, adjusted foot position and aimed along Arty's arm. "Got it. Grab your bow."

First one then the other fired, pausing to listen then adjusting aim. Arty's third shot returned a faint thud. She looked at her friend. "Think maybe one of our boats got loose from its mooring?"

Athy ran into the lighthouse and came back with a small wooden table, shielded lamp, urn of lamp oil and bundle of clothes. She turned the table upside down, set it next to her then squatted over the other items. "I'll rig, you shoot."

Watching her wrap cloth around arrows and dip them in oil, Arty pointed to the table. "Why did you bring that if you aren't going to use it?"

Athy set four arrows afire. "If it's the enemy, what do you think they will do when they see fire arrows coming at them? Shoot quickly then put your arms down to your sides."

As the arrows streaked in high arcs, Athy grabbed the table, held it over her head and squeezed close to Arty. A salvo of arrows rained down around them, several sticking in the table and one passing through a crack, hitting Arty's left shoulder. Athy kicked the fire into the water and Arty snapped off the arrow's shaft. Grimacing, she said, "Probably best to leave the head for later."

Loud drumbeats, war cries and sounds of oars commenced. Somewhere down the jetty, the only way back to land for them, a ship crashed, followed by the noise of warriors disembarking. Athy slung off her coat and helped Arty remove hers as two more ships crashed against the jetty. Athy said, "Heck of a way to make landings. The way back is going to be a tad arduous. You up to it?"

"Do or die," Arty answered, pointing at the prow of a ship coming out of the fog directly at them. "A case of wine says that I reach land before you!"

They ran, dodging, wounding and killing as the sounds of crashing ships and attacking warriors filled the harbor. Neither expected to reach the island.

***

IN THE TEMPLE KITCHENS, A HANDSOME YOUNG MAN with tousled black curls came in from the terrace rubbing sleep from his eyes. Seydi looked up from sharpening a heavy cleaver and knife. "Better go back and sleep while you can, Nadius. It's going to be a trying day."

Drawn to her like bees to flowers, he swelled his bare, muscular chest and flirted. "I would've worked without any sleep at all if I'd known you had duty, pretty Seydi."

She rewarded him with a receptive smile and fruit water, stirred by a dainty little finger. "I guarantee it is extra sweet, just the way you prefer."

He drank with aggressive gulps, smacked his lips and leered. "Got anything else for me?" To his chagrin, she returned to sharpening the cleaver and acted as if he was not there, so he went to the others. "Any idea what's going on in Cadi-sum? Big fires are burning, but can't tell what they are with all this fog."

As everyone went outside to look, Nadius fell to the ground moaning and holding his stomach. Judi ran inside to get a lamp while Maidservant knelt and asked what was wrong. Behind her, Seydi said something, but she did not understand because Judi ran back with the lamp and they saw Nadius' contorted face. Then Judi dropped the lamp and doubled up beside him. Maidservant jumped up yelling for help.

Seydi slapped and shoved her toward Main Court. "I already told you it is time, moron. Aren't you supposed to be at Leto's looking for documents or something else as useless?"

Maidservant ran, as much to escape the horror on the terrace as to do her duty.

The Priests who guarded the entrance were dead in the hallway. She ran up the stairs. One of the Priests who picked up the meals was belly down across the table in front of the door to the third floor. Metys lay in the hall farther on with the bound documents from Leto's secret room wrapped in her arms. She tugged them free, hurried back to the table and rolled the Priest off, but before she had a chance to examine the documents, a familiar voice came from behind her. "I see that you got it. Any problems?"

She whipped around. "No, Master. Everyone is dead."

"Well done!" He grabbed her by the ears, bent her backwards over the table and leaned close as if he meant to kiss her; instead, he fast-spoke an incantation. "That begins your next phase."

A terrible wrenching sensation erupted in her mid-section. It traveled up into her throat. Stinking green-yellow matter came out her mouth and nose. She had to sit up to keep from choking. She could not think clearly or make her eyes stay in focus. Then she saw her master was already down the hall at the top of the stairs with the documents.

He called out. "You have a little time, but don't rest too long. The building is on fire."

She must have blacked out for a few minutes. The building was full of smoke and the upper floors became an inferno by the time she stumbled outside into crowds of hysterical Temple members shoving, pushing and fighting to escape to nowhere. Knocked down and trampled, she crawled into shrubbery, coughed and threw up again. Then her eyes cleared and she sat enjoying the pretty flames for a time.

She did not know when or why, but she joined in the fighting. It was fun tripping, kicking and hitting people, especially as she seemed impervious to the battering she received back. She had never felt so free and alive. Then someone pounded her to the ground and she saw that she was in front of the kitchens and baths. Two huge creatures fought Priests on the walk in front of her and she enjoyed that for a while before stumbling around the side to the terrace.

She leaned precariously over the safety wall, watching the surreal spectacle of Cadi-sum burning. Then the battle noise grew louder, spoiling the mood. Irritated, she started to the kitchens but tripped and sprawled over something. A wedge of light from the ajar kitchen door illuminated Nadius and Judi's bodies, hacked to pieces. She realized she was hungry and thirsty, feelings not experienced for a long time, and went inside to see if there were leftovers she could have with wine.

Arty had a sword wound in the left side. So far, it had not slowed her, but Athy was concerned because it was too serious to heal without stopping and their pursuers were only seconds behind. They whipped through the harbor area and gate to Eao Avenue, where they dodged crowds of Scholars and townspeople cheering their pursuers until they saw them close up. Then they screamed and ran.

Athy and Arty sped up through town to the high intersection, saw with dismay the massive fire in the western sky over Cadi-sum, and continued up the mountain past the House of Kalli and the hill with the merchant's mansion to take the shortcut to the Temple. They hoped to lose the warriors chasing them in the dark woods. Darting from one twisting lane to another, they worked their way toward Boiling River footbridge.

Except for the occasional snarl, their pursuers were eerily silent now they were off the road. Unlike the attackers they faced during Hariset's feint, these had strangely shaped feet that made odd scrabbling noises on hard surfaces. Athy glanced back. "I liked it better when we could hear how close they are."

Arty, struggling to maintain speed, gasped, "What do you reckon they are?"

"Reminds me of a pack of wild animals more than anything else. Are you able to fight?"

"My shoulder is numb. Can't lift my arm."

Athy dipped her head to the right, letting an arrow pass between them. "That's bad. You might be poisoned. Does it hurt much?"

"Pain in my side's keeping my mind off it. Uh, how did you know that arrow was coming?"

"Don't know, just did. We're almost to the bridge. Can you make it up First Test?"

She sounded anything but certain. "Faster than you."

Athy glanced her way, but it was too dark to make out her face. "Say the word and I'll carry you piggyback."

"Eat bat dung!"

"Come on. I can do it, even with all the weight you've gained."

Arty laughed a little. "Thanks, but go suck fish guts."

They reached the long stretch to the bridge. Two hulking shadows were on it. Athy shot one then Arty warned, "Another one is behind those shrubs to the right." Athy fired two arrows into them in quick succession then Arty stopped her shooting the remaining warrior. "I'll do it. He has a short spear I can use one-handed."

With no time to argue, Athy pirouetted in the air and killed the closest pursuer, gaining them a few precious seconds. Meanwhile, Arty bound ahead onto the bridge, dodged a jab and trapped the spear under her arm as she head-butted the warrior over the guard rope backwards.

Athy stopped in the middle of the bridge and shot the first two warriors onto it. She caught Arty struggling up First Test and helped her. The steep incline slowed the warriors and they gained a little ground. At the top, the Temple plateau was ablaze and in complete pandemonium. Athy said, "Doesn't look good for us."

***

As DAYLIGHT BRIGHTENED THE FOG, Maidservant wrung out the dishrag then stopped to stare at it before she resumed blotting the front of her tunic. She kept telling herself she might as well stop because it mashed the vomit, blood and icky flesh into the fabric when she rubbed, but her mind no longer seemed in control of the rest of her.

Four screaming Prospects ran in from Main Court hallway. A heavy spear struck one in the back with such force it propelled his body halfway across the room. The others fled out the terrace door. Three gargantuan brutes in studded leather armor squeezed out of the hall one at a time. The first went to shake the body off his spear. The second came for Maidservant with the biggest knife she had ever seen. The third, by far the largest and most ferocious, pushed and shoved the other two toward the terrace, yelling the girl was his and that he would kill them, too. They blustered and threatened, but it was only token bravado before they did as he said.

It did not occur to Maidservant to wonder why she understood their guttural language or why she was not afraid. In fact, she kind of lost track while they argued and went back to rubbing her tunic. She was frustrated, because no matter how much soap she used, it would not come off.

Enormous feet covered with scraggly fur moved into her field of vision. Folded under and walked on, the big claws made scraping sounds on the floor. Oh, that's gross and must hurt, she thought. Then she shaded her eyes to the oil lamps hanging from the ceiling and gazed into a dark bestial face with thick leathery lips and nose, jagged teeth and a gruesome, pus-filled socket where the second big yellow eye once had been. He held a spiked club cocked back over his head. It was bigger than she was, and the same kind of stuff on her clothes ran down the weapon over his hand, dripping on her and the floor. She shook the fist with the dishrag at his big unblinking eye. "You're making a mucking mess! Get the hell out of my kitchen!"

A rumbling noise came from deep inside him, his sides shook and his mouth twisted into something resembling a sneer.

She shook her fist again. "You won't think it's so damned funny when I put my foot up your butt! Get out, I said!"

He bent down so his face was close to hers and growled menacingly. She stretched up on tiptoes and glared, not giving an inch. Seconds ticked by. He lowered the club slightly and took a step back. "Duty?"

"Yeah, yeah, duty. Now get your big monkey face out of my sight! Go bother someone else!" She wrung out the rag. "I'm never going to finish my work with all these stupid interruptions."

The brute hesitated then squeezed out the terrace doorway sideways, pulling the club after him.

A short time later, Athy came in from Main Court holding up Arty, who passed out as they entered.

It aggravated Maidservant. Why was everyone so filthy, bloody and making messes for her to cleanup? She waved them toward the terrace. "I'll rinse blood off the plates and bring you food and drink directly. Imagine you'll want wine to warm you up, in spite of the early hour."

Athy slapped her face. "Snap out of it! Don't you see that Arty is hurt? Do you hear the fighting outside? There's a body on the floor. Can you comprehend what's going on? Well, can you?"

Maidservant pulled away from her. "I'm not blind, Athy."

"Where are Leto and the others?"

"Dead, I reckon." She went down on all fours and began wiping up blood around Arty just as gruff voices came from outside Main Court hallway.

Athy picked up Arty and hurried toward the storage room. "We'll hide in there."

Maidservant got up off the floor. "I'll tell them you went out through the terrace. That is where everyone is going tonight in spite of the fact it needs cleaning."

Stopping in the doorway, Athy whispered frantically. "You have to hide with us! They'll kill you!"

Maidservant shook her head. "They won't hurt me. Don't worry, I'll protect you."

A man with braided black hair and bronze armor decorated with gold and silver scrollwork entered. Six warriors shuffled into a semi-circle around the wall behind him. The largest and fiercest was the one-eyed club bearer. Maidservant, bent over the sink, gave a quick glance then continued working, which the man considered a lack of respect. He noted her disgusting state and looked back at the brute. "You think this worthless creature serves someone important, do you? Well, I say she dies!" He slammed the counter beside her with a heavy cudgel.

Startled, Maidservant whipped around. Behind the man, the giant brute loomed, again with the club poised to strike. Then a new voice came from the hallway. "I don't know who you are, but you'll leave the girl alone if you know what's good for you."

Instantly, the big warrior was with the others, club by his side, as if he had not moved. No one else seemed to have noticed. Maidservant rubbed her eyes and slapped herself as her master, wearing an expensive wig, fragrant oil that preceded him and an elegant tunic, strode into the room, put a kerchief to his nose and sniffed loudly.

"Well, well," the man remarked, "what kind of dandy do we have here? Seize him."

The warriors grabbed him with the intention of pushing him down to the floor, but with no more than a shrug, he threw them back against the wall. "Touch me again and I'll burn the flesh off your bones."

The man signaled the soldiers into defensive position, hooked the cudgel on his belt and drew a curvilinear dagger. "Identify yourself."

"I am someone you should fear."

The man laughed. "Really? I am General Perius, first in service to Shelitine, Fourth of the Six. I doubt you know who that is, but I count the people I fear on one hand."

The man blew his nose into the handkerchief. "I never understood why someone with your good reputation would leave the service of Coeus for a conniver like Shelitine."

Insulting one of the Six in a room full of those who served was sure invitation to hard death, but Perius immediately dropped to his knees, put down the knife and prostrated, forehead to the floor. "Forgive me, Lord. I did not recognize you. Down, dogs! Show respect."

Confused, the warriors knelt, placed weapons on the floor next to them and followed the general's example. Tesi-Ra reached down and raised Perius' head. "I like correct decisions reached quickly. I offer you two choices: pledge service to me and incur Shelitine's wrath, or remain faithful to her and displease me."

Perius picked up his dagger by the blade, presented it to Tesi-Ra and leaned back, exposing his throat. "My life is yours, Lord, to do as you will."

Tesi-Ra placed the sharp edge to Perius' jugular. "Are you certain? It gives me the right to take satisfaction for your insults."

Perius stretched his neck tighter and stared fearlessly into Tesi-Ra's eyes. "It is my great honor to serve or die as you see fit, Lord."

Tesi-Ra snapped off the blade with his thumb and tossed it aside. "Shelitine and I have argued long over settlement of an old debt. I'll send word I've accepted you and this army as full payment, and you needn't worry about retribution. She will be angry at first then consider it a bargain. I'm promoting you to Senior General of all my forces, effective immediately."

Perius hid his surprise and pleasure well. "Has General Antwah been killed, Lord?"

"Not yet. I suggest you inform him of the change before he hears it elsewhere and has time to prepare objections. That would be bothersome."

Perius jumped up and saluted. "On your feet, curs. Salute Lord Tesi-Ra, First of the Six!"

Tesi-Ra nodded to Maidservant, clutching the rag to her chest and watching in a disinterested kind of way. "She is my trusted servant and instrumental in this victory. I think you should apologize to her."

Back down to the floor Perius and the warriors went, bowing to Maidservant, only this time keeping their weapons.

Tesi-Ra placed his hand on her small shoulder and beamed down like a proud father. "You'll feel better soon, but for now, you must stay in this building where it's safe. Oh, by any chance, did you happen to see where those two friends of yours ran off to?"

Maidservant could not believe the men bowed to her, or that her master honored her, but she would not betray her friends. She composed herself to sound truthful when she told the lie, but his grip tightened, hurting so badly she looked up and put a hand on his---a silent plea to stop. But he looked away from her, and she followed his gaze to her other hand, the one clutching the rag and pointing to the cupboard.

Athy killed one warrior and critically wounded another before they wrestled her to the floor. Without the one-eyed brute, they could not have held her down, even with one on each limb. All the while, Arty lay unconscious nearby.

Perius spoke with a note of respect. "We chased these two from the harbor. They run like the wind and killed countless assault warriors. Persuaded to serve, they could be of great use to us."

Tesi-Ra stood over Athy, but she stared unwaveringly at Maidservant, pressed back against the counter, terrified. He kicked her in the ribs. "Pay attention! Will you swear allegiance to save your life?"

Athy arched off the floor and fell back under the weight of the warriors. "You can make me scream until I die, but I won't do your bidding. Go ahead, do your worse."

Tesi-Ra went to Arty. "Well said, but I know your weakness."

Athy jerked a leg free and kicked the warrior trying to grab it back in the groin. The brute kept hold of the other one, caught the kicking one with his free hand and snapped the ankle. Then he squeezed, making her scream while Tesi-Ra examined Arty. "The arrow was poisoned, but she can be saved if we act fast. Will you serve me?"

The brute stopped torturing so Athy could answer. "I'd rather die than serve you, and so would she."

"Serve me, or I'll have her healed then burned alive every minute of her long life with you chained to watch. Just think how she will writhe, scream and curse you for not saving her from such a horrible fate."

Athy fast-spoke an incantation that caused the warriors holding her arms to recoil. She jerked free and sat up, but the brute did not react to the spell and used her ankle to force submission.

Tesi-Ra smiled. "You please me, young Priest. If you pledge allegiance, I'll give your friend a peaceful death. How does that sound?"

Athy turned her head to Maidservant. "If you give me her, too."

He chuckled. "You hate her so much and don't even know she poisoned everyone in the Watchers' building, including your mother. Then she burnt it down just in case she missed someone. My little servant has turned out to be quite the scamp, don't you think?"

Athy cursed him.

Tesi-Ra bent close to her face. "Hate has a delicious flavor. It melts in the mouth, sets the soul afire and enables abilities otherwise hidden. Tell you what. Perhaps, if things work out, I'll give you Seydi to vent your anger on, but not right away. There are still issues to be ironed out."

Athy spit on him. "How can you do that to your own daughter?"

He hit her, breaking the nose. "I want your intelligence as well as fighting abilities. I punish stupidity. Does that make matters any clearer for you?"

Athy turned her face to the side so the blood ran out of her nose and mouth instead of choking her. "Yes. I should have realized she might be something else."

"No more discussion. Will you serve me or watch your friend suffer the rest of your lives?"

Athy agreed.

Tesi-Ra motioned to the brute. "Can you tie her up without help?"

The giant turned Athy onto her stomach, pulled her arms back and bound them to the ankles with no regard for the broken one. Then he shoved her onto her side facing Tesi-Ra, who dug his fingers into her face and used tortured visions of Arty to force complete submission.

When she passed out, he went to Perius. "She is too strong mentally and physically to take chances before she is completely under our control. Keep her tied until we are certain transformation is well underway. Then I'll exploit her hate for the girl to bend her to our ways and enhance her power."

Perius nodded to Arty. "Want me to kill her, or simply let the poison run its course?"

Tesi-Ra gave him a withering stare. "You heard what I said about using intelligence, didn't you? She is as valuable as the other one. Take her to our best healers. When she recovers, I'll make her serve us, too. It will be too late for Athy to do anything about it."

To the relief of Perius, an officer ran in from the terrace. "Lords, we've located the entrance to the underground sleep areas. Soon as the fires burn out, we'll go inside. Meanwhile, the dead, wounded and prisoners are outside awaiting inspection."

Tesi-Ra was pleased. "That was fast. We still haven't accounted for the Head Priest and must try to find out if anyone knows where a Temple member named Envoy went. Moreover, a Priest named San-zeus is on the other side of the island and serves me. Send for him to help with interrogations. In the meantime, place guards outside this building and don't allow anyone in or out until I return."

***

MAIDSERVANT SQUATTED NEXT TO ATHY, relieved she was awake but concerned the ropes binding her swollen leg cut so deeply. She attempted to dab blood from her face with the rag, but Athy pulled her head away. "Get that filthy thing away from me!"

Maidservant tried to put her confused thoughts into words that made sense, but they would not come out right. "Wrapped your ankle with wet cloths. Your nose is bleeding all over the floor, though."

"Leave me alone, you monster!"

"The Lady said I must do the right thing, but didn't understand I never get to decide anything. No one cares what I want." Her eyes went out of focus and head lolled for a few seconds then she reached for Athy's face with the rag again.

Athy moved her head away again. "Stop!"

Maidservant stuck her filth-encrusted foot in front of Athy's face. "I am not a monster. I don't have gross feet." She giggled and pulled it back. "They are gross, but not the same way. Stepped in something, I guess."

She paused and tried to gather her thoughts again. "I want you to understand. It was same as when mousey ate the pill. Metys had the documents, but she was already dead. Then he took them. Don't know why. He can't do anything without me, except burn them maybe, like in Egypt." She noticed Athy staring at something behind her, turned to look then jumped up, flailing arms and screaming. "No! Go away!"

It took time for Athy to recognize Seydi leaning against the back wall next to the doorway to the baths. Having just come out of the pool, rivulets of water streamed off her. She had on her yellow Prospect's tunic, but it was torn, plastered to her and had an odd orange hue. She wore no wig or makeup. Her arms hung languid to the sides, fingertips loosely grasping a bloody cleaver and long knife. Then Athy looked from her to Maidservant several times with surprise and amazement. "Your faces are perfectly identical. Are you related?"

Seydi came off the wall toward them, brandishing the blades. "Don't compare me to that ugly worm!"

Suddenly, Maidservant screamed and jumped in front of her. "No! It's a trick! She died!"

Seydi shoved her. "Get out of the way!"

Crying, Maidservant came back. "It can't be."

Seydi slung her away. "And everyone said you were the smart one. Do you remember the guard with the pockmarks, the one who scared you so much? Don't shake your head. I know you do. Well, he didn't make me cry. Got him to put another girl in my place, but he didn't count on my price being so high. Skewered and burned him like a side of meat, and now, it's your turn."

Maidservant yelled, "But you're older than me!"

Seydi licked blood from the flat side of the knife blade then smiled and shook her head. "You just can't stand hearing about this, can you? Found my way into service easily enough, but it took nearly seven years before I earned rank that granted long life. Tesi-Ra probably preserved you immediately in case he needed your special abilities in the future. Revival is rare when they keep someone that way, and I was satisfied thinking of you sleeping forever amongst the other worms. Then I heard of an Egyptian girl with exceptional academic abilities awakened to act the part of a rich merchant's daughter, only extreme remaking damaged her and they needed someone else. I knew in my bones it was you, so I volunteered."

Her laughter was shrill. "I almost killed you before realizing you would not allow yourself to recognize the sister you betrayed. I did so enjoy torturing you day in, day out then making you forget. Ironic, is it not; the Great Lord, his daughter and her little slave, so intertwined by secrets?"

Maidservant looked around, dazed and confused. "Do you ever go back to Egypt to visit Mother's family?"

Seydi walked slowly toward her, dragging the point of the knife along the wall, a sound that made skin crawl. "It happened hundreds of years ago, moron."

Maidservant began moaning. Seydi backhanded her, snapping her head to the side. "If you'd kept your mouth shut like I told you, they would've saved both of us, but you only cared for yourself, reading everything they stuck in front of you."

Maidservant shook her head. "No!"

Seydi hit her again. "You only cared for yourself and left me to die. That's what happened and you know it."

Maidservant put her hands over her face. "I was so afraid, Joi-ket."

Seydi threw the cleaver at her head, but anger made her miss. Then she spoke through clenched teeth. "Don't call me by that common name. I am Czn-tanth, favorite Blood Daughter of the One Master. Soldiers should bow to me, not you. Tesi-Ra should favor me, not you. You should stay in your place and not try to take the position I've worked for so hard." She lunged with the knife.

Maidservant punched her in the face, knocking her down. Then she stood looking at her fist as if seeing it for the first time.

Czn-tanth jumped up. "So, he's began the next step of the little twerp's transformation, has he? Well, that you're stronger will make killing you more fun." The knife sliced up Maidservant's left cheek, barely missing the eye.

Maidservant screamed and bolted into Main Court hallway.

Czn-tanth expected to catch her in a few steps, but Maidservant zipped past guards, zigzagged through mobs of celebrating warriors and gained distance. Czn-tanth heard someone yell to stop, but ignored it and cast off her Cloak of Shadows as she reached First Test to use her full power.

Terrified, Maidservant realized she could not make it to the shortcut through the woods and veered into one of the narrow, steam-filled drainage passages without thinking where it went.

Czn-tanth was familiar with the passages because the Temple made Prospects conduct projects in them, but in her excitement, mistook the one they were in for another that was longer. Then she had a fleeting glimpse of Maidservant leaping full-speed off the top rail of the barrier fence, tried to stop and crashed through it.

Masculine hands pulled her back, took her by the wrists and slammed her into the passage walls all the way out to First Test. Then he swung her in a wide arc down onto her back. In excruciating pain, she stared up at Tesi-Ra, Perius and several soldiers, thinking he would not dare kill her with servants of Shelitine watching. Yet, he jerked her up and crunched her down again. "I've had enough games from you."

Now, she was terribly afraid. "Did I catch her in time? Did I save her?"

He threw her into the wall and she fell in a bloody heap. "We saw you chasing her with a knife."

She had to have more time to heal. "She went crazy. She tried to cut herself, but I wrestled the knife from her. Then she ran to throw herself into Boiling River. She was unbelievably fast. Did you do something to enhance her speed?"

He stomped on her leg, breaking and crushing more bones. "I know you think having Perius here will save you, but he is my general now. Tell me what really happened."

She was out of ideas, but did not give up. She dangled her tongue. Slobber bubbled from her mouth. Her legs and arms jerked. She rolled her eyes and babbled incoherent nonsense.

Tesi-Ra turned to Perius. "Take these men and attend to Antwah. I'll be along when I'm finished here."

As soon as they were alone, Tesi-Ra grabbed Czn-tanth off the ground and shook her. "Did you alter your looks just to provoke me? Do you want to suffer incredibly more before I kill you or have you lost your mind?"

She could not stand more damage. "Remember the two sisters in Pharaoh's Library? I'm the one you and the worm abandoned to die. Surely, you can understand why I want to kill her and don't like you very much, can't you?"

He looked at her closer. "Well, well. How did you escape and rise so fast in rank?"

She told him her story then added, "I have many powerful abilities that no one suspects until it is too late, Lord. I am more skilled than anyone thinks. I can be useful."

He considered then dumped her back on the road. "We'll see. But for now, if you can heal yourself before marauders find you, I'll allow you to live, long as you stay out of my way and pay retribution for my servant."

***

ALMOST HEALED, CZN-TANTH ROLLED ON THE GROUND next to the avenue hugging her chest, giggling and singing. "Dead sister. Dead sister. I am so happy today. Dead sister. Dead sister. Can't come out to play."

A huge shadow moved over her, taking it all away. Angry, she sat up, saw the disfigured face and recognized one of Perius' warriors. "Don't stand so close. What do you want?"

The giant extended a hand more than sufficient to wrap around her. "May I assist you, Lady Czn-tanth?"

She could kill any remade warrior, yet experienced tremendous fear of this one. Startled, she scooted to the wall, certain he meant to throw her in the river. After a few long seconds, he lumbered off down the avenue. Relieved, she got up and hobbled back to the Temple, looking back often over her shoulder.

TWENTY-TWO

THE BOOK OF MAIDSERVANT: THE LAST HEAD PRIEST

MAIDSERVANT WOKE UP TO DISTANT SOUNDS OF MARCHING. She was just inside the front entrance of the House of Kalli against the wall on the yellow floor, so no one could see her from the avenue. Her last memories were landing in an eddying pool of steaming muck near the bank of Boiling River. She had put a hand down to keep from falling then somehow climbed out before losing consciousness.

She looked at her left arm, from hand to elbow resembling a boiled bird with loose skin hanging off it. Worse, her feet and legs halfway to the knees were raw meat---swollen, blistered and bleeding. Obviously, someone had done something to take away the pain and carried her here, but why just shove her inside then, presumably, leave?

She heard scraping claw sounds coming up the avenue from the direction of Eao as well as growls and snarls. She knew what they were. Packs of ferocious creatures resembling dogs had been in Main Court attacking people while somewhat under the control of a handler. Likely, they would rip her to shreds before she could let anyone know she served. If she had to die, fine, but not like that. Frantic, she pushed up, leaned against the wall then pushed off toward the bridge, leaving bloody streaks as she stiff-legged across the floor.

Pain in her feet was intense. To waste no steps, she concentrated following the joint where the green and yellow tiles met, but halfway to the bridge, she heard the creatures enter the building. She turned around, hoping the handler would stop them, but they were alone. The largest bound on all fours ahead of the others. It leaped, reaching out for her with black-tipped claws. She threw up her hands and shrieked.

Lightning flashed from the black corner, blasting the attacker to pieces. Thunder rumbled across the room. Maidservant gaped at the creatures, which had stopped, then resumed shuffling to the bridge.

More creatures ran into the building and joined the pack. After a brief spate of growling and biting to establish leadership, the new leader howled and the chase resumed.

Meanwhile, Maidservant had reached the bridge and found a female warrior propped against a rail post near the middle. A black helm lay beside her and she did not have a weapon drawn. Then she saw it was Leto with two arrows in the stomach and a dark pool of blood around her. Neither spoke, exchanging stares as she passed. The creatures were almost to the bridge when she reached the other end, planted her feet on the red floor and faced the bull. "Dead! Dead! Dead! Dead! Cruel! Cruel! Cruel! Cruel!"

She opened her eyes to the ceiling resting against the top rails of the bridge, not enough room for her to stand up, even if she could. The walls were tight against the sides and ends. She had not considered how claustrophobic it would be and fought down a panic attack.

"I can't believe you're the one."

Maidservant made herself sit up. Leto still sat in the same spot. The light came from a small globe above her. "What happened to the creatures chasing me?"

"I don't know. Everything went pitch black, I made a light and it was like this."

"How did I get here from the end of the bridge?"

"You crawled."

"Why would I do that?"

"It wasn't easy. You resisted."

She pulled up her knees to look at her feet and legs because they felt much better. The skin was shiny pink where the burns had been and a couple of toes were missing nails, but everything seemed to work okay. "Why can't you mind your own business?"

"Someone with greater skills than mine had already started your healing. Who was it?"

She did not answer.

Leto motioned her to come closer. "I had to rest before I could do your arm and face. I can do it now, I think."

"Don't bother. I'm going to die in here."

"Don't be ridiculous." She reached into a leather pack hanging on her shoulder, pulled out the four statues and set them on the bridge. "I brought these for you. Kalli's seer said that you'd know what to do with them. Is it true?"

"She also foretold that only the Head Priest comes out of the tomb alive, and that's you, not me, so you can stick them and Kalli's plan up your butt."

"How do you know what the seer said?" Getting no answer, she shrugged. "Anyway, you've got it wrong."

Maidservant pulled something off her left hand that might have been a fingernail and flipped it at her. "You think you know so much. I can read better than you."

"I abandoned the Temple to those monsters to bring these to you!"

"If I get my hands on them, I'll smash them to bits."

Grimacing, Leto reached into the bag, took out a small vial and fumbled to open the top but could not seem to make her fingers work right. "You can sit alone in the dark and rot, for all I care."

Maidservant edged closer. "What is that?"

"Poison, in case I was captured."

"Hey, those are Athy's arrows in your gut, aren't they?"

"She and Arty thought I was the enemy. Couldn't call out, because they would've stopped and been killed, though I imagine I only postponed the inevitable."

Maidservant laughed nastily. "Athy already serves my master, and soon Arty will, too. Guess this is not your day."

Leto stared then dropped the vial and grabbed a large jar from the bag. "On second thought, damned if I'll allow you to escape the destiny you are so eager to avoid. When I break the seal, sleep fog will fill the chamber, and there's nothing you can do about it. "

"The prophecy said I die. You will live."

She gave her that irritating smirk. "Yeah, keep believing that. The jars for your awakening are in my pack. Sleep tight."

Maidservant lunged, grabbed the poison vial from beside Leto and scooted away. Leto franticly worked trying to peel back the seal of the sleep fog with her thumbnail. Maidservant pulled the vial open and sucked down the contents. Immediately, all her energy drained and she slouched over. "You go save the world. I'm done."

In deep stupor, Maidservant became aware of Leto crossing her arms over her chest. Relieved a Kallistian would know the proper Egyptian way to prepare a body for death, she sighed. Then Leto cupped her hands over the cut on her face, healing it. Slowly, realization came, but it took a while to say it. "No sleep fog. You would have smashed the jar."

Leto twisted Maidservant's head to the side to the clean nasal passages and she saw Leto still propped against the bridge with the blank stare of death's void. Yet, Leto turned her up again, shook out a cloth and placed it over her face. Then she heard Leto speaking. "Praise to Mighty Atlas. Praise to loyal, brave and dutiful DoSo. Praise to Rhea, strongest of all the Head Priests.

Finally, praise to wretched Leto for serving Kalli and not killing this vile creature."

The light illuminating the cloth on Maidservant's face went out.

***

ON THE HILL ACROSS FROM WHERE THE HOUSE OF KALLI HAD BEEN, a line of warriors watched fearfully as dense emerald fog swirled precisely within the perimeters of the site and formed the shape of a huge dome high above it. Along the avenue, they could make out a dark shadow in the mists resembling a fortress wall with an entrance between two towers near the center. Atop each tower, the shadowy shapes of enormous cats, one a lion, the other a tiger, prowled with shining yellow eyes. Suddenly, the lion shook its great head and roared at the same instant the tiger lunged forward and snarled. The warriors, directly across the avenue from them, fell back in horror, except for Tesi-Ra, Perius and the one-eyed brute.

Tesi-Ra glanced at the soldiers cowering behind shields. "At least you have one well-trained man. Order everyone but him to attack between the towers. Let's see what happens."

Eager to redeem their standing, the warriors charged down the hill, across the road and into the fog. The big cats turned and disappeared into the interior. Screams and snarling ensued. Two warriors staggered back out onto the avenue, floundered and gasped until they died. It was very quick.

Tesi-Ra shook his head. "I believe the cats are illusions. The fog is the real danger, a poison of some kind. More worrisome, I sense powerful old magic somewhere out near the center."

Perius nodded. "Yes, I feel it, too. Kalli, do you think?"

He shrugged. "We'll need someone with stronger abilities in these matters to tell more. Station the armies around this place while I go send word to the Master. He's not going to be pleased. I think we have sprung Kalli's trap."

PART TWO

OF

DR PAUL BENJAMIN'S

TRANSLATIONS

TWENTY-THREE

THE BOOK OF THE HERO ARIADNE: RESURRECTION

MY FATHER, ERMITICUS IV, KING OF THE KEFTIU EMPIRE, named me Ariadne after his mother, who died one hundred and sixty years before I was born. My mother, Queen Malidia, was long lived, too, but I was never told exactly how long because their longevity and the fact they were first and foremost Priests of the Temple of Light were their greatest secrets, kept from me until the fateful day my mother blurted it out and I left them forever.

Nearly all Priests took great care not to have children because long life was not hereditary. Only the Temple granted it to Initiates they decided would become Priests someday. Of course, there were exceptions such as DoSo, who had four children before one of them, Kore, qualified to join the Temple and had long life bestowed. Children who did not qualify had false memories implanted then relocated to grow up somewhere else with another family. It was the Temple's harshest law and made no exceptions.

I knew nothing about any of this until word arrived that Rhea had reversed the decision of the Council and accepted me as a Prospect. Initially, they ruled I was insufficient to join them, which had angered and hurt me deeply. Strangely, it upset my parents even more, especially my mother, who was distraught for weeks.

True to my nature, my gut reaction was to tell them to stick it where the sun doesn't shine and refuse to go. That was when my mother told me that she and my father were on the verge of sending me away to live with strangers for the rest of my life, which then led to telling me about Priests, long life and how our world really worked.

As I listened with deepening resentment, my father came in, realized what she was doing and they got into a hot argument. Had the Council found out she told me before I went to Kalliste, they likely would have punished and deposed them as rulers, but that's beside the point now, because during the argument it came out that he had never forgiven her having me in the first place. Well, it ended badly with me shouting I never wanted to see them again and, without their knowing, taking the next ship to Kalliste.

A few months later, when Leto broached the subject of Priests and children during class, she looked at me as she pointed out the child would grow old while the parents remained young, causing both sides to suffer immeasurably, which she said justified the disowning of a child. Never one to keep my mouth shut, I flew into a tirade, including telling her to inform my former parents that I did not appreciate them using her to speak to me. She did not bother denying it, instead arguing that I was too opinionated, stubborn and ignorant for my own good. I told her damn right, it wasn't going to change and she could tell them that, too. She gave me a week's kitchen duty for being disrespectful. The day I finished, she asked if I had learned my lesson, and I earned two more.

I arrived at the Temple cocksure I could hold my own against anyone. I was smart, worked hard and had a knack for wrestling problems to right conclusions. Moreover, I was determined to prove the Council wrong for turning down my initial admission, especially since everyone thought the Head Priest admitted me because of who my parents were. Truth be told, so did I, making me even more determined to be first in all my classes.

Turns out, most Prospects could do extraordinary things with little or no effort. Anywhere else, they called it magic. It did not take long for me to evaluate my classmates' abilities against mine then consider future Initiate vacancies. Pure and simple, I realized I wasn't good enough. My solution was to try harder, but I lost confidence, despaired and made foolish mistakes. Rightly, I expected to be in the first group asked to leave.

Then the Head Priest moved me ahead of others more deserving and inexplicably paired me with a brilliant and incredibly beautiful Prospect named Cytheria. I was certain she would be angry teamed with such a dunderhead and avoided her until one night, without warning, she burst into my room in Prospect Village. I knew her looks were amazing, of course, but had never seen her close up before. She took my breath away, and her smile left me speechless, which is really saying something. Then she did this big awkward curtsy, almost falling over sideways, laughed and hugged the air out of me.

"Hi," she said, so loud it hurt my ears, "call me Cythe. Sorry you've been stuck with such an unmannered oaf. Do you have anything to eat while we get to know each other? They stopped letting me have thirds at evening meal. Said I eat too much and might get fat. Between you and me, that is what I am trying to do. I'm tired of everyone ogling me all the time. Bet you feel the same way about everyone making a big deal about you being a royal thingamabob. Right?"

It makes me cry, thinking about her now. Impossibly, she was many times sweeter than she was pretty. When I became frustrated, complained too much or cried, Cythe would look at me with those crystal blue eyes and, in her silliest deep voice, declare, "But who knows what higher purpose Destiny holds for Princess Aria? She must…prepare…prepare." Eventually, everyone said it, especially when drinking. Made us laugh every time, too. Yeah, those were the good times.

Seems like yesterday that Leto took Cythe and me from Jellyfish House to the catacombs under the Temple. Passages ran in every direction, and it confused us. We did not have any idea all that even existed. They placed us side-by-side on two low stone beds in a gigantic, dimly lit room with long rows of sleepers.

Cythe was afraid, and I reached over to hold her hand. She gave me the warmest smile as sleep claimed her first. Then I felt terribly alone until Leto came and stood at my feet, stern as always. You'd think she would at least try to smile at a time like that. A Priest bent over me, adjusted the pillow block and whispered, "Ten years will seem no more than ten minutes. Have no concern. We'll watch over you." The last thing I remember was a glow around Cythe. At the time, I thought it was my imagination or the elixir did something to my eyes.

It is hard, but I must stop thinking so much about the past. Remembering is morbid and useless, because when I woke up, that world was gone.

***

GRUNTING INSISTENTLY, A MONSTROUS FEMALE CREATURE shook me awake by the shoulders. I stared, astounded and horrified. She obviously wanted me to do something, but I could do nothing except to recoil from her ugliness and putrid breath. Another gruesome creature peered over her shoulder then splashed a bucket of gross, oily liquid in my face. Later, I would learn it was what now passed for water. They left me on the cold earthen floor, naked and shivering.

I can't describe those moments properly. The chamber was a horror of crushed, broken skeletons strewn all around, and I knew they had to be the remains of the other sleepers. Desperately, I searched for something to indicate Cythe's fate, in spite of knowing how stupid and impossible it was. I wanted to scream and pinch myself out of the nightmare, but I could not move.

The two women---I didn't know it then, but that is what they once had been---returned and dragged me by the feet into another room with more torches and gross piles of animal and human remains everywhere. Now I could see they were completely naked except for dirt and grime, and their feet were grotesque with thick dark toenail-claws scrabbling when they shuffled across the floor. I really thought they planned to butcher and eat me.

One jammed filthy fingers into the corners of my mouth to hold it open and jerked my head back by the hair. Two amphorae of the vilest liquids ever created burned all the way down my throat into the stomach. When I refused to take more, they forced it into my mouth and held it and my nose closed until I swallowed. I nearly choked to death before I got enough down to satisfy them.

They dragged me into a small, dark room and locked me inside. The floor was cold and wet. Tiny scurrying creatures bit and stung until I regained use of my hands and squashed them. More always came, and it became both battle and pastime with no winners, only losers. I never saw or knew what they were, which was maybe for the best, I think.

Occasionally, one of the women forced more liquid down my throat. Since I no longer thought they meant to kill me, I shouted abuse and cursed them. They responded to everything by grunting like hogs. One day I grunted back until finally one slapped me, dragged me into the hall and grabbed a torch off the wall. I thought she was going to shove it in my face, but she opened her mouth and showed where her tongue used to be. I threw up. Then I was ashamed, for I realized I wasn't the only victim in this place. For what it is worth, I never yelled at them again and we got along.

Time means nothing in darkness, especially with unchanging routine. Madness and sanity can overlap, too. At some point, I realized I had been having conversations with Cythe for a long time. Whether that helped me hold onto a few threads of reality, I don't know, but I did. Yeah, I couldn't have done it without her.

The women came in with two wide boards and used them to carry me along a winding passage. It was very dark, but after so long in the room, I could see a little. We went a long ways up a gradual incline, and I wondered if it might be a tunnel to the outside, but then they took a side passage and carried me into a good-sized room with an oil lamp, lumpy bag filled with dirt for a bed, and large earthen pot for a toilet. They left, and that was the last time I saw them.

***

A GIRL WITH DARK EYES, NORMAL FEET AND CAKED-ON FILTH all over her, ran in with dirty sack-like garment for me. In spite of many rips and tears, it was nicer than the rags swinging loosely from her skinny shoulders. Seeing clothes made me embarrassed, for I had been naked so long I had stopped thinking about it. She hurried out and returned with an encrusted bowl of foul broth, wormy slab of flour cake and piece of not quite rotten fruit. Washed down with brackish water from a leaking cup, I threw it up later, but it will always be among the best meals I ever had. Best of all, she left the oil lamp so I would not be in the dark all the time. The next day, I tried to ask questions but she shook her head, grunted and showed me her tongueless mouth. She could understand me, but that was all. Soon, I realized it was the same for everyone working in this place.

Sometimes, everything shook. I'd felt it often in the dark cell, but wasn't sure it was real. Now, however, I could see things shaking or falling when it was particularly bad. Once, I even fell. It was most peculiar.

I counted each meal as a day, though they seemed extremely too long. Then the girl showed up scooting a rickety stepstool in front of her. It had three steps each side and an unusually wide top. At a different time and place, it would have been hilarious watching her point at me as she walked circles around the room, climbing up and over the stool. Even so, I understood long before I got up off the bed and did it. She was delighted, relatively speaking, because changes in her expression were so subtle that no one would notice except a...a... What was I, anyway? Prisoner? Inmate? Patient? Lunatic? Maybe parts of all of them.

Sitting on the floor in a corner, Imaginary Cythe laughed. "You're a lard butt, that's what. Can't you move any faster than that?"

After that, I passed time trading barbs with Cythe and walking around the room. Then one day the girl came in and trod along behind me. After a while, I forgot she was there and resumed talking to Cythe. Then the girl started grunting, and I realized she knew what I was doing and talked to her, too. From then on, she joined us for a walk every day, sometimes for hours, and the three of us had some great conversations.

I think the time the strange girl spent in my room were her happiest, and of all the horrors I'd experienced, nothing scared me more. Think about it.

On my side facing the wall, I had just gone to bed when the door unlocked. I assumed it was the girl, but then a man said, "Room eighty-one. The last preserved survivor. Resurrected by decree of Tesi-Ra. Do you have anything else on her?"

I jumped off the bed. Two dandified old men with magnificent gray beards and dressed in resplendent short white tunics were just outside the door. One busily wrote on a big scroll. They seemed vaguely familiar. Heart in my mouth, I said, "Hello."

The one not writing yelled, "She still has her tongue! I'll not tolerate such gross negligence, Councilor Marko. Find who's responsible and punish them before someone blames us. But first, have her tongue removed!"

"At once, Prefect Tritius." He shouted down the hall. "Summon the Head Keeper to bring the chopper to eighty-one. Now!" Then they slammed the door in my face.

I dashed around looking for something to fight them. I pulled a board off the stepstool. I wasn't very strong, but if they thought I would stand there and let them cut out my tongue, they were about to find out differently.

The door banged open. An enormous, hideous creature squeezed in sideways. He had one huge glaring yellow eye and a jagged gash with stuff running from where the other had been. His feet were like the women-wretches, only covered with long, matted hair with bigger claws. He held long metal tongs with a chopping device inside a cage built to go over the head. I could not fight this brute. No one could. He came for me. I dropped the board and screamed. Faster than I could follow, he put the cage over my head, jammed the tongs into my mouth and grabbed hold of my tongue. I felt blades positioning around it.

Then the girl was there, jumping on his feet, striking him with fists and grunting like mad. I thought he would swat her like a bug, but he bent down and listened intently, growing more furious by the second. Then he removed the apparatus and shoved Tritius and Marko out of the room. The door slammed behind them.

Acting as though nothing happened, the girl led me to the steps and motioned to go. She wouldn't take no for an answer, and finally I shuffled around the room with her following. After a time, I stopped crying and, to regain some semblance of courage, hummed a Keftiu folk song about sailors returning home from the sea. To my surprise, the girl knew it and grunted along. Then, from the hall, came deep rumbling accompaniment, and it took a moment to realize it was the brute joining in. Then Cythe said something that made me laugh. "Princess Ariadne, out for a stroll."

TWENTY-FOUR

THE BOOK OF THE HERO ARIADNE: THE WAY OF THINGS

I DO NOT KNOW HOW LONG I LIVED UNDERGROUND before they took me to meet the new masters of the world. I think it was a very long time. Looking back, my senses must have become numb to the aberrations and terrors I faced; otherwise, I would have reacted differently and not survived that day.

The door flew open and the girl rushed in grunting and waving arms frantically. Two gross boys I'd never seen before ran in behind her carrying a big earthen jar and poured water over my head. As I sputtered and fumed, the girl whipped the blanket off the bed and tried to rub dirt off my face and arms, but only succeeded streaking the oily grime coating me. Cythe laughed.

A middle-aged woman hurried in and handed the girl a somewhat clean, much mended tunic then grabbed the ragged sack covering me and tried to pull it off over my head. I held onto it and shoved her away. I pointed to the leering boys. "I'm not undressing until they go!"

The girl rolled her eyes and shoved all of them out of the room, but before she closed the door, Tritius burst in, ranting at Marko. "What do you mean she's not ready? Everyone knows that I go to audiences at the Palace at least three hours before the appointed time to show the Lords proper respect."

Bowing and wringing hands, Marko was so sequacious it would have been comical in different circumstances. "I am only thinking of you, Lord Prefect. She is not dressed and has not learned the way of things, yet."

Tritius fumed. "She can go naked and dirty for all I care. I'll not be late!"

The Head Keeper stuck his head in and grunted, none too friendly. Tritius blanched. "Very well! She can have twenty more minutes."

Finally, they led me outside. A short distance away, the three obelisks poked up through scraggly trees and underbrush. The pedestal in the pond that had designated the center of Main Court protruded out of a low, weedy mound. Nothing else identified this as the location of the Temple of Light. Tritius warned that if I spoke a single word without permission or made a fuss, he would have my tongue cut out on the spot, so I controlled my confusion and anguish.

Warm drizzle, acrid smoky haze and dark overcast made the day dismal, yet the dim daylight hurt my eyes acutely. The Keeper tied my wrists in front of me so tightly the bones ached all the way though, then he looped another rope around the first and handed the ends to Marko, who jerked me to follow him and Tritius like an animal on a leash. The girl and Keeper trailed us at some distance.

Stumbling frequently, I watched the rough rocky ground closely so as not to exacerbate the soreness of my bare feet, so didn't see the statue in an intersection of trails until we were upon it, which was fortunate, because I might have called out. It was Maidservant, perfectly life-sized and painted astonishingly realistic, standing on a short pedestal in a tattered Temple work tunic and reaching out with what appeared to be a dishrag. Except for a full head of hair, she looked identical to the last time I'd seen her.

Tritius and Marko clasped their hands to chests and bowed as they went by, then Tritius droned back over his shoulder, "Pay homage to the god, Outcast."

Dumfounded, I bowed, then kept looking back and observed the girl run to the statue and embrace it while the brute sat on the ground staring as though it was wondrous. I had so many questions that I nearly choked from not asking them.

We emerged from the overgrowth beside a busy road made of crushed seashells and gravel. Marko moved in front of me before I had a chance to get more than a glimpse. "Because you were sustained by one of the Great Lords, you will see remade creations as they truly are. You must not stare or react, for many outsiders visit the island and nothing must spoil the illusion that everyone here is the same as them. If you fail to control yourself, you will be gutted and fed to the garden."

At first, I wanted to scream. While many "regular" people like us were on the road, most were something that I now call twisted, humanity perverted into all sorts of creatures, the worst being brutes similar to the Head Keeper and the two females who had attended me. They frightened me near to death, but as no one gave me second looks, soon I gawked and studied them when Marko and Tritius did not pay me attention.

We passed through a sordid village of huts and hovels set among the charred, crumbling remains of old stone buildings. With a jolt, I realized it was Prospects' Village, where I used to live with Cythe. Children, cute in a bizarre kind of way, ran beside the road, pelting me with small stones and insults. Their vocabulary seemed limited and some just made noises. Noting how careful they were not to hit Tritius and Marko, I moved as close behind as possible, and escaped all but a few painful welts on my back and legs. Judging by all the stacks of weapons and shields, I guessed the dark misshapen inhabitants were soldiers and their families. Soon, I discovered they had low intelligence but were very cunning and dangerous, killing and eating anyone from outside their village they could.

We wound through dense, gnarly scrub and wild brambles, no vestiges whatever of the gentle green beauty that had been the earmark of Kalliste. Later, I would learn that through some trick, visitors saw it more as it used to be, and that the winding road we were on was the main way between Atlas City, old Cadi-sum, and the new Olympus City, our destination.

Clouds broke briefly and I saw the top of the mountain. It was black, barren and had fire and smoke spewing, a constant condition I would soon learn. Just then, powerful tremors shook the ground, nearly knocking me over. Tritius and Marko made a quick sidestep, hopped and had no problem.

After that, I sunk into depression and did not notice the surroundings until Tritius intoned, "Behold Olympus...City of the Gods."

Sprawled across the side of the mountain, glorious in concept and construct, the city was a masterpiece. We walked along incredible streets to an even more incredible double avenue of breathtaking proportion and elegance that ran straight up the mountain and disappeared over a high crest. Slender white columns lined the sides for no other purpose than to recreate beauty every thirty paces. Tritius intoned, "Behold...the Gods of Olympus."

In the wide grassy median, about a hundred paces apart, enormous towering statues stared down the mountain like sentinels guarding the heavens. They were stunning colors and gleamed with gold, silver leaf and precious stones.

At first, I was mesmerized. Every tree had precise green leaves, not one off-color, misshaped or wrong-sized. Every flower blossomed fully, not a petal withered or fallen. Everything was immaculate, not a smudge, not a blemish; even the city's inhabitants, vibrant with health, beauty, wealth and superiority, distinguishable in every way from the thongs of visitors; especially me, with my rags, grime and dirty feet. Too overcome at the time to realize the new masters could as easily make creatures with beautiful human facades as they could demons to rip people apart, I allowed feelings of shame, inferiority and inadequacy to consume me and lost track again.

Marko jerked the rope and hissed to pay homage to a statue towering over us. With a start, I realized it was the last one before the top of the hill and looked back over my shoulder. The city and big statues seen from on high were even more breathtaking. Suddenly, Marko twisted me around and whipped me across the face with the rope. "Obey me, Outcast! Bow to Aphrodite!"

Numbly, I bowed then looked up through painful tears at the god I had honored. A flowing blue gown led up to graceful hands cupping a pomegranate then higher to a golden breastplate etched with yellow and blue flowers blooming on green vines then to an incredible face, long yellow hair and blue eyes too perfect to be of this earth; but I, of all people, knew that they were. My heart tore in two and my mind screamed a word I dared not utter. Cythe.

I fell to my knees. Marko cuffed me on both ears and whipped me with the rope until I got up. To my credit, I didn't make a sound, though at that precise moment, I don't think I could. He jerked me up the road to Tritius, who waited impatiently at the crest of the hill. He slapped me hard across the face. "Act up at the palace, girl, and I will kill you myself!" Then, in a perfectly calm voice that had repeated the words too many times, he intoned, "Behold...the Palace of the Gods."

In the middle of an enormous valley scooped out of the side of the mountain, a blue and green crystal palace with magnificent spires shimmered and sparkled as if constructed of jewels. Around it, lush gardens stretched steeply up in every direction to a rim lined with dense, wild vegetation except where the avenue entered. I recalled Maidservant telling me about a secluded bowl-shaped meadow in the Amber Area and thought this might be the same one.

Tritius took us through a gated turnoff into a section of gardens that bypassed most of the brutish guards. We entered an area of flowers and fountains with throngs of people milling. They were even more breathtakingly exquisite and perfect than the people in town, but something about them did not ring true to me. They discussed business, war and politics without a single casual or personal comment. After I heard the same phrases repeatedly and no one bothered to look at us, I realized Tritius and Marko ignored them, not something they would do. On impulse, I stuck my elbow out, intending to brush against a tall aristocrat, and it passed right though him. Astounded, I wanted to try it again but didn't get the chance because Tritius took a path away from them.

We went around a huge octopus fountain shooting water high into the air from the arms that I recognized from Eao, a place we drank wine in the summer because it was the coolest location in the city. I touched it with my foot to make sure it was real then looked for Cythe's and my names among others scratched on the side, but Tritius turned us away again before I found them. The great palace loomed over us, the mountain towering behind it. Wide steps led up to a magnificent porticoed entrance, but Tritius took a small side door marked private.

The Great Hall of the Gods of Olympus was cavernous and luxurious. Columns and tapestries seemed to rise to the heavens. Red carpets crisscrossed the room, converging at a glorious golden throne set on a high platform. Above it, a golden sunburst shined brightly. Rich, important people packed the room, but they were not perfect because they were visitors to the island. It did not keep them from looking down their noses at me, though. I was exhausted, did not feel well and resented their superior attitudes. I glared at each and every one, in spite of Marko hissing to lower my eyes.

Tritius took us behind a curtain, pulled out a big key and opened a tall door into a small vacant room with hard spindle chairs lining one side. A set of massive wooden doors intricately carved with grotesque faces, the first ugly things I'd seen since entering the city, filled the end wall.

Tritius sat down heavily, crossed his legs and settled back for a long wait. Marko paced around the room examining murals of the palace exterior, but I thought the real reason he didn't sit was that Tritius did not say he could. Still in tow, he kept me close like a child in an expensive ceramics shop. My body throbbed painfully from unaccustomed exertion and my mind was a muddled mess.

Without warning, the big doors flew open and a tall man with long white hair and beard swept out. A flowing purple robe, gold crown and flashing scepter with crossed lightning bolts proclaimed his eminence and power---a god, if ever a god existed.

Tritius and Marko threw themselves to the floor, Marko pulling me down and shoving my face into the stone, but I had already recognized San-zeus. I sneaked another look as he paused to twist the scepter. Light flared around him and he transformed into a giant. Then he went through the door, greeted by wild cheering and heralding horns before it closed behind him. I didn't have time to think about it, though, because from beyond the double doors came a familiar nasal voice. "Bring the Outcast."

***

LOUNGING ON ORNATE RED COUCHES behind a low white marble table at the far end of the room were four giants. Tritius led us to what must have been his customary place and waited for them to acknowledge him.

In spite of seeing all sorts of monsters already, their appearances shook me to the core. Three had faces out of nightmares, but the fourth was as sharply handsome as I remembered, for it was Ambassador Hariset, but how could he be so big and why did the others defer to him?

The giant with the cruelest, calculating eyes fixed them upon Tritius. "Why bring the Outcast up the Avenue of Gods and through the Elysian Gardens, Prefect? Surely, you know we have important delegations visiting today. We want to impress them, not expose our vermin problem."

Instantly, Tritius was wet with sweat, and I could smell a strong odor of alcohol. He wrung his hands. "The Head Keeper didn't have her ready, Lord Perius, so going the long way through Hunter Forest and Stalker Gardens would have made me late."

The only female was contemptuous, running freakish long fingers with black nails through tangled red hair that seemed to move occasionally of its own accord. "Let's slit their throats and feed the garden before the Prefect soils himself and smells up the room."

The largest, strongest man stroked a braided black beard with an enormous hand that appeared capable of crushing boulders. "Ah, Shelitine's solution to every personnel problem---kill everyone."

She laughed. "Please recall that you were my mentor, Kronos."

I could tell she resented his comment though she went along with the joke. I could also tell she had no qualms about killing us, and my knees went weak with a stark suspicion that I might not leave this room alive.

Meanwhile, Hariset studied me, and it felt as if fingertips pressed the sides of my head. Petrified with fear, it was easy for me not to react. Then it stopped and he asked, "Do you know why I spared you?"

I barely made my voice work and it sounded insipid. "No, Lord Hariset."

He spoke to Tritius sharply. "Why doesn't this Outcast know the proper way to address her master, Prefect?"

Before he could respond, Shelitine asked, "What's this, Prefect? You've allowed a sleeper out of the Barrows with a tongue. The penalty for that is death, isn't it?"

Tritius was on the verge of collapse and his reply was shrill. "It's not my fault! I ordered it removed but the Keeper refused after a troublemaker, Marlie, insisted she had received special instructions to leave it in. I've filed numerous complaints about her interfering, but no one does anything. Ask Marko, he'll tell you!"

Shelitine gazed maliciously at Hariset, who appeared particularly annoyed. "You answered the Fourth of the Six before me, your master, the First. You've made too many such blunders of late. I release you from your vows to me. From now on, you may serve Lady Shelitine, if she will have you."

Tritius went to his knees to beg, and I saw how showing weakness before them could be a grave mistake. He spoke his last words. "Please, Lord Tesi-Ra, I want to serve you, not her."

Shelitine leaned across the table and ripped out Tritius' throat so fast she was already back on the couch before he slumped to the floor. Then she stared at Marko and me with a slightly amused expression while cleaning blood and muck from her hands with a narrow darting black tongue. "Where did you find such useless creatures, Tesi-Ra?"

He jumped up and came around the table to us, but I saw sly intent upon his face before he faced the others. "These two are all that remain from the Temple, other than the gods, of course. This girl was a student, but had no abilities whatsoever. In fact, she used to clean our toilets."

Shelitine regarded me suspiciously. "Then why did you keep her?"

Towering over me, he waited until I looked up at him. "She's a princess, the last royal alive from that period."

Shelitine sat bolt upright. "What family? Some lineages are not as desirable as others."

"Daughter of the last King and Queen of the Keftiu Empire, who were secretly Priests sustained by Kalli's blood. Ariadne's her name, if I remember correctly."

Shelitine jumped up, glaring. "I turned Keftiu and Kalliste inside out searching for her. Why wasn't she listed on inventories of the living?"

He feigned surprise. "My private lists were not included, of course."

It took Shelitine considerable effort to keep her anger in check. "If she has no abilities, why would you want her? You certainly have no predilection for royal blood."

He was so smooth. "Maidservant requested I spare the girl's life because she wanted her as spoils, so when I came upon her unexpectedly sleeping in the catacombs, I kept the promise in case I thought of a way she might serve the hero of our victory someday. Least I could do for someone who served me so faithfully."

Kronos elbowed Perius. "Well, I don't know what Tesi-Ra has in mind, but she's too ugly to be a brothel girl, even for enlisted ranks. If we gave her to them, they'd probably declare war on us."

"Yeah," Perius laughed. "And with those hips, she'd be too slow for archery practice. Be like hitting a double sack of grain at ten paces."

Shelitine sneered. "Royal vermin always act as if they're better than people with real abilities, lording and mastering over everyone. You still haven't said what you plan to do with her, Tesi-Ra. I'll give you a thousand for her blood."

He acted interested. "If it means so much to you, I might consider a trade."

She practically salivated. "What do you want?"

"The service of Czn-tanth."

Shelitine shook her head. "You know the Master will be displeased if I give her to you. Name anything else, and it's yours."

"No, I will keep her."

She did not hide her anger. "What do you have planned for her?"

"When we proclaimed Maidservant a god, it never occurred to anyone the islanders would worship her with such fervor or that someone would hate her so much they risk death to deface her statues and shrines."

This was news to Kronos and Shelitine. Kronos demanded, "Who would dare? Why haven't they been stopped?"

Perius had responsibility for security on the island. "We've tried everything, but the culprits have eluded all our traps so far. The islanders blame the other gods, claiming they are jealous of Maidservant and have their followers retaliating. What was a trifling matter has grown into a troubling one."

"Someone with strong abilities must be behind it," Kronos observed. "Otherwise, the soldiers would have caught them already."

Tesi-Ra agreed. "That's why I've ordered Athene to look into it, but in the meantime, Maidservant's shrines and statues must be maintained. What could be more appropriate than having a blueblood spend the rest of her life serving the one who saved her?"

Shelitine was contemptuous. "She'll just sit on her royal rump all day peeling grapes. Give her to me as a gift and you'll come out ahead."

Tesi-Ra had expected the argument. "I sent word to the military that anyone who observes her not working between dawn and dusk will receive a generous bonus. Then, for every bonus, she will lose something, beginning with fingers and toes. When she can no longer do her duty, she will nourish the gardens."

Kronos had a booming laugh. "The likes of her won't last a day outside the towns."

Tesi-Ra nodded. "The army commanders will be responsible for protecting her in their areas. If anything happens to her, they will face my judgment. She will be designated Barrows Outcast and have a small group of them working with her, too. That will keep townspeople away."

Shelitine was not satisfied. "Then why does she have her tongue, to read poetry?"

Tesi-Ra shrugged. "In all fairness, she must be able to scream for help."

Hatred all over her face, Shelitine stared at me. "She hasn't cried or showed any emotions since coming in. Didn't even ask how long she slept, and they all ask that. Perhaps you should test to make certain her mind is sound."

Tesi-Ra glanced down and I knew he could not say no. "Ask one question. It must help you in service to us or we will judge you unfit. You have one minute."

Shelitine held those awful black nails up for me to see. "Concentrate, dearie, mustn't let anything distract you. Oh look, the poor thing's trembling. Do you feel a chill?"

I did not need to think about it and mostly concentrated to make my voice sound stronger than before. "Great Lord Tesi-Ra, what prevents soldiers from lying about me not working to collect rewards?"

He gave Shelitine a smug look. "As surely they will. Serve me faithfully, and I promise either Perius or I will examine all claimants personally. After we execute a few, the others will not lie. Is that agreeable?"

Before I could answer, Shelitine spoke. "I fear we got off on the wrong foot, dearie. Is there anything you would like to know about the fates of people you knew before you slept or how to get ahead in service to us?"

The lesson of Tritius was not one I would ever forget, especially as my feet stood in his blood. I looked at Tesi-Ra and answered his question. "I am honored to serve you, Lord. Thank you."

Maybe I looked relieved. Maybe it made no difference. Tesi-Ra took my hand, gave the little finger a push with his great thumb and snapped it back like a twig. How could something so little hurt so much? I screamed in spite of myself, wondering if it would bring my death, but he smiled as my father used to when I pleased him. "Take her back to the Barrows, Marko. Choose a few Outcasts to help her. They will live in Forbidden Tomb Shrine. Her service begins at daylight tomorrow."

***

MARKO LED ME OUT A SMALL DOOR into a long corridor with windows looking out on sunlit gardens of white-pink seashell walkways, tranquil ponds and graceful pagodas. He shuffled slowly then stopped altogether, staring down. Dazed and hurting, it was a moment before I realized. "Are you all right, Marko?"

"Tritius was my brother. I cared for him all our lives."

I tried to think of something appropriate to say. "I remember both of you from Jellyfish House."

"It's forbidden to speak of the time before the Master's rule." He shook his head. "I remember you, too, Aria. I'm glad you're still alive."

"I'm sorry your brother died so horribly."

"No, don't be. It's the way of things, now. Is there anything you'd like to know?"

"Uh, why is Maidservant a god?"

The hardness in his eyes returned. "During the attack, the little coward poisoned dozens of people, including the Watchers. She stole secrets from the Head Priest. She was most responsible for the Temple's downfall. Tritius and I betrayed everyone, but she was despicable." He glanced outside. "We've got to hurry. No more talking until we're out of the gardens."

I had a thousand more questions, but figured I could ask on the way back. Mostly, I wanted to know about Cythe, of course.

But when we were almost to an arched opening into the garden, a girl came from a side hall and blocked the way. My heart jumped into my throat because she looked exactly like Maidservant, only older, but when she spoke, I recognized Seydi. At first, she seemed not to know me. She grabbed Marko and pushed him against the wall. "What are you going to do with it, Marko, leave it for the Stalkers? What if I take it? You'll keep it secret, won't you?"

He blanched. "The Council judged her fit to serve, Lady Czn-tanth."

She looked at me curiously. "It was spared? Can it do something special?"

He shook his head. "Tomorrow, she begins working in the shrines of Maidservant."

Her face darkened. "Don't tell me they've decided that scab-faced monkey will have clerics. I don't like it. I don't like it at all."

"Oh no, Lady," Marko answered in a rush. "Her status is Barrows Outcast. She will clean and repair her shrines and statues."

She put a finger under my chin, twisting in a long, red nail. "Well, if they cut out its tongue, I suppose I don't mind too much if it lives."

Marko paled even more. "She still has it. Lord Tesi-Ra made an exception."

She squeezed my throbbing hand, making me cry out. "Will wonders never cease? I would like to hear it sing more, but no time now. I'm preparing for a trip. Where's silly Tritius? I have errands for him."

Marko showed nothing. "Tesi-Ra released him from service and offered him to Shelitine, but she was not pleased."

Czn-Tanth smiled. "I bet it was bloody. Did he beg? Did he scream? Shelitine has such style. You must come tell me about it while you help me pack. This pathetic creature can find its own way back to its Barrows hole."

"Lady, please, she can't go into the garden alone. It'll be dark soon."

She licked her lips. "Are you defying me, little Marko?"

He hung his head. "No, Lady Czn-tanth."

She took the ends of the rope from him, thrust them into my hands and pushed me outside. "The garden is very pretty when the eventide lights come out. If I were you, I'd have a nice stroll and enjoy them. Really I would."

Over her shoulder, Marko emphatically mouthed, "Run."

She whipped around, narrowly missed catching him then made certain I heard her parting remark as they walked away. "Took me five hundred years to forget how stupid and ugly it was, and now it shows up again and makes me want to puke at the sight of it again."

Precious seconds ticked as I stood trying to get my head around five hundred years. Then, with a jolt, I realized nothing else mattered right now but getting away. Holding my broken finger, I remembered how fast Athy and Arty used to run and tried to make my legs do the same, though I have always been slower than a three-legged cow. Making matters worse, my mouth was parched. My hand pounded. The seashells pieces jabbed and cut my bare feet.

The rim was much farther than it looked from the palace. Lengthening shadows cast across the valley, deepening and merging as the sun dropped below the rim. Sunlight reflecting from the mountain delayed nightfall, but not for long. I fought the urge to look back, keeping my eyes straight to the front to maximize speed as Arty taught me.

Night came as I reached the edge of the forest. I fell down heavily, heart pounding in my ears, and tried to catch my breath. I could see the front garden we passed through, now lit with strange blue lights and full of people, or whatever they were, carrying on endless, useless conversations. Beyond, rising mists glowed from the lights of Olympus City, and I thought how fabulous it must look at night. Then hundreds of blue globes illuminated above the palace and floated down and out over the grounds. It was incredibly beautiful and ethereal.

In the dark gardens below, a shrub rustled then farther away, another. Evening breezes, I thought, licking my fingers and holding them up, but couldn't feel anything, probably because of the trees around me. Suddenly, shouting and fighting erupted in the forest behind me. It grew intense and moved closer. It certainly looked safer and faster to cut across the gardens to the city. I stood and started to go.

Someone grabbed my shoulder and clamped a hand over my mouth, holding me so I could not move. My assailant turned me so I could see a silhouette. It was the Barrows girl. She motioned me to follow her into the forest. I motioned to the garden. She shook her head emphatically and hurt my hand trying to pull me, but I was too much for her. She reached into her rags with the free hand and produced a large silver disk hanging on a heavy chain around her neck. She thrust it in front of my face and gestured until I understood she wanted me to turnaround and use it as a mirror.

Instead of a palace, I saw the rotting carcass of some kind of huge animal sprawled across barren, rock-strewn ground. Huge white worms with teeth and shining eyes writhed in and out of it. I rubbed my eyes, looked again and gasped. The worms had stopped, lifted up and stared in our direction. I had no idea what it meant, except that it wasn't good. Soon, I would learn the disk interpreted the corruption of anything viewed with it, not the actual physical appearance.

A big shadow rose up behind me, blocking the view. As I turned to look, a long arm snaked into the tree line, grabbed and pulled me backwards. It happened very fast, but the girl was faster. She jumped onto me and slashed out with a knife several times. The creature yelped and freed me. Then howling came from all parts of the gardens, followed by the sounds of numerous entities moving fast in our direction. A frenzied commotion of snarling, ripping and fighting commenced close in front of us.

The girl grunted, took the disk from me and grabbed my rope. She jerked me away into the forest, much rougher than Marko. I did my darnedest to keep some slack because it hurt so badly, but I was exhausted and kept running into things and stepping on her heels, earning angry grunts and shoves. I wondered how she could see since it was as dark as the Barrows catacombs. That was the answer, of course, though I did not realize it then.

Without warning, torches flared across the path in front of us. Three twisted warriors wearing smelly skins blocked the way. Waving a short sword, one growled, "Ah, tasty treats."

I tried to run, but the girl jerked me back, put a hand over her head and snapped her fingers two times---a very tiny noise. The savages hesitated, probably thinking she'd used magic, but when nothing happened, they put away their weapons and came for us with big, leathery hands, showing their purpose was not to kill us immediately. When one grabbed my arm, I screamed.

They stopped dead in their tracks, threw down the torches and turned tail. For a second, I thought stupidly that my scream scared them then noticed the girl smiling at something over my head. It was the Keeper with a huge club held ready to strike. I wondered how anyone so big could move so quietly in the scraggly forest, for I had not heard him at all.

Grunting to him nonstop, the girl cut my hands free, picked up a torch and led us the way the warriors had gone. To my amazement, she began grunting the song we'd sung in my room and the giant joined in, prodding me in the back frequently to sing, but I didn't feel like it.

The torch and the singing drew warriors like bugs to lights, but most of them got out of the way after seeing the Keeper. A few tried to stop us, but after he smashed a couple into bloody pulp, they ran. We did not detour for battles, either. For the most part, they shifted out of our way. Obviously, the Keeper had a reputation.

Bonfires burned around old Prospects' Village and there were more inhabitants than before, only now they had weapons and armor, even the children. They had barricades across the road, and if they didn't move fast enough to let us through, the Keeper shoved their junk out of the way. I swear, the whole time, he and the girl grunted that stupid song without missing a beat. The world had gone mad, and I was along for the ride.

***

FINALLY, WE REACHED MAIDSERVANT'S STATUE. The Keeper dropped down in the middle of the path, held his hand out to the girl and grunted. She gave him the disk, which he put in a big pouch he always carried then pulled out a big piece of moldy flour cake. He broke it up and shared it, grunting emphatically to the girl. Whatever he said agitated her, because she shook her head and swatted his "words" away with one hand while stuffing cake in her mouth with the other. All the while, they kept looking at me. That was the last I remembered for a while. Exhausted, I fell asleep.

First light was in the sky when I woke up. The Keeper and the girl were awake, talking quietly. Tired of them and overwhelmed by all that had happened, I dragged myself up and went to the statue. Maidservant was a god because she murdered people at the Temple. Monsters ruled us. Anything that mattered to me was five hundred years ago. I was in hell and could do nothing about it. With no warning, I threw up on the lower part of the statue then went a little mad. I screamed, grabbed handfuls of dirt and flung them in Maidservant's face. Then I just stood there. Behind me, the crazy girl and her one-eyed monster were dead silent.

Voices came down the trail from old Prospects' Village. Somehow, I remembered it was my first day of service. I pulled leaves off a shrub and began wiping the dirt and bird messes off the statue. The soldiers knew about me, all right. They watched for a while then one pantomimed me wiping, causing the others to laugh. Then their expressions became serious and they began edging closer until the Keeper jumped up with his club and chased them away.

That was when I realized I had cried the whole time, and though my hand hurt so much I could hardly bear it, I was afraid to stop working because someone might be watching from the bushes and I did not want my fingers and toes cut off. I dug dirt from the crevasses of Maidservant's hair with my fingernails and cleaned her face with spit and tears and the front of my rags. I got down on my knees to blow dirt off her feet. Loudly, I sobbed, "This is the rest of your life, Aria."

Imaginary Cythe popped her head around the statue. "I wouldn't worry about it. Someone is bound to kill you before too long."

Meanwhile, the girl sat cross-legged in the dirt watching me, cocking her head side-to-side like a puppy and scooting closer when she thought I wasn't looking. Then she was next to me tearing pieces off her dress---believe me, it didn't matter---spitting on them and helping. When we'd done all we could, she pushed my shoulder until I turned to her.

She held a stick carved crudely into the shape of a tall owl and clenched so tightly her knuckles showed white through the grime. She leaned close to me and pointed the other hand to her filthy mouth. The tip of a very pink tongue appeared and darted back in. Then she spoke. "Blogfetter says trust you, but I don't, because you're an evil priest blasphemer from the past."

Rain began falling as we stared at one another, waiting for me to say something. Finally, I managed, "Blogfetter?"

She glanced over at the brute and he nodded with a hideous expression that I would eventually recognize as friendly, though at the time I thought he fancied me for breakfast. I couldn't stand looking at him so glanced around, nervously checking the forest for prying eyes.

He grunted and the girl translated. "Stop worrying, they're gone." She looked up at the statue. "I refused to talk until I saw you loved her, too. Isn't she wonderful? Blogfetter knew her, you know."

He grunted sharply and she sighed. "He says that's not strictly true because he only met her one time while he was in service to Perius, one of the Fathers of the gods who watch over us, on the very day the impenetrable fortress of the priest blasphemers..." She shot me an accusing look. "...was breached. In a fight room to room, they came upon her alone in a kitchen. Because they thought she was an enemy, some of the warriors attacked her, but Great Perius recognized she was in service and wondrous, and made them bow down to her and pray forgiveness."

A tear made a line in the dirt on her cheek. "But afterward, the enemy took her hostage and demanded withdrawal from the island for her life, but she broke loose and cast herself into the River of Boiling Torrents rather than have victory lost for her sake. She was so noble. Blogfetter witnessed her magnificent sacrifice, giving up her life so that the righteous forces might prevail over the blasphemers. And now she watches over us always, and someday, it is said, she will return and..."

Blogfetter grunted loudly, stopping her. Irritated, she turned back to me. "He said, Marlie, you talk too much and to show you how the owl stick works. He won't leave me alone until I do it."

She handed me the talisman and opened her mouth---no tongue. She took it back and resumed speaking. "By wisdom of the gods, Outcasts are forbidden the ability to speak, so Blogfetter shouldn't work magic to restore my tongue, but he says it's for the best and I always do what he says even if it's wrong because he takes such good care of me." She gave a big nod as if these mad things made perfect sense.

I glanced over at Blogfetter, who stared back with that big unblinking yellow eye, somehow warning me not to dispute anything she said, so I swallowed all my impertinent comments. "Why are Outcasts forbidden to speak?"

She spat and gave me that look again. "Because the evil priest blasphemers hid sleeper magicians like rats in holes so they could rise up out of the ground to kill us. There are all kinds of secret passages and rooms in the Barrows. Specialists like me dig and search for them underground, though mostly, we don't find any until they wake up and come out of their own accord. Then our job is to sound alarms so Blogfetter and his guards can come to remove their tongues before they regain enough strength to use forbidden magic full force. That's why we gave up the ability to speak. So they can't force us to use their evil chants against the gods and the Fathers."

"What happens after they're captured?"

"They're taken to be judged then sent to the garden unless the Fathers make an exception, like they did with you. It does not happen very often. You were blessed, especially since you are plain looking."

Blogfetter grunted something she didn't like and they argued until finally she gave in. "I don't know why, but he wants you to know that he cared for you himself until I came to work in the Barrows. For a long time, watching over you was my main duty, but it wasn't easy because he fussed all the time that you were too dusty and had too many spider webs or bugs on you. He never listened that I was afraid you might turn me into an evil blasphemer, especially after he gave me the magic owl stick. He…"

Blogfetter grunted loudly.

She crossed her arms and glared. "You told me to tell her, didn't you? Well, that's what I'm doing. You don't like it, you tell her."

He made a sound very much resembling a human sigh then grunted a long reply. Very self-satisfied, she continued. "We followed you yesterday morning, but had to go around when they honored you by going through the heart of Olympus City. You don't know, but Outcasts are forbidden to step foot on the consecrated ground of the holy city, and Blogfetter says no other prisoner has ever been allowed in the Elysium gardens or inside the Great Hall of Zeus, either."

Blogfetter grunted again.

"He says stick to the subject, but you will tell me about them later, okay? Where was I? Oh, Blogfetter sent me around in the woods to watch the gardens in case you were sent to nourish them, so that's what I thought when you came out alone, but then you were able to escape even though no one escorted you."

She scratched her head, little white things fell out of her matted hair and wiggled on her shoulders. "Anyway, Blogfetter wonders if you know why the Fathers resurrected you, if you're now in service to one of them and for what purpose? Did they tell you whether he's supposed to remove your tongue or not? Perhaps the Prefect or his Marko will bring more instructions. Yes?"

The whole time, Blogfetter had not moved or blinked a single time. I wanted to run screaming through the woods and throw myself over a cliff or something. I stared up at the statue and tried to calm myself. Finally, I answered, "I knew Maidservant at the Temple. Apparently, before she died, she wanted me as part of her reward for service to Tesi-Ra. Now, because of that, Tesi-Ra assigned me to care for Maidservant's shrines and statues. And I get to keep my tongue, thank you."

He grunted something but Marlie was preoccupied reaching out and touching me as if I was some sort of holy relic. "You knew her? You've been bestowed the great honor of caring for her shrines in service to the First

Father? I don't understand. Why would they give a priest blasphemer such wondrous duties?"

Blogfetter grunted. Crestfallen, she asked, "Where are you to live?"

"Uh, Forbidden Tomb Shrine?"

He grunted a long response. She shook her head. He insisted until she nodded. I could tell she was scared. "No one has gone to that shrine since the first year it was built except soldiers. Either the evil god Kalli or the Head Blasphemer Priest is asleep inside tomb gathering power and preparing to spring out to destroy our world, so the armies of the Fathers remain on guard around it until that day comes. It is a very dangerous place. Are you sure they said you will live there?"

I nodded.

"Surely, someone is going with you."

"Marko is to choose workers from the Barrows to assist me."

Blogfetter grunted and the girl could not have looked more surprised. "He says we'll do it." He grunted again and she shook her head. "No, I'm not afraid, not if it's for Maidservant and you're going, too."

I was caught off-guard completely. I wanted to get away from this one-eyed, tongue-cutting monster. I blurted, "That's Marko's decision, not his!"

He growled a string of grunts so threatening that even the girl shrank back. "He says only he can protect you and Marko won't argue because the Prefect will be very happy to get us out of the Barrows. He's been trying ever since I came, because I listen to Blogfetter, not nasty Tritius and his Marko."

I spoke from the fast growing place inside where I didn't feel anything anymore. "A monster named Shelitine butchered Tritius in the palace."

Blogfetter finally blinked, but the girl angered and shook a finger at me. "Lady Shelitine is one of the Six Fathers---Tesi-Ra, Kronos, Theia, Shelitine, Coeus and Perius, in that order---so you mustn't blaspheme any of them. If she decided Tritius can better serve in the afterlife, then that is what he must do."

I was incensed. "She's a cold-blooded cretin!"

Marlie's outrage grew. "You don't have the right to question the will of the Fathers and the gods, so stop it. I'll forgive you this one time because you're sick and ignorant, but don't do it again. As for Tritius' death, it isn't a problem. His Marko will be glad to see the backsides of us, too."

I yelled, "What if I don't want you to go with me?"

Blogfetter answered with her translating as he went. "He says you've been too impolite to introduce yourself to us the whole time we've known you. He says you're an ingrate, especially after we saved and cared for you so long. We're coming with you, and you can't do anything about it, so get over yourself and live with it. You'll learn the Barrows language, too, so I don't have to keep talking with the owl stick because it's dangerous, but mainly because I talk too much and give him splitting headaches." She grinned at him with the scummiest teeth in the world. "Think you're clever, don't you?"

I don't know what possessed me. I picked up a stone and threw it, striking his putrid face. "My name's Aria. I will not learn to grunt like a hog and there's nothing you can do to make me!"

Blogfetter stood, and I thought he was going to stomp me flat, but he reached down, took my injured hand in his huge leathery one and grunted like mad into my face. I am certain Marlie edited, because it obviously frightened her. "You'll be quiet and not speak again unless he tells you. We'll leave together in the morning, or you can wait here for soldiers to kill you. Moreover, you'll learn the Barrows language or he'll fix it so you need an owl stick to talk, same as me." She stuck out her tongue and made a snipping motion with her fingers. "You understand? Yes?"

Blogfetter held his hand out to her. She took his thumb and they walked down the trail toward the Barrows, not looking back a single time. I sat there, staring down at my crooked little finger in stunned amazement because it was no longer broken.

I asked Cythe what to do, but she was gone and I knew she wouldn't be back. I looked at the ugly world around me. Tritius and Marko had figured it out; and now, so did I. If you learn the way of things, maybe you can stay alive until tomorrow. I trudged down the path after them.

TWENTY-FIVE

THE BOOK OF THE HERO ARIADNE: MY HIGHER PURPOSE

T HE MOUNTAIN RUMBLED AND SHOOK ALL NIGHT, keeping me awake, so I was I bone-tired when Marlie came for me. Blogfetter led us outside past sleepy guards. It was another smoky, misty day, but at least it was not raining. He took us through the trees to a high stone barricade and lifted us over. We were at the top of First Test, which hadn't changed except for all the broken and blackened building debris strewn down it. It was sad to see.

A third of the way down, Marlie stopped, grunted emphatically and pointed to one of the drainage trails. Blogfetter shook his head and tried to get her to go, but she wouldn't shut up or budge, no matter how much he argued. Finally, he threw up his hands and gave her the owl stick. She turned to me, very excited. "That's where Maidservant sacrificed herself. I want to go see but Blogfetter says no. He thinks I'll jump in to be with her in the afterlife as so many other devout people have. That's why they closed the road. I promised him I won't, but then he said it is too dangerous. Will you ask him? I just want to see it."

I stated the obvious. "It will be faster to do it than stand here arguing all day. You can hold onto her, can't you?"

Blogfetter glared as if it was all my fault then snatched her up and disappeared into the steam-filled passage. It was only a few minutes before he brought her back. It was the happiest I had seen her. Then something occurred to me. "Since the Barrows are so close, why haven't you come here before?"

She looked as if it was a stupid question. "It is the will of the gods that everyone stays inside assigned territory boundaries, except for officials and soldiers, of course. The barrier at the top of the road is the southern boundary for the Barrows."

"You mean you've never been anywhere else on the island?"

"Before Blogfetter chose me for the Barrows, I lived in Ruined Village, which is where an evil priest city named Eao used to be. Thankfully, the Fathers and their gods destroyed it, but the spirits of the most powerful blasphemers are lured by nearby Forbidden Tomb to lurk there at night."

I was incensed. "What a crock! Eao was a beautiful city full of fine people."

Blogfetter growled, grabbed the talking stick from Marlie and pushed me to get moving. When I tried to continue the conversation, he pushed me again then shut me up with a shake of the head.

We passed the shortcut to Boiling River footbridge, now overgrown with weeds and scrub. At the bottom of First Test, Blogfetter lifted us over another high barrier into what used to be the intersection of Cadi-sum-Temple and Eao Avenues. In the middle of it was another statue of Maidservant, identical to the one in the Barrows woods except for standing on a four-foot high pedestal to protect it from heavy traffic. Someone had disfigured the face with reddish-brown stains and broken the right arm off at the shoulder. Marlie burst out crying, spotted the arm in the grass a little ways up Olympus Way and ran to get it. Then she called Blogfetter because she couldn't lift it.

With so much traffic, I couldn't understand why no one saw who damaged the statue, but that evening I discovered everyone stayed in towns and villages behind barricades after dark because bands of warriors roamed senselessly attacking anyone they came upon. At first light, they returned to where they lived then everyone emerged, cleared away bodies and went about their business. It was insane.

Blogfetter took a table-sized cloth from his big bag and spread it on the ground. Then he set out little sealed bottles, bags of powders and mixing bowls. Amazingly dexterous with those big hands, he mixed a foul smelling concoction and thrust it in my hands with a rag. Before I realized what he was going to do, he hoisted me up onto the pedestal and motioned me to wipe the face. To my surprise, the stains came right off. Then he set Marlie beside me with freshly made paints and a set of brushes. With consummate skill and speed, she touched up the face perfectly. To say their skills amazed me would be an understatement, but I did not tell them.

When we jumped down, we received a smattering of favorable comments, though more said Barrows Outcasts were despicable and speculated why we were outside our territory. Blogfetter ignored them, repacked and led us toward old Eao, carrying the statue arm in one great hand for us to repair and take back.

The Temple Priests used to say Kalliste's gleaming white avenues were indestructible and created by ancients long forgotten, but Cythe and I thought it was just a wild story to impress lowly Prospects. Seeing the roads again after five hundred years, I marveled and thought they had told the truth.

Months later, after Marlie told a grandiose story about how the Fathers created the avenues to commemorate the vanquishing of evil priests, I asked why they built such crappy roads now, and she snapped that I should just be grateful for everything they gave us. By then, I no longer feared Blogfetter, and I had become fed up with Marlie's endless babbling about Fathers, gods and blasphemers and told them so, but I'm getting ahead of myself.

We came to a wide gray-black expanse of molten rock that had flowed from the mountain down to the sea. We crossed several more areas like it before entering the territory of Ruined Village.

Then, in a space of a few minutes, gangs of warriors attacked us twice. They were men and women, not twisted in any ways I could see. Blogfetter did not even bother taking the club off his back, hitting them with the statue arm until they ran. He did not kill them as he did many attackers we encountered. If I had been more rational, I might have taken notice and not treated him as stupidly as I did.

We reached the intersection that had been the northern boundary of Eao. Enormous rock flows completely covered the entire eastern half of the city, forming wide, fan-shaped steps all the way down to the harbor. In the bay, parts of jetties and the bottom half of the lighthouse stuck out of the water, but nothing else showed Eao ever existed. Off to the west, smoke curled from Ruined Village. It made me sad seeing so much destruction.

Blogfetter turned us the other way up the avenue and three soldiers appeared out of heavy brush on the left side, double-timed to us and halted in a line, blocking the way. One of them boomed, "State your business."

Blogfetter and Marlie looked to me for response, catching me by surprise. I squeaked, "We were sent to care for the Shrine of Maidservant."

It seemed to take a long time for my words to make it to the distant place he processed thoughts. "Only one worker has permission to enter the area."

I glanced up at Blogfetter for help but he stood there with a dumb expression as if he hadn't heard. Well, he bragged that he could protect me, didn't he? I was two-thirds as tall as the smallest of the soldiers, yet I paced in front of them and spoke with all the royalty I could infuse into words. "If you do not move out of the way and allow my party to pass, I'll have Father Tesi-Ra feed all of you to the garden!"

To my amazement and relief, they about-faced and departed faster than they'd arrived. I thought Blogfetter might at least make an appreciative grunt, but he acted as if I'd simply done what was expected.

***

To OUR RIGHT, THE FORMER SITE OF THE HOUSE OF KALLI, dense hedges stood as high and impenetrable as fortress walls. They had tight, tangled branches and prickly, five-pointed leaves intertwined with black vines full of long red thorns secreting green ooze. Along the bottom of the hedge was a five-foot band of barren ground littered with bones and decaying carcasses of small animals. Marlie pointed ahead to a high hill on the other side where a merchant's estate had been. Steps led up to a statue of Maidservant facing across the avenue. Set back a short distance was a small domed building, the shrine.

Then I saw the emerald cat and golden lion statues from the House of Kalli atop two huge vine-covered stone towers rising out of the hedge directly across from the shrine. A group of soldiers crouched on the avenue behind big shields looking up at them. Marlie whimpered and moved against Blogfetter, and I looked up again as the lion turned its head, staring down the road at us with glowing yellow eyes.

Strange, isn't it, the ridiculous thoughts you sometimes have when confronted with something unexplainable and terrifying? I remembered when Cythe, Maidservant and I scrubbed the floors in front of the statues, how Cythe and I made rude gestures, even bending over, pulling up our tunics and shaking our butts at them. Once, I climbed up and dabbed bloodstains on the fangs of the green cat then lay across its feet for Cythe and Maidservant to discover. That had been a real hoot. Well, it doesn't seem so funny, now.

Marlie and I stopped. Blogfetter reached down, picked us up around the waists and carried us up the road. The lion followed our progress while the green cat continued staring down at the soldiers. Blogfetter set us down at the steps to the shrine.

Between the two towers, a long corridor ran straight in between more hedges. Weapons, armor and body remains in all stages of deterioration littered it. I went up a few of the shrine steps to see over the front hedges. It was a huge maze, far vaster than I remembered the gardens around the House of Kalli. At its center was a grassy mound with a small, unadorned stone sepulcher. Next to it, on a raised platform, the red bull stood sentinel. Suddenly, the green cat roared, so unexpected and frightening that Marlie tripped backwards over Blogfetter's big foot. Some of the soldiers cried out.

A warrior, wearing well-worn armor with large yellow arm insignia, came down the steps from the shrine and I had to run to get out of his way. He crossed the road, stopping just short of the maze entrance. The emerald cat leaned forward and stretched down, opening a great mouth full of teeth at him. He took off his helmet and shook a fist in its face. "Go on, you mangy beast, take Mariqk's head if you dare!" It looked for a moment as if the cat would surely gobble him up, but then it drew back and both animals roared and yowled.

He strolled back to us, saluted Blogfetter with an arm across his chest then stood in front of the soldiers. "Command Sergeant Mariqk. The cats are harmless long as you don't get a case of stupid and go into the maze. Don't want to get near them shrubs, either. That green goo dripping off them is righteous poison. Get it on your skin and you're dead in a minute. Sometimes, the maze fills with green mists. If you enter them, you're dead in a minute. He pointed to Blogfetter. "Hey, aren't you that soldier they put in charge of the Barrows? Heard you were some kind of big hero a long time back. How about showing my newbies a thing or two. Go stand where Mariqk stood and show your mettle. What say you?"

Blogfetter shook his head, turned and went up the steps. Mystified, Marlie and I scrambled after him.

Mariqk barked, "Well, big doesn't always mean brave. Guess I didn't hear right about him. Now, from the left, one at a time, go over there and show your stuff. Go!"

At the top of the stairs, Maidservant's statue set on a three-foot pedestal facing the cats. It had the same kind of stains on the face as the other statue and someone had smashed the nose. It was puzzling because only soldiers came here and they worshipped her.

A flagstone walk ran twenty paces to the shrine. Four narrow steps went up to a narrow porch with four columns and the only entrance, a wide opening with no door. Inside was a single bare room with a small low altar in the middle. Trash was everywhere.

Blogfetter kicked debris out, sending mice scurrying, two of which Marlie caught then took out her knife to skin them. I made her go outside, though only after a hot argument. I knew her ways, but many things she did turned my stomach. Meanwhile, Blogfetter ignored our squabbling, laying out his pouches and bottles on the altar. When Marlie came back, he wiped blood off her face and gave her the owl stick. She was still angry with me and translated with a lot of attitude. "Under no circumstances are you to go on the avenue in front of the maze alone. Say you understand."

What was this all about? "Why?"

Immediately, she was belligerent. "Because he says so! You will go over the hill behind the shrine coming and going, but stay off the road in front of the hedges unless I am with you, and that means me, Marlie. Now say you understand."

"But why?"

She yelled, "Never! Do you understand? Yes?"

Oh, what the hell? I said I understood and stomped outside to clean the statue. Marlie followed close on my heels, probably because they thought I was going to defy them and go down to the avenue.

When evening came, we sat on the shrine steps eating soggy flour cake while Marlie and Blogfetter grunted quietly, leaving me out of the conversation as usual. I'd asked Marlie who constructed the sepulcher and maze and she told a ridiculous story about the leader of the priest blasphemers creating it to keep the armies of the Fathers at bay while the false god Kalli slept and grew strong enough to take the island back. I was reasonably sure no one at the Temple possessed abilities to create all this, but, as I stared across at it and shivered, it certainly seemed a place suitable for someone powerful as Kalli.

Night closed around us fast. The cats' eyes shined golden. Soft green light illuminated the tomb. Soldiers fed blazing bonfires on the avenue and on both sides of the maze all the way to the cliffs behind it. Patrols carrying torches moved between the fires, calling out reports every few minutes. I felt their tension. Then it struck me that they had been doing this for five hundred years and how afraid they must be of this place.

Yet, stars reflected off distant Eao Bay as they always had. Across the plains to the southwest, the lights of Atlas City shimmered and glowed. A sliver of moon came around the side of the mountain, casting purple moon shadows across the maze. Soft winds played through brush and trees, creating familiar, restful noises. I dozed and dreamed of sitting in the garden behind the House of Kalli drinking wine with Athy, Arty, Cythe and Maidservant and planting an olive tree to signify our everlasting friendship.

Marlie shook me awake. "Blogfetter says bands of raiders are nearby. Army patrols are fanning out around the hill to engage them so we're going to take a quick look. If you need anything, snap your fingers two times the way I showed you. Yes?"

I stood on the shrine steps watching the cats stare at soldiers running up and down the road as fighting drew closer. Then a skirmish erupted around big bonfires in the intersection above old Eao. In minutes, it escalated into a major battle. I climbed up on the statue for a better vantage point.

Squads rushed down the road to reinforce the intersection as it was close to being overran. If so, their next stop would be Aria. Fighting broke out not far behind the shrine, and I realized Blogfetter and Marlie might not be able to get back in time if I needed them. Still, no danger was close enough that I felt justified calling Blogfetter back, especially since Marlie would think I was just being a baby.

Then I forgot everything else as brilliant white light appeared far away on the road from Atlas City, moving incredibly fast across the plain toward us. In minutes, it reached the rear ranks of the enemy fighting for the intersection. An erratic whirlwind, it tore into their forces. The enemy ranks fragmented, broke and ran. Wild cheering went up from the defenders. I stretched on tiptoes, wishing I could get closer to see what it was.

As if granting my wish, the light flashed up the avenue. The cats jumped up, snarls echoing off the mountain. I sidled to the other side of the statue, peeked around and witnessed my second god, a giant awash in light, standing ramrod straight at the bottom of the steps. She wore a pure white tunic, gold-scaled breast armor and a white-plumed silver helm with descending nosepiece covering the top half of her face. A jeweled short sword and quiver hanging on her belt sparkled colors. Suddenly, she yelled, "Stop the infernal yowling!" and shot a glowing arrow from a silver bow through the fanged cat apparition with such velocity that it appeared in the sky as a shooting star streaking down to the sea.

Before I took my next breath, she was at the top of the stairs face-to-face with me, bow slung over her shoulder and sword out and ready. She demanded, "Who are you, and why are you here?"

She was an angry god with piercing brown eyes that I knew well, and if I had any doubts, the image of an owl glowing on the arm holding the sword dispelled them. The words just came out. "My, but you've changed, Athy."

Five hundred years ago, she would've laughed or angered, but tonight, in this awful place, she showed not a flicker of recognition as silence filled the long time between us. Then she ordered, "Show proper respect, Outcast, or I'll take your vile life as a sacrifice! On your belly!"

I dived off the statue and flopped on my stomach. I heard her strike the statue. The nose hit the ground right in front of my eyes. Then down came the arm holding out the rag, followed by a third blow so loud I imagined the entire body fractured. The cats continued a yowling fuss, but I sensed she was gone. I peeked up then jumped back onto the statue. She was far off already, streaking across the plain toward Atlas City, out of range of the soldiers' cheers.

I sat on the shrine steps crying when Marlie ran up, pointing, grunting and jumping around excitedly. Finally, Blogfetter came and gave her the owl stick. She held out her arms. "I saw Athene this close! She is so beautiful! Did you see her, Aria? Did you?"

I was devastated. Athy, the strongest, most principled person I'd ever known, was one of them. Marlie's foul breath made me feel sicker to my stomach, and I turned away to keep from retching. "No."

She saw the damage to the statue. She cried out. "Who did it?"

I started to the shrine, every step an effort. "I don't know."

She grabbed me. "Was it rogue warriors? Tell me! I'll go kill them!"

Blogfetter pulled her off, took away the owl stick and held her.

Numb, I went into the shrine and threw myself on the brush bed Blogfetter made. I thought Marlie and I would share it, something I did not relish, though probably I was as dirty as she was, but when Blogfetter stretched out in the doorway, she curled up in a ball against his back like a housecat. Then she went straight to sleep, snoring in a loud, carefree way. Eventually, I would grow used to it, but tonight, it irritated me no end as the meeting with Athy kept playing in my mind. I imagined coming face to face with Cythe and told to get on my belly. Would I be able to do it, or would I just tell them to kill me because I can't hurt more than I already do?

***

MARLIE'S LOUD GRUNT MADE ME JERK AWAKE. Her head, resting against Blogfetter, had hit the floor when he went outside suddenly. Rubbing sleep from our eyes, we went out into the mists of early morning and found him facing a line of five soldiers with drawn swords.

The one in the middle was different from the others. Authoritative, he was clad in ornate bone armor with animal claws sewn down the front and had tiny bronze bells woven into his plaited leg fur that jingled when he moved. Tension was heavy, and I knew we were about to have bad trouble.

Sergeant Mariqk was at the right end of the line and took a step forward. "Show respect for the Commander of the Tomb Guard, Colonel Vig."

Blogfetter, technically still a soldier, came to attention with his right arm across his chest. Marlie and I, scared and bewildered, just stared open-mouthed.

Commander Vig had a big voice. "I was informed one of you can speak. Tell me why Outcasts are inside my jurisdiction, and be quick about it."

I replied none too steadily. "We were sent here by the Fathers to live and care for Maidservant's shrines."

He took a long look at the statue. "Is this an example of your work?"

"It was damaged during the fighting last night."

"Then it should have been repaired last night. You're shirking your duty."

Was he seeking the reward? "Duty requires us to repair it first thing this morning. We're here to do it now."

He jabbed his short sword at Blogfetter and Marlie. "I punished the man who allowed these undesirables unauthorized entry to my area. Order them to leave immediately, and I won't execute them."

I did not know what else to do. I clasped my hands behind my back as my father did when inspecting troops, looked Vig up and down then gave a curt nod toward Blogfetter. "This warrior is under orders not to leave my side. If I have to go to keep you from killing him, so be it. You can explain to Lord Tesi-Ra why I cannot perform the job he gave me."

He stared down at me like a hungry wolf. "Maybe we've just gotten off on the wrong foot. You will be my guest for dinner tonight. We'll work out a compromise. I'll send someone for you at dusk. In the meantime, none of you leave the shrine."

Then everything happened in blurry tableau, an exhibition of the grossest inhumanity imaginable. Blogfetter brought his great club down on the head of Mariqk, and it exploded like a ripe melon. In the same instant, he kicked the next man in the midsection with those big claws, and he went down, dying.

Then he stopped the club coming down over Vig's head and kept the other soldiers from reacting with a warning stare. It was more appalling than I can describe.

Vig signaled his men to lower weapons then, to my amazement, saluted Blogfetter. He showed no fear whatever. "If duty requires my life, so be it, warrior. Do you wish a bounty in return for my life, to kill me and take my command or may we have your permission to withdraw?"

Blogfetter waited several heartbeats before lowering the club. He didn't return the salute. He didn't grunt. He just stared.

Vig nodded and turned to me. "The shrine is yours to use as you see fit. I will provide basic provisions and water for long as you're here. You may travel through my areas with protection." He went down the steps, leaving his men to drag their comrades away.

I couldn't stand it any longer. I ran into the shrine threw myself on the floor in a corner. Meaning well, I suppose, Marlie followed and started picking stuff from my face and hair. It had splattered all over her, too, but she didn't seem to notice. Then Blogfetter filled the doorway blocking the light, and I screamed, "You didn't have to kill them! He was going to negotiate! You didn't have to kill them! You didn't have to…!" Marlie slapped me.

Blogfetter gave her the stick. He grunted a lot, but she said, "You did very well."

I twisted away from her, got up and ran to Blogfetter, pounding my fists into him. "I can't live with you, you murdering brute! I can't! I can't!"

I hadn't considered what he would do, but nothing prepared me for him sagging to the floor and moaning like a wounded animal. I stopped yelling and stood flabbergasted. He grunted and Marlie translated, "It was the only thing he could do. Vig would've used you, killed you and come for us. Now, he has pledged support and Blogfetter will have time to make certain he leaves us alone."

I was hysterical. "How can a monster like him do anything like that?"

He began moaning again. I had not realized yet that he killed only when he had no other choice and that having a defenseless, mouthy princess with him had greatly increased those instances.

Marlie came at me with her knife out. "You stop hurting him. He saved your stupid life."

Gross stuff in her hair dripped blood on her forehead and she didn't care. Something inside me snapped. "Give me your knife!"

Blogfetter grunted, Marlie tossed him the dagger and spoke for him again. "Please, try to calm down. These are brutal times. You must endure."

All I could think of was the knife. "Let me have it!"

Marlie shook her head and translated again. "For each of us there are paths and purposes. Sometimes, everything seems hopeless. In your case, they…"

I ran and hit him so hard in his empty eye socket that he actually winced. "Don't speak pointless garbage at me!"

He grunted sharply to Marlie, who had tears in her eyes. "He thought you made up your mind yesterday to live."

"I did, but I can't do this!"

He repeated something to Marlie several times. Perplexed, she turned to me and did her best to make her reedy voice deep. "But you must live, for who knows what higher purpose Destiny holds for Princess Ariadne? You must prepare...prepare." Then she added, "Or maybe people at the Temple were right about you being worthless."

Blogfetter gave me the knife, got up off the floor and lumbered outside. Marlie ran after him.

My head hurt as I tried to make sense of my spinning thoughts. Maybe Tritius or Marko told him what people said about me, but I didn't think so. Maybe, in all my rants to Cythe, I'd said the Destiny thing aloud, though I certainly didn't remember it, and I certainly never used Cythe's silly voice. I shook my head. What difference did it make? My destiny---what a laugh.

I noticed my fingers bleeding. Marlie's knife was extremely sharp and I held the blade. I stared at it then pulled a handful of leaves from my bed and wiped gore off my face as best I could. The rest could stay until we went somewhere to bathe. Yeah, why not? What difference it make, anyway? I plodded outside to give Marlie her knife and help repair Maidservant.

TWENTY-SIX

THE BOOK OF ATHENE: GODS AND FATHERS

T
HE VILLA SPRAWLED ON THE ATLAS CITY WATERFRONT SITES where the houses of Leto, Selene and Atlas once stood. It featured an extravagant courtyard stretched around an oblong, blue-bottomed crystalline pool that looked out onto the harbor through tall archways supported by graceful white columns. Other than the Olympus Palace, the dwelling was the largest and finest on the island.

A willowy, dark-haired young woman in a sheer dressing gown emerged from one of the high arched entrances on the back of the house, paused under an elaborate awning then walked languidly into the sweltering sunlight to the edge of the pool. Lost in thought, she watched ships passing until a female voice from the house broke into her reverie. "Oh, there you are. Hope you don't mind me letting myself in."

In full armored regalia, the intruder was more than twice the height of the woman, and that did not count the double row of golden plumes on her helm. She strode purposefully from under the awnings, emerald breastplate and leggings reflecting light around the courtyard like a green starburst. The woman, irritated at being disturbed, showed it when she spoke. "Aren't you hot wearing all that god paraphernalia?"

She lifted off the helm, revealing plastered-down short red hair and a fair freckled face streaming sweat. "Yeah. This new armor doesn't fit right, either. It's chafing me raw in all the wrong places."

"Then why are you wearing it?"

The reply was sharp. "Better I should ask why you aren't wearing yours. You know that several important delegations are visiting Olympus this week to have gods preside over the signing of treaties. They're running all over the island, gawking and getting into everything. Perius and I could use your help keeping an eye on them."

"I have better things to do than play hostess."

"You don't do much of anything, Athy. The Fathers have noticed."

"Their opinions are no more than rain in the gutter---here today, gone tomorrow."

"Whatever the hell that means. Listen, I ran into Coeus this morning. He said you're overdue finishing history revisions and new stories about the gods. He wants them distributed to our followers at the temples before the fall festivals begin."

"I'm tired of writing fiction for nincompoops, Arty. Besides, all they do is criticize when I give them something."

"Yeah, he told me how you upset San-zeus again. I can't believe you wrote a story about him transforming into a wild bull and raping some poor girl. If you don't leave him alone, he's going to make you suffer someday."

Athy shrugged. "Originally, the story depicted him as a stinking wart hog, but he complained and Tesi-Ra made me change it. I'm sorry you're stuck helping Perius with delegations, but not enough to help. In fact, I didn't even know you were back from Messenia. How's our war going, by the way?"

"Your armies were winning when I arrived and losing when I departed. I took two of your cities. They didn't put up much of a fight. Kronos is angry you weren't there to prolong the battles and suffering, not that it would've changed the outcome."

Athy stuck a foot in the water, testing the temperature. "What a bother. Now I'll have to go take them back."

Arty winced. "Uh, one of them burned, I'm afraid. Not much left."

Athy did not bother asking which one. "Many dead?"

"Pretty much everyone---a bloodbath, actually. My soldiers got a little out of hand."

"Yeah, sounds like."

They remained uncomfortably silent until Arty made an awkward change of subject. "I like the idea of plants on the terrace, but don't you think the colors clash?"

Dozens of tall orange pots decorated with black, stylized battle scenes and filled with red and yellow flowers set in no particular arrangement around the pool area in jarring contrast to the aqua and dark blue tile-work, benches and tables.

Athy shrugged. "It expresses how I've felt since my last sleep. How long have you been back?"

"A week, three---what difference does it make? I don't keep track of time anymore. Mostly, I've been up at the palace helping train Shelitine's latest crop of warriors. She wonders why you aren't helping with that, too."

"Tell her I've been busy arranging flowers and stuff." She slipped the gown off and stretched, enjoying the feel of the sun. Then she half-fell, half-dove into the water, surfacing on her back near a big fountain in the middle.

She shot a stream of water from her mouth into the air. "Are you coming in or just keep sweating for your masters?"

Arty hesitated then her weapons and armor clattered to the terrace. Her form shimmered, blurred and she was normal size. She left on a padded undergarment, executed a perfect dive and came up near Athy. "Ah, I needed this, but can't stay long. I'm on my way to the Ruined Village area to see how Shelitine's new warriors are getting on. She's impatient for a report."

Athy slowly treaded a circle around her. "They're not there."

"What do you mean? Where are they?"

"They attacked Vig last night."

"Yeah, so what? It was on my orders. Tesi-Ra's going to try breaching the Tomb again and wants stronger fighters in case we're successful this time, not that there's much chance, of course. Hey, are you saying that Vig's soldiers defeated them?" She looked at Athy suspiciously. "You interfered again, didn't you?"

"I was out for a stroll and happened upon the battle. That bloodlust stuff kicked in and couldn't stop myself. Fifty-one arrows, fifty-one kills. The rest ran off, hiding somewhere on the mountain, I guess. Don't think they were up to Tesi-Ra's expectations, anyway."

Arty was incredulous. "Did you really make fifty-one kills with fifty-one shots, or was that idle bragging?"

"I did, but it's not that big a deal. I've developed a new ability. I can sense hearts beating and guide arrows to them. Deadly as hell, but sure takes the fun out of archery. Imagine you'll develop the same skill eventually."

"Yeah, suppose so." She hesitated. "The Council is going to be steamed you killed those warriors, especially Shelitine. She worked a long time making them. She may demand retribution."

"Imagine so, but it's kind of like burning down cities and butchering everyone you come across. Once you start, you just can't stop. Besides, someone should've told me what was going on."

Arty splashed her frustration. "You're under orders to remain in Atlas City and Olympus until you finish the work for Coeus."

"Yeah, but I suffered from overpowering religious fervor and had to pray for solace at Maid-Cretin's shrines."

Arty threw her hands up. "Not that again! Someday, Tesi-Ra is going to figure out you're the one damaging those stupid statues."

"Nah, he's convinced Czn-tanth is behind it. He tasked me to catch the culprits and make them confess her involvement. Ironic, huh?"

"Can't you just be satisfied the little rat's gone and let it go?"

"You know the answer to that. I'm going to keep doing it until everyone is fed up repairing the shrines and forgets she ever lived."

"Too many people worship her now."

"Perhaps I should start gutting the misguided fools until they figure out she can't help them."

"You can't kill everyone, Athy, and you can't afford to keep provoking the Fathers."

"Provoke them? Me?"

Arty pointed up to an olive tree in an orange pot on top of the pool fountain. "What did you do with the statue of you and Zeus? You know they want our likenesses everywhere. You chopped up all the murals in your house, too. The place is a shambles. Where are your servants?"

"I cleansed their memories and gave them passage away from here. I used the murals to develop a nifty new timed attack with a short sword. No big deal."

"You have a combat room for that."

"Yeah, but my way is more fun."

"Come on, Athy, is this life really so bad? Look at all we've got."

Athy went under water and came up close in front of Arty. "Do you remember Aria?"

Arty had to think. "You don't mean the useless princess Rhea always favored for no good reason, do you?"

"Yeah. Ran into her last night at Vig's."

Arty's eyes widened. "She's still alive?"

"Someone preserved her, I guess, but can't imagine why. She appeared to be a Barrows Outcast, only she can talk. I found her at Vig's perched on Maid-Cretin's statue watching the fighting. I had that killing thing afflicting me and didn't realize anyone was near until we were face-to-face. Hasn't changed a bit, either. Confronted by a god with a sword ready to kill her, first thing out of her mouth was a smart-ass remark. 'You've changed, Athy.' You know, if ever she became a deity, it'd be the God of Sarcasm."

"I'm guessing you didn't kill her."

"No, but I made her grovel in the dirt on her belly."

"That's cold."

"Better than having to explain what we are and what we do. She's better off as an Outcast than being one of us."

Arty shook her head. "Why do you keep saying crazy things like that?"

Cythe came from the house and stopped at the edge of the shade. After several long sleeps, she was so devastatingly beautiful that hundreds of people killed themselves every year because they could not bear living without her. However, with only a few weak abilities remaining after the House of Kalli damaged her, Tesi-Ra had then remade her crass, self-absorbed and dimwitted to keep her from forming close relationships with others. In essence, she was highly effective seen but not heard. She stomped her feet, metal studs on the bottom of her sandals demanding their attention. "The Council wants our attendance at a meeting starting in one hour."

Arty elbowed Athy underwater. "Can't see you very well under the awning, Cythe. Step into the sunlight so we can admire your beauty."

Smiling, she ran out a few steps and turned her head to show the best profile. "How's this?"

Arty sounded concerned. "Aren't you worried the sun will harm your creamy skin? Where are those useless slaves of yours? Shouldn't they be shading you?"

Cythe looked down at her bare arms then ran back under the awnings. "They're out front. I'll go get them."

Arty stopped her. "No, don't go yet. Come back out in the sun so we can keep your image fresh in our minds while you're gone."

She whipped around. "I know what you're doing! Stop teasing me!"

Arty laughed. "Did someone cast a smart spell on you? Usually takes five or six times before you catch on."

Cythe marched to the edge of the pool. "There's no such thing as a smart spell! Just for that, I'll wipe those smug grins off your faces. I was in Messenia recently. People on both sides of your stupid war like me best. I have more shrines, too. I had them counted. Just wait until you see the newest in Pylos. It's more glorious than anything you have anywhere."

Arty nodded. "I have to admit that you're right. I passed through Pylos a couple of days after you and saw it. Sorry I missed you."

Cythe regarded her suspiciously. "You're not teasing again, are you?"

"Not at all. It was beautiful, especially the statue of you in lavender at the entrance. The murals astounded me, and the main gate is a work of art with those delicate gold flowers and butterflies. It's really gorgeous, Cythe."

She was delighted. "Tell Athy about the coral altar. She'll want to visit first thing when she goes back."

Arty grinned. "She can't. I burned your stupid temple down when I sacked the city. Salvaged the gate, though. Going to put it in my front garden. You can come see it whenever you want."

Cythe stomped away. "You're barbarians!"

Quietly, Athy asked, "Now, who's being harsh?"

Arty laughed. "She gets on my nerves, you know? Hey, are you going to tell her about Aria? They had a big thing for one another, didn't they?"

"Doubt she remembers with that scrambled head of hers, and if she does, you know she'll do something stupid. The Fathers will not countenance their most beloved god being friends with an Outcast."

"No chance of that. She doesn't care for anything but her own reflection anymore."

"At least, she's not murdering people like us."

"Please stop saying things like that. Guess I had better get going." Arty started out of the pool.

Athy called after her. "Come back when you can't stay so long."

Arty warned, "You'd better get your butt up to the palace. I won't tell them you're lollygagging here, but you can bet Cythe will."

"Tell them I'll be along soon as I reach a good stopping place in the new story I'm writing about Zeus' warts." She dived under the water.

Arty stared for a moment then leaped the remaining distance out of the pool, dressed in a blur of speed and departed angry.

***

LOCATED AT THE RIGHT REAR SIDE OF THE PALACE OF OLYMPUS and hidden behind illusions of shimmering emerald, high stone walls embedded with pottery shards safeguarded an area containing thousands of black stone slabs face down on hard, barren ground. Supervised by a special class of Darter Imps, big misshapen creatures shuffled laboriously from one to another, lifted the slab and checked the progress of a person's remaking. Work continued day and night, imps and workers never leaving the garden except by death.

Near the center of the grounds, ebony stone steps went down a chasm to a black portal, temporary entrance to the Master's realm, called Hades in this age. Six tall, lean sentinels, black statues that came to life if an intruder set foot inside the walls, kept vigil either side of the opening. The only other way out of the area was an intricately carved wooden door identical to the entrance to the Fathers' meeting room inside the palace. It opened into the Stalker Gardens that Aria escaped.

Today, those gardens hosted the entire Council of Six, reposing behind a long table shaded by a brightly colored tent with rolled-up sides. Facing them in a line, six gods stood with heads bowed to them. Squirming on a small hard bench to one side, Czn-tanth wondered why Tesi-Ra wanted her to be here and jumped when he slammed his fist down with such force the heavy table came off the ground.

Shelitine had stood to confront him over Kronos, seated between them, and turned to point a long dagger across the table at Athy. "Has the audacity to show up late in spite of receiving timely summons then sashays in as if doing us a favor attending. This, after she killed our new warriors for no reason other than to spite me. I've had enough of her foolishness. We all have."

Coeus, Fifth of the Council, his craggy reptilian features mostly hidden inside a crimson wool hood, raised a gnarled, six-fingered hand from the folds of a heavy cloak and pointed at Athy, too. "Doesn't listen, doesn't obey,

286

causing us to fall behind with the new changes we're making to history, not to mention she writes stories ridiculing other gods."

Shelitine continued her complaints. "The last remaking failed to improve her. She is lazy, ignores instructions and has a sassy mouth. If she were mine, I'd have fed her to the garden long ago and been done with it." She pointed the dagger again. "Insolence oozes from every pore of her. She serves herself, not us, I tell you."

Athy locked eyes with Shelitine and walked to the table as if suffering for all time did not matter. "Rewriting history to gain political favor with the Master and creating fairy tales about the gods should take backseat to solving the mysteries of Forbidden Tomb. Moreover, warriors defeated by a simple girl with a bow clearly are not sufficient to the task."

Shelitine plunged the dagger into the table. "A simple girl with a bow, are you, dearie? Pull the other one, why don't you? Those soldiers had just begun training. They weren't ready to fight someone of your caliber."

Athy shrugged. "Perhaps the place to start is teaching them to stand and fight rather than turn tail and run."

Shelitine grabbed her knife out of the table. It seemed she might attack Athy, but she turned back to Tesi-Ra. "At the very least, give her a sentence of guard service in Tartaros until she learns to behave in front of her betters."

Tesi-Ra used his power to push Athy back to her place with the other gods. "As you all feel so strongly about it, I'll punish her however the majority decides after we finish our other business. Satisfied?"

Shelitine snorted. "Better than nothing."

Tesi-Ra motioned to Kronos. "Finish briefing Lady Theia."

Kronos cleared his throat. "When anyone enters the maze, the entrance closes and poison mists fill it. No object or force can penetrate the hedges. Long red needles imprison live creatures then secrete poison liquid and ooze that dissolve the remains. Even boulders resting against a hedge melt away completely in a few days. Fire has no effect. Water flows in and simply disappears."

Oldest, wisest and strangest of the Master's remade beings, Theia, Third of the Council, had returned after long absence serving in the Master's realm. She spoke from a state of trance, something she often did. "Build huge catapults. Fling warriors onto the tomb mound, careful not to land in maze pathways. Build two towers that can...that can..." Her big yellow eyes drooped almost closed. She had a huge elongated head with a heavy hooked beak, and it lolled side-to-side on a long slender neck. She snored.

Tesi-Ra went down the table and shook her neck until the eyes half-opened. "Towers decay and fall down faster than we can repair them."

She squawked irritably then came fully awake. "Build a tower either side at safe distance. Put catapults on top, throw lines across. Warriors shimmy out and drop onto the mound."

Perius scoffed. "How do we know the fog won't come when they touch the mound?"

Theia screeched angrily. "Simple! Fling anything you want onto the mound. If fog comes, then will have to build towers higher than mists reach and lower men to attack the tomb from ropes."

Tesi-Ra went back to his place. "We'll try both ideas, but first we need new warriors. Shelitine, how long will it take to remake a thousand that can stand against Athy and Arty? I don't simply want front line fighters, but new assault troops as well."

Shelitine came out of her chair again. "A thousand of that caliber? Are you serious?"

"How long will it take?"

"At least a year."

Athy walked to the table again. "It can be done in six months if we cull the best warriors from the Council's armies rather than starting from scratch."

Shelitine laughed. "Yes, but who will give up their most prized possessions? Must I remind you, little god, of our history trying to break into the maze?"

Athy shrugged. "If you plan to fail, why bother to plan?"

Shelitine began sharpening her nails with the dagger, something she did often as a warning. "Ah, to be so young, feisty and foolish again. Have a care, dearie, or that insolence may cause you a lot of pain someday."

Athy was unfazed. "Suppose I'll have to start wearing my armor backwards then."

Shelitine's head jerked up. "You're on the edge of a cliff, little god. The next step will be into an abyss, if you choose to take it."

Tesi-Ra spoke before Athy replied. "Since Athene can't refrain from being insolent and making bold, unsubstantiated claims, she will be responsible for selecting troops for remaking. Objections?" He looked up and down the table then pointed to Arty. "You will help her." He pointed to Kore. "As you preside over the Tartaros gardens, you will assist, too. Begin by resurrecting all warriors in remaking and testing their abilities. Destroy all that you find lacking the required skills. We're going to need space for new ones."

Athy, looking at Shelitine, suggested, "Rather than waste time testing, might as well assume they're all as useless as those I encountered last night and burn them."

Athy's insults entitled Shelitine to deadly retribution, but she only muttered and kept sharpening her nails, leaving the others mystified and wondering if she thought Tesi-Ra might interfere.

Kore stepped forward and nodded to Czn-tanth. "Lord Tesi-Ra, I need her kept out of Tartaros if we're to be done in time. She treats the Master's realm like a personal playground and keeps everything in constant turmoil. I can't get anything done for cleaning up her messes and stopping all the squabbles she causes among the guards and workers."

Czn-tanth came off the bench. "If you did your job correctly, I wouldn't have to punish so many!"

Kore sneered. "Oh, is that what you call it? You're nothing but a little bloodsucking...!"

Tesi-Ra used his power to slam Kore to the ground and hold her down. "I've had enough of belligerent, overbearing gods for one day. All of you need reminding who serves and who rules. To that end, I propose Czn-tanth supervise the gods in this endeavor."

Suspicious, Czn-tanth eyed him. "You're proposing they answer to me?"

"I understand your hesitation given our history," he replied, "but I think you have waited long enough for a chance to prove yourself. If you do a good job, I'll join Shelitine proposing you for the next place on the Council."

After glancing at Shelitine, she smiled. "I accept."

Shelitine stood. "Czn-tanth still carries the gold scepter I gave her. Since you are Kore's master for the time being, why not demonstrate what a fine instrument it is for dealing with underlings who insult their betters? Take the defiance off her face."

Receiving no objection from Tesi-Ra, Czn-tanth walked to Kore and unfurled the scepter chain from around her wrist. She snapped back her arm and it jerked up into her hand. As she drew back to strike, all eyes went to her.

Remade by the One Master countless times, Shelitine's abilities to kill were renowned and feared. Everyone said that when she attacked, the only possible outcome was her foe's death. Faster than a snake strike, she leapt the table, plunging the dagger at Athy's throat.

Athy had listened to the quickening beat of Shelitine's heart and began twisting her body an instant before the attack. Even so, the edge of the dagger sliced the skin on the side of her neck but reached no deeper, giving Athy enough time to complete her new step around move and plunge the sword up under Shelitine's right side ribs into the relocated heart. She was dead before she hit the ground.

The gods and their makers stared in disbelief at one another across the wide gulf of time and power separating them until Theia cackled. "This girl's remaking is superb, Tesi-Ra."

He pretended to be as shocked as they were. "And to think, I almost gave her to Perius when we took the island." He glanced down the table at his former Commander. "Remember?"

"Yes, Lord. She and Arty held their own against my best soldiers and earned a place in service. I can't believe she's developed so much in such a short time. That was an inspired move."

Kronos was impressed, too. "No wonder you want her to pick the warriors. Mine are at her disposal."

Coeus hissed. "I'll contribute."

Theia cackled again. "Anticipated the attack, she did. Found Shelitine's big secret, heart on the wrong side, too. Keep a close eye on this one, I think. May rise to the Council someday."

Czn-tanth cleared her throat and bowed to the table. She did not bother hiding her delight. "Let me be the first to congratulate your promotions, Coeus, new Fourth, and Perius, new Fifth."

Tesi-Ra sniffed. "At least wait until the body cools before asking about a promotion, Czn-tanth. Don't forget, the final decision must wait until we see how well you do leading the attack to breach the tomb. We very much look forward to heralding your victory."

If Czn-tanth's eyes could kill, Tesi-Ra would have died faster than Shelitine. She searched for any possibility of support on the faces of the others, but no one showed anything. Protesting she had only agreed to supervise the preparation of warriors would do no good whatsoever. She studied Tesi-Ra. Had he planned all this? No, how could he?

Kronos knew better. He noticed Kore exchange a knowing look with Tesi-Ra before she provoked Czn-tanth. Athy had prepared the counterattack specifically for Shelitine's signature killing move and acted in self-defense so as not to face punishment. Athy, who he never liked, was more formidable than he ever dreamed. With her, Tesi-Ra was unbeatable, especially with Shelitine out of contention.

Tesi-Ra waited, giving Czn-tanth time to protest, but she was too shrewd to fall into another trap, so he returned to business. "Zeus and Hera will go to Messenia and take over the wars from Athy and Arty. Make up a story about another feud between the gods or something. Pull the bordering countries into the conflict."

San-zeus resented having to complete the work of lesser gods, but after witnessing this latest version of steely-eyed Athy, he thought getting away for a while might be a good idea. "Your will be done, Lord. We'll depart on the evening tide."

Cythe had not looked up from her tiny bracelet mirror even during the fight, going over her face inch by inch, worrying there might be a flaw she had missed. Watching her, Tesi-Ra smiled inwardly with pleasure. "Cythe, I want you to help with the new soldiers, too. Be their inspiration to fight and die gloriously."

Only half-aware, she nodded. "Okay."

As they wrapped up business, blue lights floated out from the palace. A slight creaking noise came from the rear garden and furtive noises approached. Tesi-Ra stood and stretched. "Well, if anyone needed proof about Shelitine's soldiers, it can be heard now. Call those flat-footed oafs out where we can see them."

Kore gave a low whistle. Dozens of shadows separated from the dark. They were disappointed finding no prisoners to eat although Shelitine's bloody body excited them. They edged closer to it even though they cowered before their masters.

Suddenly, Kronos jumped at them and they scattered. Tesi-Ra laughed. "To be fair, Czn-tanth, if the soldiers can't be ready in six months, you can ask for more time."

"Oh, they'll be ready to go, Lord Tesi-Ra." What else could she do? They would treat a request for delay as failure. She glanced at Athy, Arty and Kore and had to swallow her pride. She suggested they hunt down and burn the warriors in the garden, an activity they could enjoy together. Afterward, they could go to her rooms to draw up plans over wine and a specially prepared meal.

***

LATE THAT NIGHT, THEIA QUIETLY SLIPPED OUT of the large suite of rooms she shared with Coeus and made her way to Tesi-Ra's quarters. She tapped softly and he opened the door personally.

He led her to his study, poured wine and took her into a smaller room with seating sufficiently large to accommodate her comfortably.

She was impressed. "You did not have to go to so much trouble."

"No, I am very grateful you came. I realize Coeus would not be pleased about us talking in private."

She looked at him sharply then shrugged. "I guess you mean for us to be candid with one another. Very well. Yes, it could cause a rift. Best be quick and lessen the chance of him missing me, I think. What do you wish to discuss?"

"I would like to hear your opinion about something bothering me. After years considering all aspects of this island, I always end up with the same question. Do you know any way Kalli could have devised a trap from a thousand years ago?"

Instantly agitated, Theia spilled her wine.

Tesi-Ra was concerned. "Is something the matter? Are you ill?"

She squawked. "My apology. It is possible Kalli could have done so, but this is a difficult subject for Theia. Furthermore, you will not believe me."

Intrigued, Tesi-Ra assured and persuaded until she agreed to tell him.

Theia took a deep breath and tried to compose herself. "The greatest seer who ever lived served Kalli in her last years. Could see far, far into the future and understood how to manipulate people around major events to create desired outcomes."

"Surely, I would know about someone like that if he existed."

"They were girls!"

"They? What are you talking about?"

"If you want to hear this, just listen. Young and inexperienced I was, beginning my service and sent to practice new powers in a seaport rampant with stories of a group of children imprisoned by a king in the remote Far Northlands. Supposedly, each possessed a singular miraculous ability, including an incredible predictor of the future. Not likely, I thought, but if true, why not take them for the Master? However, by the time I made the journey, mercenaries had supposedly spirited them away, but I wondered why the king holed up with his best soldiers in his fortress while lesser troops searched for them. Employing shadow magic, I visited the fat so-and-so in his bedchambers. Only took a bit of persuasion before he blurted out a very strange tale."

She closed her eyes, remembering. "A seer came to the palace, showed him visions hundreds of years in the future and said she could mold events around them---for very high prices. While negotiating, he mentioned there was no way to tell her visions were true. She flew into a rage and transformed into a completely different girl who disabled his attendants with powerful magic then absurdly tried to sell him all manner of expensive potions.

Frightened out of his wits, he played along until he could slip her drugged wine and lock her in a dungeon. But there, a third girl manifested, making ridiculous assertions about her prowess as a fighter and offering wagers of immense sums to anyone brave enough to accept a challenge. A knight called her bluff and discovered she had no money, but even then, she bragged she would have plenty after she dispatched him and the rest of the royal guard.

Fed up, the king kept them imprisoned, letting no one near except powerful experts who determined they were three separate girls using strange magic that was not cloaking. The king was intrigued, but before he could find out more, they escaped, leaving behind a dozen guards cut to pieces and a message carved in a gate vowing to return for his head if anyone pursued."

Her eyes popped open. "Well, I didn't believe his wild tale, for whoever heard of a person who is more than one? I lost my temper and he died hard. Then I found his so-called searchers hidden in deep woods near the town. Well, I was certain they had the prisoners, but I was wrong, wrong about everything. Before they died, each and every one verified the king's story in detail so I went after them, because now they were a prize of immeasurable worth."

She stopped, staring at nothing, so he prompted, "What happened next?"

She nodded and closed her eyes again. "Nearly every way station had a tale about their passing, but never was the same girl in two towns consecutively. I realized they were more in control than the king and his people knew. Moreover, it was custom in those parts to use, kill or enslave unprotected females. Yet, even the most ruthless thugs paid the ultimate price for messing with them. But overconfident they seemed to me, so I rushed ahead, barely missing catching the young spell caster asleep at an inn. However, I did get scents from warm bedcovers, and for Theia, that usually means sure death in short time."

"Then what?"

"After that, true chameleons they became, shifting and changing, changing and shifting, yet seeming to evade me more by luck than skill which kept me going until the eventful morning I followed only minutes behind into the very port town where I first heard of them. I had foreseen they might try to take a ship because unless I caught it, too, they were well away, so I knew schedules beforehand. Only two boats departed that morning, and from the same dock."

She shook her big head. "But as I rushed through a market, an old merchant woman reeking of cheap eastern perfumes grabbed me besieging help to apprehend a rude girl who left behind gold a tenth the value of an expensive journeying talisman then ran away yelling she was late boarding the boat to Egypt. The old wretch said the girl didn't know the boats had delayed departures and offered half the value of the jewelry if I returned it to her.

But, though I ran, both boats had just cast off when I arrived. Then I spotted the magician girl ducking inside a pavilion, not on the Egypt boat, but the other. I hailed the captain and emptied purses on the dock until the boat returned. Inside the pavilion, I found a pretty man wearing her clothes and grinning like a fool. She'd paid him a small fortune to wait then hide when he saw---and these are the exact words she instructed him to say---a peculiar, ugly woman with a fat waddling butt running down the dock to stop them."

Tactfully, Tesi-Ra did not laugh. "I assume that you went after the other boat."

She snorted. "She was not on that one, either. When I returned to port the next day, I discovered no one had seen the old woman before she showed up that morning to sell the young imposter's goods. I searched the storeroom and found scents untainted by those reeking perfumes that confirmed they had a fourth identity---the old woman! After that, though I searched meticulously, there was no evidence of them anywhere, and I realized they could have given me the slip anytime they wanted. I think they even allowed the king to capture them. It was just a childish game to them."

She fell silent, brooding until Tesi-Ra demanded, "What ties them to Kalli?"

Theia jerked violently as her thoughts returned to the present. "For years, I had agents searching. They seemed to be everywhere and nowhere. Then all leads vanished until I heard a seer and the others served Kalli at her last stronghold, which we were close to locating. But then, as you know, Kalli died and everyone around her vanished. Those bitches! Those infernal bitches! Lost in the past before I could take my revenge!"

"So, if I understand correctly, there's no real proof the seer or the other girls were anything more than con artists?"

"Believe Theia, Tesi-Ra, when she says those strange creatures' abilities were legitimate. If they truly served Kalli, Kalli knew the future."

Then they discussed other matters, particularly the details of preparations to break into Forbidden Tomb and Athene's potential for greatness. Mostly, though, they became better acquainted, for although both had served the Master for hundreds of years, Theia's role was as personal advisor while Tesi-Ra administered the Council conducting activities outside the inner realm.

TWENTY-SEVEN

THE BOOK OF THE HERO ARIADNE: TEN FINGERS, TEN TOES

WHY DID BLOGFETTER MAKE ME WORK SO HARD to learn the stupid grunting language if he wasn't going to talk to me? He even forced me to practice with Marlie when we traveled around the island as well as every night before he let me eat. Yet, no matter how hard I tried, I couldn't make those sounds in my throat. Finally, I concentrated learning to understand their grunting and responded by speaking, but that was not good enough for him. One night, he repeated his favorite snide comment that if I didn't have a tongue, I'd have no choice. By then, I knew it was an idle threat and told him to go to hell. After that, he stopped talking when I was around as if I would overhear a secret about blasphemers or something.

His silence continued for several days before my temper exploded. We returned to the shrine, and I started screaming at him. Marlie begged me to stop, and when I didn't, ran outside with hands over her ears. Well, gods forbid I upset his precious Marlie. He slapped me so hard my neck snapped back and I fell down, hitting my head on the altar. I couldn't sit up for several hours, but some good did come from it. I saw how worried and upset he was and realized he hadn't meant to hurt me; at least, not in any permanent kind of way. Which meant that maybe I did not have to be so afraid of him.

When I woke up, it was night and I had a wet cloth on my forehead. They were lying in the doorway, Marlie snoring as usual, so I reached to the altar, took one of his mixing jars and wadded the cloth around it. I threw as hard as I could, bouncing it off his head. He didn't move, but I could tell he was awake. Fine, I swore to myself, if you're not going to do anything, you have yourself a war. Too bad for you, Freak-face.

Next morning, I started asking questions and hurling insults at him nonstop. He thought he could wait and I would wind down. I must admit, I had not realized how difficult it was to talk so much. I was raspy with a sore throat all the time. After a few days, I had about decided I could not keep it up when I realized he no longer gave me water as frequently and we ate juicy fruits and vegetables less often. My determination ratcheted back up.

He had a potion he gave us to take away pain before healing bad wounds. I stole pinches of it to put in a water skin I carried. Not only did my throat stop hurting, it gave me unexpected energy. I went after him with renewed effort, and since Marlie never stopped spouting nonsense about gods and Fathers and how perfectly wonderful every stupid thing was, old Puke Face became pretty frazzled, even developing face tics and blinking more often. I loved it!

You'd think they'd have found a better name for Ruined Village after so long. We go often because Maidservant's newest and biggest shrine is there, built after the gods forbade them using the one across from Forbidden Tomb, which they also built, according to Old One-eye. The town grew up about a hundred feet from the westernmost lava flow. The shrine is next to the lake that used to be in Eao Plaza, the one Maidservant fell in, ironic because her statue now stands on that old Kalli pedestal.

The villagers can't understand why it keeps crumbling and expect us to fix it all the time. I suggested moving it to the shrine, but you'd think I'd cut a kid's throat or something, the way they overreacted. I've lost count how many times we've resurfaced and painted it. Talk about a waste of time job. Maidservant the god. Makes me gag.

Near the shrine is a small café cobbled together from materials salvaged from the Eao ruins, which are little more than sifted piles of rubble now. One day, the owner came out and surprised us with an invitation to eat and drink in a back storeroom, long as we stayed out of sight and paid, of course. Obviously, his business was bad, but that was all right with us, even after we discovered he charged us twice as much, because we were unwelcome to enter any other businesses on the island.

I was as excited as Marlie and Blogfetter the first few times we crowded into that grungy little room with a single small table of old ship planks resting on a small boulder. There were two rickety chairs, which Marlie and I sat on since Blogfetter was too big. He plopped down on the floor and still had to lean way over to reach the table. But then the day came when Marlie said she liked the new wall behind me. A mural showed through smoky grime--- twisting green vines with blue flowers. Was it the one from Cythe's bedroom? My heart wouldn't let me look at it again, because if I found a yellow flower, it would break. I ran out crying. They go back nearly every visit. I just wait outside. Did I tell them why? No. Have they asked? No.

I should say more about the fighting. All sorts of dangerous creatures roam the island---soldiers, militias, mercenary groups, outlaw gangs and monsters alone or in packs. Most are twisted, some are human. Except for those with uniforms and outright beasts, sometimes I can't tell them apart. Their numbers keep increasing, too. I think they come from the gardens at the palace, released periodically to keep people from exploring the island. We hear all kinds of stories about heroes vanquishing all sorts of monsters in the wilds, but I think they simply serve to cover up the truth.

Someone attacks us nearly every day. Occasionally, they try to distract Blogfetter to make off with Marlie or me, but usually they just come at us. Blogfetter's fighting abilities are diabolical, but without him, I would have been dead long ago. Marlie is not easy prey for them, either. She is fast and seems to know exactly where and when to strike an assailant. She has saved me several times, but resents my lack of fighting skills and never passes up a chance to mention it. Once, she tried to teach me to use a knife but gave up in disgust after only a few minutes.

Marlie and Blogfetter are very unlike in many ways. For instance, I've never seen him do anything to the remains of any creature other than treat it with respect. When it comes to food, he eats the same as me. Marlie is more like a wild animal. I realize it's the way of things, but when I catch her, I give her a smack or kick in the butt and chase her away. Part of her knows it's wrong, too, because she skulks and looks guilty when bodies are near rather than going after them forthrightly. Moreover, Blogfetter is the smart one, a planner. She acts on impulse and instinct. I thought the opposite when held in the Barrows. I think he intended everyone to believe she told him what to do. He is very complex. She is not.

Often, I don't think her mind's glued together right, or she is hiding something and makes up stuff. Of course, I may be as batty as Marlie. I'm certainly every bit as repulsive. When we sit together beside a road, I think we must look like two piles of trash to passersby. Judging by reactions from them sometimes, I know we smell like garbage. If we are close to Blogfetter, though, no one notices, because that big boy really makes people's eyes burn. Anyway, I'm a princess a long way from the palace, that's for sure.

That brings me to the day we went to Ruined Village and everything changed between Blogfetter and me. Marlie ran ahead so she'd have more time to wander around the village. She says it's unchanged since Blogfetter chose her to work at the Barrows, though frankly, now that I can understand her jabbering, I'm not certain she actually remembers it very well. When I ask about her family, she always changes the subject. It was hot, the sun beating down on the black sandy beach of old Eao Harbor and nary a breeze or bit of shade. I followed about ten paces behind his Hulking Ugliness, who hunched down even more than usual because I talked a mile a minute at his back about topics I couldn't when Marlie was with us. Oh, I was in rare form.

"So, Bed Wetter, do you really think everything's better with the Fathers in charge? Then why did your masters need to create gods and monsters like you to keep everyone in line? Hey, have you ever seen Aphrodite? Bet you must've. What a body, huh? I used to sleep in the same bed with her, right up against it. Think about that, why don't you? Does it put nasty thoughts in your pea-brain? Does it stir your manhood? Marlie says you're a hero for cutting your own tongue out as example to others when they put you in charge of the Barrows. I think you're stupid if you really did it. What did you do with it? Did you eat it? Bet you did.

Hey, Blood Blister, if you're such a great warrior, why aren't you active in the army? Do you prefer babysitting young girls to killing and maiming for a living? If you ask me, you're pretty darn contrary to the natural order of things. Hey, how did you know I came from a royal family? How did you know what Cythe used to say about my destiny? Did they make you stronger to compensate for being the ugliest, most repulsive creature in existence? Come on, it is not that hard of a question, even for someone with limited intelligence. Okay, don't answer. Let's talk about something else. What happened to your missing eye? Did you pop it out and eat it? Yum-m-m-my! Why not eat the other one? I'll lead you around and not let you fall off a cliff or walk into a burning building or into a big green hedge full of poison. Maybe you don't trust me. Is that it? Ha!

Hey, Smell Bad, why are so many soldiers gathering around the maze? What are those towers and contraptions they're building? I heard one of them say they're going to try to get into the tomb again. Do you know when? Hey, did you have a mother? Whatever could she have looked like? Boggles the mind, the imagination and gives me gas thinking about it. Did she tell you how many fathers you had? Is that the right word for whatever procreates with your species? Oh, I forgot! Monsters made you, didn't they? Why did they make you so much uglier than they are? Ever had a monster girlfriend? That's a dumb question, I guess. Why not ask them to make you someone who won't be terrorized to death when she sees you. Oh, by the gods! Are you a boy monster or girl monster? I've never looked! Do you have a great big…?"

He roared menacingly, turned and stomped into the surf, walking out until water was up to his waist. Then he stood there, staring across the once great harbor out to sea. I yelled that he should keep going but the noise of waves drown me out, so I waded closer and bounced seashells and stones off his head until my arm hurt. Finally, determined to allow him no peace, I swam beside him, riding swells up and down like a boat floating next to an island. Thinking I could dive and swim away if he lunged for me, I yelled, "Hey, Handsome, did you lose something?"

He turned to me and grunted. "A long time ago, everything I loved."

Well, he had finally spoken, and never was I more surprised by anything said to me. Then he surprised me even more.

"We thought victory was complete when the Temple fell, but then word came that a mysterious fog enshrouded the area around the House of Kalli. A platoon tried to enter and all of them died. Months passed, then one morning the mists were gone and we saw the sentinels, maze and tomb for the first time. Two armies attacked and perished in minutes. For a year, five of the Fathers used every resource and ability to break into the maze and failed. Then the One Master lost his temper and commanded them to remain on the island until they destroyed the tomb or it opened of its own accord since it is all that remains between them and remaking the world the way they want."

He turned for shore, causing a swell that carried me high. He reached back, gently caught my wrist and pulled me after him.

"You were sustained by Tesi-Ra, most powerful of the One Master's servants. He can look into you anytime he wants and you'll tell him everything. The less you know, the more likely you are to survive, and survive you must. But now, I've endangered you because you won't have it any other way. So please, behave. It's hard enough getting you and Marlie through each day alive without you being such a pain in the ass all the time."

He left me standing dumfounded in the surf watching foamy water tumble little shelled creatures in and out, their fates determined by forces they did not comprehend. Then I sprinted to catch up with him, the distance between us less with every step.

Since then, days interrupted by unexpected horrific events have been the routine. Sometimes it rains, sometimes it is foggy and sometimes it is sunny. Sometimes it is too cold or too hot. Regardless, I do the same things at the same places with the same people every day. We do not age or undergo physical changes other than more scars that are the same as other scars left from Blogfetter healing our wounds. I do have a harder, leaner body from constant toil, walking and staying alive. More importantly, thanks to him, I still have ten fingers, ten toes.

TWENTY-EIGHT

The Book of the Hero Ariadne: Into the Maze

I STOOD ON THE PEDESTAL OF MAIDSERVANT'S STATUE with my arm around its waist watching catapults fling bags of dirt from the avenue. It was the ninth consecutive day they tested the range with different load weights. Blogfetter came and stood next to me. "So far," I said, "every shot landed on the mound without a reaction. You were right, it seems."

He nodded and said nothing.

I wanted him to express opinions. "If they can get troops onto the mound without going through the maze, nothing will stop them breaking into the tomb. Right?"

He made a rumbling noise that sounded somewhat like a growl then grunted, "That's certainly what they think."

"Do I detect notes of doubt?"

He seemed surprised I noticed. "If Kalli had anything to do with Forbidden Tomb, it will not have such an obvious flaw in its defenses. I suspect they are in for a very nasty surprise."

He was slightly in front of me and could not see my open-mouthed surprise. "How do you know about Kalli? I haven't seen any of you monster guys sitting around campfires discussing philosophy, history or religion."

"You would do well to remember that so-called monsters come from all walks of life and retain varying amounts of knowledge after remaking. Kalli is a legendary enemy with many stories handed down through the warrior classes."

I think he felt he said too much, because he stopped talking and watched Marlie, standing on his foot laboriously blending the skin tones of Maidservant's toes with tiny brushes. How could he grunt, fart and act like a brute one moment and a gentle, well-educated scholar the next? He was the most contradictory, complex and mysterious creature I ever met.

In the field to the right of the maze, they finished pulling big rocks and logs up one of the high towers to the catapult on top. They loaded a boulder and sent it arcing over the maze past the tower on the other side. After three more launches, adjusting aim each time, they flung a big log with a rope attached directly over the other tower. Warriors, somewhat resembling monkeys, went to work, adding more ropes across then tying them together, creating something resembling a net. Meanwhile, soldiers streamed out of the camps to watch and cheer.

Marlie jumped up and pointed. "Why are the cats so quiet?"

After living close to them so long, the apparitions had become a familiar part of the scenery. Even when they made a fuss, which seemed to be about every five minutes when activity occurred around the maze, we seldom gave them much more than a glance. Today was different. Instead of yowling, the green cat sat quietly watching sandbags fall onto the mound with an occasional glance up at the towers and warriors. The golden lion, stretched out in relaxed repose, watched the activities on the avenue until Marlie climbed up beside me on the statue. Then it jumped up and stared fiercely across the avenue at us.

Just then, horns blared across the plains from the direction of Atlas City. A vast army double-timed toward us. All activity around the maze stopped. A vision of three gods astride fearsome stallion-like creatures shimmered in the sky above the army. Their magnificence brought gasps and whispers of amazement. I had a different reaction. My knees buckled and I nearly fell off the statue.

Blogfetter caught me and quietly chided to stop crying and get control of myself, but I couldn't, for my greatest fear was about to come true. Athy, a giant wearing sparkling silver armor rode on the right side. Arty, a giant in glowing emerald rode on the left. In the lead, normal-sized yet every bit as commanding because of her breathtaking appearance in a simple sky blue tunic and cloud white cape flowing off the back of the creature carrying her, Cythe shined like the sun.

The gods arrived in the intersection and soldiers ran past them up the avenue, forming lines both sides far as the steps to our shrine. These soldiers were like none we had seen. They had toothy snouts protruding from black helms with thin slits through which dark red eyes glowed. Blogfetter urged Marlie and me to hide, but seeing gods enthralled Marlie and I was not giving up a chance to meet Cythe, no matter the consequences.

The gods came up the avenue and dismounted at the bottom of the shrine steps. Suddenly, Blogfetter grabbed us, one under each arm, and started for the shrine, but I wrested free and fell onto the walk. I looked up and saw him and Marlie already inside the building, motioning franticly for me to put my head down, but I turned to shout Cythe's name. Athy stood over me already.

She smashed my face into the walk with her sandaled foot. Close to my ear, she asked, "Why are you here, again?"

"I live here."

Obviously, she had not known because she cursed and warned, "Don't move or utter a sound or I will kill you before Cythe realizes who you are."

She moved away as Arty arrived and stepped over me. Then Cythe walked on my back as if I was part of the landscape and, in the voice I cherished in my heart, complained, "Don't these filthy creatures know to get out of the way? Wasn't it trained?"

Athy replied sharply. "You know how stupid Outcasts are."

Cythe kicked the toe of her sandal into my ribs just under the arm, hurting me many ways. "I have not seen one before. Does it make itself so smelly and repugnant because it wants to be like Maidservant? Takes religion too seriously, if you ask me." She giggled and kicked me again.

Arty pulled her away. "You'll be lucky if you don't get flea bites, touching one of them. You're going to have to burn those clothes. You'll never get the odor out."

Father used to say my temper could propel the royal fleet for a year if only he could figure a way to harness it. He did not say it with humor, I'm afraid. Even in the face of certain death, I couldn't lie there imagining the disgust on their faces and do nothing. Before I realized, I was on my feet wind milling fists. "I'd rather be an Outcast than gods so full of ...!"

I'd caught Athy completely by surprise, but Arty left Cythe and elbowed me in the face, knocking me to the ground. She kicked me onto my stomach and drove a foot into my back, making me gasp for air.

Cythe said, "I didn't think they could talk."

Athy was livid. "Someone must have given it dispensation to keep its tongue and serve as a caretaker, probably for its pleasuring skills. Arty, toss it into the building with the other one, and if it sticks its nose out, kill them both!" Arty grabbed me off the ground by the hair and seat of my rags and slung me the whole distance into the shrine.

Blogfetter reached out and stopped me crashing into the back wall. It was such a mean, hateful thing to do that I hugged his massive neck and cried again. Marlie patted my back and made reassuring noises until Blogfetter said for her to go sit in the darkest corner and be very quiet. Then he told me, "I want to show you something. They won't see us, but you must not make a sound."

He carried me onto the porch, pressed the silver disk into my hands and motioned to look at them with it. I didn't want to do it, but he wouldn't take no for an answer. Left on my own, I would have looked anyway---that's just the way I am---but I could never do it again.

Two decomposed night-black vultures with jagged beaks and hate-filled eyes strutted around a bloody swan with a broken right wing dragging the ground. The swan's eyes showed suffering, fear and confusion. Its body trembled and jerked. That was when I fully understood the nature of Corruption.

But then I noticed something else. Across the avenue behind them stood the green and gold cat statues from the House of Kalli, not the apparitions. The hedges were not plants, but tangles of strange cables, pipes and tubes covered with long red needles oozing and dripping green poison. Bands of light passed through the entire mass and it went in and out of focus intermittently. I knew nothing that compared to something so bizarre, but I guessed the ancient makers of the white avenues must have created it. Then it occurred to me to look at Blogfetter and angled the mirror toward him, but he snatched it away so quickly that I'm sure he expected it. He carried me back inside to Marlie. "It'll be dark soon. Eat and go to sleep. The attack will commence at first light."

I couldn't sleep. The commotion the soldiers made did not help. Finally, I got up and climbed carefully over Blogfetter's legs, wondering if he would stop me, but he didn't move. I hesitated when I saw the gods. They were normal sized, standing near the statue under a light one of them made, guzzling wine from big drinking horns replenished frequently from two large wineskins hanging on Maidservant's outstretched arm. I eased out onto the porch and leaned against Blogfetter's belly. Apparently, long as I didn't do anything to make Cythe aware who I was, Athy and Arty would tolerate my presence, because they surely knew I was there.

Except for the soldiers' noise, the night was peaceful. The mountain cast a huge moon shadow over us, making night darker, but also emphasizing the stars and sparkling harbor. A soft breeze cleared smoke from the air, allowing sea scents to predominate. It brought back memories of when the island was beautiful. I thought of the olive tree and swearing lasting friendship with the people on the walk. We were so far apart now. I stretched and made a noise, too loudly I guess, because Athy glanced my way and did something to make me feel her irritation. Then Arty said something that made them laugh and she turned her back to me.

Well, pardon me for breathing, I thought. Guess I'm less than an irritating insect to you high and mighty gods. I started getting up, not thinking what I would do, but Blogfetter's big hand wrapped around me with a finger over my mouth. I couldn't move.

Cythe belched loudly. She used to be the queen of gross noises and, strangely, it comforted me that she still made them. She declared, "Well, she'd better show up, that's all I've got to say."

Arty's reply was slurred. "Oh, she'll be here, all right. Has to check what we're doing so she can take credit for the victory."

Athy was derisive. "Victory? What dream world are you living in? She's concerned how to put all the blame on us when we fail."

That made Arty hot. "We're not going to fail!"

"Hope you're right." Athy turned and spewed a mouthful of wine on the face of statue. "Drink up, Maid-Cretin!"

Cythe laughed. "Do it again, but try not to splatter me so much this time." Then she threw her cup of wine on Maidservant.

Marlie leaped over Blogfetter with her knife and grunting curses at the gods she had bragged about so many times, but he caught her with his other hand and pulled her down beside me. She had the angriest, most murderous look on her face I'd ever seen. Then I realized Athy stared our way again. Not wanting Marlie to get an arrow through the eye, I helped Blogfetter calm her.

Czn-tanth, illuminated by five hovering globes and carried by four magnificent male slaves in a white litter trailed by an entourage of seven grotesque creatures decked out in expensive robes and ridiculous peaked hats, arrived about an hour before dawn with as much pomp and fuss as any royalty I've seen. She got out with attendants fawning around her and went to Athy. "I am here. Begin the attack."

It startled me how much I hated the sound of her voice and was glad Cythe and Arty laughed and made crude comments as Athy simply walked away.

Czn-tanth went after her, the entourage milling behind. She grabbed Athy's shoulder and pulled her around. "I ordered you to attack!"

"We're waiting for daylight."

Czn-tanth fumed and the servants pantomimed her. "Our warriors can see in the dark. Give the order!"

"Yes, but they see better in light, and since we don't know what they're likely to face, it's best to wait, so why don't you and your little friends go have refreshments. I'll tell you when we're ready."

I felt the danger coming from Athy, and so did Czn-tanth, who backed away from her and ran into the entourage. She yelled and ordered them to return to Olympus. Then she sat on Maidservant's pedestal staring glumly as Athy, Arty and Cythe continued drinking as if she was not there.

When I encountered Czn-tanth at the palace, I assumed she made herself look like Maidservant as some kind of cruelty aimed at me, but she still had the same face. I leaned over and whispered to Blogfetter about it, and Marlie, scrunched down behind him gnawing something stolen from soldiers' garbage, overheard and jumped up to look.

Blogfetter had to hold her again, telling her repeatedly that Czn-tanth was not her, but honored Maidservant by altering her appearance. Marlie calmed down eventually, but her eyes never left Czn-tanth for a moment. A little while later, Blogfetter leaned close and whispered, "They were twins."

Astounded, I had a million questions and comments, but he kept signaling not to talk. It was shocking, given all that had happened.

***

JUST BEFORE DAWN, THE GODS TOSSED AWAY THE DRINKING HORNS. Athy and Arty put on their armor and transformed into giants. Then Cythe floated high into the air inside a shimmering bubble over the avenue and the soldiers went crazy. She made a rousing speech promising glory, riches and promotions for outstanding battle valor. As she floated back down to earth, the armies screamed love and devotion for their most glorious Aphrodite.

It was all smoke and mirrors, because Arty gave the speech, not Cythe. She stood on the hill beside them the whole time staring into a tiny mirror, not involved at all. I believe Athy made the image in the air. As for Czn-tanth, she continued staring into the distance, most likely bored by a performance she'd seen too many times. Athy raised a hand and her golden owl circled in the sky exactly as it had in Cadi-sum arena. It was the signal to begin the battle.

The catapults on the avenue hurled warriors onto the sepulcher mound, who jumped up, opened bags from the previous day and attacked the small building with hammers and chisels. On ropes high above, warriors unfurled long lines and slid down. The cats and bull watched and did nothing. The armies around the perimeter, eager to participate, surged forward and back, striking shields. So many soldiers were on the mound now, some had to be stepping into the maze, but there was no reaction. Czn-tanth made her voice heard over the battlefield. "Victory is ours!"

It seemed the maze reacted to her words. Huge doors slid out of the hedges and closed the entrance. The cats and bull jumped into the maze and vanished, but, unlike all the other times, green fog did not enshroud it. Instead, the sepulcher mound glowed with pulsating green light and spinning black clouds full of lightning materialized over the site. Then the center of the clouds dropped, forming a funnel with incredibly powerful winds that sucked warriors off the mound and ropes then flung them far outside the maze. One smashed into Maidservant's statue and Arty killed him, a mercy. Then the mouth of the funnel came down around the sepulcher and began filling with light from the bottom up.

As nothing more occurred for long minutes, the generals arranged the armies into stronger defensive positions. Czn-tanth and the gods discussed what to do next. Blogfetter, Marlie and I stood on the shrine steps watching.

Meanwhile, the light neared the top of the funnel. Suddenly, Athy stood apart from the others and shouted warnings heard by everyone. "Run! Take cover!" She and Arty, carrying Czn-tanth and Cythe, streaked past us around the shrine almost too fast to comprehend as the funnel cloud, full of poison liquid, exploded.

Blogfetter hugged Marlie and me to his chest and turned his back to howling gales splattering the shrine with green goo. For an instant, I saw something around us like a bubble with green rivulets streaming down its sides, but as everything was so fast and confused before Blogfetter jumped though the doorway and mashed us into a front corner, I may have imagined it.

I can't say how long it lasted, but it seemed forever. Finally, he set us down and told us not to move off our dry spot. He seemed not bothered at all standing in the gooey liquid with bare feet. His entire backside was sopping wet, too. Alarmed, Marlie started for him. He grunted sharply and she fell into my arms unconscious.

He shook his big head. "I thought we'd have more time. They're coming already. The poison should dissipate before Marlie wakes or it eats through the shrine walls. When the water clears, it is safe."

"How come it doesn't bother you?"

He gave me Marlie's owl stick. "No time. You are going to be on your own for a while, but I'm certain you'll be all right. If they question you, answer truthfully and without hesitation. Do your best to take care of Marlie." He ran out the doorway.

Dazed and impatient, I waited as the puddles cleared. Then I checked Marlie, took a deep breath and tiptoed across the wet floor outside. It was a sunshiny day with the appearance of a summer shower having just passed. Across the way, the cats were back on the towers, scanning up and down the avenue for someone to watch, but no one was alive that I could see. The maze was open, same as before except for the hundreds of bodies piled around it. Then the right tower collapsed, rotting away before my eyes. The other tower had already fallen.

The cats yowled as Athy and Arty came from behind the shrine followed by four soldiers. They went to the statue, surveyed the carnage then moved along the hill toward the mountain to look at the army camps. I heard Marlie stir and hurried back inside. She sat in the corner staring at the wet floor, frightened out of her wits.

I told her it was safe then did a completely stupid thing. I said Blogfetter left us. She went crazy. Then I tried to lie that he would be back soon, but she tripped me over backwards and ran outside to look for him. I chased her down the steps onto the avenue toward old Eao.

She was very fast, but just before reaching the intersection, Czn-tanth jumped from behind a tree and knocked her down. Then Cythe appeared, waving arms and shouting at Czn-tanth about needing to return to the palace to change clothes before anyone saw her.

I stopped and glanced back at Athy and Arty on the hillside. They faced the other direction. I didn't know what I should do, but then Czn-tanth pulled a knife and circled Marlie, who was incapable of doing anything but stare because she looked like Maidservant. All the while, Cythe yelled about her stupid clothes and hair.

I ran toward them, ignoring Cythe and shouting Czn-tanth to leave Marlie alone. Too late, I realized Czn-tanth had used Marlie to lure me closer. She grabbed my hair and slung me around, laughing and moving closer to the hedge. She let go, and I went headfirst into it up to my waist. Red thorns ripped my flesh and the wounds filled with the sticky green poison soaking me. It hurt so much. As I thrashed and struggled, I heard Cythe's anguished scream. "Aria!"

I turned my head just enough to see her backhand Czn-tanth in the face. It was a weak, ineffective blow. Czn-tanth staggered her with a fist to the sternum and took off after Marlie, running back toward the shrine. Gathering herself, Cythe pulled out a petite pearl-handled dagger that couldn't possibly do more than irritate someone, and ran after Czn-tanth. That was when the hedge released me, and I plopped down on my butt. Icky wet with sticky goo and bleeding from scratches and cuts all over, I cleared my throat and spat out bitter green gobs as I painfully got up.

Marlie lay on the road in front of the maze entrance holding her stomach. I thought Czn-tanth, going after Cythe, had stabbed her. I resolved to do one last thing before I died. I went after Czn-tanth, determined get as much poison on her as possible. I was almost to them before I realized they had stopped fighting to stare at me. Then from the hill, Athy shouted, "Don't kill her, Czn-tanth. The cats don't see her and we need to know why."

Everything stopped as everyone looked at the cats, gazing back and forth between the girls at the entrance and Athy, Arty and the soldiers, but not at me. Then realization struck me like a thunderbolt. When I'd come out of the shrine, the only living thing around, they hadn't looked at me once. The only time they paid attention to me, or Blogfetter for that matter, Marlie was with us. That was why he refused Mariqk's challenge to stand at the maze entrance. By the gods, the poison didn't hurt him, either, and I knew I was okay. I looked down at my bloody, poison soaked body with relief I can't express.

Then Athy shouted the soldiers to use their shields to corral me and they charged down the hill. Wild-eyed, Marlie ran straight into the maze. Having no choice, I ran after her. Behind me, Cythe cried out. "No!"

Marlie was a quarter down the corridor when she tripped over a body then sat there wailing until I caught up. I wiped my hands dry on the warrior's clothes and thrust the owl stick into her hands. "Blogfetter said to give you this until he comes back. In the meantime, you're to mind me. Get up."

She ignored me, staring wide-eyed over my shoulder. I whipped around and found Cythe reaching for me. I slapped her hand away. "I've got poison all over me. Why did you follow us in here?"

Marlie yelped. Four soldiers had entered the maze. Behind them, Athy and Arty stood on the avenue, waiting to see what happened. The gate doors slammed closed. The warriors stopped and looked up fearfully at the tops of the towers where the cats had been then at thick green mists rising from the hedges on the outer perimeter, a curtain closing us off from the world. I pulled Marlie to her feet and took Cythe's arm, trying to get them to go, but Marlie dug in her heels, shook the owl stick at me and screamed at the top of her voice. "What's happening?"

It drew the warriors' attention back to us and they approached cautiously because they were afraid of Cythe in spite of Athy telling them not to be. Soon, however, they realized she could do nothing and made a sick game of running at us and laughing at our reactions. We kept backing farther down the corridor, Marlie and Cythe's knives our only defense.

In the House of Kalli, we all had nightmares about the cat statues, but mine were the worse. Once, I woke up seeing those big yellow eyes pressed against the bedroom shutters and screamed Cythe awake. I told her I had a leg cramp, figuring I had enough problems without my friends thinking I almost peed myself over foolish dreams. After Maidservant came, I convinced myself that if someone like her could live alone with those statues, then someone like me couldn't possibly have anything to fear. I was about to discover how wrong I was about that, too.

The soldiers had tired of playing with us. It was hopeless, but we ran toward the t-intersection at the end of the corridor. Suddenly, three green cats the size of horses loped around the corner and bound toward us. Screaming, we dived to the ground. They leapt us and tore into our pursuers. It was worse than Blogfetter smashing his club down on heads, but I didn't have time to think about it, because very quickly, they turned on us.

I have to give Cythe credit. She jumped up and waggled her little dagger at them. "Be gone! Aphrodite commands it!"

For a second, she really looked like a powerful god as the cats hesitated, but then the biggest one glanced at the other two as if to say, hey, this food is being impertinent, and swatted-ripped her sideways down to the ground, where she lay looking like a bag of bloody rags. Strangely, they paid no attention to her because all three locked eyes on Marlie. Then the big one lunged.

I've never thought of myself as brave. Perhaps Cythe inspired me. I hit the cat in the nose with a short piece of a broken staff picked up from the ground as I jumped to scrunch over Marlie as if I could protect her somehow. After a few seconds of not dying, I looked up to see why. The beast was no more than a foot away, sniffing at me. Suddenly, it gathered as if to pounce then hopped over us. The others did likewise and followed the leader back around the corner.

Crying with pain, Cythe struggled up and pulled fabric out of the wounds before they healed over it. I could actually see them closing. In wonder, I asked, "How can you do that?"

She shrugged, making herself wince. "Been this way since the first sleep."

Without warning, Marlie kicked dirt on Cythe. "Defiler! Blasphemer!"

Cythe spat at her, but Marlie dodged. "Tell this despicable creature if she doesn't treat me with respect I'll turn her into a dung beetle. No, that'd be an improvement. What's she angry about, anyway?"

Marlie kicked dirt on her again. "You threw wine on her! She's a real god, not a faker like you."

Puzzled, Cythe looked to me, and I said, "She means Maidservant."

"Oh, her." She got up and started to walk away like there weren't hedges full of poison imprisoning us then came back with a look of determination. "She's no more a god than you, dirtball. She's a murdering little tramp."

Marlie waved the owl stick in the air. "Liar!"

This time, Cythe's spit hit her in the face. "She killed my family, not to mention everything that happened at the Temple."

Marlie grabbed her and I had to pull them apart. But then Cythe crouched on the ground, hiding under her arms like a frightened little girl. I knelt beside her. She reached for me then remembered the poison and drew back her hands. "I thought you were dead."

The poison was surely gone from my wet clothes, but I didn't want to take a chance so I took her hands but kept her at arms' length. "You're a god. Wow."

She unleashed a smile that melted away time, but the sparkle in her eyes was missing. She glanced down at the fresh scars on her shoulder. "Can we stop at a market? I need make-up and new clothes. Tesi-Ra will punish me for looking like this."

Marlie, determined to vent hate, tried to hit Cythe, but I shoved her away. "Blogfetter said you have to mind me. Behave, or I'll tell him you've been bad. He'll be so disappointed."

The fight went right out of her. "We should go repair her statue then."

It took me a few seconds. "We'll do it first thing after we get out of the maze. Do you have enough paint? You said you were running low."

She nodded. "I need red and white. Blogfetter will have to make some."

"I'll tell him. Now, pick up your bag, stand next to Cythe and both of you listen. Cythe, if you touch a hedge, your body will shrivel and people will say you weren't really so beautiful. Marlie, followers of Maidservant who die in this maze are reborn as evil blasphemers. That's a proven fact, so stay away from the poison."

She eyed the hedges then gave me a long, critical stare. "Is that what happened to you?"

Oh, my aching head. I pointed the way the cats had gone. "We'll go single file. Stay close and walk in my footsteps. Don't dally or wander. Understand?"

They nodded promises I knew they would break before five minutes elapsed.

TWENTY-NINE

THE BOOK OF ATHENE: A PROFOUND REVELATION

RUNNING WITH WING-ARMS TUCKED TIGHTLY AGAINST HER SIDES, the weight of Theia's massive teardrop shaped body shifted awkwardly side-to-side while her slender neck stretched so far out in front that her heavy bobbing head appeared in danger of striking the ground. Next to her, hidden inside a flowing hooded robe, Coeus seemed to glide over the terrain and be the faster of the two, but looks were deceiving. Theia had extraordinary speed and dexterity, as many adversaries discovered too late.

They sped around Maidservant's shrine and stared at the domed green mists obscuring the Forbidden Tomb maze, but that was not their most pressing concern. Theia stretched her head into the air and sniffed several times. She turned to the badly damaged shrine. "It came from there."

She went in alone because it was important that scents and signs not be disturbed if she was to sense clues about the magic user they sought, but in less than a minute, she staggered out gasping and collapsed on the steps. Coeus shouted for help as he looked for wounds, but she was too heavy for him to move and examine thoroughly.

Fortunately, Tesi-Ra, Perius and Kronos had just arrived at the intersection from Atlas City. Met by Athy, Arty, Czn-tanth and Commander Vig, the party rushed to the shrine, but nothing helped until Athy suggested moving Theia farther from it. They carried her down to the avenue and she recovered quickly.

Though she continued wheezing loudly through the holes in her hooked beak, she motioned them to help her stand. She shook her head to questions and went to Athy, across the avenue looking up intently at the mists above the big gates. Theia studied her before speaking. "You've earned my gratitude, young god."

Athy bowed to her. "I am honored, but it was just a lucky guess."

Theia returned to the others and took her accustomed place beside Coeus. "With respect, Lords, I need a few more moments to recover then will answer all your questions." She closed her eyes and appeared to go into trance.

Impatient but acquiescing, Tesi-Ra resumed lambasting Czn-tanth for the disaster.

Meanwhile, Theia silently communicated with Coeus. "I need to speak to you in private before discussing this matter with the others."

Coeus was less skillful at secret communication but sensed the importance. "Of course, dear."

"If I propose Athene for the Council against Czn-tanth, will you support?"

Unseen inside his hood, Coeus stirred uneasily. "While I do not like Czn-tanth, I do not like Athene more. Regardless, I doubt the Master allows either to survive this debacle."

She made a cooing sound. "Tesi-Ra seated the table for this endeavor so Czn-tanth can't get out of the head chair, but she's the Master's favorite. Athy killed Shelitine in a fair fight, which will impress the Master. I think he'll punish and forgive them rather than torture and sacrifice, which likely means Czn-tanth returns to court as favorite and Athy serves on the Council. If we give support now, Athy will be an ally and gain us favor with Tesi-Ra, because he has groomed her to be his other hand opposite Perius."

Coeus bridled. "Athene has a rebellious nature and I don't trust Tesi-Ra's fealty to the Master. It is a perilous investment that will result in disaster for everyone involved with him."

Theia hid her irritation by cooing again. "You are wise as always, dearest, but do not forget Shelitine was Tesi-Ra's main opposition."

Coeus' aggravation spilled out. "I am not exactly powerless and can oppose Tesi-Ra, too."

"Yes, of course you can. Perhaps, we could tell Tesi-Ra that we'll give token opposition if he proposes Athy for the Council then allow him to persuade us to his side. That way, we can renege up to the last possible moment if his influence wanes, gaining us advantage over Kronos who is moving toward supporting him. The best strategy for us, I think."

Coeus would not compromise. "I will not support Athene in any regard. Must I remind the pledge you made?"

"Of course not, dearest, of course not. I'm simply seeking your wise counsel to keep me from making wrong choices. You know how much I rely on you."

Theia squawked, opened her eyes and unceremoniously interrupted Tesi-Ra. "I sensed strong forbidden magic cast in this area and hurried here with Coeus. It originated from the little shrine, but a trap was left behind, made with magic more akin to the lost arts of alchemy and potions than channeled solely from words of power."

Tesi-Ra was intrigued. "I found references to that kind of magic in old Egyptian texts, but even they said it was long ago lost."

Theia nodded earnestly. "Yes, but scents do not lie. Potions mixed with a few words of an old Kalli spell poisoned the air when I entered."

Without warning, Kronos backhanded Czn-tanth across the face. "It can only be someone that you let escape from the maze."

She hissed, "No one came out."

"Then who the hell was it!" Kronos thundered. "Where were all of you? Who else was around?"

"We were on the shrine hill," Arty answered. "No one else was there except the shrine caretaker and another Barrows minion."

Tesi-Ra said, "The caretaker is the royal female Shelitine coveted. I can vouch she has no abilities. I know nothing of the other Outcast."

Perius spoke. "She is an islander remade to ferret out hidden sleepers in the Barrows, something at which she has proven exceptional, but she is more common than muck in other regards."

Arty said, "They were on the steps of the shrine when we ran for cover. I don't see how they could have survived unscathed unless the caretaker used magic of some kind."

Tesi-Ra snapped, "It is not her!"

Arty chose words carefully. "Please, Lord, based on what I knew of her in the past, I agree she has no abilities. Yet, after the disaster, she and the other Outcast had an altercation with Czn-tanth, who threw the caretaker into the poison hedge. She pulled free, unaffected by the poison. The cats did not react to her, either, as if she was invisible to them."

Kronos expressed the disbelief they all felt, but Tesi-Ra motioned him silent and turned to Czn-tanth. "Do you have anything to say about this? You are in charge, after all."

She did not hide how pleased she was to tell him. "Arty left out important parts. Cythe was in cahoots with the Barrows scum and they attacked me."

Tesi-Ra grabbed her off the ground and ignited blue fire up to her waist. "Cythe wouldn't attack anyone without good reason. What did you do?"

Athy took her time sauntering across the road to prolong Czn-tanth's suffering long as possible. "I think Cythe intended to assist Czn-tanth against the Outcasts, but you know how clumsy and confused she gets. However, when I ordered soldiers to capture the Outcasts, they ran into the maze and Cythe heroically led soldiers in after them. Arty, Czn-tanth and I ran to help her, but the gates closed in our faces. I'm afraid that we must assume Cythe is dead, as will Czn-tanth be if you burn her much longer."

Tesi-Ra tossed Czn-tanth aside and spoke as if losing Cythe did not bother him. "While I have no answers why the maze didn't affect the caretaker, I swear by the Master that she does not possess abilities. There must be another answer."

Theia had listened closely. "Can't be certain absolutely, but may be three scents in the old shrine, a male warrior serving us in addition to the girls. Is a reasonable conclusion given all the facts, because not only did someone use forbidden magic, he influenced the decision making of Czn-tanth and the gods, too."

She waved down their protests. "Hear me out then argue if not convinced. You ordered everyone but your most seasoned fighters pulled out of this area, yet allowed the lowest of the low to remain on the hill with you during the operation. Why do that? Not a decision of your own making, I'll wager."

Athy considered then agreed. "We saw two Outcasts, but given Tesi-Ra's and Perius' information and Theia's comments, someone else was likely there protecting them."

Commander Vig, with the small group of soldiers that survived, did not want to speak but knew he must do his duty or suffer consequences if they found out. He cleared his throat and came forward. "Lords, a warrior named Blogfetter was with them."

Perius went to him. "Do you mean the Head Keeper of the Barrows?"

"Yes sir."

"Remember him," Perius asked Tesi-Ra, "from when we took the Temple? The big one-eyed club bearer who held Athene down. I sent him to restore order in the Barrows during the worker revolt then promoted him to Head Keeper after he did an outstanding job. What else can you tell us, Vig?"

"He arrived with the caretaker, and I challenged his presence...but she insisted he was here by decree of the palace so I allowed him to remain."

Theia stretched out her neck so her face was a few inches in front of his. "Started to say something important, then didn't. Want me to get it out, or will you tell it?"

Vig blanched but answered boldly. "I demanded that he leave, but he killed members of my personal guard and spared my life after I acknowledged his superior warrior skills. It was one of the greatest displays of fighting I've witnessed."

Tesi-Ra asked, "I accept your actions to that point, but what else did you do?"

"Do, my Lord?"

"Did you report him for being absent from his assigned post? Did you get more men and attack him? Did you try to murder him in his sleep or poison his food?"

Vig searched hard for an answer that would not get him killed, but there was only the truth with Theia so close. "I gave him permission to stay with the caretaker with my protection, Lord. Thinking about it, it doesn't make sense."

Theia, rather than striking as he expected, pulled back and cackled. "An enemy standing under our noses close as our mouths, on the same patch of ground as our feet and in front of our eyes, but sensed, heard and seen only when it pleases him. Fooled Fathers, gods and generals for a long, long time. Must root out such a powerful enemy without delay."

Coeus speculated. "It could be male or female, no way of knowing for sure."

Perius shook his head. "Perhaps it is the Head Priest who disappeared when the Temple fell."

Tesi-Ra stroked his beard. "Could be Envoy, the one who vanished."

"Or a powerful enemy we do not even know," Kronos offered.

Suddenly, Theia began chanting, hopping in a circle and shaking her big backside. "Could be a forgotten priest---could be, could be. Could be a god no one suspects---could be, could be. Could be anyone---could be, could be." She stopped on one leg with the other tucked tight under the stomach and fixed her big yellow eyes upon them. "But does not matter who it could be, could be. Only matters why someone who can lurk in the shadows so easily chose to come out now. Time for something to happen, I think."

Her frivolous behavior angered Tesi-Ra. "What the hell do you mean? Speak plainly."

She unfolded one of her deformed arms and pointed to Athy, staring across the road at the fog again. "You seem fascinated by the maze today, little god."

Athy nodded. "It feels different somehow. I can see that more of the poison is rising from the hedges than ever before, but beyond that, I can't tell explain the feeling."

Theia sat down on her legs. "Your abilities are going to be extraordinary if you live long enough. My Lords, the mists do not fill the maze as they have before, but form walls around the perimeter. Easier to break into, perhaps, but many great beasts roam inside this time, entering from a place I can't tell. More importantly, the sleeper's power is reaching extraordinary levels and awakening has begun. Soon, the tomb will open."

THIRTY

THE BOOK OF THE HERO ARIADNE: THE SLEEPER

CYTHE YELLED AT MARLIE THE THIRD TIME IN FIVE MINUTES. Fed up, I stopped and yelled at her. "If she keeps stepping on your heels, let her go in front of you."

Marlie started around Cythe with a grin, leaving no doubt she had been doing it intentionally. Cythe shoved her back. "I'm not following a dirtball!"

"Please, Cythe?"

She shook her head. "Not going to happen."

Marlie swung a fist. Cythe caught her arm and twisted it. Marlie pulled her knife out with the other hand. I snatched it away and held them apart until they glared at me instead of each other. I gave Marlie the knife back. "If I see it again I'm going to throw it in a hedge."

"You'd better not. Blogfetter gave me it."

"You've been warned." I watched to make sure she put it away then positioned them side-by-side. "Keep your hands to yourselves. Let's go."

I was frustrated. It didn't seem to me that we were any closer to the center of the maze than when we started. Of course, the hedges were so high that we would not see the sepulcher mound until we turned onto a path leading to it, but I felt we should have found one by now. We came to another four-way intersection. I consulted the marks on my grimy arm, took the right way and spat on my little finger to record it. Soon, I would have to use the other arm.

Marlie yelled, "Let go, it's mine!"

Cythe had her hand, trying to pry the fingers off the talking stick. "I just want to see it a minute."

I smacked Cythe's hands away. "Leave it alone!"

She stamped her feet. "You always take her side. What's happened to you?"

My head hurt. The god, Aphrodite---temples in countries all over the world, thousands of worshippers praying and sacrificing to her---behaving like a spoiled child. I slapped her hand away again and spoke through clenched teeth. "She can't talk without the stick, Cythe."

She gave me a look I knew all too well. She was not going to stop until she got her way. I held my hand out to Marlie. "Give me the stick. I'll give it right back."

She looked around as if thinking of running. Thoughts of us separated stampeded through my head. I tried to sound calm. "I promise that she'll leave it alone. Don't forget, Blogfetter said I was to take care of you until he came back, so we have to trust each other. Okay?"

Slowly, she handed it over, and the whole time I kept a close eye on Cythe, afraid she might try to grab it. I put it behind my back so they could not see it. "Open your mouth as wide as you can so Cythe sees how you look without the talking stick."

Realizing what I was up to, Marlie grinned, stuck dirty fingers in her mouth and stretched it wide for Cythe. Maybe the sight touched Cythe's compassion way down deep under all the stuff they'd done to her, but more likely it just made her feel sick to the stomach like it did me the first time. Regardless, she left the stick alone after that.

We'd seen a few cats crossing our pathways at a distance but nothing else until we came upon three warriors' bodies ripped apart, eaten and stinking. Their water skins were intact and Marlie and Cythe took them, the smart thing to do, but I wish they'd at least wiped some of the grossness off before drinking and hadn't laughed when I did. We were unlike in so many ways, but I knew I'd be the same eventually. I shooed flies from my face and spoke my thoughts, not expecting a response. "Everyone said the cats are illusions and mists fill the maze when the gates close. Sure glad they were wrong."

Cythe said, "It's different this time."

"How do you know that?"

She shrugged and looked away.

The sun had passed its highest place in the sky. Sticky hot, exhausted and struggling to keep going, we didn't notice two huge lions running up behind us, one after the other, but they brushed by and paid no attention even when we yelled our surprise and fright. Hardly able to move my legs anymore, I called a break. Marlie dropped to sit where she stopped and asked, "Why is the sky turning green?"

I looked up at the dome forming and spoke mostly to myself. "Wonder if it was over the House of Kalli, too. No way to know, I suppose."

Cythe, stretched out on her back with hands behind her head, responded in a strange, disjointed way, pausing after each sentence. "It has always been there. No one realizes it exists until the tomb phase activates. Pretty, isn't it? Like being inside a big emerald. Green is my favorite color. Remember?"

"Yes, Cythe." I smiled though I wanted to cry because she used to be so brilliant and now failed to notice the obvious. Trapped inside a container filling with gas, we had a set amount of time to escape, find shelter or suffer the direst consequences. And how were the cats getting into the maze? Mightn't that be a way out? Ignoring protests to rest longer, I led onward.

The numbers of cats increased steadily. Since they gave the impression of hurrying to a destination, I tried following one, but couldn't keep up. Another passed and we chased it with the same result. I kept at it until we were too exhausted to run anymore. Unsure what to do, I wiped away tears hoping they wouldn't notice before I stopped for a five minute break.

Marlie complained, "Hungry!"

Cythe tugged my arm. She had ripped a piece off her ragged tunic and placed it on the ground. "Let's try counting steps through a couple of turns then backtrack."

I wondered if she'd taken leave of her senses. "We don't have time to waste."

"I think it may help."

She was so earnest and imploring, I gave in. We went thirty-six paces, turned right. Forty more paces to a four-way intersection. Left for twenty steps, turned around and started back, but the left and right turnoffs of the four-way were no longer there. I shouted, "What the hell is going on?"

Cythe nodded. "The maze changes, opening and closing passages. I think it only occurs when we go the wrong way, but then I'm unsure of myself. Got any ideas?"

I didn't know what to do, but Marlie did. "The god should lead us."

I was pessimistic that Cythe led us any better than I had, because soon as we started out she began prattling in ridiculous detail about all her fine clothes and jewelry, paying no attention to the ways she took. Several times, I started to say something then was glad I kept my mouth shut because very quickly we arrived at a corridor twice as wide. It had so many cats running along it that we were reluctant to go that way, but after watching a few minutes and realizing most went in one direction, we felt compelled.

I brought up the rear to shield the Cythe and Marlie, but I needn't have worried because the cats made great effort to avoid us. Once, in fact, as a long line of cats streamed past, two came from the other direction, stopped a good distance away and waited until they could go around. Cythe had an explanation for their behavior. They had finally realized that she was a god.

As the beasts were not a problem, I looked up to calculate how long before the poison reached us, then didn't bother because it was more than halfway down already. We had until a little after dark. I yelled to go faster, earning glares from my companions.

We reached a large square area that had a wide corridor entering from each side. At its center, a small white stone building with a peaked blue tile roof and open doorway with a small window either side. As we approached, swampy odors grew very strong. Peering inside, we could make out nothing but pitch blackness, as if outside light could not enter.

Suddenly, a snarling, wounded cat carrying a chunk of warrior's torso in its mouth bound from one of the corridors and ran straight for us. We scrambled out of the way as it rushed into the house and disappeared in a flash of light. Before we recovered, two more cats came from another corridor, jumped over Marlie and me and vanished into the building.

Crouched on the other side of the doorway, Cythe began playing with her fingers and speaking baby talk. "Poor widdle kitties, fwightened and wunning away."

Another flash, and a cat ran out of the house and took the corridor behind it. Cythe got up, all business. "We can't go this way, Aria. It is certain death."

I glanced up at the fog, no more than twenty feet above the hedges. "Where, then?" She pointed the way the cat had gone.

Mists swirled near the top of the hedges, rendering early evening so dark I could barely see my hand in front of my face. Of course, Marlie and Cythe saw well enough to keep going, and we made fast progress until Cythe, whose shoulder I held, stopped and said we had to climb over some bodies. I reached out with my foot but she pulled me back. "Stay behind me and hold onto my clothes. It's very gross."

Marlie laughed. "It's just a bunch of tore up soldiers and two cats with heads hacked off. Soldiers probably took them as trophies."

Cythe responded with the pride of a god for her subjects. "Finally, warriors worthy to serve me. Well done, my faithful servants, well done. Ariadne, tell Corrine to make a note about this so Athy can write a story about how I inspired their heroism."

I gave her a gentle shake. "Uh, we've got to get going, Cythe. Come on, help me climb over."

I felt her breath on my face. "Too bad it's forbidden to use Temple magic or I would make a light for you. I can't use the Fathers' magic because I'm impure, or at least that's what they call it. Did I tell you that most of them wanted me fed me to the garden but Tesi-Ra protected me? I'm supposed to be grateful to him, and at first I was, but now I..." She went silent.

My heart broke, but first things first. "You can still make Priest's light?"

"Of course, silly, but Tesi-Ra said if I disobey again, he'll turn me into a Crypt Tender or something worse. I don't think he'd really do it, but last time I embarrassed him, he hurt me for a long time. I have to careful because I do things without realizing." She was quiet for a few seconds. "I'm glad you're not dead."

I hugged her, carefully keeping my wet face turned away. Then I spoke quietly. "Cythe, look up at the fog then remember where it was when we started. Can you do that for me?"

It only took her a few seconds. "Well darn, guess dirtball and me don't need to worry what they'll do to us, do we? Wish you'd said something sooner." She uttered a passage and a small light globe came to life above us.

I heard a muffled squeal of surprise from Marlie and looked around. She was crouched, hacking off chunks from a cat's shoulder and stuffing her mouth. I jerked her up. "Leave it alone!"

She pulled away and scrambled over the bodies on all fours to the other side then taunted me. "Meat! Meat! Meat!"

I pulled Cythe after her, trying not to think what my bare feet stepped in. Marlie had a pile of chunks on the ground and hacking more. She glared, warning us off like a wild animal over prey, and I knew better than to confront her just then.

Suddenly, Cythe ran up the path a little ways and twirled around, the most animated I'd seen her. "Did you feel that? The whole maze just shifted and changed big time!" She squealed and pointed into the shadows of a hedge "Wow! Can you believe that's here?"

The poison fog was only minutes from us. I grabbed Cythe and hugged her, for the last time, I thought. Then I saw Maidservant's little olive tree. It had not changed any at all. I bent down and touched the leaves. There was no poison on it, nor, I realized, in the hedges. It was all in the air, coming down to kill everything in the maze.

Marlie screamed. Two huge cats were on top of the bodies poised to attack her.

It was too far for me to shoo them away, but Cythe sent the light flying at them. It bounced around the beasts, occupying their attention while Marlie ran to us. Meanwhile, Cythe pointed to a new corridor with a dim light at the end that had not been there a moment ago. "Since everything changed, the cats do not fear you anymore, Aria. Stay behind me."

We backed down the corridor, the beasts swatting and biting at the dancing light between us. For a couple of minutes all went well then they began looking more and more in our direction. Cythe created a second light and sent both flying wildly back and forth in front of them. We ran. The cats noticed and bound down the corridor after us.

It was the garden house. A light shined in the small window beside the entrance where we used to keep an oil lamp lit for Maidservant. We dashed inside and slammed the door. The bar was in its customary place in the corner or we couldn't have stopped them crashing in. They threw their bodies against the door and tore at it with their claws repeatedly, shaking the entire building. More came and tried to get in. The noise was incredible.

Marlie pulled a rug off the floor, went to a corner and rolled up inside. Cythe, after saving us brilliantly, seemed lost standing in the middle of the room. I dragged tables, chairs and anything else moveable against the door. Then, as I scrunched a heavy cabinet across the floor, the commotion stopped abruptly.

I tiptoed to the little window and pulled back the heavy curtain. I assumed a lamp burned there, but to my astonishment, it was a tiny round Priest's light. I wished I could make it move because I could see nothing outside but thick green fog reflecting light. Then I nearly panicked, thinking the fog would come in, and pulled the curtain closed again. I rolled up small rugs and put them against the crack under the door. I was too tired to do anything else. I went to Cythe. She did not seem to hear me. I waved my hand in front of her face. She didn't even blink.

I found an oil lamp and flints in the cupboard where we'd always kept them. Abundant amounts of fruits and vegetables were in the kitchen bins. That certainly made no sense to me. I went into the small bedroom, found covers thrown back and an impression still in the mattress. From the size, I knew Maidservant made it. Her clothes, and some of ours, were in the wardrobes. Then another amazing thing---the bedside basin had water in it, perfectly usable though with a dust skim on top. Shivers ran through me.

I walked Cythe into the bedroom, undressed and dropped a gown over her head, mortified by all the scars everywhere clothes did not hide, almost as many as Envoy, only hers were more from burns than cuts. I combed tangles out of her hair with my fingers and washed filth off her face and hands best that I could. I talked to her the whole time, mainly to keep from screaming. As I put her in bed I said, "I really missed you," and she mumbled, "Me, too," then sagged into my arms asleep.

***

GREENISH LIGHT SHINED THROUGH THE BEDROOM SHUTTER. I looked at Cythe, asleep on her back, snoring as usual at the ceiling. I eased out of bed and tiptoed into the other room. Marlie, still rolled in the rug, snored up a storm, too. I thought how it would be sleeping in a room with both of them and smiled in spite of everything. Then I went to the window, took a deep breath and opened the curtains.

Cats lay all along the path from the house. As quietly as I could, I moved the furniture and lifted the door bar. I called out a few times even though I could tell they were dead. I went outside.

All the fog was in the dome except for a heavy curtain around the perimeter; otherwise, everything was as I remembered from the time of the

Temple. Behind the house, the faucet dripped and the big washbasin still rocked with one leg slightly shorter. I ran up the path past the cat bodies to Maidservant's little tree, took a deep breath and jumped through the hedge.

The pathway was chock full of cat and warrior bodies, but I only had eyes for the back entrance of the House of Kalli. Then the door opened a wide crack and a warrior poked her bloody head out and fixed a pair of those red piercing eyes on me before leaning back inside and gesturing frantically to someone. I'm sure that when she looked again, she wondered if she'd imagined me because I was on the other path running for the garden house.

I sat on the edge of the bed telling Cythe what I'd found, expecting her to be as excited as me, but all she did was yawn. "Guess we'd better go check it out then."

"What about the soldiers?"

"They'll do what I tell them."

"The others attacked you."

"Only because Athy ordered them. She outranks everyone except Zeus and Hera. It won't be a problem now, I think."

It took us longer than we intended because Marlie refused to leave the house and I wouldn't go without her, in spite of Cythe insisting. Finally, though, I coaxed her outside, but then she refused to use the shortcut as no amount of arguing or reasoning would make her touch the hedges. Exasperated, I shouted, "They aren't poison anymore. They're just shrubbery."

Self-righteously, she pointed the owl stick at me. "You're just trying to turn me into a blasphemer in a way you can tell Blogfetter I did it myself."

Cythe laughed and for some stupid reason tried to shove Marlie into the hedge, but she ducked and hit Cythe in the jaw. Out came the knives. I screamed at them until they stopped. "We'll go the long way around. It'll only take a few more minutes, so you two behave."

Cat and warrior carcasses, stinking of pee, feces and decomposition, were numerous. Clouds of biting flies swarmed around them. Then we came to the olive grove overlook at the far back corner of the maze where I intended to rest, but it was too dangerous.

A wall of thick mists swirled along the edge of the cliff, kept in place by some invisible force. I thought of feeling to see if I felt something and asked Cythe if she thought I was still immune, but she could not tell. Meanwhile, Marlie decided she wanted to touch it. Luckily, I spotted her reaching and jerked her away. "Are you crazy?"

She put her hands on her hips and glared as if I was the mad one. "You said stay away from the hedges because they're poison. Then you said jump into the hedges because they're not poison. Now you tell me I can't touch the pretty fog because its poison. Well, you touched the poison and nothing happened. If I wait five minutes, you'll say I can do it. You make my head hurt. Sheesh!"

As I led them back into the maze, Cythe giggled. "It would've been easier if you'd let her do it."

I whipped around. "You saw her doing it, didn't you? I can't believe you just stood there and didn't say anything. What's the matter with you?" She looked away, the hurt on her face extreme. Marlie grinned and gave me a pat on the arm for hurting her.

We turned into a long corridor and the upper part of the House of Kalli was visible in the distance. Marlie screamed, "Where are we?" and started to run back the way we'd come, but Cythe tripped her. A fistfight ensued, and I just let them go at it until they stopped and glared at each other's swollen black eyes and bloody noses. Then Marlie burst out crying and pointed at me. "Now, I'm as evil as you."

Cythe had pushed her into the hedge. Too fed up to say anything, I prodded them to go in front of me. It was not long before we reached the corridor leading to the back door of the House of Kalli. Two helmless warriors stood there, each with a sword and putrid cat's head. They started to attack, recognized Cythe and prostrated before her.

A god again, she strode back and forth. "Heroic warriors, tell Great Cythe your names and units so I might bless and reward you." Neither moved, even after she repeated it twice more. She scratched her head. "Do you think it's because they are in such awe?"

Dully, I nodded. "Yeah, that must be it."

She positively glowed. "Seeing me up close overwhelms people. They get tongue-tied and do the craziest things. Once, in Messenia, a man brought his daughter to the temple to teach her how to sacrifice. Turned out the lamb had been the girl's pet, though, and she made an awful fuss, screaming, crying and all. By the time they got to me, he was so upset with her and flustered that he pointed to the girl instead of the animal when he said the prayer of offering. Well, I thought it was funny and made a joke by accepting and telling the priests to take her to the altar, but the stupid man believed I was serious and cursed me, which upset the priests so much they demanded the offering stand. What a mess." She laughed. "Anyway, see what I mean, don't you?"

I was appalled. "Oh, Cythe, you didn't let them sacrifice the girl, did you?"

"Of course not, silly. I'd never have a child killed, even if certain others did." She gave me a knowing look. "Nah. I gave the kid a gold plate with my likeness and sent a priest to take her home to explain to her mother what happened."

I did not have a chance to ask more questions, which probably was just as well.

"Are you two never going to shut up?" Marlie kicked the female warrior in the head with her heel until she looked up, pointed to her ears and shook her head.

After glaring at Marlie for interrupting, Cythe shouted at the warrior to no avail. Perplexed, she turned to me. "Usually, their senses are enhanced when they're remade. They feed defective specimens to the garden. I don't understand why this one can't hear."

Marlie yelled and kicked the man, a sergeant, in the head. He couldn't hear, either, but at least had enough intelligence to deduce what we wanted to know. "Great Cythe, our party killed two beasts and more came. We retreated to this place and thought it safe, but blasphemer ghosts wielded lightning and thunder against us when we tried to go beyond the entry hall." He grabbed the cat's head and held it up. "Praise to Great Cythe!"

She took the awful thing in both hands---he helped her hold it---and made great show examining it. She even made us nod heads in admiration. Then, after a great deal of pantomiming and drawing in the dirt, she made them understand they were to go to the garden house and wait. They tromped off, full of pride.

I meant it as half joke, half compliment. "Quite the performance, Great Cythe."

It hurt her feelings. She fumbled with her hands. "Yeah, it's pretty much as dirtball says. I'm a fake, mostly. The magic is all Athy and Arty. That's why they lost respect and treat me the way they do. Can't blame them, but sometimes, they're so mean I tell Tesi-Ra and he punishes them, so you can see why we don't like each other very much. It's not the same as it used to be, when people had friends. Everyone now is selfish and mean."

Marlie jerked open the door. "Are you going to stand there jabbering all day or go already?"

I almost hit her. "Didn't you hear what the sergeant said about the danger?"

She leaned in, listened and smelled the air like an animal. "Burned, stinking bodies, far off sounds of running water and cool air. No attackers nearby in ambush, so traps are the immediate concern, and that will not change whether we go now or later. No point waiting and allowing enemies time to prepare. You two know this place, yes? Go first."

In the Barrows, when it came to dark places, no one was more skilled than Marlie. I nodded and Cythe made a light that we followed down the hall. Except for the odor, everything was as we remembered.

We stopped at the threshold of the big room and Cythe sent the light ahead. A short distance away, the gross remains of warriors spread across the floor, causing me to throw up, which made Marlie laugh. Then I asked Cythe if she knew anyone who could do such horrific damage. Casually as discussing weather, she said Tesi-Ra burned people, but their bodies looked nothing like this afterward. Then she began describing awful things that others could do until Marlie made a frustrated noise and shoved by us.

Our hair crackled and stood straight up. Call it intuition, craziness or luck, but I ran out, grabbed Marlie and jerked her back into the hallway as a bolt of lightning struck near where she had been. It knocked us down. Thunder boomed, assailing our ears. Then lightning began striking randomly all over the room accompanied by thunderclaps. Holding our ears and screaming, we ran outside.

***

I STOOD A LITTLE WAYS DOWN THE PATH WITH MARLIE, who whimpered and cried on the ground with her arms wrapped tight around my legs, but my attention focused on Cythe, pressing the front of her body against the house with arms stretched out as if trying to hug it. She'd been like that for several minutes. "Uh, Cythe, what are you doing?"

Sliding down the wall to her knees, she looked back with a rapturous expression. "So old, with presence, power and abilities unto itself. Sometimes it is a protected tomb with beasts and poison maze constantly changing, sometimes a portal building with water, expanding lands and garden maze unchanging. Yet, always the same, wondrous creation. Can you feel it, Aria, can you tell?"

"Don't forget who you're talking to, Cythe."

She had tears. "Oh, but you're changing, too. You sensed danger and saved dirtball faster than lightning could strike her. Quite amazing."

"A slug moves faster than me and you know it."

During those times, I think there were two Cythes. Her expression blanked then she shrugged, got up and brushed grit from her knees. "That was a close one. What do we do now?"

"Maybe go back to the garden house and wait for the fog to clear. Everyone probably thinks we're dead so we might be able to sneak away through the garden."

All at once, Marlie lunged up, grabbed me around the neck and pulled me down to her. Her eyes were wild, unfocused. She spoke, but I heard Leto's voice. "Your time has come, Ariadne." Then she kissed me full on the mouth and wouldn't stop.

I never felt such revulsion. I pulled away from the kiss then hit her arms and hands, but she held me tight. I yelled to Cythe for help, but though she looked straight at us, she did not see or hear what was happening. Suddenly, Marlie jerked away from me across the ground backwards as if giant hands snapped a cord fastened to her spine. She slammed into the wall next to Cythe and let out a mournful wail. Cythe jolted then looked down at her with distaste. "What's the matter with you, now?"

Marlie held up her hands, showing palms.

Cythe scowled. "Yeah, they're filthy as the rest of you. Thanks for sharing."

Meanwhile, I felt very strange, as if someone much smarter and stronger than me had occupied my body. "Where's the talking stick, Marlie?"

She grunted, "I dropped it inside."

I opened the door and looked in. "The cats left me alone and the poison didn't kill me, so I think perhaps the lightning might not strike me, either. You two go back to the garden house and wait for the maze to open."

Cythe grabbed me. "Even if the lightning doesn't kill you, we are enemy to the sleeper. You can't stand up to someone like that."

Gently, I extricated myself. "I have to do this."

As only Cythe could, she looked hard and determined, soft and vulnerable at the same time. "Without you, I'm just in everyone's way. I'm going, too."

I shook my head. "I need you to take care of Marlie. Please, she can't stay by herself."

Marlie poked me in the ribs. "I'd rather puke up my guts than stay with her. Not that I'm that crazy about you, either, but just saying. Anyway, I have to get my owl stick, whether you go or not."

Cythe's light globe drifted over my head, a tiny amount of light in such a big space, but it calmed me. I took a deep breath, walked out into the big room and picked up the talking stick. It was charred but intact. I returned it to Marlie and Cythe in the hallway then walked slowly out to exploded warrior bodies. The stink was incredible and I had never felt so alone.

Then, from close behind me, Cythe whispered, "Sorry, but that's as bright as I can make the light."

I whipped around. "We agreed you two would wait in the hallway."

Cythe shook her head. "You're the one the lightning doesn't strike. We're staying close."

Marlie added, "You got that right."

I felt more like hugging than scolding them, so we pressed on. After we had gone much farther than the distance to the canal that Cythe and I remembered, I stopped and asked if she thought we went in a straight line. She said the bridge was straight ahead but could not tell how far, then added, "The room must have expanded."

That started Marlie asking questions that had answers she could not possibly understand. Cythe said she was too stupid to live. They got into another fight, and I had to shove between them. When finally I got them sorted and going again, no one said a word for a very long time until Marlie shrieked, "This is the blasphemers' fortress, isn't it?"

I calmed her down. Then Cythe, who knew the story of the fortress well because she read it to her worshippers frequently, said, "Ah, don't fib to her, Aria. This is the big old blasphemer fortress, and it's full of evil spirits waiting for smelly little dirtballs to convert."

Marlie screamed and jumped on my back. "Save me!"

I tried to spin her off. "It's just a big room."

Cythe couldn't stop laughing. "Yeah, nothing special about it, except for thunder, lightning and the river."

Just like Maidservant so long ago, she stuttered, "There's a...a river?"

Cythe chortled. "Why do you think we keep talking about getting to a bridge? Blasphemers used it dangle dirtballs upside down in the water until the dirt came off so they could cook them. Be careful one doesn't sneak up behind you."

I pulled Marlie off and hugged her. "Cythe, stop acting bat dung crazy before you get us all killed. You're just being cruel picking on her. I don't like you this way."

As quickly as she became nasty, Cythe turned sensible. "Sorry, I got carried away same as you used to. Anyway, I can make out the rails of the bridge up ahead."

"Two bodies are on it," Marlie said. "One is covered up."

Crazy Cythe came back. "How is it that someone such as you can possibly see more than a god?"

Marlie got right in her face. "Go live in the Barrows a few hundred years and maybe you'll figure it out, lamebrain. How many times do I have to tell you?"

I moved between them again. "Cythe, will you please bring the light down closer to the bridge so I can see it?"

We stood at the end of the bridge surveying the situation. A cloak covered the closest body lying at the center of the bridge. Next to it, several jars and a small bundle. Slightly farther away, the other body, a normal sized warrior, was propped against a rail post.

Cythe shook her head, "I don't believe either is the sleeper. The one warrior laid out a dead comrade then died, too. I could be wrong, though, because remade soldiers don't usually show concern for the dead."

Marlie was sarcastic. "It's the sleeper under the cloak that you've all been peeing yourselves over, though I certainly see nothing about it to be concerned about."

Cythe was snide. "You can't know that for sure. Sleepers have no aura except to people with special abilities, and that's certainly not you."

Marlie argued. "The body was covered to keep it clean. The jars and bundle are near the left hand easy to reach in the traditional way. Learn a trade so you'll know something other than half-baked opinions and spells you can't do."

I tried to stop them before it got out of control again. "Cythe, I think that must certainly be the sleeper."

Cythe shot me an angry look then yelled at Marlie. "Just because you lived like a rat underground where sleepers were kept doesn't make you an expert!"

Marlie got in her face again. "I learned resurrection arts from the same people who revived you. They still laugh when they tell how scared you were of them, and they make fart noises whenever they say Aphrodite because you were so gassy. That's the reason we worship Maidservant and not you. You're just a big, stinking joke."

I caught Cythe by the wrist, stopping her fist mere inches from Marlie's nose. Then I shoved them apart. "Enough! Shut up! Both of you!"

Cythe looked puzzled as if she did not understand why I yelled. "I don't think I can keep the light going much longer. Maybe we should go get some oil lamps. It might be dangerous when we take off the cover."

I was very tired. "Yeah, okay."

Marlie yelled, "What part of asleep don't you two understand? Sleepers can't hurt you until they wake up! It is more dangerous to leave and come back than to see who it is now."

Cythe spat on her. "No one cares what you think, dirtball."

Marlie shoved her and sprinted onto the bridge. Green light from the black corner illuminated the entire room. We all dived to the floor, but nothing happened. Cautiously, Cythe and I got up and walked onto the bridge to coax Marlie up, no easy task now that she could see the canal and shadowy statues from the tomb maze. Then she yelled, "You lied to me, Aria. This is the fortress!"

Fed up, I jerked her off the floor. "Stop being an idiot all the time!"

***

WE CROUCHED AROUND THE COVERED SLEEPER'S HEAD with me holding a corner of the cloak. Cythe had her knife out, ready to strike. Marlie rolled her eyes and shook her head at our nervousness and how long we took. I looked to Cythe for encouragement. She put a hand on mine, patted it reassuringly and smiled. We were almost ready. Then Marlie knocked our hands away and snatched the cloak back.

It was Maidservant with a jade Temple tunic tucked around her tattered work dress. The big ring of the Head Priest was around one of her small fingers. Her hands were folded on her chest. She had a thin scar from the left eye to the side of the chin. The left forearm and hand, as well as lower legs and feet, were shiny pink from healed burns.

Marlie gasped, finally remembering to breathe. "Is it really her?"

I nodded. "Yes."

"But she's smaller than me. What happened to her hair?"

"She's from a place called Egypt. Sometimes they shave their heads and wear wigs."

"They cut off their hair and wear someone else's? Why?"

Something made me look up. Cythe stood frozen, face contorted with hate and knife pulled back over her head in both hands ready to plunge into Maidservant's chest. I tackled her around the legs. She kicked free. Marlie shoved her into the rails and punched her in the mouth.

All the fight went out of her. She dropped the knife and remained standing only by hooking elbows over a rail. Then I hit Marlie across the arm and took away her knife as she went for Cythe's midsection. The three of us exchanged hate-filled stares until Cythe got her breath back.

Quietly, I said, "It's impossible to know the truth about Maidservant or anything else the way things are now, Cythe. Besides, we're no better."

She shook her head. "Everyone who serves is evil, but Maidservant is in a class of her own. Yet, it is not in me to end her life, but I take solace from knowing nothing will stop Athy killing her the instant she sees her." She turned and looked at the other body. "Leto. She disappeared the night of the attack."

I did not understand so many things. "Why would Leto dress Maidservant as Head Priest?"

Cythe put her face in her hands and burst out crying. "All this time we've waited for Kalli or an army of powerful Priests to rise from the tomb to stop those bastards, and here lies Maidservant, yet another parasite sucking good out of the world. Truly, this is the end of all hope."

THIRTY-ONE

THE BOOK OF MAIDSERVANT: CONSTANT DAYS

EXCEPT DURING REMAKING, EVERYONE EXPERIENCED LONG SLEEP as an unconscious void with no memories of it after wakening, but it was different for Maidservant. She remained constantly aware where she was, aching because she could not move on the hard bridge, blaming the Kalli woman for her predicament and despising Leto for placing a smothering cover over her face. Had her life spirit not been able to escape to the Wheel of Nun, she would have gone completely mad very quickly.

At first, she spent most of the time in the blue room bingeing on stories. Then she began wandering the ruins of Hub City with eyes closed imagining she was an Eirycian living in the heyday of the bustling metropolis. Slowly, what was a made-up game to breakup monotony became an obsession. She re-created an entire city in her extraordinary mind, plucking people from the stories to populate it then constructing relationships so layered and evolving they became another reality for her. Had she not suffered devastating panic attacks when staying too long inside the Wheel of Nun, Maidservant might have been lost inside her made up fantasy world forever.

She had no way of knowing the attacks were a safeguard the Kalli woman implanted that sent her screaming into the portal back to the Valley of Clouds to roll in grass, smell flowers and experience warm sun and fresh air until exhaustion overtook her. Then, when she opened her eyes, she would be back inside the tomb cursing the cloth on her face and calculating how many more days to add to the total. Close to the end, she reckoned nine thousand days had gone by, a staggering amount of time to a young girl. However, she was wrong. The actual number was one hundred and eighty-three thousand.

***

OUT OF BREATH AND WET WITH SWEAT, Marko stumbled through the front gardens of Olympus Palace to the octopus fountain. In a small plaza next to the Elysian Garden, Tesi-Ra, Kronos, Perius and Theia dined. He bowed and waited, fidgeting and glancing furtively at water on a nearby serving table.

Annoyed, Perius addressed him. "Why are you here without summons, Prefect?"

He never hid fear sufficiently. "Sire, sleepers are emerging from every nook and cranny of the Barrows. We can't handle so many."

Kronos frowned. "The best solution would be to find somebody to run the Barrows who can do the job."

Theia squawked. "We should have foreseen this was a possibility. The power emanating from the tomb draws them out. Likely, the numbers will keep increasing. Will need the assistance of a large number of soldiers. Not a good situation if any escape."

Tesi-Ra nodded. "I think you are right on all counts, Theia. Perius, take control of the Barrows and kill everyone---sleepers, prisoners and workers alike. Send the bodies here to nourish our new warriors. Then collapse the tunnels so no one else can get out. Leave some guards in case a few strays dig out. I'm tired dealing with that infernal place."

Marko blurted, "But what of me, Lord? What do I do?"

Tesi-Ra burned him to ash then held a cloth to his nose to block the stench. "Beginning today, we'll take turns standing vigil at the maze with the gods. Place all the island forces at full alert and send word that battle is imminent."

Watching Perius hurry away to carry out the orders, Theia nodded. "Wise precautions."

Kronos agreed. "Yes, it is time for this matter to be resolved so we can leave this infernal island."

***

MAIDSERVANT DID NOT UNDERSTAND WHAT WAS WRONG. Sitting in a crumbling opening on the top floor of the tallest building in Hub City, she dangled legs precariously and stared down into the ruins, heartbroken because no longer could she imagine her beautiful city filled with friends and activities. She had even set the blue globe in the dome in motion to play soothing musical tones, something that before had always helped her mental constructions, but strong feelings that someone watched her persisted, wrecking concentration. Desperate, she had chanced the dangerous climb up through the broken building to survey the city for evidence of someone lurking, but found nothing except the usual cold emptiness.

She wished she could let go and change this endless nightmarish life, but she had tried that once, figuring that either she would not be injured since her body was in the tomb or the fall would kill her life spirit and leave her body useless and empty. Both outcomes were acceptable to her at that point, but she had not considered a third possibility---injuring her life spirit then having to remain in the body suffering horribly while it recovered.

Suddenly, she inexplicably jammed her fingers into her mouth and began sucking them. Memories of how food and drink tasted drove all other thoughts away. Then she choked and pulled her fingers out, but it didn't help because something blocked her nose and mouth, forcing her to swallow foul liquid. Cramps knotted her midsection and burning sensations shot down her legs. She gasped and coughed.

Cold liquid doused her face and she realized Leto's accursed cloth was gone. Blurry shadows in green haze moved around her. One of them crouched close and shook her. Another, who talked almost nonstop, poured cold water over her midsection then said the name Marlie. The close one with bad breath responded by making strange noises then moved away. A third shadow stayed unmoving by her feet, staring down. The talker's face came close, peering into her eyes. What was she going to do, bite her nose? She seemed familiar but all the names she remembered at the moment were people in Hub City.

"Shake her again, Marlie."

She managed to move a hand and made a weak attempt to swat the talker away.

"She's awake!"

THIRTY-TWO

THE BOOK OF THE HERO ARIADNE: DUTY

I WANTED TO MOVE MAIDSERVANT INTO THE LIVING QUARTERS but she refused to leave the bridge so we pulled a bed and chairs out for her. Marlie stayed by her side, sleeping in a blanket next to the bed and seeing to her every need although Maidservant would not speak to her except through me, which upset Marlie very much. Maidservant and Cythe had nothing to say to each other except for Cythe calling her a murderer and demanding she explain how she could kill everyone, especially Erran and her parents. I simply couldn't believe Maidservant did all those awful things, but I only spoke to her when necessary because of an incident with Leto's body.

Marlie and I helped Maidservant up to exercise her legs and she asked to see Leto, laid out on the bridge covered with a blanket. I thought she wanted to pay respects because Leto saved her with long sleep, but instead, she cursed and kicked some of the remains into the water. Then, as I wrestled her back to bed, Marlie kicked more of the body off the bridge before Cythe, returning from the garden house, made her stop. Ironically, the only thing that made sense after that was to put the rest of the body in the water. I glanced Maidservant's way while we did it, and will never forget her triumphant sneer.

The next day, Maidservant would not speak to anyone, even when Marlie made a wreath, placed it next to the bed and knelt down to pray. But then, after I sent Cythe and Marlie to the garden house for food, she climbed off the bed and used the rails to make her way to the end of the bridge where I washed clothes in the canal. "Who does Marlie think I am?"

I hadn't noticed her. Surprised she could move around already, I did my best to hide my opinions of her. "Tesi-Ra said you were a hero for murdering and betraying everyone at the Temple and they made you a god."

She absolutely beamed. "I'm a god? He did that for me?"

I wanted to puke on her face. "Don't be so pleased. Gods don't amount to much these days."

"Now I understand why Marlie made an offering and prayed to me."

"She's an idiot."

"What am I called?"

I refrained from answering what I wanted.

"Did they give me a good name? Surely, I'm not the God Maidservant."

"Yeah, kind of sticks in the throat, doesn't it?"

It upset her and she changed the subject. "Exactly how long did I sleep?"

"Five hundred years, give or take."

She looked dismayed. "I've missed so much."

"Not really. I've only been awake a short time myself."

She was surprised. "Do you serve my master, too?"

I wanted to slap her face. "Did you really believe this world would be better than the one you destroyed?"

She was unfazed. "If I'm a god, it is. I wasn't anything in the other one, that's for sure. What do you do?"

Not a question I would answer. "What about Leto? How did she die?"

She related the story. "Funny, huh?"

"Why did Leto abandon the Temple to bring those statues here? Are you supposed to do something with them? Does it have anything to do with her dressing you as Head Priest?"

The questions agitated her. "She did it to satisfy a bunch of ridiculous prophecies made by a crazy seer who served Kalli. She said a hero would show up to save everyone, and when one didn't, they picked me to do it. I told the shining woman, I told Rhea and I told Leto, but no one listened, so now I'm telling you. I'M NOT THE ONE!"

"Please, Leto made you Head Priest so you could do something with the statues. Why won't you do it?"

"All of you acted friendly long as it didn't inconvenience you. The woman used me. Rhea used me. Envoy promised to save me then left. I found out Seydi was the sister I loved, but she wanted to kill me. I've never had a real friend or anyone do anything for me my whole life. Nobody."

"Please, you're the only one who can save us. We're your friends. Why won't you help us?"

"I'm going to give the statues to my master and teach him to recite the words of power. I will have everything I ever wanted. Nothing you can say will change my mind." She looked up at the ceiling and it opened. "Leave me alone or I'll make something bad happen to you."

I choked down all the things I wanted to say and helped her back to bed.

Several days later, I was on the bridge with Cythe watching Maidservant run and swim around the room. It amazed us how far she leaped and that she kept going nonstop.

Marlie, happily serving her new master, cleaned the area around the bed. She got on my nerves, but I pitied her as hardly anyone could have lived her life and still believed in anything, however wrong it was.

Then Cythe asked, "Is something bothering you? You've hardly spoken to me the last few days."

If I looked at her, I'd cry, so I squeezed her hand. "I have a lot on my mind."

"Did I do something to upset you?"

I shook my head but still could not look at her. More than anything, I wanted to say what she meant to me and why I was about to leave, but she would not understand and certainly interfere. Because, as it turns out, Kalli planned my destiny a thousand years ago.

The seer had foreseen that the biggest challenge to finishing the plan was Maidservant and found a child with powerful abilities who would be born into the Keftiu royal family they could mold into one of the possible solutions. Consequently, the Head Priests and Mother expected my birth before she even knew Father. Then, from infancy, she and Rhea trained and fed me concoctions of herbs and food laced with increasing amounts of maze poison that made me immune and seen by the sentinels and other safeguards as a functioning part of the House of Kalli complex.

They kept all this from Father. They were that careful to insure the people who knew about me was the smallest number possible. In fact, after training ended at age twelve, Rhea removed Mother's and my memories, so she alone knew my purpose.

When Marlie delivered Leto's message and kissed me, it triggered an unsealing of my memories and abilities. No one knew how many days my recovery would take, so it was up to me to delay Maidservant long as possible and hope I was ready when she went out of the tomb.

Although neither of my parents knew the truth about me when I left them, they did know how they were going to die, and played their parts in the plan without hesitation. Before they buried my memories, I was fervent in my beliefs, too. Now, however, I struggle to keep my word, more because of Cythe than Maidservant being so reprehensible that I'd rather cut her throat.

I went to Maidservant as Marlie helped her dress. "Do you remember the olive tree we gave you? It's still in the maze, not changed at all. Would you like to go see it?"

"No."

"I found wine in the cellar of the garden house. Probably some you gave us. We could sit at the overlook and talk as we used to. What do you say? Can't you wait until tomorrow?"

She picked up the bag with the statues and walked off the bridge with us crowded around her. "Stop trying to change my mind. I'm sick and tired of it."

Cythe tried to help me. "We've told you how things are, but you won't listen. You're not going to like it at all."

Glaring, she pointed and the double doors and windows along the front wall flew open. "Shut up!"

I got in front and stopped her. "We're your friends. We just want to help you."

"No one ever does anything for me."

I pleaded. "At least wait until tonight. We'll sneak out through the garden and you can see for yourself how things are before doing anything rash. I'm sure you'll change your mind and help us once you know. Besides, the island is very different now. Athy wants to kill you. Marauding warriors are everywhere. I can't let anything bad happen to you. You are too important to us."

"Stop lying. Get out of the way!"

Cythe helped me block her. Marlie hit Cythe with the talking stick. "She doesn't need to worry. She's a real god!"

We were nearly to the doorway. The green fog vanished. Maidservant swung the statues at me. I pushed them aside and grabbed her arm. She twisted to jerk away but could not break the grip. Startled by my sudden strength, she gaped at me. Cythe grabbed her other arm with both hands. Marlie shoved Cythe, but she held on.

***

NOT SINCE THE FABLED EIRYCIAN WARS had all the forces of the One Master walked the earth at the same time. The four armies arrayed around the maze were behind mounds of earth, boulders and felled trees in case of another poison explosion. Reinforcements camped on the plain between Atlas City and old Eao, ready to fight. Perius' personal guard defended Olympus City and provided police duties. Massive fleets of black ships stood offshore filled with assault troops. Another army camped on the north shore of Keftiu, sixty miles to the south, ready to deploy. The remainder of the One Master's forces occupied all other major islands and coastlines of countries bordering the sea in spite of the unlikelihood of an enemy making it that far.

Towering above Maidservant's statue, Kronos and Tesi-Ra stood on the shrine hill looking at the armies stretched around the fog-enshrouded tomb. Kronos' chest swelled with pride. "What a glorious, historic sight this is."

Tesi-Ra studied him then chose words carefully. "Even if we face Kalli in person, we should be victorious, but I have concerns about the times that follow. With no more powerful opposition, the gods will be sufficient to keep the weak-minded fools inflicting misery and suffering on each other."

Kronos did not show his surprise though it was extreme. Unless he was mistaken, Tesi-Ra invited a conversation that could bring suffering beyond time and imagination if one reported the other, yet he was glad for the chance to engage. "The Master has left things to us far too long and we have become more powerful than he intended. He surely plans an end to some, if not all, of us when this matter is concluded."

Tesi-Ra nodded. "I had hopes of tipping the scales more in our favor before showing my hand, but it hasn't worked out."

"You haven't found enough of the old magic or solved the riddle of its use then?"

Tesi-Ra laughed bitterly. "You know damn well I haven't, nor have you, but we can't wait any longer. Perius and I have a pact. When we finish here, we intend to kill Theia and Coeus, take control of their armies and wipe out as many of the Master's forces we can before he recalls them to Tartaros. We can't win as things are now, but it will buy us time to keep searching for old magic."

Kronos nodded. "It's a huge gamble with short odds, but I'd rather die in war than spend the rest of my life as one of his court flunkies, which is the only alternative to being returned to the Pit. If you'll have me, please count me in."

Tesi-Ra and he grasped forearms, sealing the alliance as Athy, Czn-tanth and Arty came up the hill from the avenue. Czn-tanth reported. "We heard noises in the fog that sounded like doors and windows opening."

Arty pointed to the places. "May we have permission to probe with arrows?"

Before Tesi-Ra could answer, the fog vanished and there stood the House of Kalli with sunlight streaming into the windows and double doorway, illuminating someone emerging from the shadowy interior.

Arty had the sharpest eyes. "Maidservant!"

Faster than Tesi-Ra could turn to stop her, Athy unslung her bow, fitted an arrow and sent it streaking to Maidservant's heart.

***

I KNEW EXACTLY WHAT WE'D SEE ON THE HILL ACROSS THE WAY. Tesi-Ra and Kronos are giants, Czn-tanth and Arty point to us and Athy lets fly an arrow as Tesi-Ra turns to stop her. Yes, I'm a seer of sorts, but only when unfolding events endanger me. It was my other abilities Kalli's plan most wanted, though.

When I was little, they began throwing objects at me. At first, they thought I was simply extraordinarily fast because no one could hit me. Then I started plucking them out of the air, even spears, knives and arrows shot across a room. No one understood how I did it even when I described it, but that isn't important now. I do this for my parents and Cythe, who I love.

Except for me, everything slows almost to a stop. Marlie breaks Cythe's grip on Maidservant and I let go. Athy's arrow flies straight for the little traitor's heart. I must remember to be loud and not choke on such an audacious lie. "I LOVE YOU, MAIDSERVANT!"

THIRTY-THREE

THE BOOK OF MAIDSERVANT: GOOD GIRL GONE BAD

MAIDSERVANT HEARD ARIA YELL BEHIND HER then impossibly Aria was in front of her clutching an arrow in her chest with both hands as she fell face down. Screaming and crying, Cythe threw herself on the body. Then Tesi-Ra, Kronos and Czn-tanth were there with Athy and Arty. Soldiers dragged Cythe and Aria out of the entrance and her master spoke to her. "Who else is in the building?"

She could not tear her gaze from Aria and Cythe on the avenue. It was difficult to get words out. "The bodies of warriors who got inside just before I woke up and Leto, who I found dying from arrows in the stomach when the Temple fell."

He was concerned. "There must be someone else. What of the power coming from the tomb? Look at me!"

She did as told but continued seeing Aria in her mind and speaking with no emotion. "The House of Kalli generates power on its own. Leto talked about it after she changed the building into a tomb. Then she healed me and gave me her sleep drugs because she was dying. I don't know why she saved me. We hated each other."

Tesi-Ra transformed to normal size and looked at her more closely. "You landed in the river, didn't you? How did you make it here? Did Leto help you do that, too?"

She shook her head. "No, it couldn't have been her. I don't remember much about it except wanting to die to stop the hurting."

"You must have been in great pain."

"Yes."

He patted her head. "You've done well. I am happy to have my good girl back in service. The sleep delayed your transformation, but you'll feel much better soon. Did Leto know who shot her?"

"It was Athy."

Athy shoved by the others. "Liar!"

Maidservant did not flinch. "Leto hid behind bushes when you and Arty ran by and you thought she was enemy. If you don't believe me, you put little marks on your arrows so Arty didn't take credit for your shots. The body is in the water under the bridge if you want to go see for yourself."

Czn-tanth laughed. "Athene killed the Head Priest? I'm so impressed. Hey, wait a minute---she was on your side back then, wasn't she?"

Athy whipped out her short sword, but Tesi-Ra struck the weapon from her hand. "You've done more than enough mischief for one day. I wanted the caretaker alive to find out why she was immune to the maze. Now we'll never know." He nodded to Czn-tanth. "As for you, stop causing trouble."

She shrugged and smiled prettily. "I didn't do anything."

Without warning, Maidservant slashed Czn-tanth up the left side of her face with a knife. Instantly, she retaliated, intending to strike back with nails suddenly long and sharp as razors, but Tesi-Ra knocked her down. "You don't listen, do you?"

Incensed, Czn-tanth jumped back to her feet. "I demand satisfaction! It's my right!"

More than a little pleased, Tesi-Ra looked at Maidservant, bloody knife in hand. "Why did you attack her?"

She pointed to the scar on her face in the same place. "She did it to me. I did her back."

He laughed. "Amazing what a little sleep does for some people. You did that, Czn-tanth?"

"No!"

Athy sneered. "I was there when she did it. That's why Maidservant ran from the Temple kitchen that night, Master."

Tesi-Ra forced the three girls apart as they went for one another. "Satisfaction has been served and past differences settled. Today you begin anew. The matter is closed."

Czn-tanth fumed. "I'll have a scar on my face. What of that?"

He shrugged. "Appeal to the Master if you want, but if you lose, I'll claim satisfaction, so you might want to think it over. Besides, a scar fits your personality perfectly."

Czn-tanth shoved soldiers out of the way and disappeared into the building. Tesi-Ra told Maidservant to stay with Cythe and went inside with Athy and Arty. In a few minutes they returned. Tesi-Ra bent over Cythe. "Get up! Your behavior is unbecoming."

Cythe raised her head. Never had anyone seen her so dirty, swollen-faced and wretched, yet in spite of it, her appeal remained powerful. "Please, a little more time, then I will do anything you ask."

He nodded. "One hour, then take the maid to the palace and get cleaned up so the Council can hear the details of your adventures together." He motioned to Athy, Arty and Czn-tanth. "Have the armies stand down then destroy this building and everything around it." He and Kronos changed into shining titans and went down the road with wild cheering from the armies.

Athy and Arty knew the House of Kalli and grounds were indestructible, but ordered soldiers to break the tile floors, block walls and statues with heavy hammers and axes then ate lunch and watched stoically as the efforts left not so much as a mark. Czn-tanth, who did not know, conjured demonic fire under the statues, accomplishing nothing except black soot that wiped off easily. Then she set the strongest warriors to pounding the bridge rails with hammers with no result.

Meanwhile, on the avenue, Cythe yelled at Maidservant. "What are you? Don't you feel anything for her?"

Maidservant began speaking the incantation she used on Cythe so long ago, but it only made her angry. "Doesn't work on me now, you little snake! Try that again, and I'll shove a light globe down your throat." But then she half-tripped on Aria's leg, began crying and ran down the road.

Maidservant sent Marlie to stop her with instructions to wait in the intersection then rolled Aria onto her back. She meant to tell her weak creatures die, but could not say the words for some reason. She started down the road, hesitated, and went back. She took off the necklace and pulled it around Aria's cold neck. She snapped the clasp closed.

Suddenly, as if everything had been invisible, she saw her surroundings. Demon warriors rushed by on the road, bowing and dipping weapons to her. The island was desolate from centuries of ash and lava flows, nothing much growing on it anymore. The once beautiful mountain billowed black smoke that blotted blue from the sky. The city of Eao was gone. In the intersection, Marlie and Cythe hit, cursed and stabbed knives at each other. She looked up the hill at her acid eroded statue and shrine. How absurd, how utterly absurd, everything was. She realized she was crying.

Fastidious, Aria had died as disgusting and dirty as Marlie. It was not right. Maidservant wiped off her face best she could. She pulled tangles out of her hair and arranged the rags into a semblance of the tunic it may once have been. She wanted to fold her hands the Egyptian way but could not unclench the bloody fingers from Athy's arrow. She kissed the cold forehead then stood and wiped away the tears.

"Okay. I'll stop being a good girl long as I can, but it probably won't accomplish anything but getting me killed, too."

THIRTY-FOUR

THE BOOK OF ATHENE: SPIRITS EVERLASTING

ATHY, ARTY AND CZN-TANTH CAME OUT OF THE HOUSE OF KALLI just in time to see Cythe and Marlie chasing Maidservant up the avenue past the hill and take the old shortcut into the woods. Arty was puzzled. "Why are they going that way? Those trails are overgrown."

Athy shook her head. "The ignorant leading the stupid. That's the way Maidservant always went to the Temple and Cythe probably forgot the last five hundred years."

Suddenly, Theia, Perius and Coeus led an elite squad of soldiers from behind Maidservant's shrine and hurried down the hill. Agitated, Theia snapped her hooked beak as she asked questions too fast to answer. "What happened to Forbidden Tomb? Who was inside? What is this building? Where are Tesi-Ra and Kronos? Why are you useless fools standing here doing nothing?"

Startled by the ferocity of her interrogation, the girls looked at one another rather than answering immediately.

Theia thrust out her neck, the razor sharp beak inches from Czn-tanth's face. "You're in charge. Answer or Theia will bite off your head."

Czn-tanth stammered and struggled get words out so Athy stepped forward. "The mists cleared and the House of Kalli, which stood on this spot in the time of the Temple, had reappeared. Inside, they found Head Priest Leto, dead since the Temple fell, and Maidservant, revived from long sleep by Cythe and two Outcasts, who somehow negotiated the maze to reach the tomb. I killed one of the Outcasts when they came out. That is her body on the road. Maidservant told Tesi-Ra the building somehow contains old magic, which accounted for the power emanating from the tomb. Since there is no threat, Tesi-Ra and Kronos ordered the armies to stand down and returned to Olympus."

Much calmer, Theia poked her head into the house and sniffed several times. She bent to Aria's body and sniffed it. Something puzzled her. She stretched her head high into the air, sniffing in all directions. Her eyes widened. She screeched and pointed a talon up the road. "Who went that way?"

Again, Athy answered. "Cythe, Maidservant and an Outcast."

Theia regarded them angrily. "The stench of old magic outside the building is too intense to be missed even by you nitwits. Must I rip the eyes out of your heads to make you use other senses? Must I tell you everything like ignorant children?"

They tried, but no one sensed anything out of the ordinary, not even Athy or Coeus.

Theia squawked her frustration and pointed up the road again. "It has to be coming from Maidservant, but all in the group are tainted and must die. After them!"

Athy and Arty ran, Perius following with the soldiers. Coeus remained with Theia, who held Czn-tanth behind to explain everything that happened in more detail.

It was hard going in the thick scrub, especially for Athy in titan form bulling straight ahead with her shield. Ducking debris behind her, Arty complained, "Theia says kill them, Tesi-Ra says don't. What are we going to do?"

Athy grunted as she knocked over a small tree. "Kill Maid-Cretin and leave Cythe for them to argue over."

"Do you think Maidservant is really that powerful? I didn't sense it from her."

"No, or she would've done something when I shot the arrow at her."

"I thought you meant to kill the princess. Everyone did. You never miss."

"Show respect and call her Aria."

Arty hesitated. "Uh, did I miss something?"

"Weren't you watching? When I released the arrow, she was in the shadows behind Maid-Cretin."

"Tesi-Ra shoved me when he went after you, but surely you're mistaken. Your arrows strike faster than a blink. Was there something different about your shot?"

Athy ripped a huge patch of brambles out of the ground and hurled them away. "No, and there's something else. It should have passed clean through her and killed both of them. In spite of the power and velocity behind the shot, she caught it."

"If she could do that, couldn't she have kept it from killing her?"

Athy rammed into a group of big trees that stopped her cold in her tracks. "Yeah, I believe so. Which means she meant to die."

"Then it makes no sense whatever, especially since she has no abilities."

"She had them today, and they were extraordinary."

Arty waited for her to say more, but she just stood there. "Uh, not to criticize, but nothing at all indicates they came this way. Cythe's not exactly fast, either."

Athy changed to normal size and drank some water. "Just needed to get my emotions sorted, you know? They're on the lower path we used to take to the footbridge, not far from where it crosses Olympus Avenue. I suspect they'll turn up the road toward the palace and we'll cut them off."

Arty took a deep breath. "What's eating at you? Was it killing the princess or not killing Maidservant?"

Athy's reply was harsh. "Her name was Aria!"

Maidservant, Cythe and Marlie tumbled down a high embankment and landed in a tangle of arms and legs in the uphill lane of Olympus Avenue. A team of wild-eyed creatures pulling an overloaded cart reared. Cargo tumbled out, stopping traffic in both directions. The angry driver cursed them and drew a sword just as they spotted Athy and Arty on the road higher up. They dashed to the path on the other side and disappeared into the woods.

Athy and Arty expected to catch them quickly, but the appearance of two gods caused a commotion as people left skittish animals untended to prostrate. Then Perius and the warriors appeared even farther up the mountain and raced down the avenue, trampling anyone and anything in the way. Animals bolted and pandemonium ensued.

Athy and Arty ran down the shoulder and turned onto the path full speed, but as they ducked under low branches in a tight left turn, they encountered Cythe and Marlie running back toward the road. Athy knocked them aside and hurried on. Arty glanced back over her shoulder. "They took off again. Maybe we should have found out what they are doing or at least tied them up."

Athy glared. "Do what you want, but I have to stop Maid-Cretin before she reaches the river. She doesn't know the other bank collapsed and might try jumping again."

"Then she'll have the death she escaped five hundred years ago. Poetic justice, if you ask me."

"She needs to suffer much longer than that before she dies."

Maidservant could tell by the overgrowth no one had come this way for a long time and assumed the bridge was gone. She wished Cythe had told her, but no matter, because this was the narrowest part of the gorge and she could jump it easily. Imagining the expression on Athy's face, she sped up, crashed through brush where the bridge had been and leaped off the edge precisely.

It was one of the best jumps she ever made, but too many seconds ticked by. She plummeted down into billowing clouds of steam. Then a wall of black rock rushed out of mists at her. Reflexively, she closed eyes, held arms and legs out against impact and screamed, "Master, help me!"

Her body began changing just before she hit the wall. Her hands and feet felt as if they went into the surface of the rock, keeping her from falling. Long seconds passed before she caught her breath and worked up enough courage to look.

Still changing, her arms were a pale gray-green, elongated and had two elbow joints. Her hands and feet were membranous and cup-shaped. They oozed sticky green-yellow substances that helped suction to surfaces. In wonder, she yanked the left hand free to examine, but it brushed her cheek and suctioned onto her face. Since she could not use the other hand to pull it off, she twisted and jerked until it came free, almost falling in the process. That was when the horror of what she was becoming hit her. She screamed, "No! I don't want to be like this!"

Instantly, the changing reversed. Terrified, she climbed fast as she could go before she lost grip on the smooth wet rock.

Meanwhile, Athy grabbed a succession of small limbs and vines as she skidded through brush and into space over the river gorge. Close behind, Arty caught hold of a tree branch with one hand and Athy's hair with the other. Athy reached up and held onto Arty's arm as they swung out over the river. Then they swung back and Athy dropped to safety, followed by Arty the next time. Neither said anything about it.

Arty found Maidservant's footprints quickly. "Sorry. You'll have to be satisfied she's dead and leave it at that."

Athy stared down through the gap in brush Maidservant left behind. Disbelief contorted her face. "She's not dead. She's climbing straight up the rock cliff on all fours. Tesi-Ra must've remade her."

Arty whistled. "Can you tell what she is?"

Athy's shoulders slumped slightly. "No, but already she's over the top and running up First Test toward the Barrows. She's changing back, too."

Arty gasped. "But only the Fathers have the ability to change back and forth."

Athy shook her head. "She's not that strong and is still in the remaking process. I have no idea how any of this is possible or what she is, other than strange."

"What do we do now?"

"We'll follow the river down to the avenue and take it to First Test. She'll go up the mountain beyond the Barrows, but she'll encounter soldiers and have to turn back. All we have to do is wait."

As they started to leave, Perius' soldiers arrived and reported he had gone after Cythe and sent them to help the gods.

***

PERIUS HAD CYTHE AND MARLIE CORNERED against tangles of brambles farther up the river. He had chased them back and forth across the avenue several times before catching them, and he was angry. He had wanted time to toy with Cythe before killing her, but they were not far from Olympus Avenue and he had no idea how close Athy and Arty were.

Suddenly, Cythe ran at him with a ridiculous knife and he slapped her down senseless. He reached to scoop her up but the Outcast scum jumped between them snapping fingers like crazy. He thought the audacious little freak must be out of her mind with fear. He pounded her with his fist then carried them to the riverbank, one in each hand.

He had to be mindful of details. Tesi-Ra had unnatural feelings for Cythe and might want to see the place she died, so he put them down carefully on rocks so as not to leave unintentional signs. He poked his head through the brush to make certain nothing impeded a fall to the water. He picked Cythe up and shook her awake as the Outcast got up on her knees and began chanting prayers to him. He laughed at her then dangled Cythe by the hands, making her run and leave tracks to the river. He bent down to see the tracks closer.

Marlie continued to pray as she crept up behind him and planted her feet wide. Then she put the owl stick between her teeth, took her knife in both hands and slashed across the tendon on the back of his huge right foot. He threw Cythe down and spun around.

Marlie fell on his other foot, plunging the blade to the hilt between two toes. Cursing, he kicked her off, but she kept the grip on the knife, slicing a deep wound as she flew away. She slammed into a small tree, the only thing that prevented her going into the river. Grimacing, she took the stick out of her mouth. "You're a pus head."

He reached for her, planning to tie her to the tree and dunk her until all the meat was gone from the bones, but she did not scream and plead as expected. Instead, she cocked her head and grinned. He hesitated a fatal second before starting to look around.

An enormous force drove him past Marlie, who barely managed to scramble away as he grabbed her sapling and took it with him into the river. Then she, battered and wincing from broken ribs, helped Cythe up and proudly announced, "Blogfetter takes good care of me."

Cythe staggered, trying to focus her eyes on a huge club bearer with a badly disfigured face reaching down a finger to steady her. Terrified to have an assault warrior touch her, she nonetheless mumbled a thank you.

He grunted and Marlie translated. "Don't be afraid. He'll heal you, if you want."

She looked at him again and wondered if she misheard, for his kind did not have healing abilities. "My body heals itself. Besides, you need it more than me."

Marlie nodded to his grunting. "He wonders why one of the Fathers tried to kill a god, if you feel like talking right now."

Cythe burst out crying into her hands.

Marlie sighed. "Don't take offense, Blogfetter, it's not you. She's just sad because Aria died. She liked her. I don't know why, though."

Blogfetter bent down to her, grunting urgently.

She responded with indifference. "Athene killed her. You know how it is. If it's the will of the gods then too bad for you. Aria claimed she used to be friends with her, but if you ask me, I don't think they could've been very close. I suppose I liked her some of the time, but she was too bossy. Marlie, do this. Marlie, do that. Marlie, stop talking about blasphemers so much. Got so I did it mostly to upset her."

Then her face lit. "Oh, I forgot the most important thing. The tomb changed into a big building with a river, bridge and statues of the Forbidden Tomb sentinels. We found her sleeping on the bridge with evil Head Priest Leto sacrificed at her feet. I revived her! Maidservant!"

Blogfetter's eye grew big as a platter. He grunted at Cythe. Marlie turned to her, put hands on hips and huffed. "He wants you to say she's alive. He doesn't believe me."

Cythe nodded.

Blogfetter grunted like mad and turned back and forth as if wanting to run all directions at once until Marlie grabbed a small tuft of fur on the back of his hand and yanked hard as she could. Then, while he rubbed the sore place, she reached down the armhole of her rags and pulled out the white Kalli statue tethered by a leather cord around her neck. "She told us to remove her statue and put this on the pedestal in Ruined Village Lake then meet her behind the big house. Funny thing about her, though. She doesn't have any hair and is skinny with pointy ears, a pink hand and feet. Kind of looks more like a mouse than a god." She slapped her hands over her mouth. "Oh! I didn't mean disrespect. I only meant…"

Blogfetter grunted emphatically, cutting her off.

"I just told you that we have to go to Ruined Village first!"

He grunted at Cythe. Marlie rolled her eyes. "He wants you to say whether we should go after her or go to Ruined Village. Stop! What are you doing?"

Cythe hugged the air out of her then smiled as only she could. "Thanks for saving me. From now on we'll be friends and look out for each other if that's okay with you."

Marlie's lip quivered and tears welled. "But I'm an Outcast and you're a god."

Cythe hugged her again. "Might as well get used to it. You're stuck with me."

Marlie held out the talking stick. "If ever you lose your tongue, I'll share, and you can go first."

Blogfetter interrupted again and Cythe did not need a translation. "Because we have to go to Ruined Village first. Listen to Marlie."

***

AS ATHY AND ARTY NEARED THE TOP OF FIRST TEST, the avenue tiles illuminated with lavender light and the high walls came to life with scenes of people strolling along a tree-lined boulevard. They were so lifelike Arty tried to touch a woman's arm, causing a tile-sized red square to appear under her hand, slide down the wall and reappear at the edge of the avenue. It kept trying to move under Arty's feet, but she dodged. "What is that thing?"

Athy shrugged. "Let's hurry and find Maidservant."

But when they vaulted over the barricade into the Barrows, hordes of sleepers caked in dirt and ragged burial clothes wandered aimlessly everywhere they looked. A young man, root clods tangled in his long hair and beard, lurched by them. "Is it time?"

As they readied bows, Arty asked, "Where are the soldiers? I don't see a one."

Athy was concerned. "This place is heavy with old magic. I don't sense any heartbeats, though, not even from the sleepers. They may all be illusions, but be careful. The caster may use them to get close."

They moved through the trees past the old pedestal to the Barrows entrance. A steady stream of sleepers emerged. Athy shook her head. "All this may be nothing but a ploy to divert attention from Maid-Cretin. If a threat presents itself, we'll deal with it; otherwise, let's keep searching."

They moved at a faster pace until Arty pointed through the trees. "There are four obelisks. Look, a black one."

They moved closer. No longer blurred, lines of precise ancient text shined on the surfaces. Athy was amazed. "Go find Tesi-Ra. He'll want to see this. But don't mention me. I sense Maid-Cretin coming this way from the north and I'll have her well away from here by the time you return. Warn the soldiers on First Test that it'll be their heads if I miss her and she gets by them."

Athy hid in thick shrubbery near the center of Main Court until Maidservant was close. She leaped out, planning to shoot her in the leg to stop her running, but she was not there. Instead, a glowing emerald statue of Kalli stood upon the old pedestal, all the sleepers were gone and the Barrows entrance had caved in. She spun around to make sure no one else was around, but when she turned back to the statue, a decrepit old woman in a tattered black robe stood next to it.

Badly stooped, she clutched a crude staff in trembling gnarled hands. Stringy white hair hung in tangles from her bowed head, hiding the face. Her heartbeat was weak and a little erratic, exactly as it should be from someone so old. Athy no longer sensed Maidservant anywhere. Furious, she pulled the arrow taut and moved toward the woman cautiously. "What are you doing here, hag, waiting to die?"

The reply was creaky. "I'm here to set you free."

Athy moved sideways to get a clear shot to the heart. "Is that a fact?"

The woman lifted her head as though the effort taxed her strength. The hair, clumped together, stayed in place then fell back from her face all at once, revealing Athy's mother, Metys.

Caught off guard, Athy hesitated then fired too quickly as the hag left the staff stuck in the ground, dipped under the arrow and covered the distance between them in a twinkling. She pushed the bow aside, confronting Athy with Arty's green eyes, freckled face and sassy, taunting smile. The voice was hers, too. "Slow as ever."

Athy sneered. "Cute, using my memories against me, but if that's the best you can do, you're living your last minutes."

Laughing, Arty melted back into the old woman. She raised a thin, emaciated wrist displaying a barely discernible symbol---a staring eye inside a black triangle. "Yours is a golden owl, if my muddled mind is not betrayed by so many years."

Athy showed her wrist. "How did you know?"

"A powerful seer served Kalli, and the symbol was all she could see of you. Do you realize that Corruption made you into a murderous servant by using two people you knew well? What a farce you've become, unable to kill the hated one and incapable of loving the cherished one. Want to hear more?"

Athy did not notice the woman reaching for her wrist. "Shut up!"

Powerful old magic burned into her through the symbol. She hit and kicked, jerked and twisted until she freed her arm and rolled sideways onto her knees, but the woman was gone, replaced by a vision of Maidservant jumping over the barricade at the top of First Test. She had the black Kalli statue in her hand.

Athy looked at the emerald statue then across at the black obelisk. She remembered the four statues on the Head Priest's table and guessed what Maidservant was doing. That meant Cythe was probably on the way to Ruined Village with the white statue. She had no idea what would happen once all of them were in place, but Theia was right. They must kill Maidservant and Cythe soon as possible.

But first, Athy struck the statue a flurry of blows with the sword and determined it was indestructible. She had to hurry, but after jumping the barricade onto First Test, she skidded to a stop and raised her bow.

Arty stood next to the avenue watching the murals. She turned and held up her arm, showing a handprint burned around the wrist. "Girl grabbed my arm leaving the Barrows. Next thing I know, I'm lying here next to the road. Maidservant came, jumped on that red square and it whisked her down the hill past the soldiers. I wanted to go after her, but I couldn't." She threw up.

"Enough games, witch. You don't have those ugly freckles right and Arty's backside is fatter and more lopsided."

Arty straightened, eyes flashing anger. "And you're a pimple on a frog's hind end! If you don't stop pointing that stupid bow at me, I'm going to shove it up your butt! And what's all that stuff Maidservant said about you marking arrows so I wouldn't take credit for your shots? Yeah, like I ever needed to."

Athy held up her wrist with a similar burn. "An old hag got me. Her symbol was an eye in a black triangle. Did you see what the girl had?"

"The same. I didn't sense she was cloaked though."

"Neither was mine. Don't know what we were dealing with, but it doesn't matter now, I guess. Can you run?"

"Yeah, you broke the spell. Thanks, I think."

Athy explained the statues as they ran down First Test. "You go to Ruined Village after Cythe. I'll stop Maidservant."

But Arty had noticed something. "Look at the shadows. We were at the Temple at least an hour. Surely they've done it already."

Concerned, Athy considered a few seconds. "You never know with Cythe. She may have forgotten what she was doing and gone for a swim or something. Go check it out then meet me at the House of Kalli. If you come across Cythe, kill her. There's no other choice the way things stand now."

Streaking on the avenue to old Eao, turmoil reigned on the plains around them as armies assembled in formations to join others marching toward the House of Kalli. At the first lava flow across the avenue, the soldiers from First Test circled Maidservant's red square and made a game of dodging as it went from one to another. Athy and Arty passed by so fast that debris and rocks pelted them. Then Athy veered left, a blur of light zigzagging between columns of soldiers on the shorter way up the mountain behind Maidservant's shrine while Arty went right, leaping entire units of startled warriors making way down the great lava steps to Ruined Village.

***

MASSES OF SOLDIERS PUSHED AND SHOVED trying to get inside the House of Kalli. Standing on the hill watching, Athy wondered why no officers kept order and started for the steps to take charge. She would not remember the sudden burst of power that surged from her right wrist, knocking her backwards to the ground.

She sat up on a dusty road next to a whinnying horse-creature. It had a shattered right fetlock. The bloody bodies of two young boys lay on the ground a short distance away. She remembered the scene well. It happened shortly before she became a god. They had come out of a crowd cursing her for running down some useless man who had gotten in the way of Zeus' and Hera's procession. She knew it must be something the old hag did to make her relive the incident, glanced at the bloody sword in her hand and shrugged. "Yeah, so what's the point?"

The boys stood up. Sliced open, one had insides hanging out. The other had his head twisted half around. They staggered toward her, reaching with small grasping fingers. She swung the sword but it went right through them. She kicked and hit nothing, but felt their cold hands touch her. Each said a name repeatedly. She yelled, "I don't care who you were!"

From darkness gathering behind them, multitudes of spirits with injuries of all descriptions walked toward her speaking names---an endless procession of death and accusation.

She turned to run, but nothing existed any longer except the top of the hill. She went into Maidservant's little shrine, thinking to stop them at the doorway, but it was dark as pitch inside and she could not find the way out. Then they were inside touching her, filling her with abiding sorrows, hatred and memories of lives cruelly taken.

A dervish of unspeakable power, Athy crashed wall-to-wall, trying to hurt enough physically to break their hold on her mind, but even the greatest gods have limits.

Unseen hands lifted her off the floor onto Maidservant's altar, no longer speaking their names but chanting hers. She knew what they wanted and refused to give it. The struggle continued for what seemed an eternity before they weakened. With growing defiance, she sat up. "It'll take more than illusions and memory tricks to beat me, hag! It'll take more, do you hear?"

The black dissolved. Light from the outside world shined through the doorway. She laughed, got up and dusted herself. She had won. Athene always won, and now was mightier than ever having stood against the dead as well as the living.

In a corner that seemed darker and farther away than the others did, something moved ever so slightly and the room grew colder. Tired of this ordeal, Athy picked up her sword and tried to leave, but when she reached the doorway she found herself back where she started. After trying several times, she faced the presence in the darkness. "Very well, get it over with. Come out where I can see you."

It was excruciating gradual. First, a vague shimmering form. More impression than substance. Imprecise features filling in. A girl. In rags. Staring unwaveringly through tops of vacant eyes. Hands clutching an arrow protruding from blackness on her chest. A whisper, slightly more than a trick of the mind. "You've changed, Athy."

She slumped to the floor and did not resist Aria's embrace.

THIRTY-FIVE

THE BOOK OF ATHENE: BASTING

THE TOP OF THE MOUNTAIN, after months rumbling and roaring so often that it was more routine than concern, blew up. Wading through undulant masses of warriors pushing to reach the House of Kalli, the giant shining god Athene stopped and looked up as tons of earth seemed to hang in the air and spread slowly across the sky. Then it came crashing down.

A gargantuan chunk of molten rock landed squarely on Maidservant's shrine, demolishing it. Debris killed and wounded hundreds of soldiers. When it stopped, someone wailed for Athene's protection then everyone prostrated, praying and beseeching her to help.

She had crouched with the shield over her head. Now, paying no attention to the soldiers, she gazed up at the mountain to see if any lava flowed this way. There was too much smoke to tell, so she sprinted across on the backs of warriors to the building, changed to normal size and shed the armor to be inconspicuous. With a last look at the mountain, she squeezed through the crammed entrance with her bow and short sword.

Just inside the door, she could not move in the crush of soldiers. Making matters worse, the green and yellow floors glowed from inner light so brightly it was difficult to see. She climbed onto a hulking brute's shoulder to survey the room. All the areas had illuminated, casting a breathtaking mix of colors onto the ceiling, but the brightness made it difficult to see the black and red areas across the canal clearly. She put a hand over her face and looked between fingers.

It did not make sense. While rank upon rank of soldiers jam-packed this side of the canal, the other side was empty except for a group of warriors halfway into the red area behind shields facing the black end as if expecting an attack. Her gaze left them, moved up the floor and found large numbers of dead soldiers strewn from the bridge along the line where the red and black floors joined. Then someone shouted commands and units in the yellow area along the canal raised bows to shoot across into the black area. Immediately, someone else countermanded the order, and the soldiers resumed defensive positions.

Cursing her poor eyesight, she closed eyes and projected other senses into the black area. She found three heartbeats somewhere near the center. It was Maidservant, Cythe and probably the Barrows minion. They were huddled on the floor, frightened out of their wits. There was no one else.

Then Arty climbed onto the soldier next to her. Her face was drawn and pale. Her eyes were expressionless. Normal-sized, she still wore the god armor but the breastplate neck protector hung carelessly open and drying blood had saturated the leather and fabric holding it in place. A newly healed cut made by an extremely sharp blade ran across her throat to the left ear.

Aghast, Athy stared. "Uh, what happened to your neck? Looks like it could have been…bad." She had started to say fatal.

Looking past her, Arty answered in hoarse whispers. "The gleaming white statue hung in the air over the lake. Scores of villagers gathered marveling, or so I thought as I made my way to water's edge. Only they were not villagers. They were spirits, people I'd killed. I thought there couldn't possibly be so many. That's how unfeeling and foolish I've become, because then multitudes more crawled up out of the water. They just kept coming, shoving, pulling and accusing me with the names I took from them. I fought, even used magic, but what can you do when they're already dead? I had to give them what they wanted to make them stop. I cut my throat to become one with them."

Athy could barely speak. "So, you're another spirit, come to torment me?"

Arty focused, giving her a consuming, angry stare. "You always think everything is about you. It isn't! And you always think you're right. You're not! As I lay dying, an assault warrior stood over me. Drawn by my blood, I thought, but he held me in his arms and hummed gentle sounds that warmed and soothed me as once you did. Do you ever think how it used to be?"

Athy wanted to lie to her and say yes, but the words would not come.

Arty shook her head. "I knew the soldier had to be Blogfetter of the Barrows the Lords seek. I wanted to thank him…but my throat, you know? I closed my eyes to pass from this world feeling peace I'd long forgotten." She gave a hollow laugh. "I woke up healed. And now, I must spend this undeserved gift of life in service to those I've wronged. Atonement begins here." She drew her short sword and looked down the blade dirtied by her own blood.

Athy did not flinch. "By killing me, you mean?"

"Yeah, this part is about you."

Carefully keeping hands away from weapons, Athy pointed to the floor. "Can you see her, Arty? In the shadows between the two club bearers staring up at us? If you can, you'll understand I experienced the same as you. If you can't, then kill me, because I cannot bear the guilt of what I've done alone."

Arty stared down. The sword slipped from her fingers and clattered to the floor. "How is this possible?"

Athy wanted to hug and reassure her, but that was a long time away, if ever. "Let's get down, get you out of the armor and sneak onto the bridge to find out what is going on."

***

Tesi-Ra and Kronos shoved through the entrance and made their way to the bridge where Tesi-Ra confronted Theia. "Why are you attacking my servants? They're no threat."

Theia did not back down, explaining how she detected the scent of forbidden magic outside and how Perius and two gods went after Cythe and Maidservant. How they eluded Perius and sneaked through the maze into the back of the building. How she sent her personal guard to capture them and bolts of lightning struck them down. "So, a little reluctant to agree that your maid is no threat, I am."

Tesi-Ra indicated the ceiling opening. "The lightning came through there?"

Theia shook her head. "It originated from the black corner, where your maid is trying to lead them."

He stared across the floor. "If she has that kind of power, why did they stop?"

Coeus cleared his throat nervously. "I had archers shoot volleys in front of them and warned they would be killed if they kept going."

Tesi-Ra glowered. "Then why didn't she strike you and the archers with lightning?"

Theia squawked angrily. "We don't know! Perhaps there are too many of us or she can only use it in the black area. I am certain of one thing only. The bridge has a very different feeling than the floor and is safe, so take care to stay on it, Great Lord."

He fixed a warning stare upon them. "Then why not threaten to rain arrows down on them if they don't surrender? Surely you don't need me to tell you something so obvious." They exchanged worried looks and did not respond. He roared, "Outcasts speak more freely than you two! What is going on?"

Theia's reply was just as hot. "We did! Cythe warned that when you found out we killed her for doing nothing but sitting and waiting for him, you'd want revenge, so you deal with these upstart minions, First. I'm fed up with them!"

Tesi-Ra noticed looks passing among several listening generals and his face darkened. "Order your soldiers to attack again. I want to see the lightning."

Theia shook with anger. "I need those warriors to create new ones. It will add years to the process."

His eyes narrowed. "Are you refusing a direct order in battle?"

Theia gave a brusque nod to General Splx, Commander of the Third Army. Proud and resplendent in a custom-fitted red uniform and a silver helmet adorned with a white feathered plume, he waited until all eyes were on him then strutted to the end of the bridge as if fearing nothing. However, his masters did not miss that he glanced to insure his feet remained safely on the bridge before ordering the men to attack. The soldiers reacted slowly then moved up the floor in fits and starts.

Loudly, Kronos opined, "If those are your best warriors, Theia, I'd hate to see the others."

She squawked and commanded, "Make them fight as they were trained, Splx!"

He shouted orders to officers who repeated them to the men. They cast belligerent glances and, if anything, moved slower. Splx gave Theia a shrug of futility then went back to shouting at the officers. Laughing and jibes came from the watching ranks.

Theia leaped intervening soldiers in one bound to the end of the bridge, grabbed Splx up over her head and heaved him far out onto the floor amongst the bodies. He tried to run back. She gave a piercing whistle through the holes on her beak. He changed into a hideous fat woolly creature with a horned goat's head, enormous haunches and thin legs barely sufficient to support its great weight. Wide-eyed, it staggered, waved fat arms and bleated like a frightened sheep.

Realizing they would be next to suffer Theia's wrath, the warriors scattered all directions. She whistled a complex series of tones and they transformed into fearsome creatures modeled after the One Master's most dreaded personal servants, three sisters known as the Furies of Vengeance, with clawed leather bat wings, monstrous dog bodies and writhing snakes growing out the tops of three snarling canine heads, each set upon a long twisting neck.

Again, Theia whistled.

They bound up the floor on all fours, hideously howling. They devoured the general and dead bodies, frenetic and jostling. The watching soldiers surged forward and back, shrieking and yowling. They charged into the black area after the girls, not one hesitating. From the corner lightning flashed, blasting them into pieces smoldering. A stench filled the big room, suddenly silent.

Outraged, Theia pushed through the soldiers back to Tesi-Ra. "All for nothing!"

He held a fine cloth to his nose. "Didn't feel anything indicating the girl wielded magic. Did you?"

"No!"

"But you're convinced she did it?"

"Yes!"

He took a deep breath. "I rendered her unable to use powerful magic when I made her."

"And I swear by all my senses that she possesses old magic at levels I've never before experienced!"

In spite of their history of animosity, he respected her abilities. He considered a moment then swallowed his pride and faced the black area, making it so everyone heard. "Girl, you promised to be good and obey me, didn't you?"

The reply was timorous. "Yes, Master."

He did not raise his voice. "Then why didn't you stand before answering?"

She pulled loose from Marlie and Cythe trying to hold her down. "Sorry, Master."

"That's better. Why didn't you go with Cythe to the Palace as I told you? Why did you come back here?"

"I have to put a statue on the pedestal."

"Why?"

"I promised Aria I'd do it."

He had to think whom she meant. "The dead royal? Can't make any difference to her now, can it?"

She did not answer.

He pressed. "What do you think will happen?"

Still no answer.

He sounded fatherly. "I understand how much losing a close friend can upset a person. When Athene gets here, I'll have her apologize to you for killing your friend, one god to another. For now, though, please accept my apology and know how sorry I am for your loss."

Maidservant, concentrating to resist him, could not have been more surprised and dropped her guard. "You're sorry?"

His staggered the warriors around him. "BRING IT TO ME!"

She tried to resist, but he had too strong a hold on her now. She held the statue straight out before her. She took a step. Another.

***

HIDDEN BEHIND SOLDIERS ON THE BRIDGE NEAR TESI-RA, Arty nudged Athy. "We've got to stop her or it is over."

Athy shook her head. "All I can think of is attack and hope she makes it to the pedestal before we're dead. We can't last near long enough against four of them and all those generals, though."

Arty nodded. "You'll have to shoot her then."

Athy was incredulous. "Are you nuts?"

"Remember when you hit warriors in the chest with your fist to stop their hearts then shook and pounded them back to life? Couldn't you hit Maidservant over the heart with one of those trick arrows you used to shoot fruit out of trees? Then one of us will revive her."

Athy's face expressed her opinion. "And we'll all live happily ever after. Please remember, many of those warriors died. Besides, even if I had one of the arrows, it would pierce her heart with the speed necessary to keep them from sensing and stopping it."

"You can tell where her heart is, so couldn't you just strike close to it?" She reached into her bag and pulled out an arrow. "I kept this as a reminder to never underestimate you again."

Athy stared at it then shook her head. "Too close will kill her, too far away and she'll scream her head off. Besides, Tesi-Ra will punish or kill me for interfering and we won't get to her in time."

Arty pushed the arrow toward her. "Don't forget, Maidservant is much tougher now that she is remade. Tesi-Ra always finds reasons not to kill you, too. Point out that we are the only ones who can dodge lightning and retrieve the statue for him."

Her reply was grim. "Thanks. Then he will kill me and send you."

Arty grinned. "Okay. It's not a good plan, but it will stop her giving him the statue and maybe give one of us a chance to get it to the pedestal. As it stands now, we have no hope."

Then, for the first time, Arty heard Aria's whisper. "No more time. Do it."

The Great Lords did not see the arrow but Tesi-Ra, inside Maidservant's mind, felt her pain explode in his chest. Staggering, he broke contact with her. Then he plowed through the soldiers, grabbed Athy by the neck and crashed her down on the bridge. "What are you thinking?"

His expression told her death was near. "She already put statues on the other pedestals, Lord. She had to be stopped."

He hit her in the face, smashing bones. "She was stopped!"

Another blow would finish her, but she could not speak.

His fist came down again, but Theia bent down over her, deflecting the blow. She twisted her head to look at him. "If maid girl is not responsible for lightning as you say, whoever goes onto the black floor will be dead, except maybe Athene and Artemis, who can avoid it. Moreover, odds are better sending two than one."

Tesi-Ra, at his most dangerous, glared and said nothing.

Theia continued, "Yes, I owe Athene my life, but you will regret killing her, too. Besides, if she's dead, you may order me to get the statue. Don't know whether you've noticed, but I'm too fat for lightning to miss. I might end up an overdone entrée for the troops, although it would certainly be the sweetest meat any of them ever sank teeth into." She cackled loudly, shook her backside and backed away.

It was enough time for him to regain some semblance of control over his temper. He stared down at Athy's reconstructing face. "If you can talk, tell me why you aren't dressed for battle."

In spite of incredible pain, she grinned mischievously. "Arty and I thought it prudent to remove armor so as not to attract lightning."

Everyone within hearing glanced down at breastplates, shields and weapons with concern and Tesi-Ra smiled in spite of himself. He admired her audacious nerve. Most of all, though, he liked how she infuriated him so much he wanted to rip her apart yet never quite did it. He motioned Arty to join them, pulled Athy up and spoke so everyone heard. "Retrieve the statue and I'll take it into consideration when I decide your punishment." Then he spoke so only they heard. "Bring Cythe back unharmed."

Without discussion, they trotted off the bridge and separated. Arty went straight across the red-black line to the wall and turned into the black area while Athy waited at the end of the bridge then moved parallel to her along the canal. Nothing happened.

Tesi-Ra went to Theia, standing with Coeus. "Looks like you were right. What say I contribute one hundred soldiers from my personal guard to replace some of those you lost? It will save a lot of time rebuilding your forces."

Kronos came over. "Creating the Furies was remarkable, Theia. Even Shelitine never did better, and the way you dealt with that popinjay general inspired my officers. Another hundred soldiers from my personal reserves."

Genuinely appreciative, she bowed respectfully, causing Coeus to sidle away. Tesi-Ra and Kronos, although not looking his direction, noticed.

Two officers from Perius' security forces, covered in fine ash, ran onto the bridge. One reported, "Lords, we have soldiers trapped by lava on the north side of the island. May we evacuate them by sea? Also, smoke is making breathing difficult in many places."

Tesi-Ra looked up through the opening. The smoke was very high above and no ash was visible. Then he realized no debris from the volcano's explosion had fallen into the House of Kalli. He muttered, "This infernal building."

Meanwhile, Kronos asked the men about Perius. They were perplexed. "We thought he was here. No one has seen him since this afternoon when he went in pursuit of Aphrodite."

Arty rolled Maidservant onto her side. "Good thing everyone assumes you kill anyone you shoot or they may have looked closer at her."

Athy let out a deep breath and glanced toward the bridge. "It was close. We'll remove the arrow and heal her then I will make it so she can't move until recovered."

Cythe and Marlie were a short distance away, watching warily. When Athy and Arty went to them and tried to explain Maidservant would recover, Marlie attacked Arty, who took the knife away and threw her to the floor. "Remember your place, Outcast."

Cythe pushed Arty. "She kept Perius from killing me, so leave her alone!"

Arty did not believe it. "Pull the other one, why don't you?"

Cythe was scared but stood up to her. "She has a friend, a rogue warrior named Blogfetter that she can summon. He pushed Perius into Boiling River."

The change in Arty was immediate. She helped Marlie up and gave the knife back. "If he's a friend of yours, then so are we. I'm Arty. She's Athy. How are you called?"

Marlie was stunned. She had prayed to these gods her whole life and now despised them. Athene killed Maidservant and claimed she brought her back to life, which made no sense whatever. Moreover, gods always treated Barrows dwellers like scum and now said they wanted to be friends, which made even less sense.

Cythe challenged. "Why should we believe Maidservant is recovering if you won't let us go check?"

A familiar voice whispered in her ear. "It's true, fish brains."

Cythe spun around then spat at Athy. "What a cruel trick!"

Athy's face could not have appeared more tragic. "Her spirit stayed with us instead of going to the afterlife. Arty and I can see her."

Cythe backed away. "You're crazy! Why would she want to be with you?"

"To make us remember all the people we've killed."

Arty nodded. "It's true."

Cythe looked back and forth at them then reached up suddenly to her cheek. "Something cold is touching me. I feel fingers."

Arty had tears in her eyes. "She brightened at your touch."

Athy turned away. "Let's get the statue onto that pedestal."

Meanwhile, the lords and generals arranged for the rescue and withdrawal of troops while the ranks fidgeted and whispered, eager to get out of the building. Theia, bored by logistics and administration, stood alone a short distant away on one leg half dozing. Suddenly, she sensed something wrong and looked into the black area. Arty was busy helping heal a bloody wound in Athy's right side while Cythe and the Outcast, running for the garden exit, veered toward the corner when guards stepped out of the hall. She shrieked for Tesi-Ra's attention. He yelled across the room. "Who has the statue?"

Arty pulled it out of her pouch and held it up. "Cythe acted a little crazy over Aria's death and caught Athy by surprise with a knife. We'll go get her soon as we finish this."

Embarrassed by Cythe's behavior, he ordered, "Get her now!" then turned back to business, glaring away all comments.

Theia, watching Athy and Arty herd Cythe and the Outcast into the corner, noticed something odd. She mused aloud. "What's that strange shadow following Athy? Has presence but no substance. More, then less, fading out, filling in. Ah, it's a girl. Oh, senses me, too. It's gone! Gone!" She spun around squawking.

Tesi-Ra was in the middle of giving final orders. "Can you be quiet until I finish, please?"

Annoyed, she turned back and saw Arty leaping off the pedestal. She shrieked, "Traitors! Traitors!"

THIRTY-SIX

A PINPOINT OF LIGHT BRIGHTENED AND EXPANDED over the pedestal and became a tall woman that everyone saw close up. She wore long, loose midnight-black cerements that undulated slowly in the air around her, heightening the paleness of her skin. Plaited into a single braid hanging in front of the left shoulder to the knees, platinum hair shined like polished silver. Her emerald eyes captured their gazes and held them captive as she surveyed the room.

Kronos shouted, "Lady Theia says she's only an illusion! Close your eyes and look away from her. Shake your comrades until they do the same."

With order restored, Tesi-Ra dealt with the rebellious gods. "Athene, Artemis and Aphrodite, your service to me is severed. You are sentenced to Tartaros to spend the remainder of your miserable lives tortured and begging for deaths that will be long coming."

They fell to the floor throwing up black bile and blood, yet Arty managed to speak. "You stinking coward, using magic rather than fighting us like a warrior. You are yellow, through and through."

Outraged and needing to save face before so many subordinates, Tesi-Ra changed into a titan and plowed across the bridge, trampling and knocking soldiers over the rails into the canal. A dynamo of raw power, he stormed into the black area. Only Theia's mental shriek could reach him in that state. "The lightning comes!"

Three strikes narrowly missed as he jumped and dodged back to the bridge, where soldiers doused his burning clothing. Then he went to Theia, who was spinning in circles and waving arms hysterically. He grabbed her by the throat. "You were wrong about the girl! It nearly got me killed!"

She flexed her neck muscles and broke his grip. "We were careless. The girl is not dead. And you were right that she cannot wield power directly. But she can use power endowed to this building as a weapon by reciting passages of forbidden magic and willing it to strike. Oh, none of you believe Theia, do you? Then listen for yourselves."

They heard Maidservant's labored breathing with whispered, barely audible fast-speak mixed in it. Least sensitive to such things, Kronos scoffed. "She's simply babbling prayers or other such nonsense while she dies."

"Not dying," Theia corrected. "The healing touches of our treacherous gods run through her, and those are forbidden verses repeated as Kalli's followers were once wont to do, only she…she's…"

Her eyes grew bigger and rounder as she listened. "She's not reciting passages by rote but different lines every time, and…and…no, it can't be! She understands every word! This girl knows the secret of the Eirycians! I swear, she knows!"

After a period of stunned silence and closer listening, Tesi-Ra's voice filled the room. "Girl, we can hear you."

A loud gasp. "Uh-oh."

"You're reciting Eirycian words of power, aren't you?"

Silence.

"Somehow, you've learned to understand it, haven't you?"

She broke down and blubbered. "I intended to tell you, Master, really I did, but things kept happening so fast then got all mixed up in my head until I couldn't think straight anymore. And now, I've made you hate me, same as everyone else does."

"I don't hate you!"

"Sure sounds like you do."

He controlled his voice, but it was a good thing she could not see him. "I'm just excited, that's all. It's such an amazing achievement. Get up off the floor and explain how you did it."

"Athy did something to me so I can't move. It's wearing off, though."

Coeus, most pious of all the One Master's servants, rasped, "You must kill this vile creature and everyone she has come in contact with to insure contamination does not spread, for only this magic can challenge the Master, praise be to him."

Tesi-Ra replied drily. "It seems prudent to ask her a few questions first."

Coeus insisted. "It's too dangerous, for even the mightiest may be tempted to stray by the opportunity to obtain such great power."

"Do you want to stand before the Master like an imbecile unable to answer all the questions he most certainly will ask about this girl? I surely don't."

Seeing Tesi-Ra would not back down, Coeus acquiesced though with strong reservations. "I caution you not to take it too far, my Lord."

Tesi-Ra took a deep breath to quell his anger. "Girl, you heard everything, didn't you?"

"Yes."

"How much Eirycian can you recite? Do not lie, for we will know."

She answered with no hesitation. "A few dozen paragraphs."

Tesi-Ra made her experience bee stings all over, at the same time using his most powerful spell of compelling. "TELL THE TRUTH!"

She drew blood biting her lips closed, but two words escaped. "Ten...thousand..."

Shocked, Tesi-Ra intensified the pain. "Surely you can't mean verses. What then? Words? Lines?"

It was more than she could bear. She gasped, "Years."

Coeus grabbed Theia by the arm and started pulling her away. "Do what you want, First, we won't betray you, but we will be no part of letting this dangerous creature live a moment longer. Be it on your heads, not ours."

Theia tried to reason with him. "Darling, wait. It is a ridiculous claim."

Ignoring the argument, he turned and pulled her to go. Theia leaped onto his back, rode him to the ground and eviscerated him with her talons. Then she sat on the body preening and wearing a very serene expression.

Tesi-Ra sniffed. "You surprise me, Theia."

She nodded. "You and Kronos would have killed us before we got off the bridge in spite of foolish Coeus thinking we were evenly matched. You would have been right to do it, too, for he communicated we'd go straightaway to the Master, and I would become First and he Second. But he planned naming me conspirator, too, so he could be First. Didn't care for me, not really. Thought he could shield his mind from Theia, the nasty creature did. He used me. I used him better."

Tesi-Ra gave her a long, appraising look. "What do you want?"

"To bury differences, serve you and share the girl's power, in spite of my concern she probably does not know enough verses for us to stand against the Master."

Tesi-Ra and Kronos welcomed her into the conspiracy then quietly discussed their immediate options.

Meanwhile, Maidservant listened to their conversations because Tesi-Ra had not bothered to break contact with her. She had heard Athy and Arty talking while they healed her and understood why Athy shot her and why she could not move, too. Soon, though, Tesi-Ra would resume torturing her and she could do little to defend herself this way. Deciding she had to nothing to lose by taking the initiative, she screwed up all her courage. "You know, Master, this would be much easier if you would just give me what I'm due for the magic and allow me to go on serving you."

He chuckled. "Finally, you've said something that makes sense, but you're still mentally reciting verses, too."

She was astounded he could tell. "I'm not just going to lie here and give you everything in exchange for nothing. I did learn from you, after all."

This, he understood. "Very well. What do you want?"

"What have you got?"

He thought for a moment. "I will perform the Rite of Joining to make you a full blood daughter. Then we'll make you a major god with a country to rule. You'll have riches beyond imagination, palaces and anything else your heart desires. Does that suffice?"

It was breathtakingly more than she expected. Her decision to oppose him wavered, but then the scene of Aria's death replayed in her mind and shored up her resolve. "Sounds pretty good, but what are you going to do with my sister?"

Czn-tanth had sneaked away when Coeus died because she knew they would never allow witnesses with questionable loyalty to live and her position as the Master's favorite put her at the top of the list. However, she had stopped at the other end of the bridge when Theia made her aware she would die sooner rather than later if she went any farther.

Tesi-Ra assumed Maidservant wanted her dead, too. "You may have the pleasure of torturing and killing her if you wish it."

Maidservant hoped they did not notice her true feelings when she replied, "Oh, no. I think she should be given her rightful place on the Council."

He nearly choked. "But she tried to kill you!"

"Yes, but it was mostly my fault."

"She disfigured your face. You did the same to hers."

"That was just a little family squabble between siblings."

Theia spoke in his mind. "It doesn't matter. After we get what we want from her, we'll bind these sweet sisters together and burn them in the eternal fires."

Tesi-Ra let out a long breath. "If that is what you want, girl, then so shall it be. Lady Czn-tanth, if you swear service to me, I will name you Fifth of the Council after Perius."

Czn-tanth stepped from behind a group of soldiers and strode across the bridge with nothing whatever suggesting the turmoil churning inside her. What was the little worm up to? She nodded politely when she passed Kronos and Theia but oh, how she wanted to shout obscenities in their smug faces and sing, dance and spin around laughing. She stopped before Tesi-Ra and knelt, offering up her lovely tan throat. "I am yours, Lord, for sacrifice or service, as you choose."

Tesi-Ra wanted nothing more than to watch her blood drain off the bridge into the dark water of the canal, but instead cut his hand and held it to her lips, hiding his distaste while she sucked so thirstily he felt burning all the way up his arm. "By my blood, I pledge long life to Czn-tanth for as long as she is faithful."

He pulled his hand away, disgusted how her mouth followed it hungrily, and turned back to Maidservant. "Now you may come to me and take your rightful place."

She could move now, but not enough. "What about Athy, Arty and Cythe? You promised I could have them and now you're trying to kill them. That's why I made lightning strike at you, Master---to protect my property."

In spite of himself, he lost his temper. "They betrayed us!"

She acted petulant. "Yes, but they're not yours, they're mine. I suppose I could be convinced to sell them if the price was right, though."

"You're certainly your sister's sister," he muttered under his breath so Maidservant could not hear, causing Czn-tanth, still on her knees before him, to laugh. He threatened with the knife and she scooted out of reach. He took several deep breaths to calm down. "Very well, you may have them, but they still will be punished. I'd sleep with one eye open if I were you. Now, if there's nothing else, come take your rightful place here beside me."

"I would, Master, but Athy's spell still holds me here and I am really weak."

Tesi-Ra gave Theia a sly wink. "I'll remove the spell and give you extra strength that will make you feel much better." He spoke an incantation. "Does that help?"

She got up and stretched away stiffness. She felt the sore place on her chest where the arrow wound healed. Then she waved and started for the black corner.

Tesi-Ra's voice boomed. "Where are you doing?"

She answered over her shoulder. "To get the new property you so generously gifted me."

His face darkened. "I'm in no mood for more games, girl. Tell me what you're up to or I will have the archers shoot your friends."

She whipped around. "If you do, I'll blast them with lightning until there's not one left! Then I'll blast the other soldiers to bits, too! I think I may be able to do other things, too."

He laughed. "Suddenly, you sound so mature, so resolute, but I think your waywardness may be because you want something you don't think I can give you. Is that the case?"

Again, he had surprised her. "You won't understand."

"Ah, come on, tell me. It's the least you can do before you kill everyone, isn't it?"

"You're just making fun of me, but if you must know, I want a real name so I don't have to be called Maidservant anymore."

It would have been so simple for him to give her one. Instead, he erupted, "You little idiot! You're making all this fuss over nothing! Don't you understand that as my blood daughter everyone will fear you? As for a name, you can call yourself anything you want. You can have a hundred names! A thousand! Moron!"

She shook her head. "But to you and the others, I'll always be Maidservant or just a plain girl no better than a slave. You know it's true."

"COME TO ME! NOW!"

She put her hands on her hips and tried to spit at him but was so dehydrated she could not. Then, hoping no one had noticed, she tried to sound extra belligerent. "I don't think I could resist without the remaking and extra strength you just gave me. Who's the moron now, huh?"

He motioned to two lines of warriors that had just arrived. They marched onto the red floor and turned into the black area. Every third man had a child tied spread-eagled across a shield. Tesi-Ra taunted her. "Go ahead, make me proud and kill them with lightning. Well, what are you waiting for?"

She responded, "No, I've found something better."

The soldiers crashed into an invisible force, causing several to fall down. They kicked, pushed and struck at it with weapons, but could not advance. Furious, Tesi-Ra told Theia to watch for lightning then he and Kronos joined the soldiers and used their strength to test its power. When they came back, he said, "We made a little progress but it was extremely strong. Any idea what it is?"

Theia nodded. "A blanket of pressure over the entire area except where she is, but I sensed it took nearly all her strength when you pushed, so it is unlikely she can make other magic at the same time. Send our most powerful warriors against it, and she will wear down quickly, I think."

***

FIVE ENORMOUS BRUTES CAME IN through the front entrance and marched to the bridge. Soldiers in the way climbed over each other clearing a path for them. Each wore a Crimson Helm with Golden Plumes awarded by the One Master to the most elite, battle-proven warriors. Two were sergeants armed with long battle lances. The others had battering clubs marred and dented from many campaigns and gladiatorial matches in the Tartaros arenas. They crossed the bridge saluting the great lords and continued without stopping to the soldiers in the black area. They took shields with children then pounded their shoulders against the barrier in unison, gaining a few inches forward. Tireless juggernauts, they hit relentlessly, slowly closing the distance to Maidservant, who crumpled to the floor despairing.

Tesi-Ra harangued her, weaving spells into his words to tear away resolve and resistance. He continued for half an hour then stopped suddenly. "You are stronger than I thought possible, and it is not all because of my remaking. Who else's power has shaped you? I think the time has come for you to tell me everything. Let's raise the ante, shall we?"

She began twitching then trembling then shaking so violently it seemed she might come apart, yet she doggedly kept fast-speaking and willing the building to keep the barrier in place. But she grew weaker over time as Theia predicted and the soldiers advanced faster until they were no more than two dozen strides away. Then, for no reason anyone could see, she became still and outstretched arms toward the nearest club bearer as if pleading for mercy.

Struggling against the immense pressure, it was all Arty could do to turn to Athy. "She's almost done for. If only we could do something."

Cythe, on her side next to Marlie with her head propped up on an arm, exclaimed, "Look!"

As though the invisible force did not exist, Maidservant's giant smashed one of the sergeants in the face with such force that his club's swing continued around to kill the man to his left with a crushing blow across the back. The second sergeant jabbed with his spear while the other club bearer tried to grab him, but he avoided their attacks and killed them. Then he dropped the club, pulled off the Crimson Helm and bounced it far across the floor into the canal as if the pressure field did not exist. He scooped Maidservant up in his arms as Marlie shouted, "Blogfetter will take care of her!"

Arty, using her extraordinary ability to hear, informed the others, "She said, 'I knew it was you.' He replied, 'Ties that bind us are stronger than time or any force they use to keep us apart.'"

Cythe sighed. "That's so sweet."

But Athy was concerned. "How is he talking? The Keeper of the Barrows doesn't have a tongue. And how can Maidservant possibly know him? Was there a secret back door in the tomb? And hey, Arty, how about stopping with the repeating everything they're saying and make it so we can all hear them, huh?"

Reddening, Arty hurriedly whispered an incantation, but after a few seconds, Athy carped again. "I still don't hear anything!"

Arty's face turned redder. "By the dead mice I'm going to cram down your throat, Athene, don't blame me for your weak eyes. They're not talking."

Then Tesi-Ra chided, "Why don't you step out of your cloak and show yourself, warrior? Not that I have any doubt who you are."

Mystified, Theia said, "But he is not cloaked, and I sense nothing about him except a remade assault warrior. Very strange. Very interesting. Very frightening."

Blogfetter set Maidservant back on the floor and moved a short distance away. His huge body sagged, broke apart and fell in pieces onto the floor in a sickening pile of flesh, bone and gore around the legs of a man last seen before the fall of the Temple of Light. A squeal from Cythe announced him. "Envoy!"

Arty's eyes popped. "Now I've seen everything!"

Athy had a slight smile on tightly sealed lips.

Marlie, however, was in shock, staring down at the hand where the owl stick had turned to powdery sawdust. She licked her lips and grabbed her tongue with her fingers. "Who ith that drange man?"

Tesi-Ra was unfazed. "I always suspected you were a powerful person of history. Tell me who you were and the magic used, and I'll have your body interred in a sepulcher rather than letting soldiers have it. Why, I'll even put the girl in with you when I'm done with her and erect a monument to both of you."

Envoy held his right arm over his head. A vision of Egypt's great pyramids illuminated floor to ceiling between them. They were not the restored plastered monuments Tesi-Ra knew, but sheathed in gold and sparkling jewels; and they were not static images, but showed desert heat shimmering around them. Then the scene shifted to night, the moon and stars reflecting on their sides, merging them into the cool night sky. A woman in black stepped out from the foreground shadows. Sterile moonlight illuminated her face, showing her identical to the vision watching silently from the pedestal. Envoy lowered the arm and the images vanished.

Tesi-Ra mocked. "I know ancient myths about the original wearer of those symbols and how supposedly he built the pyramids in the time of the so-called First Ones and blah...blah...blah. I also know from later texts that they wrote those ridiculous stories to frighten a superstitious populace into paying endlessly for salvation and protection. No one but the One Master, and possibly Kalli, lived since those times, so identify yourself properly before my patience wears out."

The woman on the pedestal clapped her hands. "I'll tell you who he is, dark lord, for never have I been more surprised by anything than finding this man impossibly alive in this time and place with that particular, peculiar girl. How did you manage to live so long without Kalli's sustaining, Samus? Or do you prefer the title she gave you---Thoth, Pharaoh-god of Egypt?"

Envoy faced her. "Are you Kalli, or simply a mouthy vision left behind to remind us how she abandoned her followers on this island to die same as she abandoned all others in the past?"

The light around her tinged red. "Time has not dulled that sharp tongue, Samus, but let us get back to business before one of us gets angry. Would you great lords like to know what Kalli has in store for you?"

Tesi-Ra was defiant. "It doesn't matter. Kalli can't defeat the warriors in this room, much less all the armies we stationed everywhere. Her time is past."

"Oh, she never intended to fight you. It was only necessary that you position your forces exactly as they are."

Tesi-Ra scoffed. "Surely, you aren't about to tell me a tall tale about Kalli's wondrous seer who could find ways to arrange events a thousand years into the future."

The woman laughed. "Of course not. Theia already told you about her."

Tesi-Ra sent Kronos and Czn-tanth hurrying away to take all ships and as many personnel away from the island as possible by noon the next day. They were to remain at least three miles out to sea until the eruption ran its course. Theia would wait two extra days in Atlas City with the last ship because he would stay behind with the forces in the building to retrieve the girl and give justice to his former servants.

Theia replied, "Since there is no way off the island, we should just leave her and move to safety. If nothing happens, you can collect her later and deal with the traitors."

He shook his head. "She is too big a treasure to not take the risk. However, if you sense her outside the House of Kalli, come find us in case I need help. Otherwise, be certain that no ships remain behind other than yours. As our new leader, I must insure my actions live up to your expectations and that I do nothing to arouse suspicions that I want her for myself."

Impressed that he had said what she could not, she bowed and went outside.

THIRTY-SEVEN

THE BOOK OF MAIDSERVANT: THE UNRAVELING

THE FRONT LINE OF BRUTES CRASHED into the barrier en masse. Maidservant willed the building to resist but they were too strong. The next line hit, moving even farther forward.

She glanced up at Envoy, who had his eyes closed doing something to shield them from Tesi-Ra's magic. She thought of the Eirycian stories. They insinuated Thoth died in the Life-Giver. It was just too incredible that he could have lived so long and escaped notice of the all-knowing recorder of time and history. She tried to stop thinking about it. She had a sure-fire way to find out the truth if they lived long enough. She took his hand. "Remember, don't move until everything stops."

She took away the barrier. Soldiers made for speed swarmed past the battering brutes. In any other place, they would have reached them in seconds, but since they ran from the bridge straight toward the corner, the black area expanded, carrying them away.

Tesi-Ra's forces had strung out for miles along the line of pursuit when the warriors in the lead came to a ragged halt. The quarry had disappeared over the endless horizon around them more than an hour ago. Disoriented, no walls in sight and the high ceiling glowing black, same as the floor, they could not tell directions any longer. Discussions became arguments that led to fighting.

When Tesi-Ra and the army caught up, a colonel and several soldiers were dead. Another colonel began making excuses and blaming his dead counterpart for getting lost. Annoyed, Tesi-Ra beheaded him and commanded everyone into ranks. He endowed them with extra strength and shared the ability to sense the prey's direction, which immediately bolstered confidence.

He led them across the glowing floor at astounding speeds. His intention had been to hold the girl in the building until Kronos and Czn-tanth departed the island then lure and kill Theia. Why would they think he would consider sharing ultimate power? Their naiveté amazed him.

Now, however, he would not reach the girl until long after Kronos sailed, and he still had to take her prisoner and get outside before Theia departed. It would be close unless he could force Maidservant to shrink the room back to its former dimensions, which he felt confident he could do. He shrugged away all thoughts of failure. He would rather die attempting to obtain the greatest power on earth than abandon the effort while any reasonable chance of success existed. Of course, he had no way of knowing the fate of everyone inside the House of Kalli was already sealed.

Outside, Theia ordered soldiers to stop trying to break through the doors and windows that had slammed shut. Heavy sulfurous smoke made breathing difficult. Hot ash layered every surface and burned hair and skin of all but the hardiest remade creatures. The island rumbled and shook ominously. She wondered if it would last to the next tide, much less another day, but made the same decision as Tesi-Ra. The prize was worth the risk, but she was not certain how long she would wait. She ran toward Cadi-sum, leaving the soldiers behind.

***

MAIDSERVANT AND ENVOY WERE A SHORT DISTANCE from the pedestal when everything stopped. Above Athy and the others, the woman sat dangling translucent feet over their heads. As Maidservant approached, she said, "You can't imagine how relieved I am to see you survived the attempts on your life today."

Maidservant screwed up her face. "Uh, there was only one, when I came out of the tomb."

Athy cleared her throat. "She doesn't know, but I would have killed her near the emerald statue in the Barrows area except for a sleeper interfering. Sorry again, Maidservant."

The woman spoke to Maidservant again. "Did the princess give her life to save yours?"

Maidservant looked away so Athy answered again. "Ariadne, daughter of the king and queen of Keftiu, jumped in front of an arrow meant for Maidservant."

The woman read everyone's eyes and expressions. "My, aren't you the bloody one? What were you the god of, anyway? Murder? Mayhem? Strangling children?"

Athy did not meet her eyes. "Strategies, war, wisdom, music, pottery and other things like that."

The woman laughed. "Artistic people sacrificed cuddly little animals and prayed to someone like you? Priceless!"

The voice came from nowhere. "Why don't you stuff the sarcasm up your butt and scoot on it sideways?"

The woman dropped to the floor in front of Athy, suddenly real as any of them. "Who said that?"

Athy sounded very tired. "Ariadne's spirit remained with me to make certain I never forget the awful things I've done."

The woman seemed pleased. "Now, that's retribution. Just goes to show that no matter how long you live, there's always something new."

Arty shoved in front of Athy. "We've had all the mouth we're going to take from you!"

Instantly, the woman became translucent again. She indicated Marlie. "I don't know anything about you."

She took a step back, looking around for a place to hide.

The woman shrugged. "Time is short. I've decided to make all of you Kalli's daughters. Congratulations."

Arty retorted, "We don't want another master!"

The woman pointed to a silver tray with cups of wine on the floor nearby. "You can certainly refuse, but you're going to need more strength to hold off your pursuers, especially those of you the dark lord took out of service. He will be here soon."

Athy demanded, "What's in them?"

"The black cup is wine for Maidservant. The others contain Kalli's elixir. Drink it only if you are truly free of the One Master's influence; otherwise, it will kill you." She looked at Athy when she said the last.

Athy grabbed a cup and gulped it down. Cythe followed suit then Arty and finally Marlie, but only after Cythe's encouragement. Maidservant took a black cup. Envoy kicked the tray and last cup away.

"I can tell you have given up much of your power, so that was foolish," the woman said and turned to Cythe. "Allow me to hold your right wrist then say your name and the names of your parents."

"Cytheria, raised by Plinius and Denear of Kalliste." The woman let her go, revealing the symbol of a luminous clamshell boat on blue water. Light also shined through the bodice of her ragged tunic, so she pulled down the neck and found crossed double axes emblazoned on her upper breast. "Wow, just like a Priest's."

The woman held Athy and Arty's wrists at the same time and nodded to Athy first. "Athene, daughter of Metys, Healing Priest. Never told me my father, nor did I ask." Then Arty. "Artemis, daughter of Leto, the last legitimate Head Priest, with whom I had no relationship. Never asked about my father because she would have lied."

The woman noted everyone's surprise about Arty's mother. "You lot are certainly full of stories, but no time to hear them, sorry to say." She moved to

Marlie, who was afraid to hold out her arm. The woman whispered something in her ear and her eyes widened with surprise. "You know what I am and don't care? Really?"

"But you must speak the truth and not the lies you always tell about your past."

Marlie swallowed and placed her wrist in the woman's outstretched hand. "Marlie. I tell about my family in Ruined Village, but I was birthed another place and sold to them after my first change. My lot was caring for young squallers, cleaning catch and working fields. After my second change, I baited marauders into ambushes and tended the needs of our warriors. Third change, I was a hunter-scavenger. Fourth change, I was a different kind of hunter--- not sure what the name is---then Blogfetter bartered me to become a Barrows Outcast. He is the only parent I know."

The woman left Marlie examining green grape-laden vines around her right arm from wrist to elbow, very different from the others. Then she wiped her runny nose on the back of her hand and marched resolutely to Envoy. "What did you do to him?"

He grunted, "I am Blogfetter, and I'll still take care of you, if you'll let me."

She hesitated then told Cythe what he said. After reassurance, she jumped into his arms and cried.

Meanwhile, the woman was in front of Aria, who sidestepped away, but the woman matched her steps exactly until she stopped. "I didn't think you could see me."

"I can sense the necklace you're wearing. Give me your wrist."

"In case you haven't noticed, I don't have a body."

"I'm not certain, but I think this will make you much stronger."

Long seconds passed then she placed her wrist in the woman's hand. "Ariadne, daughter of Ermiticus and Malidia, Priests and last sovereigns of the Keftiu Empire."

Arty whispered to Cythe and Marlie. "She has a symbol of a little olive tree in a pot just like the one we planted in the maze. Wait. How can she know about that?"

The woman went to Maidservant, who would not look at her, much less offer her arm. "The seer said the princess would have Kalli's necklace when she saved you, but no one could figure out how it was possible, so I chanced giving it to you and hoped for the best."

Maidservant shook her head. "She didn't have it until after she died."

The woman seemed perplexed then grabbed Maidservant's wrist and gave her a symbol of three leaping dolphins silhouetted against a big yellow sun. "I think a new name would suit you, too. How about Jnais-etieri-Rnai,

Eirycian for sunshine that breaks through clouds during a spring rain? Do you like it?"

Cythe blurted, "It's beautiful!"

But Maidservant was wretched to behold.

Hurriedly, the woman continued. "I made it so the evil inside you will remain at bay for long as you wish it to be, but I can't remove it now. You went to your master, didn't you?"

"I didn't realize that calling out to him to save me meant that, but you already knew I would do it, didn't you? Just like Aria, my fate was decided by Kalli's plan all along, wasn't it?"

Suddenly, Maidservant stood in gray nothingness, Envoy and Athy's surprised exclamations still in her ears. Then everything turned black and cold. Light flared. Again she faced the woman in the tomb where they first met. Maidservant said, "Even the amount of Eirycian you expected me to take from Nun would ruin the plan if it gets back out into the world, wouldn't it?"

"Out of curiosity, can you really recite all ten thousand years of Eirycian stories?"

"And translate them into every language Nun showed me. There is so much spinning inside my head that it gives me headaches all the time."

"That is incredible. How is possible you can remember so much?"

"You and Tesi-Ra should share notes about the freaks you create. Before he took me from my family, I could memorize most things I set my mind to. Now, I can't stop remembering everything. I think it is more curse than gift."

"Do you understand that if you shared power with your friends, it will corrupt at least one of them or end up in the wrong hands eventually? Once out in the world, it will only be a matter of time before everything ends in disaster again."

Very glum, she nodded. "I think that Samus Thoth became corrupted when he was a god trying to finish the city. The story did not say that directly, but his behavior indicated he was in its grips. That is probably why he can take the guise of a demon and live among them without detection, and it may have something to do with him living so long, too. So yes, I understand exactly what you mean."

The woman stared at her in amazement. "That's what happened to the Eirycians, if you haven't figured it out already, and they were vastly more advanced and skilled at handling such things. Their magic must be inaccessible to the world after this."

"The Temple cleansed people's memories. Can that be done to me?"

"You're too strong. There's only one solution to this situation."

She nodded. "I have to die, but can't my friends be saved?"

"The building is sealed and no one can get out now.

"That's not fair."

"No, it's not."

"Is Nun recording this?"

"Most certainly."

"Then let it record that I think Kalli is a cold-hearted witch no better than the demons she fights."

***

MAIDSERVANT WAS ON THE FLOOR, the others asking if she knew where the woman had gone and if she was all right. They helped her up and bombarded her with questions but she just stood there. Athy shushed everyone and Envoy held her until she was ready to speak. "As Kalli intended from the beginning, the building is sealed and we can't get out."

Envoy struck the pedestal an awesome blow that remarkably did no damage to him or the pedestal. "Why?"

Maidservant shook her head. "I think she expected all the Lords would be inside trying to capture me since they never trust each other, but it appears the plan failed in that regard."

Arty began checking her arrows and weapons. "Guess it should not come as a surprise after what happened to everyone at the Temple, though I still can't see why Kalli wanted everyone who believed in her dead or with the enemy."

Then Cythe changed the fate of the world. "I don't suppose any of the little houses still work, do they? Two appeared in the black area when it stopped expanding."

It took six hours hard running, and just before reaching the house, Arty spotted flickering movement along the horizon to their left. "That is light reflecting off armor and shields. They're coming this way fast."

The little building was black but stood on a square section of floor comprised of all four tile colors in no particular order. Maidservant stared at it for a time then began muttering, shaking her head and pacing back and forth. They tried to ask her questions but she refused to say anything.

Envoy threw an empty water skin through the doorway and it disappeared in a flash. Marlie said, "Same as the cat house in the maze. It goes somewhere."

Cythe sat on the floor, exhausted in spite of Athy and Arty having carried her---her arms on their shoulders---most of the way. Arty massaged her numb arms and cramping legs. Athy was behind the building quietly talking to Aria. Suddenly, Maidservant stopped pacing "They'll be here in a few minutes. Who's going first?"

Athy called to her. "Why don't you show us how it's done?"

Maidservant shook her head. "I have to go last and close the portal so they can't follow."

Envoy went to her. "Then we'll go last together. I'm not leaving you alone with Tesi-Ra."

She was defiant. "Two can't go at the same time. Someone go now! We're almost out of time."

Cythe got to her knees, held her palms a few inches above the floor and fast-spoke. A marble-sized globe of light appeared. "This will slow them down."

Arty could not help herself. "What are you going to do with that, put someone's eye out?"

Cythe laughed then flicked the globe toward the advancing horde. It bounced then rolled, picking up speed, size and brightness until it was a huge streaking mass. Reaching the enemy, it burst open, burning, blinding and scattering warriors.

Arty unslung her bow and ran to jump onto the roof of the house, but Maidservant, a blur of speed, knocked her through the doorway and she was gone. She yelled again. "Go!"

Athy vaulted over the house, grabbed Cythe, who had just sent off another ball of light, and ran into the house with her. Envoy locked eyes with Maidservant when they disappeared. She said, "Okay, I was wrong. Just take Marlie and go. I'll be right behind you."

Envoy kissed Marlie's forehead and gently pushed her inside the building. Then he faced Maidservant on knees and holding both sides of the doorway. "Do what you must. I'm not leaving without you."

She glanced at the army, splitting and running to encircle them. "I can't share forbidden power with any of you, and if I escape back out into the world, they'll keep coming after me until you're all dead and take it. You can see that, can't you?"

"Yes."

"I can never leave here."

"I know."

"Marlie needs you."

"Marlie can take care of herself. She just doesn't realize it, yet. Best get started. They will attack all sides at once."

She took a deep breath. Tears welled in her eyes. She broke down, ran to him and fell on her knees. Then she spoke a dialect so far in the past he had all but forgotten it. "Hey-ya-a-a, Samus, son of Thoth. Wouldn't you have been happier staying a Mud Man warrior with Siris and Talik than stuck here to die with a useless homeless female who has no dowry?" She reached out for him.

He started to take her embrace.

She shoved him backwards and shielded her eyes from the flash, his last word in her ears. "Why?"

MAIDSERVANT THE GOD

***

THE CIRCLE OF ENEMY WAS FIFTY PACES AWAY, watching quietly. Here and there, a child on a shield moved or cried, but most of them appeared dead already. She tried to hate the twisted warriors, but she could not do it. They were as much victims as the children, and she knew she could not kill them.

Tesi-Ra, in titan form, moved from an outer circle of troops into the one directly in front of her. "It appears your so-called friends have abandoned you."

She trembled, unable to imagine fighting him. It was absurd. Then his voice sounded inside her head ordering her to obey him. She hit herself in the face until he left her.

He laughed. "Never had anyone fight me by beating themselves up. I don't think you are likely to win that way."

Him, she hated enough to kill. Something stirred inside her. She felt its strength and knew this was what they planned her to do all along. It did not matter anymore. She took a deep breath and willed it to take her. It took less than a minute for her to change completely. As she ripped off the binding clothes, something unexpected manifested and seized control of the thing she had become. RAGE.

Foul, she was not afraid of anything. She strutted forward and back, making crude gestures and spitting at her former master and his servants. She hissed through bared teeth and flicked a long red tongue at his officers to provoke them to attack, but not one reacted. She screeched crude insults at Tesi-Ra, hoping he would lose his temper and order them to attack her, but no one took her seriously. They laughed at her puny size and ridiculed for thinking she could stand up to him.

Tesi-Ra moved forward confidently. "Now that you've changed into an imp, fool, you belong to me, the one who made you. On your knees to your master!"

A bolt of lightning knocked him to the floor with blood gushing from under his glorious armor. He jumped up, more furious than hurt. "You can't disobey me! I made you! So it has always been, so it is."

"Oh, Master," she cried. "I'm so sorry. Please, allow me to show my love for you." She turned around, bent over and raised high her tail, showing her anus. At the same time, she cursed him in a royal demon dialect she learned on Nun.

Tesi-Ra grabbed a shield with two children and led the attack. The entire inner circle of warriors charged.

No longer a weak creature like those useless children, she shrieked and leapt onto the house in a single bound. She willed salvos of lightning to strike around her, decimating them. Except for Tesi-Ra, knocked down and badly wounded, what remained of the inner circle retreated, but there was nowhere to go. She sent wave after wave of lightning, blasting warriors to pieces everywhere in the black area then struck the bodies repeatedly, determined to obliterate them into nothingness. But in her excitement and unaccustomed bloodlust, she became unfocused and lost track of her main adversary.

Tesi-Ra resorted to a physical attack, throwing the shield by edge at her. Spinning and flying at a ferocious rate, it struck in the mid-section and knocked her off the house to the floor.

Seriously hurt but back to her senses, she struggled up, startled how close he was. Grimacing, she had no time to worry about finding red tiles to place her feet. Hoping it worked, she held an arm over her head and counted words on unfamiliar short black claws to insure she did not make a mistake. "Dead! Dead! Dead! Dead! Cruel! Cruel! Cruel! Cruel!"

Thinking she called more lightning, Tesi-Ra lunged just as some invisible force lifted her off the floor and carried her through the doorway. His giant hand followed through the opening and closed around her as the House of Kalli reduced to its smallest size in an instant, crushing everything inside utterly together.

Maidservant, propelled by a powerful outflow of viscous matter, shot out the doorway of a little house into a hellish world of sulfurous heat and smoke. Gasping to breathe, she coughed-gagged as hands pulled her from thick stinking slime and performed rudimentary healing. Through the ringing in her ears, she heard Athy speaking. "E-yew, Aria, what is this mess?"

She barely made out the soft reply. "If I could, I'd throw up."

Athy again. "She transformed."

Envoy. "We've got to go. I'll carry her."

Aria. "That is not Maidservant anymore. She is a horror."

Athy. "What has she got her hands stretched around?"

Aria. "Could be a head, or worse. Leave her."

Envoy wrapped her in a blanket, slung her over his shoulder and took off running.

Hanging upside-down bouncing on his back, Maidservant vaguely wondered where the others were and if she killed them, too. Then she shook her head until she could see out a fold of the blanket. They were going up the side of the big meadow, smoke-filled and devoid of animals. Below were the rows of little houses, yet she also saw fancy dressed people milling in a garden near the Eao octopus fountain and a beautiful palace. All of it faded in and out, some things prominent then others. Suddenly, enormous globs of roaring fire plopped off the mountain, engulfing and filling the valley. It sloshed up the hill behind them. Heat burned her face as it roared closer and she shut her eyes to it. That was Maidservant's last memory on the island of Kalliste.

They went over the rim of the ridge and Athy took the lead, speeding down the Avenue of the Gods past the statues, most of them toppled. They did not look back when lava surged over the rim and splashed down through the city behind them. Leaving the outskirts, Athy chose the path through burning woods to the Temple rather than a clear way to Olympus Avenue, and that decision saved their lives because the lava raced that way, turning the road into a fiery river-avalanche all the way to the sea.

Frenzied warriors slowed them in old Prospect Village because they wanted to fight for some stupid reason. Athy killed several without slowing much then they left the rest behind. They passed Maidservant's statue and entered the Barrows. Colored shafts of light shined out of the obelisks in every direction, but Athy and Envoy did not give them a second look. They dashed through old Main Court and leaped the barricade onto First Test.

Halfway down, a youngish woman covered in dirt, soot and tatters stood pouring water over her head from one of many skins slung over bare, narrow shoulders. Lanky and jerky to the extreme, she waved them to stop, but they zipped around her.

To their shock, she caught up quickly and doused water over their heads, relieving their smoldering scalps and stinging eyes. Her buckteeth whistled when she talked. "Priest Jana. Have me a boat, last one on the island, I venture, and needed help to use it. I took your companions to it, but then the warrior girl ordered me to go find you. Says it's up to you whether I go or not. Done my part, so yes or no?"

Athy studied her. "Depends. How'd you find us?"

"Great Kalli called me her bloodhound. Like I told warrior girl, I smell power, and you lot are full of it, especially her." She eyed the bundle over Envoy's shoulder then glimpsed the face and whipped out a knife. "Demon!"

Not slowing in the least, Envoy paid no attention to her. Athy simply stared.

Jana sheathed the knife quickly. "My mistake."

Athy said, "You have enough sense not to pick stupid fights and die, at least. You can go if he doesn't object."

Envoy shrugged.

Atlas City burned and marauders were everywhere, but they had to kill only a few because most recognized Athy and stayed clear. They found Arty crouched on a private dock behind a row of palatial houses sprinkling water on an unconscious girl flat on her back. Maidservant had begun writhing and moaning so Envoy passed without a word to a small boat farther along. Athy and Jana stopped and hacked up black gobs as they studied the stranger.

Battered and burned, she had unusually good looks in spite of unfashionable dark spiky hair. The tattered dress was expensive though it was the uniform of a slave, indicating she probably was the favorite of a master or mistress, a common living arrangement in rich houses. Her arms wrapped tightly around a ridiculously huge sword held to her chest, the hilt reaching beyond the top of her head and the point well past her charred bare feet. Inscriptions and odd symbols filled the awkwardly shaped blade.

Arty scratched her scalp, sending bits of burned hair flying. "Oddest thing. I put Cythe and Marlie in the boat, rushed back here to stand watch and found her, just as you see. Didn't see anyone else. Can't get a rise out of her---in shock, most likely. Suspect she stole that sword thinking it's valuable. Must be a piece of ceremonial junk or decoration, as no one could possibly use such a heavy, unwieldy thing."

Jana urged them to go. "We'll leave her. Boat's overloaded as it is."

Arty disagreed. "No way. If it's too crowded, you can swim alongside."

Jana bristled. "Well, take that heavy monstrosity away from her." But they could not get it away without cutting her so Athy decided they should leave it alone. Jana kept tugging. Arty shoved her away. Jana called her a name. They faced off.

A series of explosions rocked the island and they had to grab one another to keep from tumbling off the bucking pier. Then tons of lava poured off the Temple plateau into the westernmost part of the city. At the same time, a river of fire roared down First Test into the east side. They grabbed the girl and jumped into the boat just before the dock shook apart.

THIRTY-EIGHT

THE BOOK OF MAIDSERVANT: DROPS IN THE OCEAN

THE PLAIN UNDER THE CONFLAGRATED CITY SWELLED, becoming a huge mound rising above the harbor. Roiling black smoke hid the island's higher elevations. Streams of lava poured into the harbor, shooting sizzling founts of steam hundreds of feet into the air. Strong outflows of wind buffeted the harbor with soot and hot ash. Spates of choppy waves, powerful crosscurrents and tumultuous semi-buoyant bubbling areas rendered the usually tranquil harbor almost unnavigable.

Making matters worse, the Kallistians had specially constructed the small boat for ferrying repair teams to vessels inside the harbor. It had no mast and only four oar stations consisting of two small bench seats either side of an extra wide midsection for carrying tools and materials. Shortened oars facilitated passage between docked vessels at the cost of reduced stroke power and maneuverability. Otherwise, the boat had a short bench in a narrow snubbed bow and another bench across the stern to accommodate manning a rudder paddle that could be mounted either side.

Athy and Envoy sat across from each other in the rowing positions closest to the stern with Jana and Arty seated behind them. Cythe and Marlie wrestled with the rudder to keep them on the shortest course through the openings in the jetties while watching for rocks. Marlie bailed when Cythe could manage alone because the boat leaked and took on water over low gunwales. Aria, energy depleted from her efforts in the House of Kalli, sat on the other end of the stern bench staring morosely at Athy. Maidservant lay next to the servant girl between the rowing positions completely covered by blankets tied loosely around her. Their heads rested on supplies to keep them out of the water sloshing in the boat bottom.

In spite of all the difficulties, they cleared the last jetty into the high-rolling sea in record time and kept going with no thought of pause or rest. No one had any idea how much time had passed or could identify the terrible noise when the great mound under the city collapsed and avalanched into the harbor en masse, throwing up a wave that crashed over the jetties and out to sea.

Athy ordered the boat turned into the wave, but its awkward shape made them slow. Fortunately, the sea bottom descended rapidly from the island and the wave lost most of its height before reaching them. Even so, it nearly swamped the boat. They bailed like mad then continued on their way with one pair rowing while the other rested.

They spent the first night going up-up-up rough swells then plunging down into deep canyons of water. In spite of the danger of nearby black ships, they kept globes around their clumsy craft or they would have perished. The sea calmed before dawn, but then they saw fleets to the north and south. Nonetheless, Athy, rowing with Envoy, declared a short break.

Jana and Arty jammed together on the narrow bow seat elbowing and glaring as if there was more space. Slouched over the rudder, Cythe half dozed. On the other end of the bench, Marlie draped over the side, seasick. Next to her, Aria watched Athy rummage in the water next to the servant girl's legs for a water skin.

Arty stretched with a loud yawn, hitting Jana in the head. "Strange about that wave getting smaller like that. Maybe that jerk Poseidon saved us."

Envoy, eating olives, stared out at the ships. "Does it strike anyone else strange they aren't coming to investigate? Though we are low in the water, they surely can see us at this distance. Someone must sense Maidservant's aura, too. It's as if they're waiting for something."

Suddenly suspicious, Athy bent over the servant girl to examine her more closely. Instantly, her eyes popped open, their gazes met and she showed Athy a vision of Theia changing into Jana. Athy spun around, dagger already in hand.

But Theia had seen the vision, too. As she transformed, she plunged talons into Arty's mid-section and slung her into Athy and Envoy, sending them backwards in a heap. Fully restored, she scooped up the blanketed Maidservant and held her between them. "Stay in your places while I signal, little gods. Nothing you can do. No, no, no."

Envoy crouched, looking for an opening. "You need her alive."

She cackled. "Yes, but I can still make her suffer tremendously. Stay back."

Athy, helping Cythe and Marlie pull Arty onto the stern seat, spun around. "Put her down and we'll allow you to swim away, Theia. I give you my word."

But Theia seemed not to hear and acted strangely. Her yellow eyes narrowed, she sniffed the air and darted wild looks from one to another of them. Then she shrieked, threw Maidservant into them and took a mighty, underhanded swipe with her talons down the center of the boat.

Afterward, everyone remembered the servant girl as an indistinct blur of movement except for two incredible images. The first, she stood perfectly balanced on tiptoes upon the starboard gunwale, left arm extended holding the sword straight out behind her while the right hand pointed to Theia, looking up at her in amazement. The second, she had her left foot planted in the bottom of the boat while the other remained on the gunwale, and the right arm was now behind her for balance as the left stretched in front holding the sword down past Theia's knees.

Theia's arm, severed cleanly from the shoulder, dropped into the boat with a bloody splash. She shrieked and leaped overboard, nearly capsizing them. A full minute passed before she surfaced far to the south and looked back to see if they had been able to tell the direction. Satisfied there were no arrows or pursuit, she thrashed toward the ships.

Meanwhile, Arty, although not healed completely, sat up soon as the boat stopped rocking. "That was brilliant! I'm Arty. Who are you?"

The girl held the pose, obviously waiting for someone to ask that very question. Adding flourishes to every move, she straddled Theia's arm, put her right hand on her hip and thrust the sword straight overhead. Staring up the blade into the sky, she declared, "Renowned! Feared! Revered! Rachel, the Sword Bane!" Then she broke up laughing.

The others laughed, too, except Athy, who inexplicably raised her bow, pointing an arrow at the girl's face. "Your cute little act isn't going to give you an opening to kill Maidservant, so don't bother trying."

Arty gaped at her. "What are you doing?"

"Her aura is identical to the witches we ran into at the Barrows though she has no symbol. I'm guessing she's insurance against Maidservant escaping. Only thing I don't understand is why she didn't attack at the dock or kill Maidservant when she was next to her."

Rachel smiled as if she had not a care in the world. "Well, you're certainly smarter than you look. I don't mean to hurt your feelings, but Theia was a much bigger danger than you are. Now, decide how you want to die---one at a time or all at once. It won't hurt as much if you simply submit and don't aggravate me."

Arty jumped up between Athy and Envoy, blocking the way to Maidservant. Behind them, Marlie and Cythe had knives out, too.

Rachel laughed and showed mock concern as she sized them up. Suddenly, however, her face filled with incredulity, and it was plain the reason was Envoy. She kicked the side of the boat. "That ninny! How could she have missed seeing the likes of you? Oh well, I'm just doing this to pass time until we all die, anyway, so no biggie. Nice to have met you. Younger, you're needed."

Another girl appeared in her place. She had sharp features and big, out of proportion hands holding a knobby staff in the same position Rachel last held the sword.

Arty yelled, "This time, I'm going to kick your butt, you witch!"

She lowered the staff and ran fingers through her long black hair. "Well, got to hand it to you, running Rachel off, but now you've inconvenienced Maligor the Younger. You can either kill the little demon or have me kill all of you. Make the right decision and I'll not rot the flesh off your bodies faster than you can count to three."

Arty waggled her knife. "One, two, three."

Athy laughed. "The spells you're casting under your bad breath are blocked by at least two us. Not as easy when we know what to expect, is it? I think we'll start by cutting off your ears."

Younger kicked bloody water on them and said, "Maligor."

The old hag materialized holding the same staff. She pointed a gnarled index finger at them. "Together, you are too strong for Maligor, so won't even bother contending. Once was a time your little gang couldn't have stood against me. Once was a time I traveled beside Great Kalli, second only to her as most powerful warrior-illusionist on earth. Fierce fighters trembled in my presence. Gifted wizards paled before my knowledge. Kings sought my counsel." She shook her grizzled head. "But no more, no more; for age brings miserable end to long life same as age brings miserable end to short life. Shame on you, forcing Maligor to suffer when my others are hale, hearty and young. Deal with them, not me, I implore you."

Athy warned, "Be careful. She's really fast."

Maligor chuckled. "That was Rachel, not me. Use your eyes. Maligor can hardly walk, she has so much pain in her legs."

"You deserve to hurt," Arty retorted, "after what you did to us."

Maligor shook a feeble fist. "We helped you find redemption. Saved the girl when you tried to kill her. Saved her again from the evil lord you invited onto the boat. Three times thanks you owe Maligor and her others, not threats ten times exaggerated."

Athy pointed her bow. "And now you want to kill her. I'm sick of all this foolishness. Unless you want to try swimming with your legs pinned together by arrows, show us the other identity, the one you're trying so hard to hide."

Maligor lifted the staff as if to protest and Athy's arrow struck deep into her right arm. She dropped the staff and sank down slowly into the bloody water, crying and trying to clutch the arrow out with old, twisted fingers unable to get a grip. "There is no one else. Please, don't hurt me. Have pity."

Arty said, "Shoot her in the other arm if you think it will help improve her memory."

Cythe had moved into the stern with Marlie to make Maidservant comfortable. She looked up, showed deep concern. "For pity's sake, you two, stop acting so heartless and cruel to that old woman."

Athy snapped, "Stay out of it, Cythe."

Maligor leaned sideways to see around Athy. "May Bolifus, most gentle god of compassion, bless and keep you, pretty young lady. I beseech you. Please tell your friends there is no one other than Rachel, Younger and Maligor."

Cythe could not have been more sympathetic, smiled friendlier or her blue eyes appeared more alluring in spite of a grimy, sooty appearance. Using magic she had forgotten for five hundred years, she coaxed, coddled and cajoled. "Tell me more, poor thing, and I'll make them leave you alone, I promise."

Maligor could not look away. She wanted to please her with every fiber of her being. "They don't understand that Great Kalli forbade summoning our other ever again because it could jeopardize the great plan. She made me new dominant and responsible for the mission. Younger and Rachel agreed, and so did our other, at the end. I must not let her out again. Please, make them understand."

Cythe smiled. "Oh, they understand very well, thank you very much."

Maligor nodded. "You're very welcome. I..." Cythe no longer seemed caring or friendly at all, but something else upset her even more. She sneered at Athy. "You couldn't tell whether there was anyone else, could you? Bluffed Maligor, didn't you?"

Arty laughed. "That's why no one gambles with her. When you look away she cheats, and she can make you look away."

No longer wretched or pathetic in the least, Maligor reached down, jerked the arrow out of her arm and tossed it into the water. She passed a hand over the wound and it healed in an instant. She indicated Envoy. "If not for you, Rachel would've offed everyone's heads or the Maligors burned the souls out of you."

Athy was out of patience. She aimed at her right eye. "Do the others die when you do?"

Maligor smiled sweet as a beloved grandmother. "Very well, you can have her, but don't blame me if you don't like it. Guess when you get right down to it, it doesn't matter anymore."

***

A PUDGY GIRL WITH LIMP BROWN HAIR, doughy complexion and dark-ringed, too-small-for-the-face eyes looked around in bewilderment until she spotted the great plume of smoke over a distant speck of island. Then she began trembling, sweating and ranting in the kind of snippy, whiney voice that engendered instant dislike.

"Cripes, spite and acrimony, not here of all places, not now, of all times. Damn Maligor. Damn Rachel. Damn that portal casting bitch-witch, Younger, for doing this to us. Damn Kalli for breathing and polluting my air so long. Damn all of you, too, for forcing Alicia to join you dying in this accursed place. Well, I'm not answering any of your questions so don't even bother asking. The lot of you can go to hell. Egad, stop staring at me as if I am responsible for your troubles!"

At a loss, Athy looked around to see if anyone had any ideas. To everyone's surprise, Maidservant, propped up in Marlie's arms, spoke out of the blanket in a voice deep, heavy and unrecognizable. "Alicia was the name of Kalli's seer."

"Yeah, yeah, I'm Seer Alicia, and you're the main subject of all my nightmares and cause of everyone's troubles. But why aren't you dead already? Don't answer, because it doesn't matter. Sending someone to kill you was never necessary. If Kalli weren't so hyper-anal and listened occasionally, Rachel and the Maligors would not have had the opportunity to bust a gut volunteering to be heroes. Kissed Kalli's butt ever chance they got. None of that explains why I'm here, though. Tell me!"

Then she noticed she sat in bloody water with Theia's arm next to her. Disgust consumed her face. "That fat pain in the butt demon was here, too? Didn't see that one coming, but looks like Rachel cleaved her, so why didn't she kill you, too? None of this is the way it's supposed to be! What messed everything up? Tell me!"

Arty demanded, "How can you not be here if the others are? You're all the same person, aren't you?"

Alicia stuck two fingers in her nose and flipped them at her. "Go diddle yourself! Isn't it enough that for a hundred years I lived through this nightmare in dribs and drabs, drips and drops, tormented near to death with the horror of it all? Someone woke me every morning demanding to know what I dreamed. Then all day it was, Alicia, are you sure? Alicia, this part disagrees with that part. Alicia, look again. Alicia, what do you mean you're tired? Alicia, what if we change this? Alicia, that can't work. We went over and over and over the blasted plan until I thought MY HEAD WOULD EXPLODE!"

She raised half up then splashed down again, staring vacantly. "But finally, finally, it was finished, and I thought I could forget all about it and have a life again, but no, no, NO!"

She repositioned the arm and lay back in the water, resting her head on it. She spoke to the sky. "Kalli wouldn't be satisfied until she sucked the light out of the rest of my life, too. Alicia will join the sleepers, she declared, for who's better than Alicia, Rachel and the Maligors to deal with all the problems we may face at the end? Well, I refused, but Rachel and the Maligors were another matter. Practically wet their pants at the chance to please Kalli, especially since they could suppress me finally. I had to give in, but only with the understanding that I would not have to experience this. All of you are supposed to be dead already. Guess you think it's a big joke on Alicia. Well, ha, ha, ha. Kiss my ass."

Cythe asked, "What's wrong with her?"

Alicia sat up and screamed, "What's wrong with me? What's wrong with you? You were on the island! You have eyes!" She shook her head. "I'm yelling at idiots."

Athy suggested, "If you explain what's going to happen, maybe we can figure a way through it."

"Yes," Arty added, "together we can do anything."

Cythe tried using the charm spell again. "It's true, you know. Just tell me and everything will be fine, you'll see."

Alicia glared at her. "La-de-da, pea-brain, you can shove that cutesy spell where the sun doesn't shine, but if all of you are so hot to know---that's a joke, by the way---I'll show you one of my dreams and see how many tries it takes before you dummies guess what you're seeing. Ready or not, here it comes." She cupped her hands over her eyes and began fast speaking.

THEY SEE THE ISLAND. The top quarter of the mountain is gone. There is not much smoke. The ground is still. Lava flows have abated. Black ships are close offshore assessing damage. A few survivors have found their way to the harbor and call out to them for rescue.

THEY SEE UNDERGROUND. Water infiltrates honeycombed rock---seeping then trickling then streaming then roaring through cracks and fissures into a vast sea of magma, pressured for untold eons and pushing to escape earthen bounds.

THEY ARE HIGH IN THE SKY staring at an image frozen in time. Most of the island has vaporized. Untold tons of earthen debris is in the sky. Walls of water thousands of feet high surround an abyss ripped out of the sea bottom that is more than one mile deep.

THE IMAGE COMES TO LIFE. The water walls collapse into the abyss, pulling in the sea for miles around. The water rebounds, throwing up enormous waves all directions. At the same time, gargantuan clouds of superheated matter spread across the surface at more than two hundred miles an hour. Poison gases and voids of oxygen snuff out any life that miraculously survived the conflagrated clouds' initial onslaught. On and on the great clouds travel, a hundred miles in every direction in less than thirty minutes.

MAIDSERVANT THE GOD

THEY SEE A SUCCESSION OF FARAWAY COASTAL AREAS. Beaches, harbors, villages and cities witness the water receding, leaving scattered pools, marooned boats and dying sea life. Multitudes of people and black clad soldiers investigate, speculate or simply gaze in wonder before waves, some hundreds of feet high, roar back over the horizon bringing utter devastation and death.

THEY SEE THE INITIAL AFTERMATH. Volcanic residue in the air causes perpetual haze. Noon is twilight and nights starless. Poison rain kills plants, insects and animals. Famine, disease, and death are rampant.

THEY SEE THE FUTURE. Balances of power have shifted, governments toppled, cultures and civilizations erased. It is a new world. Neither the new followers of the One Master nor the new followers of Kalli have advantage. The struggle to dominate begins once again.

Sobbing, Cythe wiped her eyes. "It's the end of our world."

Alicia cried, too. "Yeah, pea-brain, you got it first time."

Athy put a hand on Alicia's shoulder, trying to be reassuring. "Kalli must have been concerned about Maidservant escaping if she sent people to stop her. What else did you see?"

Alicia's tears stopped and the surliness returned instantly. "Here we go again. In one dream, the death cloud to the northwest had long twisting streamers far out in front with black ships in the gaps. Any reasonable person would conclude the mass consumed them, but Kalli argued that since my dreams are never without significance, if the girl made it onto a ship, she might survive. I mean, what are the chances?"

Athy considered. "Surely, you're not right all the time, are you?"

Alicia rolled her eyes. "Well, duh, why do you think I'm so popular? It sure as hell isn't my charming personality."

Athy pressed. "You never make mistakes?"

"I see the future! I don't make it up! Although, some people misinterpret my visions to suit their purposes or refuse to face the truth then blame me. For instance, even though there's no possibility of your little demon getting away, Kalli insisted there was because she wanted me to die with a bunch of pathetic losers in a leaky boat."

Unable to restrain herself, Athy slapped Alicia's face then thrust an oar into her hands. She motioned Envoy and Arty to take up oars and grabbed one for herself. "We need to go northwest fast as possible."

Arty pointed south. "Three ships are turning this way."

Then Athy saw that Alicia had put the oar down to pick splinters from her hand. "What do you think you're doing?"

She sneered. "This calls for magic, not sweat. Maligor."

The old woman arrived sitting in the water again. Pulling up out of the muck onto the seat, she swore, "If ever I get my hands on that seer, I'll give her a future she'll not soon forget." She stretched a hand over the side of the boat. "Where there is one, let there be twenty."

As images of the boat replicated around them moving away in different directions, Athy observed, "Those won't fool anyone."

Maligor passed her hand over the water again. "Where there is one, let there be two, and make this craft appear as false as the others." She nodded. "They won't be able to detect the difference unless they get really close."

Arty snapped, "That's great. Now bring lard butt back so she can row."

Athy readied her bow. "No, we need Rachel."

She had the sword resting across her knees. "Decided you'd rather have me kill you than breathe fire, eh? Glad to accommodate. Who's first?"

Athy asked, "Do you know how to row?"

Rachel beamed. "Of course. I won the Keftiu Singles Regatta so many times they retired the event and presented me a golden oar. Want to hear what was inscribed on it?"

Athy shook her head. "Later. Will you give your word to leave Maidservant alone and help us?"

She coolly eyed the arrow pointed at her until Athy lowered it. "It's better than just sitting around waiting to die. Yeah, thanks for asking. Who knows, maybe we will prove Alicia wrong. Of course, if that happens, we'll have to carry out our mission."

Athy nodded. "And we will stop you. But for now, let's get moving."

Rachel tied the sword to the seat and pulled Theia's arm over to rest her feet on. Then she gave a mighty pull on the oar, turning them off course. She gave them a critical look. "You'll get the hang of rowing with me if you just pay attention and follow my lead." She did it again.

Arty suggested, "Let's everybody take turns holding and hitting her."

Rachel laughed good-naturedly. "Ah, you don't have to hide how honored you feel having me captain your crew. I assure you, accolades don't go to my head."

Despite going against prevailing currents and winds, they made fast headway and left the pursuing ships behind chasing decoys. At nightfall, they went back to the two on and off rowing schedule and continued through the next day.

At twilight, they spotted two black ships to the north with only a few oars in use and making erratic progress. Deciding they must be undermanned, they went after them, but, in spite of all four rowers keeping up a fast pace throughout the night, the ships were nowhere to be seen at daylight. Athy even climbed onto Envoy's shoulders and Arty onto hers to look for them. Fatigued and distraught, they continued going northwest.

MAIDSERVANT THE GOD

***

THE NEXT DAY, MIDMORNING ARRIVED UNMERCIFULLY HOT. Athy called a break and began passing out a ration of food and water. Cythe wondered aloud whether anyone would remember them if they died here. Arty said that she hoped not. Cythe answered they had done good things, too. Then, as usual, they looked to Athy for an opinion. She expressed concern that so many stories about the gods had circulated that it was likely people would remember, but added, "Of course, they are mostly fiction and show us much better than we are."

Suddenly, from far behind them, the sound of an enormous explosion and a colossal black mushroom cloud grew in the sky. They went into action, securing oars and tying themselves to gunwales. As they worked, Athy repeated instructions for capsizing the boat and holding on under it.

A massive black tumbling firestorm interspersed with crackling blue-green lightning and thunder roared over the horizon tremendously faster than they expected from Alicia's visions. Arty made a rude gesture at it. Athy gave her a quick smile then hurried everyone into position. Cythe had tears in her eyes because she felt Aria's arm around her shoulders. Envoy held Marlie close and reached to take Maidservant into his other arm.

She rolled away and lifted the blankets and rope up off her with both arms then used them to keep her hands, still spread around something, covered. They were accustomed to all sorts of remade creatures, of course, but seeing Maidservant changed into some kind of new Darter Imp shocked them.

Slight and sleek, her soft skin was mottled aquamarine. The face was mostly hers but darker than the body with bigger, expressive brown eyes that had strange appeal. The arms had two elbows capable of bending all sorts of angles. The cup-shaped feet and hands spread and gripped whatever they touched. Her movements were quick, especially the long tail, twitching constantly into different positions.

She wanted to express her feelings for them, say that she was sorry and goodbye, but perceived the startled stares as revulsion, blame and hate. She spun the rope around the blanketed object, knotted a loop and put it around her neck as the holocaust bore down.

The sea began pitching violently. Athy yelled and they flipped the boat. In the same instant, Envoy jerked the rope holding Maidservant and grabbed for her, but she, having spent endless lifetimes speeding through the corridors of Nun balanced upon technology older than civilizations on earth, dodged him easily and used her claws to sever the last tether to their world.

***

EPILOGUE – THE SOURCE OF THE TAPES

DR BENJAMIN WAS LIVID. "You can't keep someone prisoner for a month!"

The rich man, who had just sped up to a back entrance of the house in a golf cart, reached into his shirt pocket and pulled out a folded check. "This enough?"

Dr Benjamin eyes popped. "A million dollars---are you serious?"

"It's yours regardless what you decide, but I want you to work for me."

"Are you going to tell me what is going on?"

The man patted the seat next to him. "It's easier to show you."

They barreled through the gardens into heavy forest, passed heavily armed security people and emerged in a clearing with an imposing two story brick building protected by fences, concertina wire and sandbagged guard posts. Dr Benjamin had seen nothing like it since serving in the military. To his surprise, they drove past the building to a small guard shack on the other side. A woman wearing a medical smock stepped out to meet them. The man jumped out of the cart and introduced them. "Paul, my mother, Jane."

Years ago, she had been in the news frequently as a pioneering brain surgeon and socialite wife of one of the world's richest industrialists, who died tragically after a car crash from head trauma. That led to his wife founding a private research hospital to study those types of injuries, but Dr Benjamin had vague recollections she had passed away, too. He nodded. "Nice to meet you."

She shook his hand without a word then led inside the bunker, which had nothing in it but a metal desk and folding chairs. She reached into her pocket and a steel door slid out of the wall sealing the entrance. The entire room plunged down for what seemed a long ways then jolted to a stop. They stepped into a wide fluorescent hallway with unoccupied hospital rooms either side.

Around a corner, they took a regular elevator up and exited into a bright park enclosed by two story brick walls same as the big building in the clearing.

Dr Benjamin had a strong hunch it was not the same place they had driven past. Above them appeared to be sunlit sky, but looking closer, it was artificial light. Near the center of the park, medium-sized trees shaded a dozen or so wooden benches near a burbling marble fountain. Two young female nurses sat on one of them talking quietly and eating lunch off trays. Seated on another bench with back to the elevator, a young woman in a light gray hospital robe gestured and moved as though in earnest conversation with people in front of her, only no one was there.

Jane surprised Dr Benjamin by hooking her arm around his and speaking as though continuing a previous conversation. "At present, she mouths words and doesn't make a sound. Soon, she'll begin whispering then gradually speak faster, louder and making the noises you heard on the tapes. The gestures speed up throughout, becoming too fast to follow. It's quite extraordinary to witness. Then she'll go dead silent, close her eyes and sit still as a statue until the process starts anew. At present, an entire cycle takes little more than three weeks. It took months when she first started doing it nine or so years ago."

She paused as though expecting a question so he asked the obvious. "Was she injured?"

"Fifteen years ago, people were in lines to buy tickets outside a crowded theater when two teenagers began gunning down everyone in sight because they wanted the record for most kills in a shooting spree. Struck in the head and diagnosed in permanent vegetative state, one girl had no identification and no one knew her. By sheerest happenstance, my foundation needed a new study subject and acquired her before the hospital removed life support."

She looked at her son to see whether she should continue. "I soon discovered that the accepted rules of biology and death do not apply in her case. Incredibly, all the physical injuries healed of their own accord, but since then, it is as if she erected walls between herself and the rest of the world. We are hoping you can help us find a way to break through to her."

The man stopped their conversation. "It will save time if you go meet the patient before asking more questions. Take as long as you want."

***

THE NURSES MOVED AWAY AS HE APPROACHED. His upbringing, beliefs and experiences in no way prepared him for what he faced. He stared down at the gesturing girl then knelt to see her better while struggling for reasonable explanations other than an elaborate hoax.

Seventeen at most. Small in stature. Brunette. A faint scar on the left cheek almost to the eye. Left arm and hand had a lighter, slightly pink skin tone, as did portions of the lower legs visible between tops of burly socks and the robe.

In spite of reason insisting how absurd it was, he followed the gesturing right hand for a good look at the wrist. No symbol, but faded smudges of colors.

On impulse, he gently caught a hand between thumb and forefinger and she ceased all movement instantly. He whispered an early Egyptian dialect. "Forgive an old man's interruption, young lady, but I want to help you. My name is Paul."

She tugged the hand away and continued the silent recitations.

He watched her lips intently then took a jab at speaking an obscure Greek precessor language, this time without touching her. "If you permit, I will call you Sunshine, the kind Eirycians referred to as Jnais-etieri-Rnai."

It was but an instant. She stopped. Only her brown eyes moved, darting a quick look at him. Then, wondering how an old man she did not know could possibly be here, she resumed reciting stories to friends gathered around a table in her imaginary world of Hub City, a closed place in her mind that she no longer felt compelled to leave.

END

ABOUT THE AUTHOR

B C Howell grew up in Greensboro, North Carolina and graduated from the University of North Carolina. He has lived and worked in numerous places in the United States as well as Asia and Europe, and now resides in Arizona. Unwavering interests in writing, ancient history, mythology, science fiction and fantasy have been passions since childhood.

Made in the USA
San Bernardino, CA
06 December 2015